Men of
Honour

**Can love heal the hearts of two
damaged men?**

**Bestselling authors Diana Palmer
and Suzanne Brockmann introduce
us to two women determined to
prove that it can...**

We're proud to present

SILHOUETTE SPOTLIGHT

a second chance to enjoy two bestselling novels by favourite authors every month— they're back by popular demand!

April 2004
Men of Honour
featuring
Frisco's Kid by Suzanne Brockmann
Man of Ice by Diana Palmer

May 2004
Everything For Marriage
featuring
A River To Cross by Laurie Paige
The Cougar by Lindsay McKenna

June 2004
His Virgin Seductress
featuring
The Oldest Living Married Virgin by Maureen Child
Maddy Lawrence's Big Adventure by Linda Turner

Men of Honour

Suzanne Brockmann
Diana Palmer

SILHOUETTE®

*First published in Great Britain 2004
Silhouette Books, Eton House, 18-24 Paradise Road,
Richmond, Surrey TW9 1SR*

MEN OF HONOUR © Harlequin Books S.A. 2004

The publisher acknowledges the copyright holders of the
individual works as follows:

Frisco's Kid © Suzanne Brockmann 1997
Man of Ice © Diana Palmer 1996

ISBN 0 373 04962 5

64-0404

*Printed and bound in Spain
by Litografia Rosés S.A., Barcelona*

Frisco's Kid

SUZANNE BROCKMANN

SUZANNE BROCKMANN

wrote her first romance in 1992 and fell in love with the genre. She writes full-time, along with singing and arranging music for her professional a cappella singing group called Vocomotive, organizing a monthly benefit coffeehouse at her church and managing the acting careers of her two young children, Melanie and Jason. She and her family are living happily ever after in a small town outside Boston.

For my cousin, Elise Kramer, who played with and loved my mother, then me and now my children too, as if we were her own kids. With all my love Elise, this one's for you.

1

Frisco's knee was on fire.

He had to lean heavily on his cane to get from the shower to the room he shared with three other vets, and still his leg hurt like hell with every step he took.

But pain was no big deal. Pain had been part of Navy Lt. Alan "Frisco" Francisco's everyday life since his leg had damn near been blown off more than five years ago during a covert rescue operation. The pain he could handle.

It was this cane that he couldn't stand.

It was the fact that his knee wouldn't—couldn't—support his full weight or fully extend that made him crazy.

It was a warm California day, so he pulled on a pair of shorts, well aware that they wouldn't hide the raw, ugly scars on his knee.

His latest surgery had been attempted only a few months ago. They'd cut him open all over again, trying, like Humpty Dumpty, to put all the pieces back together. After the required hospital stay, he'd been sent here, to this physical therapy center, to build up strength in his leg, and to see if the operation had worked—to see if he had more flexibility in his injured joint.

But his doctor had been no more successful than the legendary King's horses and King's men. The operation hadn't improved Frisco's knee. His doctor couldn't put Frisco together again.

There was a knock on the door, and it opened a crack.

"Yo, Frisco, you in here?"

It was Lt. Joe Catalanotto, the commander of SEAL Team Ten's Alpha Squad—the squad to which, an aeon of pain and frustration and crushed hopes ago, Frisco had once belonged.

"Where else would I be?" Frisco said.

He saw Joe react to his bitter words, saw the bigger man's jaw tighten as he came into the room, closing the door behind him. He could see the look in Joe's dark eyes—a look of wary reserve. Frisco had always been the optimist of Alpha Squad. His attitude had always been upbeat and friendly. Wherever they went, Frisco had been out in the street, making friends with the locals. He'd been the first one smiling, the man who'd make jokes before a high-altitude parachute jump, relieving the tension, making everyone laugh.

But Frisco wasn't laughing now. He'd stopped laughing five years ago, when the doctors had walked into his hospital room and told him his leg would never be the same. He'd never walk again.

At first he'd approached it with the same upbeat, optimistic attitude he'd always had. *He'd* never walk again? Wanna make a bet? He was going to do more than walk again. He was going to bring himself back to active duty as a SEAL. He was going to run and jump and dive. No question.

It had taken years of intense focus, operations and physical therapy. He'd been bounced back and forth from hospitals to physical therapy centers to hospitals and back again. He'd fought long and hard, and he *could* walk again.

But he couldn't run. He could do little more than limp along with his cane—and his doctors warned him against doing too much of that. His knee couldn't support his weight, they told him. The pain that he stoically ignored was a warning signal. If he wasn't careful, he'd lose what little use he did have of his leg.

And that wasn't good enough.

Because until he could run, he couldn't be a SEAL again.

Five years of disappointment and frustration and failure had worn at Frisco's optimism and upbeat attitude. Five years of itching to return to the excitement of his life as a Navy SEAL;

of being placed into temporary retirement with no real, honest hope of being put back into active duty; of watching as Alpha Squad replaced him—*replaced* him; of shuffling along when he *burned* to run. All those years had worn him down. He wasn't upbeat anymore. He was depressed. And frustrated. And angry as hell.

Joe Catalanotto didn't bother to answer Frisco's question. His hawklike gaze took in Frisco's well-muscled body, lingering for a moment on the scars on his leg. "You look good," Joe said. "You're keeping in shape. That's good. That's real good."

"Is this a social call?" Frisco asked bluntly.

"Partly," Joe said. His rugged face relaxed into a smile. "I've got some good news I wanted to share with you."

Good news. Damn, when was the last time Frisco had gotten *good* news?

One of Frisco's roommates, stretched out on his bed, glanced up from the book he was reading.

Joe didn't seem to mind. His smile just got broader. "Ronnie's pregnant," he said. "We're going to have a kid."

"No way." Frisco couldn't help smiling. It felt odd, unnatural. It had been too long since he'd used those muscles in his face. Five years ago, he'd have been pounding Joe on the back, cracking ribald jokes about masculinity and procreation and laughing like a damn fool. But now the best he could muster up was a smile. He held out his hand and clasped Joe's in a handshake of congratulations. "I'll be damned. Who would've ever thought *you'd* become a family man? Are you terrified?"

Joe grinned. "I'm actually okay about it. Ronnie's the one who's scared to death. She's reading every book she can get her hands on about pregnancy and babies. I think the books are scaring her even more."

"God, a *kid,*" Frisco said again. "You going to call him Joe Cat, Junior?"

"I want a girl," Joe admitted. His smile softened. "A redhead, like her mother."

"So what's the other part?" Frisco asked. At Joe's blank look, he added, "You said this was partly a social call. That means it's also partly something else. Why else are you here?"

"Oh. Yeah. Steve Horowitz called me and asked me to come sit in while he talked to you."

Frisco slipped on a T-shirt, instantly wary. Steve Horowitz was his doctor. Why would his doctor want *Joe* around when he talked to Frisco? "What about?"

Joe wouldn't say, but his smile faded. "There's an officer's lounge at the end of the hall," he said. "Steve said he'd meet us there."

A talk in the officer's lounge. This was even more serious than Frisco had guessed. "All right," he said evenly. It was pointless to pressure Joe. Frisco knew his former commander wouldn't tell him a thing until Steve showed up.

"How's the knee?" Joe asked as they headed down the corridor. He purposely kept his pace slow and easy so that Frisco could keep up.

Frisco felt a familiar surge of frustration. He hated the fact that he couldn't move quickly. Damn, he used to break the sprint records during physical training.

"It's feeling better today," he lied. Every step he took hurt like hell. The really stupid thing was that Joe knew damn well how much pain he was in.

He pushed open the door to the officer's lounge. It was a pleasant enough room, with big, overstuffed furniture and a huge picture window overlooking the gardens. The carpet was a slightly lighter shade of blue than the sky, and the green of the furniture upholstery matched the abundant life growing outside the window. The colors surprised him. Most of the time Frisco had spent in here was late at night, when he couldn't sleep. In the shadowy darkness, the walls and furniture had looked gray.

Steven Horowitz came into the room, a step behind them. "Good," he said in his brisk, efficient manner. "Good, you're here.'' He nodded to Joe. ''Thank you, Lieutenant, for coming by. I know your schedule's heavy, too.''

''Not too heavy for this, Captain,'' Joe said evenly.

''What exactly is 'this'?'' Frisco asked. He hadn't felt this uneasy since he'd last gone out on a sneak-and-peek—an information-gathering expedition behind enemy lines.

The doctor gestured to the couch. ''Why don't we sit down?''

''I'll stand, thanks.'' Frisco had sat long enough during those first few years after he'd been injured. He'd spent far too much time in a wheelchair. If he had his choice, he'd never sit again.

Joe made himself comfortable on the couch, his long legs sprawled out in front of him. The doctor perched on the edge of an armchair, his body language announcing that he wasn't intending to stay long.

''You're not going to be happy about this,'' Horowitz said bluntly to Frisco, ''but yesterday I signed papers releasing you from this facility.''

Frisco couldn't believe what he was hearing. ''You did *what?*''

''You're out of here,'' the doctor said, not unkindly. ''As of fourteen hundred hours today.''

Frisco looked from the doctor to Joe and back. Joe's eyes were dark with unhappiness, but he didn't contradict the doctor's words. ''But my physical therapy sessions—''

''Have ended,'' Horowitz said. ''You've regained sufficient use of your knee and—''

''Sufficient for *what?*'' Frisco asked, outraged. ''For hobbling around? That's not good enough, dammit! I need to be able to run. I need to be able to—''

Joe sat up. ''Steve told me he's been watching your chart for weeks,'' the commander of Alpha Squad told Frisco quietly. ''Apparently, there's been no improvement—''

''So I'm in a temporary slump. It happens in this kind of—''

''Your therapist has expressed concern that you're overdoing it.'' Horowitz interrupted him. ''You're pushing yourself too hard.''

''Cut the crap.'' Frisco's knuckles were white as he gripped his cane. ''My time is up. That's what this is about, isn't it?'' He looked back at Joe. ''Someone upstairs decided that I've had my share of the benefits. Someone upstairs wants my bed emptied, so that it can be filled by some other poor son of a bitch who has no real hope of a full recovery, right?''

''Yeah, they want your bed,'' Joe said, nodding. ''That's certainly part of it. There's limited bed space in every VA facility. You know that.''

''Your progress has begun to decline,'' the doctor added. ''I've told you this before, but you haven't seemed to catch on. Pain is a signal from your body to your brain telling you that something is wrong. When your knee hurts, that does *not* mean push harder. It means back off. Sit down. Give yourself a break. If you keep abusing yourself this way, Lieutenant, you'll be back in a wheelchair by August.''

''I'll *never* be back in a wheelchair. Sir.'' Frisco said the word *sir,* but his tone and attitude said an entirely different, far-less-flattering word.

''If you don't want to spend the rest of your life sitting down, then you better stop punishing a severely injured joint,'' Dr. Horowitz snapped. He sighed, taking a deep breath and lowering his voice again. ''Look, Alan, I don't want to fight with you. Why can't you just be grateful for the fact that you can stand. You can *walk.* Sure, it's with a cane, but—''

''I'm going to run,'' Frisco said. ''I'm not going to give up until I can run.''

''You can't run,'' Steven Horowitz said bluntly. ''Your knee won't support your weight—it won't even properly extend. The best you'll manage is an awkward hop.''

''Then I need another operation.''

''What you need is to get on with your life.''

''My life requires an ability to run,'' Frisco said hotly. ''I don't know too many active-duty SEALs hobbling around with a cane. Do you?''

Dr. Horowitz shook his head, looking to Joe for help.

But Joe didn't say a word.

"You've been in and out of hospitals and PT centers for five years," the doctor told Frisco. "You're not a kid in your twenties anymore, Alan. The truth is, the SEALs don't need you. They've got kids coming up from BUD/S training who could run circles around you even if you *could* run. Do you really think the top brass are going to want some old guy with a bum knee to come back?"

Frisco carefully kept his face expressionless. "Thanks a lot, man," he said tightly as he gazed sightlessly out of the window. "I appreciate your vote of confidence."

Joe shifted in his seat. "What Steve's saying is harsh—and not entirely true," he said. "Us 'old guys' in our thirties have experience that the new kids lack, and that usually makes us better SEALs. But he's right about something—you *have* been out of the picture for half a decade. You've got more to overcome than the physical challenge—as if that weren't enough. You've got to catch up with the technology, relearn changed policies...."

"Give yourself a break," Dr. Horowitz urged again.

Frisco turned his head and looked directly at the doctor. "No," he said. He looked at Joe, too. "No breaks. Not until I can walk without this cane. Not until I can run a six-minute mile again."

The doctor rolled his eyes in exasperation, standing up and starting for the door. "A six-minute mile? Forget it. It's *not* going to happen."

Frisco looked out the window again. "Captain, you also said I'd never walk again."

Horowitz turned back. "This is *different*, Lieutenant. The truth—whether you believe it or not—is that the kind of physical exertion you've been up to is now doing your knee more damage than good."

Frisco didn't turn around. He stood silently, watching bright pink flowers move gently in the breeze.

"There are other things you can do as a SEAL," the doctor said more gently. "There are office jobs—"

Frisco spun around, his temper exploding. "I'm an expert in ten different fields of warfare, and you want me to be some kind of damn pencil pusher?"

"Alan—"

Joe stood up. "You've at least got to take some time and think about your options," he said. "Don't say no until you think it through."

Frisco gazed at Joe in barely disguised horror. Five years ago they'd joked about getting injured and being sucked into the administrative staff. It was a fate worse than death, or so they'd agreed. "You want me to think about jockeying a desk?" he said.

"You could teach."

Frisco shook his head in disbelief. "That's just perfect, man. Can't you just see me writing on a blackboard…?" He shook his head in disgust. "I would've expected *you* of all people to understand why I could never do that."

"You'd still be a SEAL," Joe persisted. "It's that or accept your retirement as permanent. *Some*one's got to teach these new kids how to survive. Why can't you do it?"

"Because I've been in the middle of action," Frisco nearly shouted. "I know what it's like. I want to go back there, I want to *be* there. I want to be *doing,* not…teaching. *Damn!*"

"The Navy doesn't want to lose you," Joe said, his voice low and intense. "It's been five years, and there's *still* been nobody in the units who can touch you when it comes to strategic warfare. Sure, you can quit. You can spend the rest of your life trying to get back what you once had. You can lock yourself away and feel sorry for yourself. Or you can help pass your knowledge on to the next generation of SEALs."

"Quit?" Frisco said. He laughed, but there was no humor in it at all. "I can't quit—because I've already been kicked out. Right, Captain Horowitz? As of fourteen hundred hours, I'm outta here."

There was silence then—silence that settled around them all, heavy and still and thick.

"I'm sorry," the doctor finally said. "I've got to do what is best for you and for this facility. We need to use your bed for someone who really could use it. You need to give your knee a rest before you damage it further. The obvious solution was to send you home. Someday you'll thank me for this." The door clicked as it closed behind him.

Frisco looked at Joe. "You can tell the Navy that I'm not going to accept anything short of active duty," he said bluntly. "I'm not going to teach."

There was compassion and regret in the bigger man's dark eyes. "I'm sorry," Joe said quietly.

Frisco glared up at the clock that was set into the wall. It was nearly noon. Two more hours, and he'd have to pack up his things and leave. Two more hours, and he wouldn't be a Navy SEAL, temporarily off the active duty list, recovering from a serious injury. In two hours he'd be *former* Navy SEAL Lt. Alan Francisco. In two hours, he'd be a civilian, with nowhere to go, nothing to do.

Anger hit him hard in the gut. Five years ago, it was a sensation he'd rarely felt. He'd been calm, he'd been cool. But nowadays, he rarely felt anything besides anger.

But wait. He *did* have somewhere to go. The anger eased up a bit. Frisco had kept up the payments on his little condo in San Felipe, the low-rent town outside of the naval base. But…once he arrived in San Felipe, then what? He would, indeed, have nothing to do.

Nothing to do was worse than nowhere to go. What *was* he going to do? Sit around all day, watching TV and collecting disability checks? The anger was back, this time lodging in his throat, choking him.

"I can't afford to continue the kind of physical therapy I've been doing here at the hospital," Frisco said, trying to keep his desperation from sounding in his voice.

"Maybe you should listen to Steve," Joe said, "and give your leg a rest."

Easy for Joe to say. Joe was going to stand up and walk out of this hospital without a cane, without a limp, without his entire life shattered. Joe was going to go back to the home he shared with his beautiful wife—who was pregnant with their first child. He was going to have dinner with Veronica, and later he'd probably make love to her and fall asleep with her in his arms. And in the morning, Joe was going to get up, go for a run, shower, shave and get dressed, and go into work as the commanding officer of SEAL Team Ten's Alpha Squad.

Joe had everything.

Frisco had an empty condo in a bad part of town.

"Congratulations about the baby, man," Frisco said, trying as hard as he could to actually mean it. Then he limped out of the room.

2

There was a light on in condo 2C.

Mia Summerton stopped in the parking lot, her arms straining from the weight of her grocery bags, and looked up at the window of the second-floor condo that was next to her own. Apartment 2C had remained empty and dark for so many years, Mia had started to believe that its owner would never come home.

But that owner—whoever he was—was home tonight.

Mia knew that the owner of 2C was, indeed, a ''he.'' She got a better grip on the handles of her cloth bags and started for the outside cement stairs that led up to the second story and her own condo. His name was Lt. Alan Francisco, U.S.N., Ret. She'd seen his name in the condo association owner's directory, and on the scattered pieces of junk mail that made it past the post office's forwarding system.

As far as Mia could figure out, her closest neighbor was a retired naval officer. With no more than his name and rank to go on, she had left the rest to her imagination. He was probably an older man, maybe even elderly. He had possibly served during the Second World War. Or perhaps he'd seen action in Korea or Vietnam.

Whatever the case, Mia was eager to meet him. Next September, her tenth graders were going to be studying American history, from the stock market crash through to the end of the Vietnam conflict. With any luck, Lt. Alan Francisco, U.S.N., Ret., would be willing to come in and talk to her class, tell his story, bring the war he'd served in down to a personal level.

And that was the problem with studying war. Until it could be understood on a personal level, it couldn't be understood at all.

Mia unlocked her own condo and carried her groceries inside, closing the door behind her with her foot. She quickly put the food away and stored her cloth grocery bags in the tiny broom closet. She glanced at herself in the mirror and adjusted and straightened the high ponytail that held her long, dark hair off her neck.

Then she went back outside, onto the open-air corridor that connected all of the second-floor units in the complex.

The figures on the door, 2C, were slightly rusted, but they still managed to reflect the floodlights from the courtyard, even through the screen. Not allowing herself time to feel nervous or shy, Mia pressed the doorbell.

She heard the buzzer inside of the apartment. The living room curtains were open and the light was on inside, so she peeked in.

Architecturally, it was the mirror image of her own unit. A small living room connected to a tiny dining area, which turned a corner and connected to a galley kitchen. Another short hallway led back from the living room to two small bedrooms and a bath. It was exactly the same as her place, except the layout of the rooms faced the opposite direction.

His furniture was an exact opposite of Mia's, too. Mia had decorated her living room with bamboo and airy, light colors. Lieutenant Francisco's was filled with faintly shabby-looking mismatched pieces of dark furniture. His couch was a dark green plaid, and the slipcovers were fraying badly. His carpeting was the same forest green that Mia's had been when she'd first moved in, three years ago. She'd replaced hers immediately.

Mia rang the bell again. Still no answer. She opened the screen and knocked loudly on the door, thinking if Lieutenant Francisco *was* an elderly man, he might be hard of hearing....

"Looking for someone in particular?"

Mia spun around, startled, and the screen door banged shut, but there was no one behind her.

"I'm down here."

The voice carried up from the courtyard, and sure enough, there was a man standing in the shadows. Mia moved to the railing.

"I'm looking for Lieutenant Francisco," she said.

He stepped forward, into the light. "Well, aren't you lucky? You found him."

Mia was staring. She knew she was staring, but she couldn't help herself.

Lt. Alan Francisco, U.S.N., Ret., was no elderly, little man. He was only slightly older than she was—in his early thirties at the most. He was young and tall and built like a tank. The sleeveless shirt he was wearing revealed muscular shoulders and arms, and did very little to cover his powerful-looking chest.

His hair was dark blond and cut short, in an almost boxlike military style. His jaw was square, too, his features rugged and harshly, commandingly handsome. Mia couldn't see what color his eyes were—only that they were intense, and that he examined her as carefully as she studied him.

He took another step forward, and Mia realized he limped and leaned heavily on a cane.

"Did you want something besides a look at me?" he asked.

His legs were still in the shadows, but his arms were in the light. And he had tattoos. One on each arm. An anchor on one arm, and something that looked like it might be a mermaid on the other. Mia pulled her gaze back to his face.

"I, um..." she said. "I just...wanted to say...hi. I'm Mia Summerton. We're next-door neighbors," she added lamely. Wow, she sounded like one of her teenage students, tongue-tied and shy.

It was more than his rugged good looks that was making her sound like a space cadet. It was because Lt. Alan Francisco was a career military man. Despite his lack of uniform, he was standing there in front of her, shoulders back, head held high—the Navy version of G.I. Joe. He was a warrior not by draft but by choice. He'd chosen to enlist. He'd chosen to perpetuate everything Mia's antiwar parents had taught her to believe was wrong.

He was still watching her as closely as she'd looked at him. "You were curious," he said. His voice was deep and accentless. He didn't speak particularly loudly, but his words carried up to her quite clearly.

Mia forced a smile. "Of course."

"Don't worry," he said. He didn't smile back. In fact, he hadn't smiled once since she'd turned to look over the railing at him. "I'm not loud. I don't throw wild parties. I won't disturb you. I'll stay out of your way and I hope you'll have the courtesy to do the same."

He nodded at her, just once, and Mia realized that she'd been dismissed. With a single nod, he'd just dismissed her as if she were one of his enlisted troops.

As Mia watched, the former Navy lieutenant headed toward the stairs. He used his cane, supporting much of his weight with it. And every step he took looked to be filled with pain. Was he honestly going to climb those stairs…?

But of course he was. This condo complex wasn't equipped with elevators or escalators or anything that would provide second-floor accessibility to the physically challenged. And this man was clearly challenged.

But Lieutenant Francisco pulled himself up, one painful step at a time. He used the cast-iron railing and his upper-body strength to support his bad leg, virtually hopping up the stairs. Still, Mia could tell that each jarring movement caused him no little amount of pain. When he got to the top, he was breathing hard, and there was a sheen of sweat on his face.

Mia spoke from her heart as usual, not stopping to think first. "There's a condo for sale on the ground floor," she said. "Maybe the association office can arrange for you to exchange your unit for the…one on the…"

The look he gave her was withering. "You still here?" His

voice was rough and his words rude. But as he looked up again, as for one brief moment he glanced into her eyes, Mia could see myriad emotions in his gaze. Anger. Despair. Shame. An incredible amount of shame.

Mia's heart was in her throat. "I'm sorry," she said, her gaze dropping almost involuntarily to his injured leg. "I didn't mean to—"

He moved directly underneath one of the corridor lights, and held up his right leg slightly. "Pretty, huh?" he said.

His knee was a virtual railroad switching track of scars. The joint itself looked swollen and sore. Mia swallowed. "What—" she said, then cleared her throat. "What… happened…?"

His eyes were an odd shade of blue, she realized, gazing up into the swirl of color. They were dark blue, almost black. And they were surrounded by the longest, thickest eyelashes she'd ever seen on a man.

Up close, even despite the shine of perspiration on his face, Mia had to believe that Lt. Alan Francisco was the single most attractive man she had ever seen in her entire twenty-seven years.

His hair was dark blond. Not average, dirty blond, but rather a shiny mixture of light brown with streaks and flashes of gold and even hints of red that gleamed in the light. His nose was big, but not too big for his face, and slightly crooked. His mouth was wide. Mia longed to see him smile. What a smile this man would have, with a generous mouth like that. There were laugh lines at the corners of his mouth and his eyes, but they were taut now with pain and anger.

"I was wounded," he said brusquely. "During a military op."

He had been drinking. He was close enough for Mia to smell whiskey on his breath. She moved back a step. "Military…op?"

"Operation," he said.

"That must have been…awful," she said. "But…I wasn't aware that the United States has been involved in any naval battles recently. I mean, someone like, oh, say…the *President* would let us all know if we were at war, wouldn't he?"

"I was wounded during a search-and-rescue counterterrorist operation in downtown Baghdad," Francisco said.

"Isn't Baghdad a little bit inland for a sailor?"

"I'm a Navy SEAL," he said. Then his lips twisted into a grim version of a smile. "*Was* a Navy SEAL," he corrected himself.

Frisco realized that she didn't know what he meant. She was looking up at him with puzzlement in her odd-colored eyes. They were a light shade of brown and green—hazel, he thought it was called—with a dark brown ring encircling the edges of her irises. Her eyes had a slightly exotic tilt to them, as if somewhere, perhaps back in her grandparents' generation, there was Asian or Polynesian blood. Hawaiian. That was it. She looked faintly Hawaiian. Her cheekbones were wide and high, adding to the exotic effect. Her nose was small and delicate, as were her graceful-looking lips. Her skin was smooth and clear and a delicious shade of tan. Her long, straight black hair was up in a ponytail, a light fringe of bangs softening her face. Her hair was so long, that if she wore it down, it would hang all the way to her hips.

His next-door neighbor was strikingly beautiful.

She was nearly an entire twelve inches shorter than he was, with a slender build. She was wearing a loose-fitting T-shirt and a pair of baggy shorts. Her shapely legs were that same light shade of brown and her feet were bare. Her figure was slight, almost boyish. Almost. Her breasts may have been small, but they swelled slightly beneath the cotton of her shirt in a way that was decidedly feminine.

At first glance, from the way she dressed and from her clean, fresh beauty, Frisco had thought she was a kid, a teenager. But up close, he could see faint lines of life on her face, along with a confidence and wisdom that no mere teenager could possibly exude. Despite her youthful appearance, this Mia Summerton was probably closer to his own age.

"Navy SEALs," he explained, still gazing into her remarkable hazel eyes, "are the U.S. military's most elite special operations group. We operate on sea, in the air and on land. SEa, Air, Land. SEAL."

"I get it," she said, with a smile. "Very cute."

Her smile was crooked and made her look just a little bit goofy. Surely she knew that her smile marred her perfect beauty, but that didn't keep her from smiling. In fact, Frisco was willing to bet that, goofy or not, a smile was this woman's default expression. Still, her smile was uncertain, as if she wasn't quite sure he deserved to be smiled at. She was ill at ease—whether that was caused by his injury or his imposing height, he didn't know. She *was* wary of him, however.

"'Cute' isn't a word used often to describe a special operations unit."

"Special operations," Mia repeated. "Is that kind of like the Green Berets or the Commandos?"

"Kind of," Frisco told her, watching her eyes as he spoke. "Only, smarter and stronger and tougher. SEALs are qualified experts in a number of fields. We're all sharpshooters, we're all demolitions experts—both underwater and on land—we can fly or drive or sail any jet or plane or tank or boat. We all have expert status in using the latest military technology."

"It sounds to me as if you're an expert at making war." Mia's goofy smile had faded, taking with it much of the warmth in her eyes. "A professional soldier."

Frisco nodded. "Yeah, that's right." She didn't like soldiers. *That* was her deal. It was funny. Some women went for military men in a very major way. At the same time, others went out of their way to keep their distance. This Mia Summerton clearly fell into the second category.

"What do you do when there's no war to fight? Start one of your own?"

Her words were purposely antagonistic, and Frisco felt himself bristle. He didn't have to defend himself or his former profession to this girl, no matter how pretty she was. He'd run into plenty of her type before. It was politically correct these days to be a pacifist, to support demilitarization, to support limiting funds for defense—without knowing the least little thing about the current world situation.

Not that Frisco had anything against pacifists. He truly believed in the power of negotiation and peace talks. But he followed the old adage: walk softly and carry a big stick. And the Navy SEALs were the biggest, toughest stick America could hope to carry.

And as for war, they were currently fighting a great big one—an ongoing war against terrorism.

"I don't need your crap." Frisco turned away as he used his cane to limp toward the door of his condo.

"Oh, my opinion is crap?" She moved in front of him, blocking his way. Her eyes flashed with green fire.

"What I *do* need is another drink," Frisco announced. "Badly. So if you don't mind moving out of my way…?"

Mia crossed her arms and didn't budge. "I'm sorry," she said. "I confess that my question *may* have sounded a bit hostile, but I don't believe that it was *crap.*"

Frisco gazed at her steadily. "I'm not in the mood for an argument," he said. "You want to come in and have a drink—please. Be my guest. I'll even find an extra glass. You want to spend the night—even better. It's been a long time since I've shared my bed. But I have no intention of standing here arguing with you."

Mia flushed, but her gaze didn't drop. She didn't look away. "Intimidation is a powerful weapon, isn't it?" she said. "But I know what you're doing, so it won't work. I'm not intimidated, Lieutenant."

He stepped forward, moving well into her personal space, backing her up against the closed door. "How about now?" he asked. "Now are you intimidated?"

She wasn't. He could see it in her eyes. She *was* angrier, though.

"How typical," she said. "When psychological attack doesn't work, resort to the threat of physical violence." She smiled at him sweetly. "I'm calling your bluff, G.I. Joe. What are you going to do now?"

Frisco gazed down into Mia's oval-shaped face, out of ideas, although he'd never admit that to her. She was *supposed* to have turned and run away by now. But she hadn't. Instead, she was still here, glaring up at him, her nose mere inches from his own.

She smelled amazingly good. She was wearing perfume— something light and delicate, with the faintest hint of exotic spices.

Something had stirred within him when she'd first given him one of her funny smiles. It stirred again and he recognized the sensation. Desire. Man, it had been a long time....

"What if I'm not bluffing?" Frisco said, his voice no more than a whisper. He was standing close enough for his breath to move several wisps of her hair. "What if I really do want you to come inside? Spend the night?"

He saw a flash of uncertainty in her eyes. And then she stepped out of his way, moving deftly around his cane. "Sorry, *I'm* not in the mood for casual sex with a jerk," she retorted.

Frisco unlocked his door. He should have kissed her. She'd damn near dared him to. But it had seemed wrong. Kissing her would have been going too far. But, Lord, he'd wanted to....

He turned to look back at her before he went inside. "If you change your mind, just let me know."

Mia laughed and disappeared into her own apartment.

3

"Yeah?" Frisco rasped into the telephone. His mouth was dry and his head was pounding as if he'd been hit by a sledgehammer. His alarm clock read 9:36, and there was sunlight streaming in underneath the bedroom curtains. It was bright, cutting like a laser beam into his brain. He closed his eyes.

"Alan, is that you?"

Sharon. It was his sister, Sharon.

Frisco rolled over, searching for something, *any*thing with which to wet his impossibly dry mouth. There was a whiskey bottle on the bedside table with about a half an inch of amber liquid still inside. He reached for it, but stopped. No way was he going to take a slug of that. Hell, that was what his old man used to do. He'd start the day off with a shot—and end it sprawled, drunk, on the living room couch.

"I need your help," Sharon said. "I need a favor. The VA hospital said you were released and I just couldn't believe how lucky my timing was."

"How big a favor?" Frisco mumbled. She was asking for money. It wasn't the first time, and it wouldn't be the last. His older sister Sharon was as big a drunk as their father had been. She couldn't hold a job, couldn't pay her rent, couldn't support her five-year-old daughter, Natasha.

Frisco shook his head. He'd been there when Tasha was born, brought into the world, the offspring of an unknown father and an irresponsible mother. As much as Frisco loved his sister, he knew damn well that Sharon *was* irresponsible. She floated through life, drifting from job to job, from town to town, from man to man. Having a baby daughter hadn't rooted Sharon in any one place.

Five years ago, back when Natasha was born, back before his leg had damn near been blown off, Frisco had been an optimist. But even he hadn't been able to imagine much happiness in the baby's future. Unless Sharon owned up to the fact that she had a drinking problem, unless she got help, sought counseling and finally settled down, he'd known that little Natasha's life would be filled with chaos and disruption and endless change.

He'd been right about that.

For the past five years, Frisco had sent his sister money every month, hoping to hell that she used it to pay her rent, hoping Natasha had a roof over her head and food to fill her stomach.

Sharon had visited him only occasionally while he was in the VA hospital. She only came when she needed money, and she never brought Natasha with her—the one person in the world Frisco would truly have wanted to see.

"This one's a major favor," Sharon said. Her voice broke. "Look, I'm a couple of blocks away. I'm gonna come over, okay? Meet me in the courtyard in about three minutes. I broke my foot, and I'm on crutches. I can't handle the stairs."

She hung up before giving Frisco a chance to answer. Sharon broke her foot. Perfect. Why was it that people with hard luck just kept getting more and more of the same? Frisco rolled over, dropped the receiver back onto the phone, grabbed his cane and staggered into the bathroom.

Three minutes. It wasn't enough time to shower, but man, he needed a shower badly. Frisco turned on the cold water in the bathroom sink and then put his head under the faucet, both drinking and letting the water flow over his face.

Damn, he hadn't meant to kill that entire bottle of whiskey last night. During the more than five years he'd been in and out of the hospital and housed in rehabilitation centers, he'd never had more than an occasional drink or two. Even before his injury, he was careful not to drink too much. Some of the guys went out at night and slammed home quantities of beer and whiskey—enough to float a ship. But Frisco rarely did. He didn't want to be like his father and his sister, and he knew enough about it to know that alcoholism could be hereditary.

And last night? He'd meant to have one more drink. That was all. Just one more to round down the edges. One more to soften the harsh slap of his release from the therapy center. But one drink had turned into two.

Then he'd started thinking about Mia Summerton, separated from him by only one very thin wall, and two had become three. He could hear the sound of her stereo. She was listening to Bonnie Raitt. Every so often, Mia would sing along, her voice a clear soprano over Bonnie's smoky alto. And after three drinks, Frisco had lost count.

He kept hearing Mia's laughter, echoing in his head, the way she'd laughed at him right before she'd gone into her own condo. It had been laughter loaded with meaning. It had been "a cold day in hell" kind of laughter, as in, it would be a cold day in hell before she'd even deign to so much as *think* about him again.

That was good. That was exactly what he wanted. Wasn't it?

Yes. Frisco splashed more water on his face, trying to convince himself that that was true. He didn't want some neighbor lady hanging around, giving him those goddamned pitying looks as he hobbled up and down the stairs. He didn't need suggestions about moving to a lousy ground-floor condo as if he were some kind of cripple. He didn't need self-righteous soapbox speeches about how war is not healthy for children and other living things. If anyone should know *that*, he sure as hell should.

He'd been in places where bombs were falling. And, yes, the bombs had military targets. But that didn't mean if a bomb accidentally went off track, it would fail to explode. Even if it hit a house or a church or a school, it was gonna go off. Bombs had no conscience, no remorse. They fell. They ex-

ploded. They destroyed and killed. And no matter how hard
the people who aimed those bombs tried, civilians ended up
dead.

But if a team of SEALs was sent in before air strikes became necessary, those SEALs could conceivably achieve
more with fewer casualties. A seven-man team of SEALs such
as the Alpha Squad could go in and totally foul up the enemy's communication system. Or they could kidnap the enemy's military leader, ensuring chaos and possibly reopening
negotiations and peace talks.

But more often than not, because the top brass failed to
realize the SEALs' full potential, they weren't utilized until
it was too late.

And then people died. Children died.

Frisco brushed his teeth, then drank more water. He dried
his face and limped back into his bedroom. He searched for
his sunglasses to no avail, uncovered his checkbook, pulled
on a clean T-shirt and, wincing at the bright sunlight, he
headed outside.

The woman in the courtyard burst into tears.

Startled, Mia looked up from her garden. She'd seen this
woman walk in—a battered, worn-out-looking blonde on
crutches, awkwardly carrying a suitcase, followed by a very
little, very frightened red-haired girl.

Mia followed the weeping woman's gaze and saw Lieutenant Francisco painfully making his way down the stairs. Wow,
he looked awful. His skin had a grayish cast, and he was
squinting as if the brilliant blue California sky and bright sun-
shine were the devil's evil doing. He hadn't shaved, and the
stubble on his face made him look as if he'd just been rolled
from a park bench. His T-shirt looked clean, but his shorts
were the same ones he'd had on last night. Clearly he'd slept
in them.

He'd obviously had "another" drink last night, and quite
probably more than that afterward.

Fabulous. Mia forced her attention back to the flowers she

was weeding. She had been convinced beyond a shadow of a doubt that Lt. Alan Francisco was *not* the kind of man she even wanted to have for a friend. He was rude and unhappy and quite possibly dangerous. And now she knew that he drank way too much, too.

No, she was going to ignore condo 2C from now on. She would pretend that the owner was still out of town.

The blond woman dropped her crutches and wrapped her arms around Francisco's neck. "I'm sorry," she kept saying, "I'm sorry."

The SEAL led the blonde to the bench directly across from Mia's garden plot. His voice carried clearly across the courtyard—she couldn't help but overhear, even though she tried desperately to mind her own business.

"Start at the beginning," he said, holding the woman's hands. "Sharon, tell me what happened. From the beginning."

"I totaled my car," the blonde—Sharon—said, and began to cry again.

"When?" Francisco asked patiently.

"Day before yesterday."

"That was when you broke your foot?"

She nodded. Yes.

"Was anyone else hurt?"

Her voice shook. "The other driver is still in the hospital. If he dies, I'll be up on charges of vehicular manslaughter."

Francisco swore. "Shar, if he dies, he'll be dead. That's a little bit worse than where you'll be, don't you think?"

Blond head bowed, Sharon nodded.

"You were DUI." It wasn't a question, but she nodded again. DUI—driving under the influence. Driving drunk.

A shadow fell across her flowers, and Mia looked up to see the little red-haired girl standing beside her.

"Hi," Mia said.

The girl was around five. Kindergarten age. She had amazing strawberry blond hair that curled in a wild mass around her round face. Her face was covered with freckles, and her eyes were the same pure shade of dark blue as Alan Francisco's.

This had to be his daughter. Mia's gaze traveled back to the blonde. That meant Sharon was his...wife? Ex-wife? Girlfriend?

It didn't matter. What did she care if Alan Francisco had a *dozen* wives?

The red-haired girl spoke. "I have a garden at home. Back in the old country."

"Which old country is that?" Mia asked with a smile. Kindergarten-age children were so wonderful.

"Russia," the little girl said, all seriousness. "My real father is a Russian prince."

Her *real* father, hmm? Mia couldn't blame the little girl for making up a fictional family. With a mother up on DUI charges, and a father who was only a step or two behind...Mia could see the benefits of having a pretend world to escape to, filled with palaces and princes and beautiful gardens.

"Do you want to help me weed?" Mia asked.

The little girl glanced over at her mother.

"The bottom line is that I have no more options," Sharon was tearfully telling Alan Francisco. "If I voluntarily enter the detox program, I'll win points with the judge who tries my case. But I need to find someplace for Natasha to stay."

"No way," the Navy lieutenant said, shaking his head. "I'm sorry. There's no way in hell I can take her."

"Alan, please, you've got to help me out here!"

His voice got louder. "What do I know about taking care of a kid?"

"She's quiet," Sharon pleaded. "She won't get in the way."

"I don't want her." Francisco had lowered his voice, but it still carried clearly over to Mia. And to the little girl—to Natasha.

Mia's heart broke for the child. What an awful thing to overhear: Her own father didn't want her.

"I'm a teacher," Mia said to the girl, hoping she wouldn't hear the rest of her parents' tense conversation. "I teach older children—high school kids."

Natasha nodded, her face a picture of concentration as she imitated Mia and gently pulled weeds from the soft earth of the garden.

"I'm supposed to go into detox in an hour," Sharon said. "If you don't take her, she'll be a ward of the state—she'll be put into foster care, Alan."

"There's a man who works for my father the prince," Natasha told Mia, as if she, too, were trying desperately not to listen to the other conversation, "who only plants flowers. That's all he does all day. Red flowers like these. And yellow flowers."

On the other side of the courtyard, Mia could hear Alan Francisco cursing. His voice was low, and she couldn't quite make out the words, but it was clear he was calling upon his full sailor's salty vocabulary. He wasn't angry at Sharon—his words weren't directed at her, but rather at the cloudless California sky above them.

"My very favorites are the blue flowers," Mia told Natasha. "They're called morning glories. You have to wake up very early in the morning to see them. They close up tightly during the day."

Natasha nodded, still so seriously. "Because the bright sun gives them a headache."

"Natasha!"

The little girl looked up at the sound of her mother's voice. Mia looked up, too—directly into Alan Francisco's dark blue eyes. She quickly lowered her gaze, afraid he'd correctly read the accusations she knew were there. How could he ignore his own child? What kind of man could admit that he didn't want his daughter around?

"You're going to be staying here, with Alan, for a while," Sharon said, smiling tremulously at her daughter.

He'd given in. The former special operations lieutenant had given in. Mia didn't know whether to be glad for the little girl, or concerned. This child needed more than this man could give her. Mia risked another look up, and found his disturbingly blue eyes still watching her.

"Won't that be fun?" Sharon hopefully asked Natasha.

The little girl considered the question thoughtfully. "No," she finally said.

Alan Francisco laughed. Mia hadn't thought him capable, but he actually smiled and snorted with laughter, covering it quickly with a cough. When he looked up again, he wasn't smiling, but she could swear she saw amusement in his eyes.

"I want to go with you," Natasha told her mother, a trace of panic in her voice. "Why can't I go with you?"

Sharon's lip trembled, as if she were the child. "Because you can't," she said ineffectively. "Not this time."

The little girl's gaze shifted to Alan and then quickly back to Sharon. "Do we know him?" she asked.

"Yes," Sharon told her. "Of course we know him. He's your uncle Alan. You remember Alan. He's in the Navy...?"

But the little girl shook her head.

"I'm your mom's brother," Alan said to the little girl.

Her brother. Alan was Sharon's brother. Not her husband. Mia didn't want to feel anything at that news. She refused to feel relieved. She refused to feel, period. She weeded her garden, pretending she couldn't hear any of the words being spoken.

Natasha gazed at her mother. "Will you come back?" she asked in a very small voice.

Mia closed her eyes. But she did feel. She felt for this little girl; she felt her fear and pain. Her heart ached for the mother, too, God help her. And she felt for blue-eyed Alan Francisco. But what she felt for him, she couldn't begin to define.

"I always do," Sharon said, dissolving once more into tears as she enveloped the little girl in a hug. "Don't I?" But then she quickly set Natasha aside. "I've got to go. Be good. I love you." She turned to Alan. "The address of the detox center is in the suitcase."

Alan nodded, and with a creak of her crutches, Sharon hurried away.

Natasha stared expressionlessly after her mother, watching until the woman disappeared from view. Then, with only a very slight tightening of her lips, she turned to look at Alan.

Mia looked at him, too, but this time his gaze never left the little girl. All of the amusement was gone from his eyes, leaving only sadness and compassion.

All of his anger had vanished. All of the rage that seemed to burn endlessly within him was temporarily doused. His blue eyes were no longer icy—instead they seemed almost warm. His chiseled features looked softer, too, as he tried to smile at Natasha. He may not have wanted her—he'd said as much—but now that she was here, it seemed as if he were going to do his best to make things easier for her.

Mia looked up to see that the little girl's eyes had filled with tears. She was trying awfully hard not to cry, but one tear finally escaped, rolling down her face. She wiped at it fiercely, fighting the flood.

"I know you don't remember me," Alan said to Natasha, his voice impossibly gentle. "But we met five years ago. On January 4."

Natasha all but stopped breathing. "That's my birthday," she said, gazing across the courtyard at him.

Alan's forced smile became genuine. "I know," he said. "I was driving your mom to the hospital and…" He broke off, looking closely at her. "You want a hug?" he asked. "Because I could really use a hug right now, and I'd sure appreciate it if you could give me one."

Natasha considered his words, then nodded. She slowly crossed to him.

"You better hold your breath, though," Alan told her ruefully. "I think I smell bad."

She nodded again, then carefully climbed onto his lap. Mia tried not to watch, but it was nearly impossible not to look at the big man, with his arms wrapped so tentatively around the little girl, as if he were afraid she might break. But when

Natasha's arms went up and locked securely around his neck, Alan closed his eyes, holding the little girl more tightly.

Mia had thought his request for a hug had been purely for Natasha's sake, but now she had to wonder. With all of his anger and his bitterness over his injured leg, it was possible Alan Francisco hadn't let anyone close enough to give him the warmth and comfort of a hug in quite some time. And everyone needed warmth and comfort—even big, tough professional soldiers.

Mia looked away, trying to concentrate on weeding her last row of flowers. But she couldn't help but overhear Natasha say, "You don't smell bad. You smell like Mommy—when she wakes up."

Alan didn't look happy with that comparison. "Terrific," he murmured.

"She's grouchy in the morning," Natasha said. "Are you grouchy in the morning, too?"

"These days I'm afraid I'm grouchy all the time," he admitted.

Natasha was quiet for a moment, considering that. "Then I'll keep the TV turned down really quiet so it doesn't bother you."

Alan laughed again, just a brief exhale of air. Still, it drew Mia's eyes to his face. When he smiled, he transformed. When he smiled, despite the pallor of his skin and his heavy stubble and his uncombed hair, he became breathtakingly handsome.

"That's probably a good idea," he said.

Natasha didn't get off his lap. "I don't remember meeting you before," she said.

"You wouldn't," Alan said. He shifted painfully. Even Natasha's slight weight was too much for his injured knee, and he moved her so that she was sitting on his good leg. "When we first met, you were still inside your mom's belly. You decided that you wanted to be born, and you didn't want to wait. You decided you wanted to come into the world in the front seat of my truck."

"Really?" Natasha was fascinated.

Alan nodded. "Really. You came out before the ambulance could get there. You were in such a hurry, I had to catch you and hold on to you to keep you from running a lap around the block."

"Babies can't run," the little girl scoffed.

"Maybe not *regular* babies," Alan said. "But you came out doing the tango, smoking a cigar and hollering at everybody. Oh, baby, were you loud."

Natasha giggled. "Really?"

"Really," Alan said. "Not the tango and the cigar, but the loud. Come on," he added, lifting her off his lap. "Grab your suitcase and I'll give you the nickel tour of my condo. You can do…something…while I take a shower. Man, do I need a shower."

Natasha tried to pick up her suitcase, but it was too heavy for her. She tried dragging it after her uncle, but she was never going to get it up the stairs. When Alan turned back to see her struggle, he stopped.

"I better get that," he said. But even as he spoke, a change came over his face. The anger was back. Anger and frustration.

Mia was only one thought behind him, and she realized almost instantly that Alan Francisco was not going to be able to carry Natasha's suitcase up the stairs. With one hand on his cane, and the other pulling himself up on the cast-iron railing, it wasn't going to happen.

She stood up, brushing the dirt from her hands. However she did this, it was going to be humiliating for him. And, as with all painful things, it was probably best to do it quickly—to get it over with.

"I'll get that," she said cheerfully, taking the suitcase out of Natasha's hand. Mia didn't wait for Alan to speak or react. She swept up the stairs, taking them two at a time, and set the suitcase down outside the door to 2C.

"Beautiful morning, isn't it?" she called out as she went into her own apartment and grabbed her watering can.

She was outside again in an instant, and as she started down the stairs, she saw that Alan hadn't moved. Only the expression on his face had changed. His eyes were even darker and angrier and his face was positively stormy. His mouth was tight. All signs of his earlier smile were gone.

"I didn't ask for your help," he said in a low, dangerous voice.

"I know," Mia said honestly, stopping several steps from the bottom so she could look at him, eye to eye. "I figured you wouldn't ask. And if *I* asked, I knew you would get all mad and you wouldn't let me help. This way, you can get as mad as you want, but the suitcase is already upstairs." She smiled at him. "So go on. Get mad. Knock yourself out."

As Mia turned and headed back to her garden, she could feel Alan's eyes boring into her back. His expression hadn't changed—he *was* mad. Mad at her, mad at the world.

She knew she shouldn't have helped him. She should have simply let him deal with his problems, let him work things out. She knew she shouldn't get entangled with someone who was obviously in need.

But Mia couldn't forget the smile that had transformed Alan into a real human being instead of this rocky pillar of anger that he seemed to be most of the time. She couldn't forget the gentle way he'd talked to the little girl, trying his best to set her at ease. And she couldn't forget the look on his face when little Natasha had given him a hug.

Mia couldn't forget—even though she knew that she'd be better off if she could.

4

Frisco started to open the bathroom door, but on second thought stopped and wrapped his towel around his waist first.

He could hear the sound of the television in the living room as he leaned heavily on his cane and went into his bedroom, shutting the door behind him.

A kid. What the hell was he going to do with a kid for the next six weeks?

He tossed his cane on the unmade bed and rubbed his wet hair with his towel. Of course, it wasn't as if his work schedule were overcrowded. He'd surely be able to squeeze Natasha in somewhere between "Good Morning, America" and the "Late Show with David Letterman."

Still, little kids required certain specific attention—like food at regular intervals, baths every now and then, a good night's sleep that didn't start at four in the morning and stretch all the way out past noon. Frisco could barely even provide those things for himself, let alone someone else.

Hopping on his good leg, he dug through his still-packed duffel bag, searching for clean underwear. Nothing.

It had been years since he'd had to cook for himself. His kitchen skills were more geared toward knowing which cleaning solutions made the best flammable substances when combined with other household products.

He moved to his dresser, and found only a pair of silk boxers that a lady friend had bought him a lifetime ago. He pulled on his bathing suit instead.

There was nothing to eat in his refrigerator besides a lemon and a six-pack of Mexican beer. His kitchen cabinets contained only shakers of moisture-solidified salt and pepper and an ancient bottle of tabasco sauce.

The second bedroom in his condo was nearly as bare as his cabinets. It had no furniture, only several rows of boxes neatly stacked along one wall. Tasha was going to have to crash on the couch until Frisco could get her a bed and whatever other kind of furniture a five-year-old girl needed.

Frisco pulled on a fresh T-shirt, throwing the clothes he'd been wearing onto the enormous and ever-expanding pile of dirty laundry in the corner of the room…some of it dating from the last time he'd been here, over five years ago. Even the cleaning lady who'd come in yesterday afternoon hadn't dared to touch it.

They'd kicked him out of the physical therapy center before laundry day. He'd arrived here yesterday with two bags of gear and an enormous duffel bag filled with dirty laundry. Somehow he was going to have to figure out a way to get his dirty clothes down to the laundry room on the first floor— and his clean clothes back up again.

But the first thing he had to do was make sure his collection of weapons were all safely locked up. Frisco didn't know much about five-year-olds, but he was certain of one thing— they didn't mix well with firearms.

He quickly combed his hair and, reaching for the smooth wood of his cane, he headed toward the sound of the TV. After he secured his private arsenal, he and Tasha would hobble on down to the grocery store on the corner and pick up some chow for lunch and…

On the television screen, a row of topless dancers gyrated. Frisco lunged for the off switch. Hell! His cable must've come with some kind of men's channel—the Playboy Channel or something similar. He honestly hadn't known.

"Whoa, Tash. I've got to program that off the remote control," he said, turning to the couch to face her.

Except she wasn't sitting on the couch.

His living room was small, and one quick look assured him

that she wasn't even in the room. Hell, that was a relief. He limped toward the kitchen. She wasn't there, either, and his relief turned to apprehension.

"Natasha…?" Frisco moved as quickly as he could down the tiny hallway toward the bedrooms and bathroom. He looked, and then he looked again, even glancing underneath his bed and in both closets.

The kid was gone.

His knee twinged as he used a skittering sort of hop and skip to propel himself back into the living room and out the screen door.

She wasn't on the second-floor landing, or anywhere in immediate view in the condo courtyard. Frisco could see Mia Summerton still working, crouched down among the explosion of flowers that were her garden, a rather silly-looking floppy straw hat covering the top of her head.

"Hey!"

She looked up, startled and uncertain as to where his voice had come from.

"Up here."

She was too far away for him to see exactly which shade of green or brown her eyes were right now. They were wide though. Her surprise quickly changed to wariness.

He could see a dark V of perspiration along the collar and down the front of her T-shirt. Her face glistened in the morning heat, and she reached up and wiped her forehead with the back of one arm. It left a smudge of dirt behind.

"Have you seen Natasha—you know, the little girl with red hair? Did she come down this way?"

Mia rinsed her hands in a bucket of water and stood up. "No—and I've been out here since you went upstairs."

Frisco swore and started down past his condo door, toward the stairs at the other side of the complex.

"What happened?" Mia came up the stairs and caught up with him easily.

"I got out of the shower and she was gone," he told her curtly, trying to move as quickly as he could. Damn, he didn't want to deal with this. The morning sun had moved high into the sky and the brightness still made his head throb—as did every jarring step he took. It was true that living with him wasn't going to be any kind of party, but the kid didn't have to run away, for God's sake.

But then he saw it.

Sparkling and deceptively pure looking, the alluring blue Pacific Ocean glimmered and danced, beckoning in the distance. The beach was several blocks away. Maybe the kid was like him and had salt water running through her veins. Maybe she caught one look at the water and headed for the beach. Maybe she wasn't running away. Maybe she was just exploring. Or maybe she was pushing the edge of the obedience envelope, testing him to see just what she could get away with.

"Do you think she went far? Do you want me to get my car?" Mia asked.

Frisco turned to look at her and realized she was keeping pace with him. He didn't want her help, but dammit, he needed it. If he was going to find Tasha quickly, four eyes were definitely better than two. And a car was far better than a bum knee and a cane when it came to getting someplace fast.

"Yeah, get your car," he said gruffly. "I want to check down at the beach."

Mia nodded once then ran ahead. She'd pulled her car up at the stairs that led to the parking lot before he'd even arrived at the bottom of them. She reached across the seat, unlocking the passenger's side door of her little subcompact.

Frisco knew he wasn't going to fit inside. He got in anyway, forcing his right knee to bend more than it comfortably could. Pain and its accompanying nausea washed over him, and he swore sharply—a repetitive, staccato chant, a profane mantra designed to bring him back from the edge.

He looked up to find Mia watching him, her face carefully expressionless.

"Drive," he told her, his voice sounding harsh to his own ears. "Come on—I don't even know if this kid can swim."

She put the car into first gear and it lurched forward. She took the route the child might well have taken if she was, indeed, heading for the beach. Frisco scanned the crowded sidewalks. What exactly had the kid been wearing? Some kind of white shirt with a pattern on it…balloons? Or maybe flowers? And a bright-colored pair of shorts. Or was she wearing a skirt? Was it green or blue? He couldn't remember, so he watched for her flaming red hair instead.

"Any sign of her?" Mia asked. "Do you want me to slow down?"

"No," Frisco said. "Let's get down to the water and make sure she's not there first. We can work our way back more slowly."

"Aye, aye, sir." Mia stepped on the gas, risking a glance at Alan Francisco. He didn't seem to notice her military-style affirmative. He was gripping the handle up above the passenger window so tightly that his knuckles were white. The muscles in his jaw were just as tight, and he kept watching out the window, searching for any sign of his tiny niece in the summertime crowd.

He'd shaved, she noticed, glancing at him again. He looked slightly less dangerous without the stubble—but only slightly.

He'd hurt his knee getting into her car, and Mia knew from the paleness of his face underneath his tan that it hurt him still. But he didn't complain. Other than his initial explosion of profanity, he hadn't said a word about it. Finding his niece took priority over his pain. Obviously it took priority, since finding Natasha was important enough for him to call a temporary truce with Mia and accept her offer of help.

She was signaling to make the left into the beach parking lot when the man finally spoke.

"There she is! With some kid. At two o'clock—"

"Where?" Mia slowed, uncertain.

"Just stop the car!"

Francisco opened the door, and Mia slammed on the brakes,

afraid he would jump out while the car was still moving. And then she saw Natasha. The little girl was at the edge of the parking lot, sitting on the top of a picnic table, paying solemn attention to a tall African-American teenage boy who was standing in front of her. Something about the way he wore his low-riding, baggy jeans was familiar. The kid turned, and Mia saw his face.

"That's Thomas King," she said. "That boy who's with Natasha—I know him."

But Francisco was already out of the car, moving as fast as he could with his limp and his cane toward the little girl.

There was nowhere to park. Mia watched through the wind-shield as the former Navy lieutenant descended upon his niece, pulling her none-too-gently from the table and setting her down on the ground behind him. She couldn't hear what he was saying, but she could tell that it wasn't a friendly greeting. She saw Thomas bristle and turn belligerently to-ward Francisco, and she threw on her hazard lights and left the car right where it was in the middle of the lot as she jumped out and ran toward them.

She arrived just in time to hear Thomas say, "You raise one hand to that girl and I'll clean the street with your face."

Alan Francisco's blue eyes had looked deadly and cold when Mia first ran up, but now they changed. Something shifted. "What are you talking about? I'm not going to *hit* her." He sounded incredulous, as if such a thing would never have occurred to him.

"Then why are you shouting at her as if you are?" Thomas King was nearly Francisco's height, but the former SEAL had at least fifty pounds of muscle over him. Still, the teenager stood his ground, his dark eyes flashing and narrowed, his lips tight.

"I'm not—"

"Yes, you are," Thomas persisted. He mimicked the older man. "'What the hell are you doing here? Who the hell gave you permission to leave...' I thought you were going to slam her—and *she* did, too."

Frisco turned to look at Natasha. She had scurried underneath the picnic table, and she looked back at him, her eyes wide. "Tash, you didn't think…"

But she had thought that. He could see it in her eyes, in the way she was cowering. Man, he felt sick.

He crouched down next to the table as best he could. "Natasha, did your mom hit you when she was angry?" He couldn't believe softhearted Sharon would hurt a defenseless child, but liquor did funny things to even the gentlest of souls.

The little girl shook her head no. "Mommy didn't," she told him softly, "but Dwayne did once and I got a bloody lip. Mommy cried, and then we moved out."

Thank God Sharon had had that much sense. Damn Dwayne to hell, whoever he was. What kind of monster would strike a five-year-old child?

What kind of monster would scare her to death by shouting at her the way he just had?

Frisco sat down heavily on the picnic table bench, glancing up at Mia. Her eyes were soft, as if she could somehow read his mind.

"Tash, I'm sorry," he said, rubbing his aching, bleary eyes. "I didn't mean to scare you."

"This some kind of *friend* of yours?" the black kid said to Mia, his tone implying she might want to be more selective in her choice of friends in the future.

"He's in 2C," Mia told the boy. "The mystery neighbor— Lt. Alan Francisco." She directed her next words to Frisco. "This is Thomas King. He's a former student of mine. He lives in 1N with his sister and her kids."

A former…student? That meant that Mia Summerton was a teacher. Damn, if he had had teachers who looked like her, he might've actually gone to high school.

She was watching him now with wariness in her eyes, as if he were a bomb on a trick timer, ready to blow at any given moment.

"Lieutenant," Thomas repeated. "Are you the badge?"

"No, I'm not a cop," Frisco said, tearing his eyes away

from Mia to glance at the kid. "I'm in the Navy...." He caught himself, and shook his head, closing his eyes briefly. "I *was* in the Navy."

Thomas had purposely crossed his arms and tucked both hands underneath them to make sure Frisco knew he had no intention of shaking hands.

"The lieutenant was a SEAL," Mia told Thomas. "That's a branch of special operations—"

"I *know* what a SEAL is," the kid interrupted. He turned to run a bored, cynical eye over Frisco. "One of those crazy freaks that ride the surf and crash their little rubber boats into the rocks down by the hotel in Coronado. Did *you* ever do that?"

Mia was watching him again, too. Damn but she was pretty. And every time she looked at him, every time their eyes met, Frisco felt a very solid slap of mutual sexual awareness. It was almost funny. With the possible exception of her exotic fashion-model face and trim, athletic body, everything about the woman irritated him. He didn't want a nosy neighbor poking around in his life. He didn't need a helpful do-gooder getting in his face and reminding him hourly of his limitations. He had no use for a disgustingly cheerful, flower-planting, antimilitary, unintimidatable, fresh-faced girl-next-door type.

But every single time he looked into her hazel eyes, he felt an undeniable surge of physical attraction. Intellectually, he may have wanted little more than to hide from her, but physically... Well, his body apparently had quite a different agenda. One that included moonlight gleaming on smooth, golden tanned skin, long dark hair trailing across his face, across his chest and lower.

Frisco managed a half smile, wondering if she could read his mind now. He couldn't look away from her, even to answer Thomas's question. "It's called rock portage," he said, "and, yeah. I did that during training."

She didn't blush. She didn't look away from him. She just steadily returned his gaze, slightly lifting one exotic eyebrow.

Frisco had the sense that she did, indeed, know exactly what he was thinking. *Cold day in hell.* She hadn't said those exact words last night, but they echoed in his mind as clearly as if she had.

It was just as well. He was having a pure, raw-sex reaction to her, but she wasn't the pure, raw type. He couldn't picture her climbing into his bed and then slipping away before dawn, no words spoken, only intense pleasure shared. No, once she got into his bed, she would never get out. She had "girl-friend" written all over her, and that was the last thing he needed. She would fill his apartment with flowers from her garden and endless conversation and little notes with smiley faces on them. She'd demand tender kisses and a clean bath-room and heart-to-heart revelations and a genuine interest in her life.

How could he begin to be interested in *her* life, when he couldn't even muster up the slightest enthusiasm for his own?

But he was getting *way* ahead of himself here. He was assuming that he'd have no trouble getting her into his bed in the first place. That might've been true five years ago, but he wasn't exactly any kind of prize anymore. There was no way a girl like Mia would want to be saddled with a man who could barely even walk.

Cold day in hell. Frisco looked out at the blinding blueness of the ocean, feeling his eyes burn from the glare.

"What's a SEAL doing with a kid who can't swim?" Thomas asked. Most of the anger had left the teenager's eyes, leaving behind a cynical disdain and a seemingly ancient wea-riness that made him look far older than his years. He had scars on his face, one bisecting one of his eyebrows, the other marking one of his high, pronounced cheekbones. That, com-bined with the fact that his nose had been broken more than once, gave him a battle-worn look that erased even more of his youth. But except for a few minor slang expressions, Thomas didn't speak the language of the street. He had no discernible accent of any kind, and Frisco wondered if the kid had worked as hard to delete that particular tie with his past and his parents as he himself had.

"Natasha is the lieutenant's niece," Mia explained. "She's going to stay with him for a few weeks. She just arrived today."

"From Mars, right?" Thomas looked under the table and made a face at Natasha.

She giggled. "Thomas thinks I'm from Mars 'cause I didn't know what that water was." Natasha slithered on her belly out from underneath the table. The sand stuck to her clothes, and Frisco realized that she was wet.

"A little Martian girl is the only kind of girl I can think of who hasn't seen the ocean before," Thomas said. "She didn't even seem to know kids shouldn't go into the water alone."

Mia watched a myriad of emotions cross Alan Francisco's face. The lifeguard's flag was out today, signaling a strong undertow and dangerous currents. She saw him look at Thomas and register the fact that the teenager's jeans were wet up to his knees.

"You went in after her," he said, his low voice deceptively even.

Thomas was as nonchalant. "I've got a five-year-old niece, too."

Francisco pulled himself painfully up with his cane. He held out his hand to Thomas. "Thanks, man. I'm sorry about before. I'm…new at this kid thing."

Mia held her breath. She knew Thomas well, and if he'd decided that Alan Francisco was the enemy, he'd never shake his hand.

But Thomas hesitated only briefly before he clasped the older man's hand.

Again, a flurry of emotions flickered in Francisco's eyes, and again he tried to hide it all. Relief. Gratitude. Sorrow. Always sorrow and always shame. But it was all gone almost before it was even there. When Alan Francisco tried to hide his emotions, he succeeded, tucking them neatly behind the ever-present anger that simmered inside of him.

He managed to use that anger to hide everything quite nicely—everything except the seven-thousand-degree nuclear-powered sexual attraction he felt for her. That he put on display, complete with neon signs and million-dollar-a-minute advertising.

Good grief, last night when he'd made that crack about wanting her to share his bed, she'd thought he'd been simply trying to scare her off.

She had been dead wrong. The way he'd looked at her just minutes ago had nearly singed her eyebrows off.

And the *truly* stupid thing was that the thought of having a physical relationship with this man didn't send her running for her apartment and the heavy-duty dead bolt that she'd had installed on her door. She couldn't figure out why. Lt. Alan Francisco was a real-life version of G.I. Joe, he was probably a male chauvinist, he drank so much that he still looked like hell at noon on a weekday *and* he carried a seemingly permanent chip on his shoulder. Yet for some bizarre reason, Mia had no trouble imagining herself pulling him by the hand into her bedroom and melting together with him on her bed.

It had nothing to do with his craggy-featured, handsome face and enticingly hard-muscled body. Well, yes, okay, so she wasn't being completely honest with herself. It had at least a *little* bit to do with that. It was true—the fact that the man looked as if he should have his own three-month segment in a hunk-of-the-month calendar was not something she'd failed to notice. And notice, and notice and notice.

But try as she might, it was the softness in his eyes when he spoke to Natasha and his crooked, painful attempts to smile at the little girl that she found hard to resist. She was a sucker for kindness, and she suspected that beneath this man's outer crust of anger and bitterness, and despite his sometimes crude language and rough behavior, there lurked the kindest of souls.

"Here's the deal about the beach," Alan Francisco was saying to his niece. "You never come down here without a grown-up, and you never, *ever* go into the water alone."

"That's what Thomas said," Tasha told him. "He said I might've drownded."

"Thomas is right," Francisco told her.

"What's drownded?"

"Drowned," he corrected her. "You ever try to breathe underwater?"

Tash shook her head no, and her red curls bounced.

"Well, don't try it. People can't breathe underwater. Only fish can. And you don't look like a fish to me."

The little girl giggled, but persisted. "What's drownded?"

Mia crossed her arms, wondering if Francisco would try to sidestep the issue again, or if he would take the plunge and discuss the topic of death with Natasha.

"Well," he said slowly, "if someone goes into the water, and they can't swim, or they hurt themselves, or the waves are too high, then the water might go over their head. Then they can't breathe. Normally, when the water goes over your head it's no big deal. You hold your breath. And then you just swim to the surface and stick your nose and mouth out and take a breath of air. But like I said, maybe this person doesn't know how to swim, or maybe their leg got a cramp, or the water's too rough, so they can't get up to the air. And if there's no air for them to breathe…well, they'll die. They'll drown. People need to breathe air to live."

Natasha gazed unblinkingly at her uncle, her head tilted slightly to one side. "I don't know how to swim," she finally said.

"Then I'll teach you," Francisco said unhesitatingly. "Everyone should know how to swim. But even when you *do* know how to swim, you still don't swim alone. That way, if you *do* get hurt, you got a friend who can save you from drowning. Even in the SEALs we didn't swim alone. We had something called swim buddies—a friend who looked out for you, and you'd look out for him, too. You and me, Tash, for the next few weeks, we're going to be swim buddies, okay?"

"I'm outta here, Ms. S. I don't want to be late for work."

Mia turned to Thomas, glad he'd broken into her reverie.

She'd been standing there like an idiot, gazing at Alan Francisco, enthralled by his conversation with his niece. "Be careful," she told him.

"Always am."

Natasha crouched down in the sand and began pushing an old Popsicle stick around as if it were a car. Thomas bent over and ruffled her hair. "See you later, Martian girl." He nodded to Francisco. "Lieutenant."

The SEAL pulled himself up and off the bench. "Call me Frisco. And thanks again, man."

Thomas nodded once more and then was gone.

"He works part-time as a security guard at the university," Mia told Francisco. "That way he can audit college courses in his spare time—spare time that doesn't exist because he also works a full day as a landscaper's assistant over in Coronado."

He was looking at her again, his steel blue eyes shuttered and unreadable this time. He hadn't told *her* she could call him Frisco. Maybe it was a guy thing. Maybe SEALs weren't allowed to let women call them by their nicknames. Or maybe it was more personal than that. Maybe Alan Francisco didn't want her as a friend. He'd certainly implied as much last night.

Mia looked back at her car, still sitting in the middle of the parking lot. "Well," she said, feeling strangely awkward. She had no problem holding her own with this man when he came on too strong or acted rudely. But when he simply stared at her like this, with no expression besides the faintest glimmer of his ever-present anger on his face, she felt off balance and ill at ease, like a schoolgirl with an unrequited crush. "I'm glad we found—*you* found Natasha…" She glanced back at her car again, more to escape his scrutiny than to reassure herself it was still there. "Can I give you a lift back to the condo?"

Frisco shook his head. "No, thanks."

"I could adjust the seat, see if I could make it more comfortable for you to—"

"No, we've got some shopping to do."

"But Natasha's all wet."

"She'll dry. Besides, I could use the exercise."

Exercise? Was he kidding? "What you could use is a week or two off your feet, in bed."

Just like that, he seemed to come alive, his mouth twisting into a sardonic half smile. His eyes sparked with heat and he lowered his voice, leaning forward to speak directly into her ear. "Are you volunteering to keep me there? I knew sooner or later you'd change your mind."

He knew nothing of the sort. He'd only said that to rattle and irritate her. Mia refused to let him see just how irritated his comment had made her. Instead, she stepped even closer, looking up at him, letting her gaze linger on his mouth before meeting his eyes, meaning to make him wonder, and to make him squirm before she launched her attack.

But she launched nothing as she looked into his eyes. His knowing smile had faded, leaving behind only heat. It magnified, doubling again and again, increasing logarithmically as their gazes locked, burning her down to her very soul. She knew that he could see more than just a mere reflection of his desire in her eyes, and she knew without a doubt that she'd given too much away. This fire that burned between them was not his alone.

The sun was beating down on them and her mouth felt parched. She tried to swallow, tried to moisten her dry lips, tried to walk away. But she couldn't move.

He reached out slowly. She could see it coming—he was going to touch her, pull her close against the hard muscles of his chest and cover her mouth with his own in a heated, heart-stopping, nuclear meltdown of a kiss.

But he touched her only lightly, tracing the path of a bead of sweat that had trailed down past her ear, down her neck and across her collarbone before it disappeared beneath the collar of her T-shirt. He touched her gently, only with one finger, but in many ways it was far more sensual, far more intimate than even a kiss.

The world seemed to spin and Mia almost reached for him. But sanity kicked in, thank God, and instead she backed away.

"When I change my mind," she said, her voice barely louder than a whisper, "it'll be a cold day in July."

She turned on legs that were actually trembling—*trembling*—and headed toward her car. He made no move to follow, but as she got inside and drove away, she could see him in the rearview mirror, still watching her.

Had she convinced him? She doubted it. She wasn't sure she'd even managed to convince herself.

5

"Okay, Tash," Frisco called down from the second-floor landing where he'd finally finished lashing the framework to the railing. "Ready for a test run?"

She nodded, and he let out the crank and lowered the rope down to her.

The realization had come to him while they were grocery shopping. He wasn't going to be able to carry the bags of food he bought up the stairs to his second-floor condominium. And Tasha, as helpful as she tried to be when she wasn't wandering off, couldn't possibly haul all the food they needed up a steep flight of stairs. She could maybe handle one or two lightweight bags, but certainly no more than that.

But Frisco had been an expert in unconventional warfare for the past ten years. He could come up with alternative, creative solutions to damn near any situation—including this one. Of course, this wasn't war, which made it that much easier. Whatever he came up with, he wasn't going to have to pull it off while underneath a rain of enemy bullets.

It hadn't taken him long to come up with a solution. He and Tasha had stopped at the local home building supply store and bought themselves the fixings for a rope-and-pulley system. Frisco could've easily handled just a rope to pull things up to the second-floor landing, but with a crank and some pulleys, Natasha would be able to use it, too.

The plastic bags filled with the groceries they'd bought were on the ground, directly underneath the rope to which he'd attached a hook.

"Hook the rope to one of the bags," Frisco commanded his niece, leaning over the railing. "Right through the handles—that's right."

Mia Summerton was watching him.

He'd been hyperaware of her from the moment he and Tash had climbed out of the taxi with all of their groceries. She'd been back in her garden again, doing God knows what and watching him out of the corner of her eye.

She'd watched as he'd transferred the frozen food and perishables into a backpack he'd bought and carried them inside. She'd watched as he'd done the same with the building supplies and set them out on the second-floor landing. She'd watched as he awkwardly lowered himself down to sit on the stairs with his tool kit and began to work.

She'd watched, but she'd been careful never to let him catch her watching.

Just the same, he felt her eyes following him. And he could damn near smell her awareness.

Man, whatever it was that they'd experienced back on the beach... He shook his head in disbelief. Whatever it was, he wanted some more. A whole lot of more. She'd looked at him, and he'd been caught in an amazing vortex of animal magnetism. He hadn't been able to resist touching her, hadn't been able to stop thinking about exactly where that droplet of perspiration had gone after it had disappeared from view beneath her shirt. It hadn't taken much imagination to picture it traveling slowly between her breasts, all the way down to her softly indented belly button.

He'd wanted to dive in after it.

It had been damn near enough to make him wonder if he'd seriously underrated smiley-face-endowed notes.

But he'd seen the shock in Mia's eyes. She hadn't expected the attraction that had surged between them. She didn't want it, didn't want him. Certainly not for a single, mind-blowing sexual encounter, and *definitely* not for anything longer term. That was no big surprise.

"I can't get it," Natasha called up to him, her face scrunched with worry.

Mia had kept to herself ever since they'd arrived home. Her offers to help had been noticeably absent. But now she stood up, apparently unable to ignore the note of anxiety in Tasha's voice.

"May I help you with that, Natasha?" She spoke directly to the little girl. She didn't even bother to look up at Frisco.

Frisco wiped the sweat from his face as he watched Tasha step back and Mia attach the hook to the plastic handles of the grocery bags. It had to be close to ninety degrees in the shade, but when Mia finally did glance up at him there was a definite wintry chill in the air.

She was trying her damnedest to act as if she had not even the slightest interest in him. Yet she'd spent the past hour and a half watching him. Why?

Maybe whatever this was that constantly drew his eyes in her direction, whatever this was that had made him hit his thumb with his hammer more times than he could count, whatever this was that made every muscle in his body tighten in anticipation when he so much as *thought* about her, whatever this uncontrollable sensation was—maybe she felt it, too.

It was lust and desire, amplified a thousandfold, mutated into something far more powerful.

He didn't want her. He didn't want the trouble, didn't want the hassle, didn't want the grief. And yet, at the same time, he wanted her desperately. He wanted her more than he'd ever wanted any woman before.

If he'd been the type to get frightened, he would've been terrified.

"We better stand back," Mia warned Tasha as Frisco began turning the crank.

It went up easily enough, the bag bulging and straining underneath the weight. But then, as if in slow motion, the bottom of the plastic bag gave out, and its contents went plummeting to the ground.

Frisco swore loudly as a six-pack shattered into pieces of

brown glass, the beer mixing unappetizingly with cranberry juice from a broken half-gallon container, four flattened tomatoes and an avocado that never again would see the light of day. The loaf of Italian bread that had also been in the bag had, thankfully, bounced free and clear of the disaster.

Mia looked down at the wreckage, and then up at Alan Francisco. He'd cut short his litany of curses and stood silently, his mouth tight and his eyes filled with far more despair than the situation warranted.

But she knew he was seeing more than a mess on the courtyard sidewalk as he looked over the railing. She knew he was seeing his life, shattered as absolutely as those beer bottles.

Still he took a deep breath, and forced himself to smile down into Natasha's wide eyes.

"We're on the right track here," he said, lowering the rope again. "We're definitely very close to outrageous success." Using his cane, he started down the stairs. "How about we try double bagging? Or a paper bag inside of the plastic one?"

"How about cloth bags?" Mia suggested.

"Back away, Tash—that's broken glass," Alan called warningly. "Yeah, cloth bags would work, but I don't have any."

Alan, Mia thought. When had he become Alan instead of Francisco? Was it when he looked down at his niece and made himself smile despite his pain, or was it earlier, at the beach parking lot, when he'd nearly lit Mia on fire with a single look?

Mia ran up the stairs past him, suddenly extremely aware that he'd taken off his shirt nearly an hour ago. His smooth tanned skin and hard muscles had been hard to ignore even from a distance. Up close it was impossible for Mia not to stare.

He wore only a loose-fitting, bright-colored bathing suit, and it rode low on his lean hips. His stomach was a washboard of muscles, and his skin gleamed with sweat. And that other tattoo on his bicep was a sea serpent, not a mermaid, as she'd first thought.

"I've got some bags," Mia called out, escaping into the coolness of her apartment, stopping for a moment to take a long, shaky breath. What was it about this man that made her heart beat double time? He was intriguing; she couldn't deny that. And he exuded a wildness, a barely tamed sexuality that constantly managed to captivate her. But so what? He was sexy. He was gorgeous. He was working hard to overcome a raftload of serious problems, making him seem tragic and fascinating. But these were not the criteria she usually used to decide whether or not to enter into a sexual relationship with a man.

The fact was that she *wasn't* going to sleep with him, she told herself firmly. Definitely probably not. She rolled her eyes in self-disgust. Definitely *probably …?*

It had to be the full moon making her feel this way. Or— as her mother might say—maybe her astrological planets were lined up in some strange configuration, making her feel restless and reckless. Or maybe as she neared thirty, her body was changing, releasing hormones in quantities that she could no longer simply ignore.

Whatever the reason—mystical or scientific—the fact remained that she would *not* have sex with a stranger. Whatever happened between them, it wasn't going to happen until she'd had a chance to get to know this man. And once she got to know him and his vast collection of both physical and psychological problems, she had a feeling that staying away from him wasn't going to be so very difficult.

She took her cloth grocery bags from the closet and went back outside. Alan was crouched awkwardly down on the sidewalk, attempting to clean up the mess.

"Alan, wait. Don't try to pick up the broken glass," she called down to him. "I've got work gloves and a shovel you can use to clean it up." She didn't dare offer to do the work for him. She knew he would refuse. "I'll get 'em. Here— catch."

She threw the bags over the railing, and he caught them with little effort as she turned to go back inside.

Frisco looked at the printed message on the outside of the bags Mia had tossed him and rolled his eyes. Of course it had to be something political. Shaking his head, he sat down on the grass and began transferring the undemolished remainder of the groceries into the cloth bags.

"'Wouldn't it be nice if we fully funded education, and the government had to hold a bake sale to buy a bomber?'" he quoted from the bags when Mia came back down the stairs.

She was holding a plastic trash bag, a pair of work gloves and what looked rather suspiciously like a pooper-scooper. She gave him a crooked smile. "Yeah," she said. "I thought you would like that."

"I'd be glad to get into a knock-down, drag-out argument about the average civilian's ignorance regarding military spending some other time," he told her. "But right now I'm not really in the mood."

"How about if I pretend you didn't just call me ignorant, and *you* pretend I don't think you're some kind of rigid, militaristic, dumb-as-a-stone professional soldier?" she said much too sweetly.

Frisco had to laugh. It was a deep laugh, a belly laugh, and he couldn't remember the last time he'd done that. He was still smiling when he looked up at her. "That sounds fair," he said. "And who knows—maybe we're both wrong."

Mia smiled back at him, but it was tentative and wary.

"I didn't get to thank you for helping me this morning," he said. "I'm sorry if I was…"

Mia gazed at him, waiting for him to finish his sentence. Unfriendly? Worried? Upset? Angry? Inappropriate? Too sexy for words? She wondered exactly what he was apologizing for.

"Rude," he finally finished. He glanced over at Natasha. She was lying on her back in the shade of a palm tree, staring up at the sky through both her spread fingers and the fronds, singing some unintelligible and probably improvised song. "I'm in way over my head here," he admitted with another crooked smile. "I don't know the first thing about taking care of a kid, and…" He shrugged. "Even if I did, these days I'm not exactly in the right place psychologically, you know?"

"You're doing great."

The look he shot her was loaded with amusement and disbelief. "She was under my care for not even thirty minutes and I managed to lose her." He shifted his weight, trying to get more comfortable, wincing slightly at the pain in his leg. "While we were walking home, I talked to her about setting up some rules and regs—basic stuff, like she has to tell me if she's going outside the condo, and she's got to play inside the courtyard. She looked at me like I was speaking French." He paused, glancing back at the little girl again. "As far as I can tell, Sharon had absolutely no rules. She let the kid go where she pleased, when she pleased. I'm not sure anything I said sunk in."

He pulled himself up with his cane, and carried one of the filled cloth bags toward the hook and rope, sidestepping the puddle of broken glass, sodden cardboard and cranberry juiced-beer.

"You've got to give her time, Alan," Mia said. "You've got to remember that living here without her mom around has to be as new and as strange to her as it is to you."

He turned to look back at her as he attached the hook to the cloth handles. "You know," he said, "generally people don't call me Alan. I'm Frisco. I've been Frisco for years." He started up the stairs. "I mean, Sharon—my sister—she calls me Alan, but everyone else calls me Frisco, from my swim buddy to my CO.…"

Frisco looked down at Mia. She was standing in the courtyard, watching him and not trying to hide it this time. Her gardening clothes were almost as filthy as his, and several strands of her long, dark hair had escaped from her ponytail. How come he felt like a sweat-sodden reject from hell, while she managed to look impossibly beautiful?

"CO?" she repeated.

"Commanding Officer," he explained, turning the crank.

The bag went up, and this time it made it all the way to the second floor.

Mia applauded and Natasha came over to do several clumsy forward rolls in the grass in celebration.

Frisco reached over the railing and pulled the bag up and onto the landing next to him.

"Lower the rope. I'll hook up the next one," Mia said.

It went up just as easily.

"Come on, Tash. Come upstairs and help me put away these supplies," Frisco called, and the little girl came barreling up the stairs. He turned back to look down at Mia. "I'll be down in a minute to clean up that mess."

"Alan, you know, I don't have anything better to do and I can—"

"Frisco," he interrupted her. "Not Alan. And *I'm* cleaning it up, not you."

"Do you mind if I call you Alan? I mean, after all, it is your *name*—"

"Yeah, I mind. It's not my name. Frisco's my name. Frisco is who I became when I joined the SEALs." His voice got softer. "Alan is nobody."

Frisco woke to the sound of a blood-chilling scream.

He was rolling out of bed, onto the floor, reaching, searching for his weapon, even before he was fully awake. But he had no firearm hidden underneath his pillow or down alongside his bed—he'd locked them all up in a trunk in his closet. He wasn't in the jungle on some dangerous mission, catching a combat nap. He was in his bedroom, in San Felipe, California, and the noise that had kicked him out of bed came from the powerful vocal cords of his five-year-old niece, who was supposed to be sound asleep on the couch in the living room.

Frisco stumbled to the wall and flipped on the light. Reaching this time for his cane, he opened his bedroom door and staggered down the hallway toward the living room.

He could see Natasha in the dim light that streamed down

the hallway from his bedroom. She was crying, sitting up in a tangle of sheets on the couch, sweat matting her hair.

"Hey," Frisco said. "What the h…uh… What's going on, Tash?"

The kid didn't answer. She just kept on crying.

Frisco sat down next to her, but all she did was cry.

"You want a hug or something?" he asked, and she shook her head no and kept on crying.

"Um," Frisco said, uncertain of what to do, or what to say. There was a tap on the door.

"You want to get that?" Frisco asked Natasha.

She didn't respond.

"I guess I'll get it then," he said, unlocking the bolt and opening the heavy wooden door.

Mia stood on the other side of the screen. She was wearing a white bathrobe and her hair was down loose around her shoulders. "Is everything all right?"

"No, I'm not murdering or torturing my niece," Frisco said flatly and closed the door. But he opened it again right away and pushed open the screen. "You wouldn't happen to know where Tash's On/Off switch is, would you?"

"It's dark in here," Mia said, stepping inside. "Maybe you should turn on all the lights so that she can see where she is."

Frisco turned on the bright overhead light—and realized he was standing in front of his neighbor and his niece in nothing but the new, tight-fitting, utilitarian white briefs he'd bought during yesterday's second trip to the grocery store. Good thing he'd bought them, or he quite possibly would have been standing there buck naked.

Whether it was the sudden light or the sight of him in his underwear, Frisco didn't know, but Natasha stopped crying, just like that. She still sniffled, and tears still flooded her eyes, but her sirenlike wail was silenced.

Mia was clearly thrown by the sight of him—and determined to act as if visiting with a neighbor who was in his underwear was the most normal thing in the world. She sat down on the couch next to Tasha and gave her a hug. Frisco excused himself and headed down the hall toward his bedroom and a pair of shorts.

It wasn't really that big a deal—Lucky O'Donlon, Frisco's swim buddy and best friend in the SEAL unit, had bought Frisco a tan-through French bathing suit from the Riviera that covered far less of him than these briefs. Of course, the minuscule suit wasn't something he'd ever be caught dead in....

He threw on his shorts and came back out into the living room.

"It must've been a pretty bad nightmare," he heard Mia saying to Tasha.

"I fell into a big, dark hole," Tash said in a tiny voice in between a very major case of hiccups. "And I was screaming and screaming and *screaming,* and I could see Mommy way, way up at the top, but she didn't hear me. She had on her mad face, and she just walked away. And then water went up and over my head, and I knew I was gonna drownd."

Frisco swore silently. He wasn't sure he could relieve Natasha's fears of abandonment, but he would do his best to make sure she didn't fear the ocean. He sat down next to her on the couch and she climbed into his lap. His heart lurched as she locked her little arms around his neck.

"Tomorrow morning we'll start your swimming lessons, okay?" he said gruffly, trying to keep the emotion that had suddenly clogged his throat from sounding in his voice.

Natasha nodded. "When I woke up, it was so dark. And someone turned off the TV."

"I turned it off when I went to bed," Frisco told her.

She lifted her head and gazed up at him. The tip of her nose was pink and her face was streaked and still wet from her tears. "Mommy always sleeps with it on. So she won't feel lonely."

Mia was looking at him over the top of Tasha's red curls. She was holding her tongue, but it was clear that she had something to say.

"Why don't you make a quick trip to the head?" he said to Tasha.

She nodded and climbed off his lap. "The head is the bathroom on a boat," she told Mia, wiping her runny nose on her hand. "Before bedtime, me and Frisco pretended we were on a pirate boat. He was the cap'n."

Mia tried to hide her smile. So *that* was the cause of the odd sounds she'd heard from Frisco's apartment at around eight o'clock.

"We also played Russian Princess," the little girl added.

Frisco actually blushed—his rugged cheekbones were tinged with a delicate shade of pink. "It's after 0200, Tash. Get moving. And wash your face and blow your nose while you're in there."

"Yo ho ho and a bottle of rum," Mia said to him as the little girl disappeared down the hallway.

The pink tinge didn't disappear, but Frisco met her gaze steadily. "I'm doomed, aren't I?" he said, resignation in his voice. "You're going to tease me about this until the end of time."

Mia grinned. "I *do* feel as if I've been armed with a powerful weapon," she admitted, adding, "Your Majesty. Oh, or did you let Natasha take a turn and be the princess?"

"Very funny."

"What I would give to have been a fly on the wall...."

"She's five years old," he tried to explain, running his hand through his disheveled blond hair. "I don't have a single toy in the house. Or any books besides the ones I'm reading— which are definitely inappropriate. I don't even have paper and pencils to draw with—"

She'd gone too far with her teasing. "You don't have to explain. Actually, I think it's incredibly sweet. It's just... surprising. You don't really strike me as the make-believe type."

Frisco leaned forward.

"Look, Tash is gonna come back out soon. If there's something you want to tell me without her overhearing, you better say it now.''

Mia was surprised again. He hadn't struck her as being extremely perceptive. In fact, he always seemed to be a touch self-absorbed and tightly wrapped up in his anger. But he was right. There *was* something that she wanted to ask him about the little girl.

''I was just wondering,'' she said, ''if you've talked to Natasha about exactly where her mother is right now.''

He shook his head.

''Maybe you should.''

He shifted his position, obviously uncomfortable. ''How do you talk about things like addiction and alcoholism to a five-year-old?''

''She probably knows more about it than you'd believe,'' Mia said quietly.

''Yeah, I guess she would,'' he said.

''It might make her feel a little bit less as if she's been deserted.''

He looked up at her, meeting her eyes. Even now, in this moment of quiet, serious conversation, when Mia's eyes met his, there was a powerful burst of heat.

His gaze slipped down to the open neckline of her bathrobe, and she could see him looking at the tiny piece of her night-gown that was exposed. It was white, with a narrow white eyelet ruffle.

He wanted to see the rest of it—she knew that from the hunger in his eyes. Would he be disappointed if he knew that her nightgown was simple and functional? It was plain, not sexy, made from lightweight cotton.

He looked into her eyes again. No, he wouldn't be disappointed, because if they ever were in a position in which he would see her in her nightgown, she would only be wearing it for all of three seconds before he removed it and it landed in a pile on the floor.

The bathroom door opened, and Frisco finally looked away as their pint-size chaperon came back into the living room.

"I'd better go." Mia stood up. "I'll just let myself out."

"I'm hungry," the little girl said.

Frisco pulled himself to his feet. "Well, let's go into the kitchen and see what we can find to eat." He turned to look back at Mia. "I'm sorry we woke you."

"It's all right." Mia turned toward the door.

"Hey, Tash," she heard Frisco say as she let herself out through the screen door, "did your mom talk to you at all about where she was going?"

Mia shut the door behind her and went back into her own apartment.

She took off her robe and got into bed, but sleep was elusive. She couldn't stop thinking about Alan Francisco.

It was funny—the fact that Mia had found out he'd been kind enough to play silly make-believe games with his niece made him blush, yet he'd answered the door dressed only in his underwear with nary a smidgen of embarrassment.

Of course, with a body like his, what was there to be embarrassed about?

Still, the briefs he'd been wearing were brief indeed. The snug-fitting white cotton left very little to the imagination. And Mia had a *very* vivid imagination.

She opened her eyes, willing that same imagination not to get too carried away. Talk about make-believe games. She could make believe that she honestly wasn't bothered by the fact that Alan had spent most of his adult life as a professional soldier, and *Alan* could make believe that he wasn't weighed down by his physical challenge, that he was psychologically healthy, that he wasn't battling depression and resorting to alcohol to numb his unhappiness.

Mia rolled over onto her stomach and switched on the lamp on her bedside table. She was wide-awake, so she would read. It was better than lying in the dark dreaming about things that would never happen.

Frisco covered the sleeping child with a light blanket. The television provided a flickering light and the soft murmur of voices. Tasha hadn't fallen asleep until he'd turned it on, and he knew better now than to turn it off.

He went into the kitchen and poured himself a few fingers of whiskey and took a swallow, welcoming the burn and the sensation of numbness that followed. Man, he needed that. Talking to Natasha about Sharon's required visit to the detox center had *not* been fun. But it had been necessary. Mia had been right.

Tash had had no clue where her mother had gone. She'd thought, in fact, that Sharon had gone to jail. The kid had heard bits and pieces of conversations about the car accident her mother had been involved in, and thought Sharon had been arrested for running someone over.

Frisco had explained how the driver of the car Sharon had struck was badly hurt and in the hospital, but not dead. He didn't go into detail about what would happen if the man were to die—she didn't need to hear that. But he did try to explain what a detox center was, and why Sharon couldn't leave the facility to visit Natasha, and why Tash couldn't go there to visit her.

The kid had looked skeptical when Frisco told her that when Sharon came out of detox, she wouldn't drink anymore. Frisco shook his head. A five-year-old cynic. What was the world coming to?

He took both his glass and the bottle back through the living room and outside onto the dimly lit landing. The sterile environment of air-conditioned sameness in his condo always got to him, particularly at this time of night. He took a deep breath of the humid, salty air, filling his lungs with the warm scent of the sea.

He sat down on the steps and took another sip of the whiskey. He willed it to make him relax, to put him to sleep, to carry him past these darkest, longest hours of the early morning. He silently cursed the fact that here it was, nearly 0300 again, and here he was, wide awake. He'd been so certain when he'd climbed into bed tonight that his exhaustion would carry him through and keep him sound asleep until the morning. He hadn't counted on Tasha's 0200 reveille. He drained his glass and poured himself another drink.

Mia's door barely made a sound as it opened, but he heard it in the quiet. Still, he didn't move as she came outside, and he didn't speak until she stood at the railing, looking down at him.

"How long ago did your dog die?" he asked, keeping his voice low so as not to wake the other condo residents.

She stood very, very still for several long seconds. Finally she laughed softly and sat down next to him on the stairs. "About eight months ago," she told him, her voice velvety in the darkness. "How did you know I had a dog?"

"Good guess," he murmured.

"No, really... Tell me."

"The pooper-scooper you lent me to clean up the mess in the courtyard was a major hint," he said. "And your car had—how do I put this delicately?—a certain canine perfume."

"Her name was Zu. She was about a million years old in dog years. I got her when I was eight."

"Z-o-o?" Frisco asked.

"Z-u," she said. "It was short for Zu-zu. I named her after a little girl in a movie—"

"It's a Wonderful Life," he said.

Mia gazed at him, surprised again. "You've seen it?"

He shrugged. "Hasn't everybody?"

"Probably. But most people don't remember the name of George Bailey's youngest daughter."

"It's a personal favorite." He gave her a sidelong glance. "Amazing that I should like it, huh? All of the war scenes in it are incidental."

"I didn't say that...."

"But you were thinking it." Frisco took a sip of his drink. It was whiskey. Mia could smell the pungent scent from where she was sitting. "Sorry about your dog."

"Thanks," Mia said. She wrapped her arms around her knees. "I still miss her."

"Too soon to get another, huh?" he said.

She nodded.

"What breed was she? No, let me guess." He shifted slightly to face her. She could feel him studying her in the darkness, as if what he could see would help him figure out the answer.

She kept her eyes averted, suddenly afraid to look him in the eye. Why had she come out here? She didn't usually make a habit of inviting disaster, and sitting in the dark a mere foot away from this man was asking for trouble.

"Part lab, part spaniel," Frisco finally said, and she did look up.

"You're half-right—although cocker spaniel was the only part I could ever identify. Although sometimes I thought I saw a bit of golden retriever." She paused. "How did you know she was a mix?"

He lowered his eyebrows in a look of mock incredulousness. "Like you'd ever get a dog from anywhere but the pound...? And probably from death row at the pound, too, right?"

She had to smile. "Okay, obviously you've figured me out completely. There's no longer any mystery in our relationship—"

"Not quite. There's one last thing I need you to clear up for me."

He was smiling at her in the darkness, flirting with her, indulging in lighthearted banter. Mia would have been amazed, had she not learned by now that Alan Francisco was full of surprises.

"What are you doing still awake?" he asked.

"I could ask the same of you," she countered.

"I'm recovering from my talk with Tasha." He looked down into his glass, the light mood instantly broken. "I'm not sure I helped any. She's pretty jaded when it comes to her mom." He laughed, but there was no humor in it. "She has every right to be."

Mia looked over toward Frisco's condo. She could see the

flicker of the television through a gap in the curtains. "She's not still up, is she?"

He sighed, shaking his head no. "She needs the TV on to sleep. I wish *I* could find a solution to not sleeping that's as easy."

Mia looked down at the drink in his hand. "That's probably not it."

Frisco didn't say anything—he just looked at her. To Mia's credit, she didn't say another word. She didn't preach, didn't chastise, didn't lecture.

But after several long moments when he didn't respond, she stood up.

"Good night," she said.

He didn't want her to leave. Oddly enough, the night wasn't so damned oppressive when she was around. But he didn't know what to say to make her stay. He could've told her that he wasn't like Sharon, that he could stop drinking when and if he wanted to, but that would have sounded exactly like a problem drinker's claim.

He could've told her he was strong enough to stop—he just wasn't strong enough right now to face the fact that the Navy had quit on him.

Instead, he said nothing, and she quietly went inside, locking her door behind her.

And he poured himself another drink.

6

Mia's legs burned as she rounded the corner onto Harris Avenue. She was nearly there, down to the last quarter mile of her run, so she put on a burst of speed.

There was construction going on just about a block and a half from the condo complex. Someone was building another fast-food restaurant—just what this neighborhood needed, she thought.

They'd poured the concrete for the foundation, and the project was at a temporary standstill while the mixture hardened. The lot was deserted. Several A&B Construction Co. trucks were parked at haphazard angles among huge hills of displaced dirt and broken asphalt.

A little girl sat digging on top of one of those hills, her face and clothing streaked with dirt, her red hair gleaming in the sunlight.

Mia skidded to a stop.

Sure enough, it was Natasha. She was oblivious to everything around her, digging happily in the sun-hardened dirt, singing a little song.

Mia tried to catch her breath as she ducked underneath the limp yellow ribbon that was supposed to warn trespassers off the construction sight.

"Natasha?"

The little girl looked down at her and smiled. "Hi, Mia."

"Honey, does your uncle know where you are?"

"He's asleep," Tasha said, returning to her digging. She'd found a plastic spoon and a discarded paper cup and was filling it with dirt and stirring the dirt as if it were coffee. She had mud covering close to every inch of her exposed skin—which was probably good since the morning sun was hot enough to give her a bad sunburn. "It's still early. He won't be up 'til later."

Mia glanced at her watch. "Tash, it's nearly ten. He's got to be awake by now. He's probably going crazy, looking for you. Don't you remember what he told you—about not leaving the courtyard, and not even going out of the condo without telling him?"

Tasha glanced up at her. "How can I tell him when he's asleep?" she said matter of factly. "Mommy always slept until after lunchtime."

Mia held out her hands to help Tasha down from the dirt pile. "Come on. I'll walk you home. We can check to see if Frisco's still asleep."

The little girl stood up and Mia swung her down to the ground.

"You *are* dirty, aren't you?" she continued as they began walking toward the condo complex. "I think a bath is in your immediate future."

Tasha looked at her arms and legs. "I already had a bath—a mud bath. Princesses always have mud baths, and they never have more than one bath a day."

"Oh?" Mia said. "I thought princesses always had bubble baths right after their mud baths."

Tasha considered that thoughtfully. "I never had a bubble bath."

"It's very luxurious," Mia told her. What a sight they must've made walking down the street—a mud-encrusted child and an adult literally dripping with perspiration. "The bubbles go right up to your chin."

Natasha's eyes were very wide. "Really?"

"Yeah, and I just happen to have some bubble-bath soap," Mia told her. "You can try it out when we get home—unless you're absolutely certain you don't want a second bath today...?"

"No, princesses can only have one *mud* bath a day," Tasha told her in complete seriousness. "It's okay if they have a mud bath *and* a bubble bath."

"Good." Mia smiled as they entered the condo courtyard.

The complex was still pretty quiet. Most of the residents had left for work hours ago. Still, it was summer vacation for the few kids who lived in the building. Mia could hear the distant strains of television sets and stereo systems. Tasha followed her up the stairs to unit 2C.

The door was ajar and Mia knocked on the screen. "Hello?" she called, but there was no answer. She leaned on the bell. Still nothing.

Mia looked at the mud caked on Natasha's body and clothes. "You better wait out here," she told the little girl.

Tasha nodded.

"*Right* here," Mia said in her best teacher's voice, pointing to the little spot of concrete directly in front of Frisco's door. "Sit. And don't go *any*where, do you understand, miss?"

Tasha nodded again and sat down.

Feeling very much like a trespasser, Mia opened the screen door and went inside. With the curtains closed, the living room was dim. The television was on, but the volume was set to a low, barely discernible murmur. The air was cool, almost cold, as if the air conditioner had been working overtime to compensate for the slightly opened door. Mia turned off the TV as she went past.

"Hello?" Mia called again. "Lieutenant Francisco…?"

The condo was as silent as a tomb.

"He's gonna be grumpy if you wake him up," Tasha said, up on her knees with her nose pressed against the screen.

"I'll take my chances," Mia said, starting down the hall toward the bedrooms.

She *was* tiptoeing, though. When she reached the end of the hall, she glanced quickly into the bathroom and the smaller of the two bedrooms. Both were empty. The larger bedroom's door was half-closed, and she crept closer. Taking a deep breath, she pushed it open as she knocked.

The double bed was empty.

In the dimness, she could see that the sheets were twisted into a knot. The blanket had been kicked onto the floor, and the pillows were rumpled, but Alan Francisco was not still lying there.

There was not much furniture in the room—just the bed, a bedside table and a dresser. The setup was Spartan. The top of his dresser held only a small pile of loose change. There were no personal items, no knickknacks, no souvenirs. The sheets on the bed were plain white, the blanket a light beige. The closet door hung open, as did one of the drawers in the modest-size dresser. Several duffel bags sagged nearby on the floor. The whole place had a rather apathetic feel, as if the person living here didn't care enough to unpack, or to hang pictures on the wall and make the place his own.

There was nothing that gave any sense of personality to the resident of the room, with the exception of an enormous pile of dirty laundry that seemed to glower from one dark corner. That and a nearly empty bottle of whiskey standing on Frisco's bedside table were the only telling things. And the bottle, at least, certainly told quite a bit. It was similar to the bottle he'd had outside last night—except *that* bottle had been nearly full.

No wonder Tasha hadn't been able to wake him.

But eventually he *had* awakened and found the little girl gone. He was probably out searching for her right now, worried near out of his mind.

The best thing *they* could do was stay put. Eventually, Frisco would come back to see if Natasha had returned.

But the thought of hanging out in Frisco's condo wasn't extremely appealing. His belongings may have been impersonal to the point of distastefulness, but she felt as if by being there, she was invading his privacy.

Mia turned to leave when a gleam of reflected light from the closet caught her eye. She switched on the overhead light.

It was amazing. She'd never seen anything like it in her entire life. A naval uniform hung in the closet, bright white and crisply pressed. And on the upper left side of the jacket, were row after row after row after row of colorful medals. And above it—the cause of that reflected light—was a pin in the shape of an eagle, wings outspread, both a gun and a trident clasped in its fierce talons.

Mia couldn't imagine the things Frisco had done to get all of those medals. But because there were so many of them, there was one thing that she suddenly did see quite clearly. Alan Francisco had a dedication to his job unlike anyone she'd ever met. These medals told her that as absolutely as if they could talk. If he had had one or two medals—sure, that would have told her he was a brave and capable soldier. But there had to be more than ten of these colorful bars pinned to his uniform. She counted them quickly with her finger. Ten...*eleven*. Eleven medals surely meant that Frisco had gone above and beyond the call of duty time after time.

She turned, and in the new light of her discovery, his bedroom had an entirely different look to it. Instead of being the room of a someone who didn't care enough to add any personal touches, it became the room of a man who'd never taken the time to have a life outside of his dangerous career.

Even the whiskey bottle looked different. It looked far more sad and desperate than ever before.

And the room *wasn't* entirely devoid of personal items. There was a book on the floor next to the bed. It was a collection of short stories by J. D. Salinger. *Salinger.* Who would've thought...?

"Mia?"

Natasha was calling her from the living room door.

Mia turned off the light on her way out of Frisco's room. "I'm here, hon, but your uncle's not," she said, coming into the living room.

"He's not?" Tasha scrambled to her feet to get out of the way of the opening screen door.

"What do you say we go next door and see about that bubble-bath soap of mine?" Mia continued, shutting the heavy wooden door to unit 2C tightly behind her. "I'll write a note for your uncle so that he knows you're at my place when he gets back.''

She'd call Thomas, too. If he was home, he might be willing to go out looking for the Navy lieutenant, to tell him Natasha was safe.

"Let's go right into the bathroom," Mia told Tasha as she opened her screen door and unlocked the dead bolt to her condo. "We'll pop you directly into the tub, okay?"

Natasha hung back, her eyes very wide in her mud-streaked face. "Is Frisco gonna be mad at me?"

Mia gazed at the little girl. "Would you blame him very much if he was?"

Tasha's face fell as she shook her head, her lips stretching into that unmistakable shape children's mouths made when they were about to cry. "He was asleep."

"Just because he's sleeping doesn't mean you can break his rules," Mia told her.

"I was gonna come home before he woke up...."

Aha. Mia suddenly understood. Natasha's mother had frequently slept off her alcoholic binges until well past noon, unknowing and perhaps even uncaring of her daughter's private explorations. It was tantamount to neglect, and obviously Tasha expected the same treatment from Frisco.

Something was going to have to change.

"If I were you," Mia advised her, "I'd be good and ready to say I'm sorry the moment Frisco gets home."

Frisco saw the note on his door from down in the courtyard. It was a pink piece of paper taped to the outside of the screen, and it lifted in the first stirrings of a late-morning breeze. He hurried up the stairs, ignoring the pain in his knee, and pulled the note from the door.

"Found Natasha," it said in clean, bold printing. Thank *God*. He closed his eyes briefly, grateful beyond belief. He'd searched the beach for nearly an hour, terrified his niece had broken his rule and gone down to the ocean again. Hell, if she would break his rule about leaving the condo, she could just as well have broken his rule about never swimming alone.

He'd run into a lifeguard who'd told him he'd heard a rumor that a kid's body had washed up on the beach early in the morning. Frisco's heart had damn near stopped beating. He'd waited for nearly forty-five minutes at a pay phone, trying to get through to the shore patrol, trying to find out if the rumor was true.

It turned out that the body that had washed up in the surf had been that of a baby seal. And with that relief had come the knowledge that he'd wasted precious time. And the search had started again.

Frisco opened his eyes and found he had crumpled the pink paper. He smoothed it out to read the rest. "Found Natasha. We're at my place. Mia."

Mia Summerton. Saving the day again.

Leaning on his cane, he went toward Mia's door, catching his reflection in his living room window. His hair was standing straight up, and he looked as if he were hiding from the sunlight behind his dark sunglasses. His T-shirt looked slept in, and his shorts *were* slept in. He looked like hell and he *felt* worse. His head had been pounding from the moment he'd stumbled out into the living room and found that Natasha was gone again. No, strike that. His head had been pounding from the moment he'd opened his eyes. It had risen to a nearly unbearable level when he'd discovered Tash was AWOL. It was still just shy of intolerable.

He rang the doorbell anyway, well aware that in addition to the not-so-pretty picture he made, he didn't smell too damn good, either. His shirt reeked of a distillery. He hadn't been too picky when he snatched it off the floor of his room this morning on his way out the door to search for Tash. Just his luck, he'd grabbed the one he'd used to mop up a spilled glass of whiskey last night.

The door swung open, and Mia Summerton stood there, looking like something out of a sailor's fantasy. She was wearing running shorts that redefined the word *short,* and a midriff-baring athletic top that redefined the word *lust*. Her hair was back in a single braid, and still damp from perspiration.

"She's here, she's safe," Mia said in way of greeting. "She's in the tub, getting cleaned up."

"Where did you find her?" His throat felt dry and his voice came out raspy and harsh.

Mia looked back into her condo unit and raised her voice. "How you doing in there, Tasha?"

"Fine," came a cheery reply.

She opened the screen door and stepped outside. "Harris Avenue," she told Frisco. "She was over on Harris Avenue, playing in the dirt at that construction site—"

"*Dammit!* What the *hell* does she think she's doing? She's five years old! She shouldn't be walking around by herself or—God!—playing on a *construction* site!" Frisco ran one hand down his face, fighting to control his flare of anger. "I know that yelling at the kid's not going to help...." He forced himself to lower his voice, to take a deep breath and try to release all of the frustration and anger and worry of the past several hours. "I don't know what to do," he admitted. "She blatantly disobeyed my orders."

"That's not the way she sees it," Mia told him.

"The rule was for her to tell me when she went outside. The rule was to stay in the courtyard."

"In her opinion, all bets are off if Mom—or Uncle Frisco—can't drag themselves out of bed in the morning." Mia fixed him with her level gaze. Her eyes were more green than brown in the bright morning sun. "She told me she thought she'd be back before you even woke up."

"A rule is a rule," Frisco started.

"Yeah, and *her* rule," Mia interrupted, "is that if you climb into a bottle, she's on her own."

Frisco's headache intensified. He looked away, unable to meet her gaze. It wasn't that she was looking at him accusingly. There was nothing even remotely accusative in her eyes. In fact, her eyes were remarkably gentle, softening the harshness of her words.

"I'm sorry," she murmured. "That was uncalled for."

He shook his head, uncertain as to whether he was agreeing with her or disagreeing with her.

"Why don't you come inside?" Mia said, holding open the screen door for him.

Mia's condo might as well have been from a different planet than his. It was spacious and open, with unspotted, light brown carpeting and white painted bamboo-framed furniture. The walls were freshly painted and clean, and potted plants were everywhere, their vines lacing across the ceiling on a system of hooks. Music played softly on the stereo. Frisco recognized the smoky Texas-blues-influenced vocals of Lee Roy Parnell.

Pictures hung on the wall—gorgeous blue and green watercolors of the ocean, and funky, quirkily colorful figures of people walking along the beach.

"My mother's an artist," Mia said, following his gaze. "Most of this is her work."

Another picture was that of the beach before a storm. It conveyed all of the dangerous power of the wind and the water, the ominous, darkening sky, the rising surf, the palm trees whipped and tossed—nature at her most deadly.

"She's good," Frisco said.

Mia smiled. "I know." She raised her voice. "How's it going in bubbleland, Natasha?"

"Okay."

"While she was out playing in the dirt, she gave herself a Russian princess mud bath." With a wry smile, she led Frisco into the tiny kitchen. It was exactly like his—and nothing like his. Magnets of all shapes and sizes covered the refrigerator, holding up photos of smiling people, and notes and coupons and theater schedules. Fresh fruit hung in wire baskets that were suspended from hooks on the ceiling. A coffee mug in the shape of a cow wearing a graduate's cap sat on the counter next to the telephone, holding pencils and pens. The entire room was filled with little bits and pieces of Mia. "I managed to convince her that true royalty always followed a mud bath with a bubble bath."

"Bless you," Frisco said. "And thank you for bringing her home."

"It was lucky I ran that way." Mia opened the refrigerator door. "I usually take a longer route, but I was feeling the heat this morning." She looked up at Frisco. "Ice tea, lemonade or soda?"

"Something with caffeine, please," Frisco told her.

"Hmm," Mia said, reaching into the back of the fridge and pulling out a can of cola. She handed it to him. "And would you like that with two aspirin or three?"

Frisco smiled. It was crooked but it was a smile. "Three. Thanks."

She motioned to the small table that was in the dining area at the end of the kitchen, and Frisco lowered himself into one of a pair of chairs. She had a napkin holder in the shape of a pig and tiny airplanes for salt and pepper shakers. There were plants everywhere in here, too, and a fragile wind chime directly over his head, in front of a window that looked out over the parking lot. He reached up and brushed the wind chime with one finger. It sounded as delicate and ghostly as it looked.

The doors to her kitchen cabinets had recently been replaced with light, blond wood. The gleaming white countertop looked new, too. But he only spared it half a glance, instead watching Mia as she stood on tiptoes to reach up into one of the cabinets for her bottle of aspirin. She was a blinding mixture of muscles and curves. He couldn't look away, even when she turned around. Great, just what she needed. Some loser leering at her in her own kitchen. He could see her apprehension and discomfort in her eyes.

She set the bottle of aspirin down in front of him on the table and disappeared, murmuring some excuse about checking on Natasha.

Frisco pressed the cold soda can against his forehead. When

Mia returned, she was wearing a T-shirt over her running gear. It helped, but not a lot.

He cleared his throat. A million years ago, he had been so good at small talk. "So...how far do you run?" Cripes, he sounded like some kind of idiot.

"Usually three miles," she answered, opening the refrigerator again and taking out a pitcher of ice tea. She poured herself a glass. "But today I only went about two and a half."

"You gotta be careful when it's hot like this." Man, could he sound any more lame? *Lame?* Yeah, that was the perfect word to describe him, in more ways than one.

She nodded, turning to look at him as she leaned back against the kitchen counter and took a sip of her tea.

"So...your mother's an artist."

Mia smiled. Damn, she had a beautiful smile. Had he really thought that it was goofy-looking just two days ago?

"Yeah," she said. "She has a studio near Malibu. That's where I grew up."

Frisco nodded. This was where he was supposed to counter by telling her where he came from. "I grew up right here in San Felipe, the armpit of California."

Her smile deepened. "Armpits have their purpose—not that I agree with you and think that San Felipe is one."

"You're entitled to your opinion," he said with a shrug. "To me, San Felipe will always be an armpit."

"So sell your condo and move to Hawaii."

"Is that where your family's from?" he asked.

She looked down into her glass. "To tell you the truth, I'm not really sure. I think I must have some Hawaiian or Polynesian blood, but I'm not certain."

"Your parents don't know?"

"I was adopted from an overseas agency. The records were extremely sketchy." She looked up at him. "I went through a phase, you know, when I tried to find my birth parents."

"Birth parents aren't always worth finding. I would've been better off without knowing mine."

"I'm sorry," Mia said quietly. "There was a time when I

might've said that you can't possibly mean that, or that that couldn't possibly be true. But I've been teaching at an urban high school for over five years, and I'm well aware that most people didn't have the kind of childhood or the kind of parents that I did.'' Her eyes were a beautiful mixture of brown and green and compassion. ''I don't know what you might have gone through, but…I *am* sorry.''

''I've heard that teaching high school is a pretty dangerous job these days, what with guns and drugs and violence,'' Frisco said, trying desperately to bring the conversation out of this dark and ultrapersonal area. ''Did they give you any special kind of commando training when you took the job?''

Mia laughed. ''No, we're on our own. Thrown to the wolves naked, so to speak. Some of the teachers have compensated by becoming real drill sergeants. I've found that positive reinforcement works far better than punishment.'' She took another sip of her ice tea, gazing at him speculatively over the top of her glass. ''In fact, you might want to consider that when you're dealing with Natasha.''

Frisco shook his head. ''What? Give her a cookie for running away? I don't think so.''

''But what kind of punishment will possibly get through to her?'' Mia persisted. ''Think about it. The poor kid's already been given the ultimate punishment for a five-year-old—her mommy's gone. There's probably nothing else that you can take away from her that will matter. You can yell at her and make her cry. You can even frighten her and make her afraid of you, and maybe even give her worse nightmares. But if you reward her when she *does* follow your rules, if you make a really big deal about it and make her feel as if she's worth a million bucks, well, she'll catch on much more quickly.''

He ran his fingers through his hair. ''But I can't just ignore what she did this morning.''

''It's difficult,'' Mia admitted. ''You have to achieve a balance between letting a child know her behavior is unacceptable, and not wanting to reward the child's bad behavior by giving her too much attention. Kids who crave attention often misbehave. It's the easiest way to get a parent or teacher to notice them.''

Frisco pushed his mouth up into another smile. "I know some so-called grown-ups who operate on the same principle.''

Mia gazed at the man sitting at her kitchen table. It was amazing. He looked as if he'd been rolled from a park bench, yet she still found him attractive. What would he look like, she wondered, shiny clean and dressed in that uniform she'd found in his closet?

He'd probably look like someone she'd go out of her way to avoid. She'd never been impressed by men in uniform. It wasn't likely that she'd be impressed now.

Still, all those medals...

Mia set her empty glass down and pushed herself off the counter. "I'll get Tasha out of the tub,'' she told Frisco. "You probably have things to do—she told me you promised to take her shopping for furniture for her bedroom.''

"Yeah.'' Frisco nodded and pulled himself clumsily to his feet. "Thanks again for bringing her home.''

Mia smiled and slipped down the hall toward the bathroom. Considering their rocky start, they'd actually achieved quite a nice, neighborly relationship.

Nice and neighborly—that's exactly where they were going to leave it, too. Despite the fact that this man had the ability to make her blood heat with a single look, despite the fact that she genuinely liked him more and more each time they met, she *was* going to be careful to keep her distance.

Because the more Mia found out about her neighbor, the more she was convinced that they were absolute polar opposites.

7

It was pink. It was definitely, undeniably pink. Its back was reminiscent of a scallop shell, and its arms were scrolled. Its cushions were decorated with shiny silver buttons that absolutely, positively could not have been comfortable to sit upon.

It was far too fancy to be called a couch or even a sofa. It was advertised as a "settee."

For Natasha, it was love at first sight.

Fortunately for Frisco, she didn't spot it until they were on their way *out* of the furniture store.

She sat down on it and went into Russian princess mode. Frisco was so tired, and his knee and head ached so badly, he sat down, too.

"Kneel in front of the Russian princess," Tash commanded him sternly.

Frisco put his head back and closed his eyes. "Not a chance, babe," he mumbled.

After Tash's bath at Mia's place, he'd taken her home, then they'd both suited up and headed to the beach for the kid's first swimming lesson. The current had still been quite strong, and he'd kept his fingers solidly locked on Tash's bathing suit the entire time.

The kid was fearless. Considering that she hadn't even seen the ocean before yesterday, she was entirely enthusiastic about the water. At the end of the week, she'd be well on her way to swimming like a fish.

Frisco shook his head. How on earth had Sharon's kid managed to live to the ripe old age of five without having even *seen* the ocean? Historically, the Franciscos were coastline people. His old man had worked on a fishing boat for years. Vacations were spent at the water. Frisco and his two older brothers had loved the beach. But not Sharon, he remembered suddenly. Sharon had damn near drowned when she was hardly any older than Natasha was now. As an adult, Sharon moved inland, spending much of her time in Las Vegas and Reno. Tash had been born in Tucson, Arizona. Not much beachfront property there.

After the swimming lesson and a forty-five-minute lecture on why Tash had to follow Frisco's rules, they'd dragged themselves home, had lunch, changed and gone shopping for furniture for Frisco's second bedroom.

They'd found this particular store in the Yellow Pages. It was right around the corner, and—the advertisement boasted—it had free, same-day delivery. Frisco had picked out a simple mattress, box spring and metal-framed bed, and Tash had chosen a pint-size bright yellow chest of drawers. Together, they'd found a small desk and chair and a petite bookshelf.

"Can we get this, Frisco?" Tash now asked hopefully.

He snorted as he opened his eyes. "A *pink* couch? Man, are you kidding?"

As usual, she answered his rhetorical question as if he'd asked it seriously. "No."

"Where the hell would we put it?" He glanced at the price tag. It was supposedly on sale, marked down to a mere small fortune.

"We could put it where that other icky one is."

"Great. Just what that condo needs." Shaking his head, Frisco pulled himself to his feet. "Come on. If we don't hurry, the delivery truck is going to beat us home. We don't want them to deliver your new furniture to some other kid."

That got Tasha moving, but not without one final lovelorn glance at the pink sofa.

They were only two blocks from home, but Frisco flagged down a cab. The sun was merciless, and his knee was damn near making him scream with pain. His head wasn't feeling too great, either.

There was no sign of Mia out in her garden in the condo courtyard. Her door was tightly shut, and Frisco found himself wondering where she had gone.

Bad mistake, he told himself. She had been making it clear that she didn't want to be anything more than a neighbor. She didn't want the likes of him sniffing around her door.

Mia actually thought he was a drunk, like his old man and his sister. It was entirely possible that if he wasn't careful, she would be proven right.

No more, he vowed, pulling himself up the stairs. Tonight, if insomnia struck, he'd tough it out. He'd face the demons who were at their ugliest in the wee hours of the morning by spitting in their faces. If he awoke in the middle of the night, he'd spend the time working out, doing exercises that would strengthen his leg and support his injured knee.

He unlocked the door to his condo and Tasha went inside first, dashing through the living room and down the hall to the bedrooms.

Frisco followed more slowly, each painful step making him grit his teeth. He needed to sit down and get his weight off his knee, elevate the damn thing and ice the hell out of it.

Tasha was in her bedroom, lying down on the wall-to-wall carpeting. She was flat on her back on the floor, staring up at the ceiling.

As Frisco stood in the doorway and watched, she scrambled to her feet and then lay down on the floor in another part of the room.

"What are you doing?" he asked as she did the exact same thing yet a third time.

"I'm picking where to put the bed," Tash told him from her position on the floor.

Frisco couldn't hide his smile. "Good idea," he said. "Why don't you work on that for a while? I'm gonna chill for a few minutes before the delivery truck comes, okay?"

"'Kay."

He headed back into the kitchen and grabbed an ice pack from the freezer. He moved into the living room and sat on his old plaid couch, swinging his injured leg up and onto the cushions. The ice felt good, and he put his head back and closed his eyes.

He had to figure out a way to move those boxes out of Tash's room. There were a half a dozen of them, and they were all too ungainly for him to carry with only one arm. But he could drag 'em, though. That would work. He could use a blanket or sheet, and wrestle the boxes on top of it, one at a time. With the box firmly trapped in the sheet like a fish in a fishing net, he could pull the sheet, sliding the box along the rug out of Tash's room and into his own and...

Frisco held his breath. He'd sensed more than heard the movement of Tasha crossing the living room floor, but now he heard the telltale squeak of the front door being opened.

He opened his eyes and sat up, but she was already out the door.

"Natasha! *Damn* it!"

His cane had slipped underneath the couch and he scrambled for it, grabbing it and moving quickly to the door.

"Tash!"

He supported himself on the railing near his rope and pulley setup. Natasha looked up at him from the courtyard, eyes wide.

"Where the *hell* are you going?" he growled.

"To see if Thomas is home."

She didn't get it. Frisco could tell just from looking at the little girl that she honestly didn't understand why he was upset with her.

He took a deep breath and forced his racing pulse to slow. "You forgot to tell me where you were going."

"You were asleep."

"No, I wasn't. And even if I was, that doesn't mean you can just break the rules."

She was silent, gazing up at him.

Frisco went down the stairs. "Come here." He gestured

with his head toward one of the courtyard benches. He sat down and she sat next to him. Her feet didn't touch the ground, and she swung them back and forth. "Do you know what a rule is?" he asked.

Tasha chewed on her lower lip. She shook her head.

"Take a guess," Frisco told her. "What's a rule?"

"Something you want me to do that I don't want to do?" she asked.

It took all that he had in him not to laugh. "It's more than that," he said. "It's something that you *have* to do, whether or not you want to. And it's always the same, whether I'm asleep or awake."

She didn't get it. He could see her confusion and disbelief written clearly on her face.

He ran one hand down his face, trying to clear his cobweb-encrusted mind. He was tired. He couldn't think how to explain to Natasha that she *had* to follow his rules all of the time. He couldn't figure out how to get through to her.

"Hi, guys."

Frisco looked up to see Mia Summerton walking toward them. She was wearing a summery, sleeveless, flower-print dress with a long, sweeping skirt that reached almost all the way to the ground. She had sandals on her feet and a large-brimmed straw hat on her head and a friendly smile on her pretty face. She looked cool and fresh, like a long-awaited evening breeze in the suffocating late-afternoon heat.

Where had she been, all dressed up like that? On a lunch date with some boyfriend? Or maybe she wasn't coming, maybe she was going. Maybe she was waiting for her dinner date to arrive. Lucky bastard. Frisco scowled, letting himself hate the guy, allowing himself that small luxury.

"There's a furniture truck unloading in the driveway," Mia said, ignoring his dark look. In fact, she was ignoring him completely. She spoke directly to Tash. "Does that pretty yellow dresser belong to you, by any chance?"

Natasha jumped up, their conversation all but forgotten.

"Me," she said, dashing toward the parking lot. "It belongs to me!"

"Don't run too far ahead," Frisco called out warningly, pulling himself to his feet. He tightened his mouth as he put his weight on his knee, resisting the urge to wince, not wanting to show Mia how much he was hurting. "And do not step off that sidewalk."

But Mia somehow knew. "Are you all right?" she asked him, no longer ignoring him, her eyes filled with concern. She followed him after Natasha, back toward the parking lot.

"I'm fine," he said brusquely.

"Have you been chasing around after her all day?"

"I'm fine," he repeated.

"You're allowed to be tired," she said with a musical laugh. "I baby-sat a friend's four-year-old last week, and I practically had to be carried out on a stretcher afterward."

Frisco glanced at her. She gazed back at him innocently. She was giving him an out, pretending that the lines of pain and fatigue on his face were due to the fact that he wasn't used to keeping up with the high energy of a young child, rather than the result of his old injury.

"Yeah, right."

Mia knew better than to show her disappointment at Frisco's terse reply. She wanted to be this man's friend, and she'd assumed they'd continue to build a friendship on the shaky foundation they'd recently established. But whatever understanding they'd reached this morning seemed to have been forgotten. The old, angry, tight-lipped Frisco had returned with a vengeance.

Unless...

It was possible his knee was hurting worse than she thought.

A delivery man approached. "You Alan Francisco?" he asked, not waiting for a reply before he held out his clipboard. "Sign at the *X*."

Frisco signed. "It's going up to Unit 2C. It's right at the top of the stairs—"

"Sorry, pal, this is as far as I go." The man didn't sound even remotely apologetic. "My instructions are to get it off the truck. You've got to take it from here."

"You're kidding." Frisco's voice was flat, unbelieving. The furniture was standing there on the asphalt, next to the delivery vehicle.

The man closed the sliding back door of his truck with a crash. "Read the small print on your receipt. It's free delivery—and you got exactly what you paid for."

How was Frisco supposed to get all this up a flight of stairs? Mia saw the frustration and anger in his eyes and in the tight set of his mouth.

The man climbed into the cab and closed the door behind him.

"I bought this stuff from your store because you advertise a free delivery," Frisco said roughly. "If you're not going to deliver it, you can damn well load it up and take it back."

"First of all, it's not *my* store," the man told him, starting the engine with a roar and grinding the gears as he put it into first, "and secondly, you already signed for it."

It was all Frisco could do to keep himself from pulling himself up on the running board and slamming his fist into the man's surly face. But Tash and Mia were watching him. So he did nothing. He stood there like a damned idiot as the truck pulled away.

He stared after it, feeling helpless and impotent and frustrated beyond belief.

And then Mia touched his arm. Her fingers felt cool against his hot skin. Her touch was hesitant and light, but she didn't pull away even when he turned to glare down at her.

"I sent Tasha to see if Thomas is home," she said quietly. "We'll get this upstairs."

"I hate this," he said. The words were out of his mouth before he could stop them. They were dripping with despair and shame. He hadn't meant to say it aloud, to reveal so much of himself to her. It wasn't a complaint, or even self-pity. It was a fact. He hated his limitations.

Her brown-green eyes grew warmer, more liquid. She slid her hand all the way down to his, and intertwined their fingers. "I know," she said huskily. "I'm so sorry."

He turned to look at her then, to *really* look at her. "You don't even like me," he said. "How can you stand to be so nice?"

"I *do* like you," she said, trying to step back, away from the intensity of his gaze. But he wouldn't let go of her hand. "I want to be your friend."

Friend. She tugged again, and this time he released her. She wanted to be his friend. He wanted so much more....

"Yo, Frisco!"

Frisco turned. The voice was as familiar to him as breathing. It was Lucky O'Donlon. He'd parked his motorcycle in one of the visitor's spaces, and now sauntered toward them. He was wearing his blue dress uniform and looked to be one hundred percent spit and polish. Frisco knew better.

"Hey, guy, having a tag sale or something?" Lucky's wide smile and warm blue eyes traveled lazily over the furniture, Frisco's damned cane, and Mia. He took an especially long time taking in Mia. "You gonna introduce me to your friend?"

"Do I have a choice?"

Lucky held out his hand to Mia. "I'm Lt. Luke O'Donlon, U.S. Navy SEALs. And you are…?"

Mia smiled. Of course she would smile. No one could resist Lucky. "Mia Summerton. I'm Frisco's neighbor."

"I'm his swim buddy."

"*Former* swim buddy."

Lucky shook his head. "No such thing." He looped his arm around Frisco's neck and smiled at Mia. "We went through BUD/S together. That makes you swim buddies for life."

"BUD/S is basic training for SEALs," Frisco translated for her, pushing Lucky away from him. "Where are you going, dressed like that?"

"Some kind of semiformal affair at the OC. A shindig for

some top brass pencil pusher who's being promoted.'' He grinned at Frisco, but his gaze kept returning to Mia. "I thought maybe you'd want to come along."

Frisco snorted. "Dream on, man. I hated those parties when I was required to go."

"Please?" Lucky begged. "I need someone to keep me company or I'll spend all night dancing with the admiral's wife, trying to keep her from grabbing my butt." He smiled at Mia and winked.

"Even if I wanted to," Frisco told him, "which I *don't*, I couldn't. I'm taking care of my sister's kid for the next six weeks." He gestured to the furniture. "This is supposed to be for her bedroom."

"The kid's either fond of the outdoors, or you got yourself some kind of snafu here."

"Number two," Frisco said.

"Yo, neighbor babe," Lucky said, picking up one end of the mattress. "You look healthy. Grab the other end."

"Her name is Mia," Frisco said.

"Excuse me," Lucky said. "Mia babe, grab the other end."

Mia was laughing, thank God. As Frisco watched, she and Lucky carried the mattress into the courtyard. He could hear Mia's laughter long after they moved out of sight.

As Frisco picked up the lightweight bookcase and carried it slowly toward the courtyard, he could also hear Tasha's excited chirping, and Thomas King's rich voice coming toward him.

"Hey, Navy." Thomas nodded a greeting as he passed. He knew better than to offer to take the bookcase from Frisco on his way out to the parking lot.

"Thanks for helping out, man," Frisco said to him.

"No problem," the teenager replied.

No problem. It was possible that this whole deal wasn't a problem for anybody—except Frisco.

He set the bookcase down at the bottom of the stairs, and looked up to see Lucky come out of his condo, with Tasha in his arms. He was tickling the little girl, and she was giggling. Mia was right behind them, and she was laughing, too.

He'd never seen Mia look so beautiful or relaxed. Lucky leaned toward her and said something into her ear, and she laughed again. She started down the stairs, and Lucky watched her go, his eyes following the movement of her hips.

Frisco had to look away. He couldn't blame Lucky. At one time, the two of them had been so much alike. They still were alike in so many ways. It didn't surprise him that his best friend would be attracted to Mia, too.

It took all of ten minutes to transport Tasha's furniture into her bedroom and to move the boxes that were in there into Frisco's room.

Thomas headed off to work, and Mia made her excuses and disappeared into her condo—after smiling at the big deal Lucky made out of shaking her hand once again.

"She, uh, said you guys were just friends, huh?" Lucky said much too casually as Frisco walked him to his bike.

Frisco was silent, wondering what he could possibly say to that statement. If he agreed, then Lucky would be dropping by all the time, asking Mia out, working his famous O'Donlon charm and persistence until she gave in. And she would give in. No one could resist Lucky. And then Frisco would have to watch as his best friend dated and probably seduced this woman that he wanted so badly.

It was true. He wanted Mia. And dammit, he was going to do everything in his power to get her.

"She's wrong," he told Lucky. "We're more than friends. She just doesn't know it yet."

If Lucky was disappointed, he hid it well. And it didn't take long for his disappointment to turn into genuine pleasure. "This is great. This means you're coming back," he said.

"To the SEALs?" Frisco shook his head. "Man, haven't you heard, I'm—"

"No," Lucky interrupted. "I meant to the world of the living."

Frisco gazed at his friend. He didn't understand. He was

alive. He'd had five years of pain and frustration to prove that.

"Call me sometime," Lucky said, strapping on his motor-cycle helmet. "I miss you, man."

Frisco awoke to the sound of an electronic buzzer. It was loud as hell and it was right in his ear and...

He sat up, wide-awake.

It was the sound of the booby trap he'd rigged to the front door last night before he went to bed. Tasha was AWOL again, dammit.

He pulled on a pair of shorts as he rolled out of bed, and grabbed his cane from the floor.

Oh, Lord, he was tired. He may have gone to bed last night, but he hadn't gone to sleep. It couldn't have been more than two hours ago that he'd finally closed his eyes. But he'd done it. He'd stared down the night without even a sip of whiskey to help him along.

He may have been exhausted, but he wasn't hung over.

And that was damn good, because if he had been, the sound of this blasted buzzer would have taken the top of his head clear off.

He quickly disconnected it. It was a simple system, de-signed for the circuit to break if the door was open. If the circuit was broken, the buzzer would sound.

He pulled the door the rest of the way open and...

Tasha, with Mia directly behind her, stood on the other side of the screen door.

Tash was still wearing her pajamas. Mia was wearing her bathing suit underneath a pair of shorts and a T-shirt. Frisco could see the brightly colored strap that tied up and around her neck.

"Good morning," she said.

Frisco glared at Tash. "Where the h—"

Mia cut him off. "Tasha was coming over to visit me," she told Frisco, "but she remembered that she was supposed to tell you first where she was going." She looked down at the little girl. "Right, Tash?"

Tasha nodded.

Tasha remembered? Mia remembered was more like it.

Mia mouthed "Positive reinforcement" over Tasha's head.

Frisco swallowed his frustration. All right. If Mia thought he could get through to Tasha this way, he'd give it a shot. Somehow he mustered up far more enthusiasm than he felt. "Excellent job remembering," he said to the little girl, opening the screen door and letting both Tasha and Mia inside.

He forced himself to smile, and Natasha visibly brightened. Jeez, maybe there *was* something to this.

He scooped the little girl into his arms and awkwardly spun her around until she began to giggle, then collapsed with her onto the couch. "In fact," he continued, "you are so *amazingly* excellent, I think you should probably get a medal. Don't you?"

She nodded, her eyes wide. "What's a medal?"

"It's a very special pin that you get for doing something really great—like remembering my rules," Frisco told her. He dumped her off his lap and onto the soft cushions of the couch. "Wait right here—I'll get it."

Mia was standing near the door, and as she watched, Frisco pushed himself off the couch and headed down the hall to his bedroom.

"Getting a medal is a really big deal." Frisco raised his voice so they could hear him in the living room. "It requires a very special ceremony."

Tasha was bouncing up and down on the couch, barely able to contain her excitement. Mia had to smile. It seemed that Frisco understood the concept of positive reinforcement.

"Here we go," he said, coming back into the living room. He caught Mia's eye and smiled. He looked like hell this morning. He looked more exhausted than she'd ever seen him. He'd clearly been sound asleep mere moments ago. But somehow he seemed more vibrant, his eyes more clear. And the smile that he'd sent her was remarkably sweet, almost shy.

Mia's heart was in her throat as she watched him with his little niece.

"For the remarkable remembering of my rules and regs, including rule number one—'Tell Frisco where you're going before you leave the condo,'" he intoned, "I award Natasha Francisco this medal of honor."

He pinned one of the colorful bars Mia had seen attached to his dress uniform onto Tasha's pajama shirt.

"Now I salute you and you salute me," he whispered to the little girl after he attached the pin.

He stood at sharp attention, and snapped a salute. Tasha imitated him remarkably well.

"The only time SEALs ever salute is when someone gets a medal," Frisco said with another glance in Mia's direction. He pulled Tasha back to the couch with him. "Here's the deal," he told her. "In order to keep this medal, you have to remember my rules all day today. Do you remember the rules?"

"Tell you when I want to go outside...."

"Even when I'm asleep. You have to wake me up, okay? And what else?"

"Stay here...."

"In the courtyard, right. And...?"

"No swimming without my buddy."

"Absolutely, incredibly correct. Gimme a high five."

Natasha giggled, slapping hands with her uncle.

"Here's the rest of the deal," he said. "Are you listening, Tash?"

She nodded.

"When you get enough of these medals, you know what happens?"

Tasha shook her head no.

"We trade this thing in," Frisco told her, smacking the back of the couch they were sitting on with one hand, "for a certain pink sofa."

Mia thought it was entirely possible that the little girl was going to explode with pleasure.

"You're going to have to work really hard to follow the rules," Frisco was telling her. "You've got to remember that the reason I want you to obey these rules is because I want you to be safe, and it really gets me upset when I don't know for certain that you're safe. You have to think about that and remember that, because I know you don't want to make me feel upset, right?"

Tasha nodded. "Do you have to follow *my* rules?"

Frisco was surprised, but he hid it well. "What are *your* rules?"

"No more bad words," the little girl said without hesitation.

Frisco glanced up at Mia again, chagrin in his eyes. "Okay," he said, looking back at Tasha. "That's a tough one, but I'll try."

"More playing with Mia," Tasha suggested.

He laughed nervously. "I'm not sure we can make that a rule, Tash. I mean, things that concern you and me are fine, but…"

"I'd love to play with you," Mia murmured.

Frisco glanced up at her. She couldn't possibly have meant that the way it sounded. No, she was talking to Natasha. Still… He let his imagination run with the scenario. It was a very, *very* good one.

"But we don't have to make a rule about it," Mia added.

"Can you come to the beach with us for my swimming lesson?" Tasha asked her.

Mia hesitated, looking cautiously across the room at Frisco. "I don't want to get in the way."

"You've already got your bathing suit on," he pointed out.

She seemed surprised that he'd noticed. "Well, yes, but…"

"Were you planning to go to a different beach?"

"No… I just don't want to…you know…" She shrugged and smiled apologetically, nervously. "Interfere."

"It wouldn't be interfering," Frisco told her. Man, he felt as nervous as she sounded. When had this gotten so hard? He used to be so good at this sort of thing. "Tasha wants you to come with us." Perfect. Now he sounded as if he wanted her to come along as a playmate for his niece. That wasn't it at all. "And I...I do, too," he added.

Jeez, his heart was in his mouth. He swallowed, trying to make it go back where it belonged as Mia just gazed at him.

"Well, okay," she finally said. "In that case, I'd love to come. If you want, I could pack a picnic lunch...?"

"Yeah!" Tasha squealed, hopping around the room. "A picnic! A picnic!"

Frisco felt himself smile. A picnic on the beach with Mia. He couldn't remember the last time he'd felt such anticipation. And his anticipation was for more than his wanting to see what her bathing suit looked like, although he was feeling plenty of that, too. "I guess that's a yes. But it shouldn't be just up to you to bring the food."

"I'll make sandwiches," Mia told him, opening the door. "You guys bring something to drink. Soda. Or beer if you want it."

"No beer," Frisco said.

She paused, looking back at him, her hand on the handle of the screen door.

"It's another one of the rules I'm going to be following from now on," he said quietly. Natasha had stopped dancing around the room. She was listening, her eyes wide. "No more drinking. Not even beer."

Mia stepped away from the door, her eyes nearly as wide as Tasha's. "Um, Tash, why don't you go put on your bathing suit?"

Silently Tasha vanished down the hallway.

Frisco shook his head. "It's not that big a deal."

Mia clearly thought otherwise. She stepped closer to him, lowering her voice for privacy from Tasha's sensitive ears. "You know, there are support groups all over town. You can find a meeting at virtually any time of day—"

Did she honestly think his drinking was *that* serious a problem? "Look, I can handle this," he said gruffly. "I went overboard for a couple of days, but that's all it was. I didn't

drink at all while I was in the hospital—right up 'til two days
ago. These past few days—you haven't exactly been seeing
me at my best.''

"I'm sorry," she murmured. "I didn't mean to imply…"

"It's no big deal."

She touched his arm, her fingers gentle and cool and so soft
against his skin. "Yes, it is," she told him. "To Natasha, it's
a *very* big deal."

"I'm not doing it for Tash," he said quietly, looking down
at her delicate hand resting on the corded muscles of his forearm, wishing she would leave it there, but knowing she was
going to pull away. "I'm doing it for myself."

8

"Is Thomas really a king?"

Mia looked up from the sand castle she was helping Tasha build. The little girl was making dribble turrets on the side of the large mound using wet sand and water from a plastic pail that Mia had found in her closet. She had remarkable dexterity for a five-year-old, and managed to make most of her dribbles quite tall and spiky.

"Thomas's last name is King," Mia answered. "But here in the United States, we don't have kings and queens."

"Is he a king somewhere else? Like I'm a princess in Russia?"

"Well," Mia said diplomatically, "you might want to check with Thomas, but I think King is just his last name."

"He looks like a king." Natasha giggled. "He thinks I'm from Mars. I'm gonna marry him."

"Marry who?" Frisco asked, sitting down in the sand next to them.

He'd just come out of the ocean, and water beaded on his eyelashes and dripped from his hair. He looked more relaxed and at ease than Mia had ever seen him.

"Thomas," Tasha told him, completely serious.

"Thomas." Frisco considered that thoughtfully. "I like him," he said. "But you're a little young to be getting married, don't you think?"

"Not now, silly," she said with exasperation. "When I'm a grown-up, of course."

Frisco tried to hide his smile. "Of course," he said.

"You can't marry my mom cause you're her brother, right?" she asked.

"That's right," Frisco told her. He leaned back in the sand on his elbows. Mia tried not to stare at the way the muscles in his arms flexed as they supported his weight. She tried to pull her gaze away from his broad shoulders and powerful chest and smooth, tanned skin. This wasn't the first time she'd seen him without a shirt, after all. She should be getting used to this....

"Too bad," Tash said with a sigh. "Mommy's always looking for someone to marry, and I like you."

Frisco's voice was husky. "Thanks, Tash. I like you, too."

"I didn't like Dwayne," the little girl said. "He scared me, but Mommy liked living in his house."

"Maybe when your mom comes back, the two of you could live a few doors down from me," Frisco said.

"You could marry Mia," Tasha suggested. "And move in with her. And we could live in your place."

Mia glanced up. Frisco met her eyes, clearly embarrassed. "Maybe Mia doesn't want to get married," he said.

"Do you?" the little girl asked, looking up from her hand-iwork to gaze at Mia with those pure blue eyes that were so like Frisco's.

"Well," she said carefully. "Someday I'd like to get married and have a family, but—"

"She does," Tasha informed her uncle. "She's pretty and she makes good sandwiches. You should ask her to marry you." She stood up and, taking her bucket, went down to the edge of the water, where she began to chase waves up the sand.

"I'm sorry about that," Frisco said with a nervous laugh. "She's...you know, *five*. She's heavily into happily ever after."

"It's all right," Mia said with a smile. "And don't worry. I won't hold you to any promises that Tasha makes on your behalf." She brushed the sand from her knees and moved back onto the beach blanket she'd spread out.

Frisco moved to join her. "That's good to know." He turned to look at Mia, his warm gaze skimming up her legs, lingering on her red two-piece bathing suit and the enormous amount of skin it exposed, before settling on her face. "She's right, though. You *are* pretty, and you make damn good sandwiches."

Mia's pulse was racing. When had it started to matter so much whether or not this man thought that she was pretty? When had the urge disappeared—the urge to cover herself up with a bulky T-shirt every time he looked at her with that heat in his eyes? When had her heart started to leap at his crooked, funny smiles? When had he crossed that boundary that defined him as more than a mere friend?

It had started days ago, with that very first hug he had given Natasha in the courtyard. He was so gentle with the child, so patient. Mia's attraction to him had been there from the start, yet now that she had come to know more of him, it was multilayered, existing on more complicated levels than just basic, raw sexual magnetism.

It was crazy. Mia knew it was crazy. This was not a man with whom she could picture herself spending the rest of her life. He'd been trained as a killer—a professional soldier. And if that wasn't enough, he had barrels of anger and frustration and pain to work through before he could be considered psychologically and emotionally healthy. And if *that* wasn't enough, there was the fact of his drinking.

Yes, he'd vowed to stop, but Mia's experience as a high school teacher had made her an expert on the disease of alcoholism. The best way to fight it was not to face it alone, but to seek help. He seemed hell-bent on handling it himself, and more often than not, such a course would end in failure.

No, if she were smart, she'd pack up her beach bag right now and get the heck out of there.

Instead, she put more sunblock on her face. "I went into your kitchen to help Natasha load the cooler with soda," she said. "And I noticed you had only one thing stuck onto your refrigerator. A list."

He glanced at her, his expression one of wariness. "Yeah?"

"I wasn't sure," she said, "but...it looked like it might've been a list of things that you have difficulty doing with your injured knee."

The list had included things like run, jump, skydive, bike, and climb stairs.

He gazed out at the ocean, squinting slightly in the brightness. "That's right."

"You forgot to include that you're no longer able to play on the Olympic basketball team, so I added that to the bottom," she said, her tongue firmly in her cheek.

He let loose a short burst of air that might've been called a laugh if he'd been smiling. "Very funny. If you'd looked carefully, you'd have noticed that the word *walk* was at the top. I crossed it off when I could walk. I intend to do the same with the rest of those things on that list."

His eyes were the same fierce shade of blue as the sky.

Mia rolled onto her stomach and propped her chin up in her hands. "Tell me about this amazing pink couch," she said. "What's that all about?"

This time Frisco *did* laugh, and the lines around his eyes crinkled with genuine amusement. He stretched out next to her on the blanket, making sure he could still see Tasha from where they lay. "Oh, that," he said. "It's gonna look great in my living room, don't you think? Dirt brown and ugly green go real well with pink and silver."

Mia smiled. "You'll have to redecorate. Maybe a white carpet and lots of Art Deco type mirrors on the walls would work."

"And it would be so me," he said, deadpan.

"Seriously, though," Mia said. "If anything will give Tasha incentive to follow your rules, that will. She's only mentioned it five thousand times today already."

"Tell me the truth," Frisco said, supporting his head with one hand as he gazed at her. "Did I go too far? Did I cross the line from positive reinforcement into sheer bribery?"

Mia shook her head, caught in the intense blue of his eyes. "You're giving her the opportunity to earn something that she truly wants, along with learning an important lesson about following rules. That's not bribery."

"I feel like I'm taking the point and heading into totally uncharted territory," Frisco admitted.

Mia didn't understand. "Taking the point...?"

"If you take the point, if you're the pointman," he explained, "that means you lead the squad. You're the first guy out there—the first guy either to locate or step on any booby traps or land mines. It's a pretty intense job."

"At least you know that Natasha's not suddenly going to explode."

Frisco smiled. "Are you sure about that?"

With amusement dancing in his eyes, a smile softening his face and the ocean breeze gently ruffling his hair, Frisco looked like the kind of man Mia would go far out of her way to meet. He looked charming and friendly and pleasant and sinfully handsome.

"You're doing a wonderful job with Tasha," she told him. "You're being remarkably consistent in dealing with her. I know how hard it is not to lose your temper when she disobeys you—I've seen you swallow it, and I know that's not easy. And giving her that medal—that was brilliant." She sat up, reaching for the T-shirt Tasha had been wearing over her bathing suit. "Look." She held it up so he could see. "She's so proud of that medal, she asked me to pin it onto this shirt for her so she could wear it to the beach. If you keep this up, it's only a matter of time before she'll remember to follow your rules."

Frisco had rolled over onto his back and was shielding his eyes from the glare of the sun with one hand as he looked up at her. He sat up now, in one smooth effortless motion, glancing back at Natasha, checking briefly to be sure the little girl was safe.

She was crouched in the sand halfway between the blanket and the water, starting a new dribble castle.

"I'm doing a wonderful job and I'm brilliant?" he said with a half smile. "Sounds like you're giving *me* a little positive reinforcement here."

Natasha's T-shirt was damp and Mia spread it out on top of the cooler to dry in the sun. "Well...maybe," she admitted with a sheepish smile.

He touched her gently under her chin, pulling her head up so that she was forced to look at him.

His smile had faded, and the amusement in his eyes was gone, replaced by something else entirely, something hot and dangerous and impossible to turn away from.

"I like my positive reinforcement delivered a little differently," he told her, his voice no more than a husky whisper.

His gaze flickered down to her mouth, then up again to meet her eyes, and Mia knew that he was going to kiss her. He leaned forward slowly, giving her plenty of time to back away. But she didn't move. She couldn't move. Or maybe she just plain didn't want to move.

She felt him sigh as his lips met hers. His mouth was warm and sweet, and he kissed her so softly. He touched her lips gently with his tongue, waiting until she granted him access before he deepened the kiss. And even then, even as she opened herself to him, he kissed her breathtakingly tenderly.

It was the sweetest kiss she'd ever shared.

He pulled back to look into her eyes, and she could feel her heart pounding. But then he smiled, one of his beautiful, heart-stoppingly perfect crooked smiles, as if he'd just found gold at the end of a rainbow. And this time she reached for him, wrapping her arms up around his neck, pressing herself against him, stabbing her fingers up into the incredible softness of his hair as she kissed him again.

This time it was pure fire. This time he touched her with more than just his lips, pulling her even harder against his chest, running his hands along the bare skin of her back, through her hair, down her arms as he met her tongue in a kiss of wild, bone-melting intensity.

"Frisco! Frisco! The ice-cream truck is here! Can I get an ice cream?"

Mia pushed Frisco away from her even as he released her. He was breathing as hard as she was, and he looked thoroughly shaken. But Natasha was oblivious to everything but the ice-cream truck that had pulled into the beach parking lot.

"Please, please, please, please, please," she was saying, running in circles around and around the beach blanket.

Frisco looked up toward the end of the beach, where the ice-cream truck was parked, and then back at Mia. He looked as shocked and as stunned as she felt. "Uh," he said. He leaned toward her and spoke quickly, in a low voice. "Can you take her? I can't."

"Of course." She quickly pulled on her T-shirt. God, her hands were shaking. She glanced up at him. "Is your knee all right?"

He dug a five-dollar bill out of his wallet and handed it to her with a weak grin. "Actually, it has nothing to do with my knee."

Suddenly Mia understood. She felt her cheeks heat with a blush. "Come on, Tasha," she said, pulling her hair out from the collar of her T-shirt as she led the little girl up the beach.

What had she just done?

She'd just experienced both the sweetest and the most arousing kisses of her entire life—with a man she'd vowed to stay away from. Mia stood in line with Tasha at the ice-cream truck, trying to figure out her next move.

Getting involved with Frisco was entirely out of the question. But, oh, those kisses… Mia closed her eyes. Mistake, she told herself over and over. She'd already made the mistake—to continue in this direction would be sheer foolishness. So okay. He was an amazing mixture of sweetness and sexiness. But he was a man who needed saving, and she knew better than to think she could save him. To become involved would only pull her under, too. Only he could save himself from his unhappiness and despair, and only time would tell if he'd succeed.

She'd have to be honest with him. She'd have to make sure he understood.

In a fog, she ordered Tasha's ice cream and two ice bars for herself and Frisco. The trek back to the blanket seemed endlessly long. The sand seemed hotter than before and her feet burned. Tasha went back to her sand castle, ice cream dripping down her chin.

Frisco was sitting on the edge of the blanket, soaking wet, as if he'd thrown himself into the ocean to cool down. That was good. Mia wanted him cooled down, didn't she?

She handed him the ice pop and tried to smile as she sat down. "I figured we could all use something to cool us off, but you beat me to it."

Frisco looked at Mia, sitting as far from him as she possibly could on the beach blanket, and then down at the ice bar in his hands. "I kind of liked the heat we were generating," he said quietly.

Mia shook her head, unable even to look him in the eye. "I have to be honest. I hardly even know you and…"

He stayed silent, just waiting for her to go on.

"I don't think we should… I mean, I think it would be a mistake to…" She was blushing again.

"Okay." Frisco nodded. "That's okay. I…I understand." He couldn't blame her. How could he blame her? She wasn't the type who went for short-term ecstasy. If she played the game, it would be for keeps, and face it, he wasn't a keeper. He was not the kind of man Mia would want to be saddled with for the rest of her life. She was so full of life, and he was forced to move so slowly. She was so complete; he was less than whole.

"I should probably get home," she said, starting to gather up her things.

"We'll walk you back," he said quietly.

"Oh, no—you don't have to."

"Yeah, we do, okay?"

She glanced up at him, and something she saw in his eyes or on his face made her know not to argue. "All right."

Frisco stood up, reaching for his cane. "Come on, Tash, let's go into the water one last time and wash that ice cream off your face."

He tossed the unopened ice pop into a garbage can as he walked Natasha down to the ocean. He stared out at the water and tried his damnedest not to think about Mia as Tasha rinsed the last of her ice cream from her face and hands. But he couldn't do it. He could still taste her, still feel her in his arms, still smell her spicy perfume.

And for those moments that he'd kissed her, for those incredible few minutes that she'd been in his arms, for the first time since the last dose of heavy-duty pain medication had worn off five years ago, he'd actually forgotten about his injured knee.

Natasha didn't seem to notice the awkward silence. She chattered on, to Mia, to Frisco, to no one in particular. She sang snatches of songs and chanted bits of rhymes.

Mia felt miserable. Rejection was never fun, from either the giving or the receiving end. She knew she'd hurt Frisco by backing away. But her worst mistake had been to let him kiss her in the first place.

She wished she'd insisted that they take her car to the beach, rather than walk. Frisco was a master at hiding his pain, but she could tell from the subtle changes in the way he held himself and the way he breathed that he was hurting.

Mia closed her eyes briefly, trying not to care, but she couldn't. She *did* care. She cared far too much.

"I'm sorry," she murmured to Frisco as Natasha skipped ahead of them, hopping over the cracks in the sidewalk.

He turned and looked at her with those piercing blue eyes that seemed to see right through to her very soul. "You really are, aren't you?"

She nodded.

"I'm sorry, too," he said quietly.

"Frisco!" Natasha launched herself at him, nearly knocking him over.

"Whoa!" he said, catching her in his left arm while he used his right to balance both of their weight with his cane. "What's wrong, Tash?"

The little girl had both of her arms wrapped tightly around his waist, and she was hiding her face in his T-shirt.

"Tash, what's going on?" Frisco asked again, but she didn't move. Short of yanking the child away from himself, he couldn't get her to release him.

Mia crouched down next to the little girl. "Natasha, did something scare you?"

She nodded yes.

Mia pushed Tasha's red curls back from her face. "Honey, what scared you?"

Tasha lifted her head, looking at Mia with tear-filled eyes. "Dwayne," she whispered. "I saw Dwayne."

Mia looked up at Frisco, frowning her confusion. "Who…?"

"One of Sharon's old boyfriends." He pulled Natasha up and into his arms. "Tash, you probably just saw someone who reminded you of him."

Natasha shook her head emphatically as Mia stood up. "I saw Dwayne," she said again, tears overflowing onto her cheeks and great gulping sobs making her nearly impossible to understand. "I saw him."

"What would he be doing here in San Felipe?" Frisco asked the little girl.

"He'd be looking for Sharon Francisco," a low voice drawled. "That's what he'd be doing here."

Natasha was suddenly, instantly silent.

Mia gazed at the man standing directly in front of them. He was a big man, taller and wider even than Frisco, but softer and heavily overweight. He was wearing a dark business suit that had to have been hand tailored to fit his girth, and lizard-skin boots that were buffed to a gleaming shine. His shirt was dark gray—a slightly lighter shade of the same black of his suit, and his tie was a color that fell somewhere between the two. His hair was thick and dark, and it tumbled forward into his eyes in a style reminiscent of Elvis Presley. His face was fifty pounds too heavy to be called handsome, with a distinctive hawklike nose and deep-set eyes that were now lost among the puffiness of his excess flesh.

In one big, beefy hand, he held a switchblade knife that he opened and closed, opened and closed, with a rhythmic hiss of metal on metal.

"My sister's not here," Frisco said evenly.

Mia felt him touch her shoulder, and she turned toward him. His eyes never left Dwayne and the knife in the man's right hand as he handed her Natasha. "Get behind me," he murmured. "And start backing away."

"I can see that your sister's not here," the heavy man had a thick New Orleans accent. The gentlemanly old South politeness of his speech somehow made him seem all the more frightening. "But since you have the pleasure of her daughter's company, I must assume you know of her whereabouts."

"Why don't you leave me your phone number," Frisco suggested, "and I'll have her call you."

Dwayne flicked his knife open again, and this time he didn't close it. "I'm afraid that's unacceptable. You see, she owes me a great deal of money." He smiled. "Of course, I could always take the child as collateral...."

Frisco could still sense Mia's presence behind him. He heard her sharp intake of breath. "Mia, take Tash into the deli on the corner and call the police," he told her without turning around.

He felt her hesitation and anxiety, felt the coolness of her fingers as she touched his arm. "Alan..."

"Do it," he said sharply.

Mia began backing away. Her heart was pounding as she watched Frisco smile pleasantly at Dwayne, always keeping his eyes on that knife. "You know I'd die before I'd let you even touch the girl," the former SEAL said matter-of-factly. Mia knew that what he said was true. She prayed it wouldn't come to that.

"Why don't you just tell me where Sharon is?" Dwayne

asked. "I'm not interested in beating the hell out of a poor, pathetic cripple, but I will if I have to."

"The same way you had to hit a five-year-old?" Frisco countered. Everything about him—his stance, his face, the look in his eyes, the tone of his voice—was deadly. Despite the cane in his hand, despite his injured knee, he looked anything but poor and pathetic.

But Dwayne had a knife, and Frisco only had his cane— which he needed to use to support himself.

Dwayne lunged at Frisco, and Mia turned and ran for the deli.

Frisco saw Mia's sudden movement from the corner of his eye. Thank God. It would be ten times easier to fight this enormous son of a bitch knowing that Mia and Tash were safe and out of the way.

Dwayne lunged with the knife again, and Frisco sidestepped him, gritting his teeth against the sudden screaming pain as his knee was forced to twist and turn in ways that it no longer could. He used his cane and struck the heavyset man on the wrist, sending the sharp-bladed knife skittering into the street.

He realized far too late that he had played right into Dwayne's hand. With his cane up and in the air, he couldn't use it to support himself. And Dwayne came at him again, spinning and turning with the graceful agility of a much smaller, lighter man. Frisco watched, almost in slow motion, as his opponent aimed a powerful karate kick directly at his injured knee.

He saw it coming, but as if he, too, were caught in slow motion, he couldn't move out of the way.

And then there was only pain. Sheer, blinding, excruciating pain. Frisco felt a hoarse cry rip from his throat as he went down, hard, onto the sidewalk. He fought the darkness that threatened to close in on him as he felt Dwayne's foot connect violently with his side, this time damn near launching him into the air.

Somehow he held on to the heavy man's leg. Somehow he

brought his own legs up and around, twisting and kicking and tripping, until Dwayne, too, fell onto the ground.

There were no rules. One of Dwayne's elbows landed squarely in Frisco's face, and he felt his nose gush with blood. He struggled to keep the bigger man's weight off of him, trying to keep Dwayne pinned as he hit him in the face again and again.

Another, smaller man would've been knocked out, but Dwayne was like one of those pop-up punching bag dolls. He just kept coming. The son of a bitch went for his knee again. There was no way he could miss, and again pain ripped into Frisco like a freight train. He grabbed hold of Dwayne's head and slammed it back against the sidewalk.

There were sirens in the distance—Frisco heard them through waves of nausea and dizziness. The police were coming.

Dwayne should have been out for the count, but he scrambled up and onto his feet.

"You tell Sharon I want that money back," he said through bruised and bleeding lips before he limped away.

Frisco tried to go after him, but his knee crumbled beneath his weight, sending another wave of searing pain blasting through him. He felt himself retch and he pressed his cheek against the sidewalk to make the world stop spinning.

A crowd had gathered, he suddenly realized. Someone pushed through the mob, running toward him. He tensed, moving quickly into a defensive position.

"Yo, Lieutenant! Whoa, back off, Navy, it's me, *Thomas.*"

It was. It was Thomas. The kid crouched down next to Frisco on the sidewalk.

"Who ran *you* over with a truck? My God…" Thomas stood up again, looking into the crowd. "Hey, someone call an ambulance for my friend! *Now!*"

Frisco reached for Thomas.

"Yeah, I'm here, man. I'm here, Frisco. I saw this big guy running away—he looked only a little bit better than you do,"

Thomas told him. "What happened? You make some kind of uncalled-for fat joke?"

"Mia," Frisco rasped. "She's got Natasha...at the deli. Stay with them...make sure they're okay."

"You're the one who looks like you need help—"

"I'm *fine*," Frisco ground out between clenched teeth. "If you won't go to them, I will." He searched for his cane. Where the hell was his cane? It was in the street. He crawled toward it, dragging his injured leg.

"God," Thomas said. His eyes were wide in amazement that Frisco could even move. For once he actually looked only eighteen years old. "You stay here, I'll go find them. If it's that important to you..."

"Run," Frisco told him.

Thomas ran.

9

The hospital emergency room was crowded. Mia was ignored by the nurses at the front desk, so she finally gave up and simply walked into the back. She was stepped around, pushed past and nearly knocked over as she searched for Frisco.

"Excuse me, I'm looking for—"

"Not now, dear," a nurse told her, briskly moving down the hallway.

Mia heard him before she saw him. His voice was low, and his language was abominable. It was definitely Alan Francisco.

She followed the sound of his voice into a big room that held six beds, all filled. He was sitting up, his right leg stretched out in front of him, his injured knee swollen and bruised. His T-shirt was covered with blood, he had a cut on his cheekbone directly underneath his right eye and his elbows and other knee looked abraded and raw.

A doctor was examining his knee. "That hurt, too?" he asked, glancing up at Frisco.

Yes, was the gist of the reply, minus all of the colorful superlatives. A new sheen of sweat had broken out on Frisco's face, and he wiped at his upper lip with the back of one hand as he braced himself for the rest of the examination.

"I thought you promised Tasha no more bad words."

Startled, he looked up, and directly into her eyes. "What are you doing here? Where's Tash?"

Mia had surprised him. And not pleasantly, either. She

could see a myriad of emotions flicker across his face. Embarrassment. Shame. Humiliation. She knew he didn't want her to see him like this, looking beaten and bloodied.

"She's with Thomas," Mia told him. "I thought you might want…" What? She thought he might want a hand to hold? No, she already knew him well enough to know he wouldn' need or want that. She shook her head. She'd come here purely for herself. "*I* wanted to make sure you were al right."

"I'm fine."

"You don't look fine."

"Depends on your definition of the word," he said. "I my book, it means I'm not dead."

"Excuse me, miss, but is Mr. Francisco a friend of yours?" It was the doctor. "Perhaps you'll be able to convince him t take the pain medication we've offered him."

Mia shook her head. "No, I don't think I'll be able to d that. He's extremely stubborn—and it's Lieutenant, not Mr If he's decided that he doesn't want it—"

"Yes, he *has* decided he doesn't want it," Frisco interjected. "And he also *hates* being talked about as if he weren' in the room, so do you mind…?"

"The medication would make him rest much more comfortably—"

"Look, all I want you to do is X-ray my damn knee an make sure it's not broken. Do you think *maybe* you can d that?"

"He's a lieutenant in which organization?" the docto asked Mia.

"Please ask him directly," she said. "Surely you can re spect him and not talk over his head this way."

"I'm with the Navy SEALs—*was* with the SEALs," Frisc said.

The doctor snapped closed Frisco's patient clipboard. "Per fect. I should have known. Nurse!" he shouted, already strid ing away. "Send this man to X-ray, and then arrange a trans fer over to the VA facility up by the naval base.…"

Frisco was watching Mia, and when she turned to look at him, he gave her a half smile. "Thanks for trying."

"Why don't you take the pain medicine?" she asked.

"Because I don't want to be stoned and drooling when Dwayne comes back for round two."

Mia couldn't breathe. "Comes back?" she repeated. "Why? Who was he anyway? And what did he want?"

Frisco shifted his weight, unable to keep from wincing. "Apparently my darling sister owes him some money."

"How much money?"

"I don't know, but I'm going to find out." He shook his head. "I'm gonna pay Sharon a little visit in the morning— to hell with the detox center's rules."

"When I saw that knife he was holding…" Mia's voice shook and she stopped. She closed her eyes, willing back the sudden rush of tears. She couldn't remember the last time she'd been that scared. "I didn't want to leave you there alone."

She opened her eyes to find him watching her, the expression on his face unreadable. "Didn't you think I could take that guy and win?" he asked softly.

She didn't need to answer him—she knew he could read her reply in her eyes. She knew how painful it was for him to walk, even with a cane. She knew his limitations. How could he have taken on a man as big as Dwayne—a man who had a knife, as well—and not been hurt? And he *had* been hurt. Badly, it looked like.

He laughed bitterly, looking away from her. "No wonder you damn near ran away from me on the beach. You don't think I'm much of a man, do you?"

Mia was shocked. "That's not true! That's not why—"

"Time to go down to X-ray," a nurse announced, pushing a wheelchair up to Frisco's bed.

Frisco didn't wait for the nurse to help him. He lifted himself off the bed and lowered himself into the chair. He jostled his knee, and it had to have hurt like hell, but he didn't say a word. When he looked up at Mia, though, she could see all of his pain in his eyes. "Just go home," he said quietly.

"They're backed up down there—this could take a while, a few hours even," the nurse informed Mia as she began pushing Frisco out of the room. "You can't come with him, so you'll just be sitting out in the waiting room. If you want to leave, he could call you when he's done."

"No, thank you," Mia said. She turned to Frisco. "Alan, you are *so* wrong about—"

"Just go home," he said again.

"No," she said. "No, I'm going to wait for you."

"Don't," he said. He glanced up at her just before the nurse pushed him out the door. "And don't call me Alan."

Frisco rode in the wheelchair back to the ER lobby with his eyes closed. His X-rays had taken a few aeons longer than forever, and he had to believe Mia had given up on him and gone home.

It was nearly eight o'clock at night. He was still supposed to meet with the doctor to talk about what his X-rays had shown. But he'd seen the film and already knew what the doctor was going to say. His knee wasn't broken. It was bruised and inflamed. There may have been ligament damage, but it was hard to tell—his injury and all of his subsequent surgeries had left things looking pretty severely scrambled.

The doctor was going to recommend shipping him over to the VA hospital for further consultation and possible treatment.

But that was going to have to wait. He had Natasha at home to take care of, and some lunatic named Dwayne to deal with.

"Where are you taking him?" It was Mia's musical voice. She was still here, waiting for him, just as she'd said. Frisco didn't know whether to feel relieved or disappointed. He kept his eyes closed, and tried not to care too much either way.

"The doctor has to take a look at the X-rays," the nurse told her. "We're overcrowded tonight. Depending on how things go, it could be another five minutes or two hours."

"May I sit with him?" Mia asked.

"Sure," the nurse said. "He can wait out here as well as anyplace else."

Frisco felt his wheelchair moved awkwardly into position, heard the nurse walk away. Then he felt Mia's cool fingers touch his forehead, pushing his hair back and off his face.

"I know you're not really asleep," she said.

Her hand felt so good in his hair. Too good. Frisco reached up and caught her wrist as he opened his eyes, pushing her away from him. "That's right," he said. "I'm just shutting everything out."

She was gazing at him with eyes that were a perfect mixture of green and brown. "Well, before you shut me out again, I want you to know—I don't judge whether or not someone is a *man* based on his ability to beat an opponent into a bloody pulp. And I wasn't running away from *you* on the beach today."

Frisco shut his eyes again. "Look, you don't have to explain why you don't want to sleep with me. If you don't, then you don't. That's all I need to know."

"I was running away from myself," she said very softly, a catch in her voice.

Frisco opened his eyes. She was looking at him with tears in her beautiful eyes and his heart lurched. "Mia, don't, really…it's all right." It wasn't, but he would have said or done anything to keep her from crying.

"No, it's not," she said. "I really want to be your friend, but I don't know if I can. I've been sitting here for the past few hours, just thinking about it, and…" She shook her head and a tear escaped down her cheek.

Frisco was lost. His chest felt so tight, he could barely breathe, and he knew the awful truth. He was glad Mia had waited for him. He was glad she'd come to the hospital. Yeah, he'd also been mortified that she'd seen him like this, but at the same time, her presence had made him feel good. For the first time in forever he didn't feel so damned alone.

But now he'd somehow made her cry. He reached for her,

cupping her face with his hand and brushing away that tear with his thumb. "It's not that big a deal," he whispered.

"No?" she said, looking up at him. She closed her eyes and pressed her cheek more fully into the palm of his hand. She turned her head slightly and brushed his fingers with her lips. When she opened her eyes again, he could see a fire burning, white-hot and molten. All sweetness, all girlish innocence was gone from her face. She was all woman, pure female desire as she gazed back at him.

His mouth went totally, instantly dry.

"You touch me, even just like this, and I feel it," she said huskily. "This chemistry—it's impossible to ignore."

She was right, and he couldn't help himself. He pushed his hand up and into the softness of her long, dark hair. She closed her eyes again at the sensation, and he felt his heart begin to pound.

"I know you feel it, too," she whispered.

Frisco nodded. Yes. He traced the soft curve of her ear, then let his hand slide down her neck. Her skin was so smooth, like satin beneath his fingers.

But then she reached for his hand, intertwining their fingers, squeezing his hand, breaking the spell. "But for me, that's not enough," she told him. "I need more than sexual chemistry. I need…love."

Silence. Big, giant silence. Frisco could hear his heart beating and the rush of his blood through his veins. He could hear the sounds of other people in the waiting room—hushed conversations, a child's quiet crying. He could hear a distant television, the clatter of an empty gurney being wheeled too quickly down the hall.

"I can't give you that," he told her.

"I know," she said softly. "And that's why I ran away." She smiled at him, so sweetly, so sadly. The seductive temptress was gone, leaving behind this nice girl who wanted more than he could give her, who knew enough not even to ask.

Or maybe she knew enough not to *want* to ask. He was no prize. He wasn't even whole.

She released his hand, and he immediately missed the warmth of her touch.

"I see they finally got you cleaned up," she said.

"I did it myself," he told her, amazed they could sit here talking like this after what she'd just revealed. "I went into the bathroom near the X-ray department and washed up."

"What happens next?" Mia asked.

What had she just revealed? Nothing, really, when it came down to it. She'd admitted that the attraction between them was powerful. She'd told him that she was looking for more than sex, that she wanted a relationship based on love. But she hadn't said that she wanted *him* to love her.

Maybe she was glossing over the truth. Maybe she'd simply omitted the part about how, even if he *was* capable of giving her what she wanted, she had no real interest in any kind of a relationship with some crippled has-been.

"The doctor will look at my X-rays and he'll tell me that nothing's broken," Frisco told her. "Nothing he can see, anyway."

How much of that fight had she seen? he wondered. Had she seen Dwayne drop him with a single well-placed blow to his knee? Had she seen him hit the sidewalk like a stone? Had she seen Dwayne kick him while he was down there, face against the concrete like some pathetic hound dog too dumb to get out of the way?

And look at him now, back in a wheelchair. He'd sworn he'd never sit in one of these damned things again, yet here he was.

"Dammit, Lieutenant, when I sent you home to rest, I meant you should *rest,* not start a new career as a street fighter." Captain Steven Horowitz was wearing his white dress uniform and he gleamed in the grimy ER waiting room. What the hell was *he* doing here?

"Dr. Wright called and said he had a former patient of mine in his emergency room, waiting to get his knee X-rayed. He said this patient's knee was swollen and damaged from a previous injury, and on top of that, it looked as if it had recently been hit with a sledgehammer. Although apparently this patient claimed there were no sledgehammers involved in the fight he'd been in,'' Horowitz said, arms folded across his chest. "The *fight* he'd been in. And I asked myself, now, which of my former knee-injury patients would be *stupid* enough to put himself into a threatening situation like a *fight* that might irrevocably damage his injured knee? I came up with Alan Francisco before Wright even mentioned your name.''

"Nice to see you, too, Steve," Frisco said, wearily running his hand through his hair, pushing it off his face. He could feel Mia watching him, watching the Navy captain.

"What were you thinking?"

"Allow me to introduce Mia Summerton," Frisco said. "Mia, I know you're going to be disappointed, but as much as Steve looks like it, he *isn't* the White Power Ranger. He's really only just a Navy doctor. His name's Horowitz. He answers to Captain, Doctor, Steve, and sometimes even God."

Steven Horowitz was several years older than Frisco, but he had an earnestness about him that made him seem quite a bit younger. Frisco watched him do a double take as he looked at Mia, with her long, dark hair, her beautiful face, her pretty flowered sundress that revealed her smooth, tanned shoulders and her slender, graceful arms. He watched Steve look back at his own bloody T-shirt and battered face. He knew what the doctor was thinking—what was *she* doing with him?

Nothing. She was doing nothing. She'd made that more than clear.

Horowitz turned back to Frisco. "I looked at the X-rays—I think you may have been lucky, but I won't be able to know for certain until the swelling goes down." He pulled a chair over, and looked at the former SEAL's knee, probing it lightly with gentle fingers.

Frisco felt himself start to sweat. From the corner of his eye, he saw Mia lean forward, as if she were going to reach for his hand. But he closed his eyes, refusing to look at her, refusing to need her.

She took his hand anyway, holding it tightly until Steve was through. By then, Frisco was drenched with sweat again, and he knew his face must've looked gray or maybe even green. He let go of her hand abruptly, suddenly aware that he was damn near mashing her fingers.

"All right," Steve finally said with a sigh. "Here's what I want you to do. I want you to go home, and I want you to stay off your feet for the next two weeks." He took his prescription pad from his leather bag. "I'll give you something to make you sleep—"

"And I won't take it," Frisco said. "I have a…situation to deal with."

"What kind of situation?"

Frisco shook his head. "It's a family matter. My sister's in some kind of trouble. All you need to know is that I'm not taking anything that's going to make me sleep. I won't object to a local painkiller, though."

Steven Horowitz laughed in disgust. "If I give you that, your knee won't hurt. And if your knee doesn't hurt, you're going to be up running laps, doing God knows what kind of damage. No. No way."

Frisco leaned forward, lowering his voice, wishing Mia weren't listening, hating himself for having to admit his weaknesses. "Steve, you know I wouldn't ask for it if I weren't in serious pain. I *need* it, man. I can't risk taking the stuff that will knock me out."

The doctor's eyes were a flat, pale blue, but for a brief moment, Frisco saw a flare of warmth and compassion behind the customary chill. Steve shook his head. "I'm going to regret doing this. I *know* I'm going to regret doing this." He scribbled something on his pad. "I'm going to give you something to bring down the swelling, too. Go easy with it." He glared at Frisco. "In return, you have to *promise* me you won't get out of this wheelchair for two weeks."

Frisco shook his head. "I can't promise that," he said. "In fact, I'd rather die than stay in this chair for a minute longer than I have to."

Dr. Horowitz turned to Mia. "His knee has already been permanently damaged. It's something of a miracle that he can even walk at all. There's nothing he can do to make his knee any better, but he *could* make things worse. Will you please try to make him understand—"

"We're just friends," she interrupted. "I can't make him do anything."

"Crutches," Frisco said. "I'll use crutches, but no chair, all right?"

He didn't look at Mia. But he couldn't stop thinking about the way her eyes had looked filled with tears, and the way that had made him feel. She was wrong. She was dead wrong. She didn't know it, but she had the power to damn well make him do anything.

Maybe even fall in love with her.

Mia pulled the car up near the emergency room entrance. She could see Frisco through the windows of the brightly lit lobby, talking to the doctor. The doctor handed Frisco a bag, and then the two men shook hands. The doctor vanished quickly down the hallway, while Frisco moved slowly on his crutches toward the automatic door.

It slid open with a whoosh, and then he was outside, looking around.

Mia opened the car door and stood up. "Over here." She saw his surprise. This wasn't her car. This thing was about twice the size of her little subcompact—he wouldn't have any trouble fitting inside it. "I traded cars with a friend for a few days," she explained.

He didn't say a word. He just put the bag the doctor had given him into the middle of the wide bench seat and slid his crutches into the back. He climbed in carefully, lowering himself down and using both hands to lift his injured leg into the car.

She got in next to him, started the powerful engine and pulled out of the driveway. She glanced at Frisco. "How's your knee doing?"

"Fine," he said tersely.

"Do you really think Dwayne's going to come back?"

"Yep."

Mia waited for him to elucidate, but he didn't continue. He obviously wasn't in a talkative mood. Not that he ever was, of course. But somehow the fairly easygoing candidness of their previous few conversations had vanished.

She knew his knee was anything but fine. She knew it hurt him badly—and that the fact that he'd been unable to defeat his attacker hurt him even more.

She knew that his injured knee and his inability to walk without a cane made him feel like less of a man. It was idiotic. A man was made up of so much more than a pair of strong legs and an athletic body.

It was idiotic, but she understood. Suddenly she understood that the list she'd seen on Frisco's refrigerator of all the things he couldn't do wasn't simply pessimistic whining, as she'd first thought. It was a recipe. It was specific directions for a magical spell that would make Frisco a man again.

Jump, run, skydive, swim, stretch, bend, extend…

Until he could do all those things and more, he wasn't going to feel like a man.

Until he could do all those things again… But he wasn't going to. That Navy doctor had said he wasn't going to get any better. This was it. Frisco had come as far as he could—and the fact that he could walk at all was something of a miracle at that.

Mia pulled the car into the condominium parking lot and parked. Frisco didn't wait for her to help him out of the car. Of course not. Real men didn't need help.

Her heart ached for him as she watched him pull out his crutches from the back seat. He grimly positioned them under his arms, and carrying the bag that the doctor had given him, swung toward the courtyard.

She followed more slowly.

Jump, run, skydive, swim, stretch, bend, extend…

It wasn't going to happen. Dr. Horowitz knew it. Mia knew it. And she suspected that deep inside, Frisco knew it, too.

She followed him into the courtyard and could barely stand to watch as he pulled himself painfully up the stairs.

He was wrong. He was wrong about it all. Moving onto the ground floor wouldn't make him less of a man. Admitting that he had physical limitations—that there were things he could no longer do—that wouldn't make him less of a man, either.

But relentlessly questing after the impossible, making goals that were unattainable, setting himself up only for failure—that would wear him down and burn him out. It would take away the last of his warmth and spark, leaving him bitter and angry and cold and incomplete. Leaving him less of a man.

10

Frisco sat in the living room, cleaning his handgun.

When Sharon's charming ex-boyfriend Dwayne had pulled out his knife this afternoon, Frisco had felt, for the first time in a while, the noticeable lack of a sidearm.

Of course, carrying a weapon meant concealing that weapon. Although he was fully licensed to carry whatever he damn well pleased, he couldn't exactly wear a weapon in a belt holster, like a cop or an old West gunslinger. And wearing a shoulder holster meant he'd have to wear a jacket over it, at least out in public. And—it was a chain reaction—if he wore a jacket, he'd have to wear long pants. Even *he* couldn't wear a jacket with shorts.

Of course, he could always do what Blue McCoy did. Blue was the Alpha Squad's XO—Executive Officer and second in command of the SEAL unit. Blue rarely wore anything other than cutoffs and an old worn-out, loose olive-drab fatigue shirt with the sleeves removed. And he always wore one of the weapons he carried in a shoulder holster underneath his shirt, the smooth leather directly against his skin.

Frisco's knee twinged, and he glanced at the clock. It was nearly 0300. Three o'clock in the morning.

Steve Horowitz had given him a number of little vials filled with a potent local pain reliever similar to novocaine. It wasn't yet time for another injection, but it was getting close. Frisco had given himself an injection at close to nine o'clock, after Mia had driven him home from the hospital.

Mia...

Frisco shook his head, determined to think about anything but Mia, separated from him by only a few thin walls, her hair spread across her pillow, wearing only a tantalizingly thin cotton nightgown. Her beautiful soft lips parted slightly in sleep....

Yeah, he was a master at self-torture. He'd been sitting here, awake for hours, spending most of his time remembering—hell, *reliving*—the way Mia had kissed him at the beach. Dear, sweet God, what a kiss that had been.

It wasn't likely he was going to get a chance to kiss her like that again. She'd made it clear that she wouldn't welcome a repeat performance. If he knew what was best, he'd stay far, far away from Mia Summerton. That wasn't going to be hard to do. From now on, she was going to be avoiding him, too.

A loud thump from the bedroom made him sit up. What the hell was that?

Frisco grabbed his crutches and his handgun and moved as quickly as he could down the hall to Tasha's room.

He'd bought a cheap portable TV. It was quite possibly the most expensive night-light and white noise machine in the world. Its bluish light flickered, illuminating the small room.

Natasha was sitting on the floor, next to her bed, sleepily rubbing her eyes and her head. She was whimpering, but only very softly. Her voice almost didn't carry above the soft murmurings of the television.

"Poor Tash, did you fall out of bed?" Frisco asked her, moving awkwardly through the narrow doorway and into the room. He slipped the safety onto his weapon and slid it into the pocket of his shorts. "Come on, climb back up. I'll tuck you in again."

But when Tasha stood up, she staggered, almost as if she'd had too much to drink, and sat back down on her rear end. As Frisco watched, she crumpled, pressing her forehead against the wall-to-wall carpeting.

Frisco leaned his crutches against the bed and bent down

to pick her up. "Tash, it's three in the morning. Don't play silly games."

Lord, the kid was on fire. Frisco felt her forehead, her cheek, her neck, double-checking, praying that he was wrong, praying that she was simply sweaty from a nightmare. But with each touch, he knew. Natasha had a raging fever.

He lifted her and put her in her bed.

How could this have happened? She'd been fine all day today. She'd had her swimming lesson with her usual enthusiasm. She'd gone back into the water over and over again with her usual energy. True, she'd been asleep when he'd returned from the hospital, but he'd chalked that up to exhaustion after the excitement of the day—watching Uncle Frisco get the living daylights kicked out of him by old, ugly Dwayne had surely been tiring for the kid.

Her eyes were half-closed and she pressed her head against her pillow as if it hurt, still making that odd, whimpering sound.

Frisco was scared to death. He tried to judge how high her fever was by the touch of his hand, and she seemed impossibly, dangerously hot.

"Tasha, talk to me," he said, sitting next to her on the bed. "Tell me what's wrong. Tell me your symptoms."

Cripes, listen to him. *Tell me your symptoms.* She was five years old, she didn't know what the hell a symptom was. And from the looks of things, she didn't even know she was here, couldn't hear him, couldn't see him.

He had medical training, but most of it was first-aid. He could handle gunshot wounds, knife wounds, burns and lacerations. But sick kids with sky-high fevers...

He had to get Natasha to the hospital.

He could call a cab, but man, he wouldn't be able to get Tasha down the stairs. He could barely make it himself with his crutches. He certainly couldn't do it carrying the girl, could he? It would be far too dangerous to try. What if he dropped her?

"I'll be right back, Tash," he told her, grabbing his

crutches and heading out toward the kitchen telephone, where he kept his phone book.

He flipped the book open, searching for the phone number for the local cab company. He quickly dialed. It rang at least ten times before someone picked up.

"Yellow Cab."

"Yeah," Frisco said. "I need a cab right away. 1210 Midfield Street, unit 2C. It's the condo complex on the corner of Midfield and Harris?"

"Destination?"

"City Hospital. Look I need the driver to come to the door. I got a little girl with a fever, and I'll need help carrying her down—"

"Sorry, sir. Our drivers do not leave their vehicles. He'll wait for you in the parking lot."

"Didn't you hear what I just said? This is an emergency. I have to get this kid to the hospital." Frisco ran his hand through his hair, trying to curb his anger and frustration. "I can't get her down the stairs by myself. I'm…" He nearly choked on the words. "I'm physically disabled."

"I'm sorry, sir. The rule is for our drivers' safety. However, the cab you requested will arrive in approximately ninety minutes."

"Ninety minutes? I can't wait *ninety* minutes!"

"Shall I cancel your request for a cab?"

"Yes." Cursing loudly, Frisco slammed down the phone.

He picked it up again and quickly dialed 911. It seemed to take forever before the line was picked up.

"What is the nature of your emergency?"

"I have a five-year-old with a very high fever."

"Is the child breathing?"

"Yes—"

"Is the child bleeding?"

"No, I said she's got a fever—"

"I'm sorry, sir. We have quite a number of priority calls and a limited number of ambulances. You'll get her to the hospital faster if you drive her yourself."

Frisco fought the urge to curse. "I don't have a car."

"Well, I can put you on the list, but since your situation isn't life or death per se, you risk being continuously bumped down as new calls come in," the woman told him. "Things usually slow down by dawn."

Dawn. "Forget it," Frisco said, hanging up none too gently.

Now what?

Mia. He was going to have to ask Mia for help.

He moved as quickly as he could back down the hall to Tasha's room. Her eyes were closed, but she was moving fitfully. She was still as hot to the touch. Maybe even hotter.

"Hang on, kid," Frisco said. "Hang on, princess. I'll be back in a sec."

He was starting to be able to move pretty nimbly with the crutches. He made it into the living room and out of the front door before he'd even had time to think.

But as he rang Mia's bell again and again, as he opened up the screen and hammered on the heavy wooden door, as he waited for her to respond, he couldn't help but wonder.

What the hell was he doing? He'd just spent the past six hours resolving to stay away from this woman. She didn't want him—she'd made that more than clear. So here he was, pounding on her door in the middle of the night, ready to humiliate himself even further by having to ask for help carrying a featherweight forty-pound little girl down the stairs.

The light went on inside Mia's apartment. She opened the door before she'd even finished putting on her bathrobe.

"Alan, what's wrong?"

"I need your help." She would never know how much it cost him to utter those words. It was only for Natasha that he would ask for help. If it had been himself in there, burning up with fever, he wouldn't've asked. He would have rather died. "Tasha's sick. She's got a really high fever—I want to take her over to the hospital."

"All right," Mia said without hesitation. "Let me throw

on a pair of shorts and some sneakers and I'll pull the car around to the outside stairs.''

She moved to go back toward her bedroom and her clothes, but he stopped her.

"Wait."

Mia turned back to the door. Frisco was standing on the other side of the screen, crutches under his arms. He was staring away from her, down at the carpeting. When he looked up, all of his customary crystal anger was gone from his eyes, leaving only a deeply burning shame. He could barely hold her gaze. He looked away, but then he forced himself to look up again, this time steadily meeting her eyes.

"I can't carry her down the stairs."

Mia's heart was in her throat. She knew what it had taken for him to say those words, and she so desperately didn't want to say the wrong thing in response. She didn't want to make light of it, but at the same time, she didn't want to embarrass him further by giving it too much weight.

"Of course not," she said quietly. "That would be dangerous to try on crutches. I'll get the car, then I'll come back up for Natasha."

He nodded once and disappeared.

She'd said the right thing, but there was no time to sag with relief. Mia dashed into her bedroom to change her clothes.

"An *ear* infection?" Frisco repeated, staring at the emergency room doctor.

This doctor was an intern, still in his twenties, but he had a bedside manner reminiscent of an old-fashioned, elderly country doctor, complete with twinkling blue eyes and a warm smile.

"I already started her on an antibiotic, and I gave her something to bring down that fever," he said, looking from Frisco to Mia, "along with a decongestant. That'll keep her knocked out for a while. Don't be surprised if she sleeps later than usual in the morning."

"That's it?" Frisco asked. "It's just an ear infection?" He

looked down at Tasha, who was sound asleep, curled up in the hospital bed. She looked impossibly small and incredibly fragile, her hair golden red against the white sheets.

"She may continue to experience the dizziness you described for a day or two," the doctor told them. "Keep her in bed if you can, and make sure she finishes the *entire* bottle of antibiotic. Oh, and ear plugs next time she goes swimming, all right?"

Frisco nodded. "You sure you don't want to keep her here for a while?"

"I think she'll be more comfortable at home," the young doctor said. "Besides, her fever's already gone down. Call me if she doesn't continue to improve."

An ear infection. Not encephalitis. Not appendicitis. Not scarlet fever or pneumonia. It still hadn't fully sunk in. Tash was going to be all right. An ear infection wasn't life threatening. The kid wasn't going to die. Frisco still couldn't quite believe it. He couldn't quite shake the tight feeling in his chest—the incredible fear, the sense of total and complete helplessness.

He felt Mia touch his arm. "Let's get her home," she said quietly.

"Yeah," he said, looking around, trying to collect himself, wondering when the relief was going to set in and push away this odd sensation of tightness and fear. "I've had enough of this place for one day."

The ride home was shorter than he remembered. He watched as Mia carried Tash back up the stairs and into his condo. She gently placed the still sleeping child into bed, and covered her with a sheet and a light blanket. He watched, trying not to think about the fact that she was taking care of Tasha because he couldn't.

"You ought to try to get some sleep, too," Mia told him, whispering as they went back down the hallway to the living room. "It's nearly dawn."

Frisco nodded.

Mia's face was in the shadows as she stood at the doorway, looking back at him. "Are you all right?"

No. He wasn't all right. He nodded. "Yeah."

"Good night, then." She opened the screen door.

"Mia…"

She stopped, turning back to face him. She didn't say a word, she just waited for him to speak.

"Thank you." His voice was husky, and to his horror he suddenly had tears in his eyes. But it was dark in the predawn, and there was no way she could have noticed.

"You're welcome," she said quietly and closed the door behind her.

She disappeared, but the tears that flooded his eyes didn't do the same. Frisco couldn't stop them from overflowing and running down his face. A sob escaped him, shaking him, and like ice breaking up on a river, another followed, faster and harder until, God, he was crying like a baby.

He'd honestly thought Tasha was going to die.

He had been totally terrified. Him, Frisco, terrified. He'd gone on rescue missions and information-gathering expeditions deep into hostile territory where he could've been killed simply for being American. He'd sat in cafés and had lunch, surrounded by the very people who wouldn't have hesitated to slit his throat had they known his true identity. He'd infiltrated a terrorist fortress and snatched back a cache of stolen nuclear weapons. He'd looked death—his own death—in the eye on more than one occasion. He'd been plenty scared all those times; only a fool wouldn't have been. That fear had been sharp edged, keeping him alert and in control. But it was nothing compared to the sheer, helpless terror he'd felt tonight.

Frisco stumbled back into the sanctuary of his bedroom, unable to stanch the flow of his tears. He didn't want to cry, dammit. Tasha was safe. She was okay. He should have enough control over his emotions to keep the intensity of his relief from wiping him out this way.

He clenched his teeth and fought it. And lost.

Yeah, Tasha was safe. For now. But what if he hadn't been able to get her to the hospital? It had been good that he'd brought her in when he did, the doctor had said. Her fever had been on the verge of becoming dangerously high.

What if Mia hadn't been home? What if he hadn't been able to get Tash down the stairs? Or what if during the time he spent figuring out how to get Tash to the hospital, her fever *had* risen dangerously high? What if his inability to do something so simple as carry a child down a set of stairs had jeopardized her life? What if she had died, because he lived on the second floor? What if she had died, because he was too damn proud to admit the truth—that he was physically disabled.

He'd said the words tonight when he spoke to the cab dispatcher. *I'm physically disabled.* He wasn't a SEAL anymore. He was a crippled man with a cane—crutches now—who might've let a kid die because of his damned pride.

Frisco sat down on his bed and let himself cry.

Mia set her purse down on her kitchen table with an odd-sounding thunk. She lifted it up and set it down again. Thunk.

What was in there?

She remembered even before she opened the zipper.

Natasha's medicine. Frisco had picked up Tasha's antibiotic directly from the hospital's twenty-four-hour pharmacy.

Mia took it out of her purse and stared at it. Tash wasn't due for another dose of the liquid until a little before noon, unless she woke up earlier.

She'd better take it over now, rather than wait.

She left her apartment and went over to Frisco's. All of his windows were dark. Damn. She opened the screen door, wincing as it screeched, and tried the door knob.

It was unlocked.

Slowly, stealthily, she let herself in. She'd tiptoe into the kitchen, put the medicine in the fridge and...

What was that...? Mia froze.

It was a strange sound, a soft sound, and Mia stood very, very still, hardly daring to breathe as she listened for it again.

There it was. It was the sound of ragged breathing, of nearly silent crying. Had Tasha awoken? Was Frisco already so soundly asleep that he didn't hear her?

Quietly Mia crept down the hall toward Tasha's bedroom and peeked in.

The little girl was fast asleep, breathing slowly and evenly.

Mia heard the sound again, and she turned and saw Frisco in the dim light that filtered in through his bedroom blinds.

He was sitting on his bed, doubled over as if in pain, his elbows resting on his legs, one hand covering his face; a picture of despair.

The noise she had heard—it was Frisco. Alan Francisco was weeping.

Mia was shocked. Never, *ever* in a million years had she expected him to cry. She would have thought him incapable, unable to release his emotions in such a visible, expressive way. She would have expected him to internalize everything, or deny his feelings.

But he was crying.

Her heart broke for him, and silently she backed away, instinctively knowing that he would feel ashamed and humiliated if he knew she had witnessed his emotional breakdown. She crept all the way back into his living room and out of his apartment, holding her breath as she shut the door tightly behind her.

Now what?

She couldn't just go back into her own condominium, knowing that he was alone with all of his pain and fears. Besides, she was still holding Tasha's medicine.

Taking a deep breath, knowing full well that even if Frisco *did* come to the door, he might very well simply take the medicine and shut her out, she rang the bell.

She knew he heard it, but no lights went on, nothing stirred. She opened the screen and knocked on the door, pushing it open a few inches. "Alan?"

"Yeah," his voice said raspily. "I'm in the bathroom. Hang on, I'll be right out."

Mia came inside again, and closed the door behind her. She stood there, leaning against it, wondering if she should turn on the lights.

She heard the water running in the bathroom sink and could picture Frisco splashing his face with icy water, praying that she wouldn't be able to tell that he'd been crying. She left the lights off.

And he made no move to turn them on when he finally appeared at the end of the darkened hallway. He didn't say anything; he just stood there.

"I, um...I had Tasha's medicine in my purse," Mia said. "I thought it would be smart to bring it over now instead of...in the morning...."

"You want a cup of tea?"

His quiet question took her entirely by surprise. Of all the things she'd imagined he'd say to her, inviting her to stay for a cup of tea was not one of them. "Yes," she said. "I would."

His crutches creaked as he went into the kitchen. Mia followed more hesitantly.

He didn't turn on the overhead lamp. He didn't need to. Light streamed in through the kitchen window from the brightly lit parking lot. It was silvery and it made shadows on the walls, but it was enough to see by.

As Frisco filled a kettle with water from the faucet, Mia opened the refrigerator door and put Tasha's medicine inside. As she closed the door, she saw that list that he kept there on the fridge, the list of all the things he could no longer do—the list of things that kept him, in his eyes, from being a man.

"I know it was hard for you to come and ask me for help tonight," she said softly.

Using only his right crutch for support, he carried the kettle to the stove and set it down. He didn't say a word until after he'd turned the burner on. Then he turned to face her. "Yeah," he said. "It was."

"I'm glad you did, though. I'm glad I could help."

"I actually…" He cleared his throat and started again. "I actually thought she was going to die. I was scared to death."

Mia was startled by his candidness. *I was scared to death.* Another surprise. She never would have expected him to admit that. Ever. But then again, this man had been surprising her right from the start.

"I don't know how parents handle it," he said, pushing down on top of the kettle as if that would make the water heat faster. "I mean, here's this kid that you love more than life itself, right? And suddenly she's so sick she can't even stand up." His voice tightened.

"The thing that kills me is that if I had been the only one left in the world, if it had been up to me and me alone, we wouldn't't've made it to that hospital. I'd still be here, trying to figure out a way to get her down those stairs." He turned suddenly, slamming his hand down on top of the counter in frustration and anger. "I *hate* feeling so damned helpless!"

His shoulders looked so tight, his face so grim. Mia wrapped her arms around herself to keep from reaching for him. "But you're not the only one left in the world. You're *not* alone."

"But I *am* helpless."

"No, you're not," she told him. "Not anymore. You're only helpless if you refuse to ask for help."

He laughed, an exhale of bitter air. "Yeah, right—"

"Yeah," she said earnestly. "*Right.* Think about it, Alan. There are things that we all don't do, things that we probably couldn't do—look at your shirt," she commanded him, stepping closer. She reached out and touched the soft cotton of his T-shirt. She lifted it, turning it over and bringing the factory-machine-sewn hem into the light from the kitchen window. "You didn't sew this shirt, did you? Or weave the cotton to make the fabric? Cotton grows in fields—you knew that, right? Somehow a whole bunch of people did something to that little fluffy plant to make it turn into this T-shirt. Does it mean that you're helpless just because you didn't do it yourself?''

Mia was standing too close to him. She could smell his musky, masculine scent along with some kind of decadently delicious after-shave or deodorant. He was watching her, the light from the window casting shadows across his face, making his features craggy and harsh. His eyes gleamed colorlessly, but the heat within them didn't need a color to be seen. She released her hold on his T-shirt but she didn't back away. She didn't want to back away, even if it meant spontaneous combustion from the heat in his eyes.

"So what if you can't make your own clothes?" she continued. "The good people at Fruit of the Loom and Levi's will make them for you. So what if you can't carry Tasha down the stairs. *I'll* carry her for you."

Frisco shook his head. "It's not the same."

"It's *exactly* the same."

"What if you're not home? What then?"

"Then you call Thomas. Or your friend, what's-his-name…Lucky. And if they're not home, you call someone else. Instead of this," she said, gesturing toward the list on his refrigerator, "you should have a two-page list of friends you can call for help. Because you're only helpless if you have no one to call."

"Will they run on the beach for me?" Frisco asked, his voice tight. He stepped closer to her, dangerously closer. His body was a whisper away from hers, and she could feel his breath, hot and sweet, moving her hair. "Will they get back in shape for me, get reinstated as an active-duty SEAL for me? And then will they come along on my missions with me, and run when I need to run, and swim against a two-knot current when I need to swim? Will they make a high-altitude, low-opening jump out of an airplane for me? Will they fight when I need to fight, and move without making a noise when I need to be silent? Will they do all those things that I'd need to do to keep myself and the men in my unit alive?"

Mia was silent.

"I know you don't understand," he said. The teakettle started to hiss and whistle, a lonely, high-pitched keening sound. He turned away from her, moving toward the stove. He hadn't touched her, but his presence and nearness had been nearly palpable. She sagged slightly as if he had been holding her up, and backing away, she lowered herself into one of his kitchen chairs. As she watched, he removed the kettle from the heat and took two mugs down from the cabinet. "I wish I could make you understand."

"Try."

He was silent as he opened the cabinet again and removed two tea bags. He put one into each mug, then poured in the steaming water from the kettle. He set the kettle back onto the stove and was seemingly intent on steeping the tea bags as he began, haltingly, to speak.

"You know that I grew up here in San Felipe," he said. "I also told you that my childhood wasn't a barrel of laughs. That was sort of an understatement. Truth was, it sucked. My old man worked on a fishing boat—when he wasn't too hung over to get out of bed. It wasn't exactly like living an episode of 'Leave it to Beaver,' or 'Father Knows Best.'" He looked at her, the muscle in his jaw tight. "I'm going to have to ask you to carry the mugs of tea into the living room for me."

"Of course." Mia glanced at him from the corner of her eyes. "That wasn't really so hard, was it?"

"Yes, it was." With both crutches securely under his arms, Frisco led the way into the living room. He switched on only one lamp and it gave the room a soft, almost golden glow. "Excuse me for a minute," he said, then vanished down the hallway to his bedroom.

Mia put both mugs down on the coffee table in front of the plaid couch and sat down.

"I wanted to check on Tash," he said, coming back into the living room, "and I wanted to get *this*." He was holding a paper bag—the bag the doctor had given him at the hospital. He winced as he sat down on the other side of the long couch and lifted his injured leg onto the coffee table. As Mia watched, he opened the bag and took out a syringe and a small vial. "I need to have my leg up. I hope you don't mind if I do this out here."

"What exactly is it that you're doing?"

"This is a local painkiller, kind of like novocaine," he explained, filling the syringe with the clear liquid. "I'm going to inject it into my knee."

"*You're* going to *inject* it into… You're kidding."

"As a SEAL, I've had training as a medic," he said. "Steve gave me a shot of cortisone in the hospital, but that won't kick in for a while yet. This works almost right away, but the down side is that it wears off after a few hours, and I have to remedicate. Still, it takes the edge off the pain without affecting my central nervous system."

Mia turned away, unable to watch as he stuck the needle into his leg.

"I'm sorry," he murmured. "But it was crossing the border into hellishly painful again."

"I don't think I could ever give myself a shot," Mia admitted.

He glanced over at her, his mouth twisted up into a near smile. "Well, it's not my favorite thing in the world to do, either, but can you imagine what would have happened tonight if I'd taken the painkiller Steve wanted to prescribe for me? I would never have heard Tasha fall out of bed. She'd still be in there, on the floor, and I'd be stupid, drooling and unconscious in my bed. This way, my knee gets numb, not my brain."

"Interesting philosophy from a man who drank himself to sleep two nights in a row."

Frisco could feel the blessed numbing start in his knee. He rolled his head to make his shoulders and neck relax. "Jeez, you don't pull your punches, do you?"

"Four-thirty in the morning is hardly the time for polite conversation," she countered, tucking her legs up underneath her on the couch and taking a sip of her tea. "If you can't be baldly honest at four-thirty in the morning, when can you be?''

Frisco reached up with one hand to rub his neck. "Here's a baldly honest truth for you, then—and it's true whether it's 0430 or high noon. Like I said before, I'm not drinking anymore.''

She was watching him, her hazel eyes studying him, looking for what, he didn't know. He had the urge to turn away or to cover his face, afraid that somehow she'd be able to see the telltale signs of his recent tears. But instead, he forced himself to hold her gaze.

"I can't believe you can just quit," she finally said. "Just like that. I mean, I look at you, and I can tell that you're sober, but…''

"The night we met, you didn't exactly catch me at my best. I was…celebrating my discharge from the Navy—toasting their lack of faith in me." He reached forward, picked up his mug of tea and took a sip. It was too hot and it burned all the way down. "I told you—I don't make a habit out of drinking too much. I'm not like Sharon. Or my father. Man, he was a bastard. He had two moods—drunk and angry, and hung over and angry. Either way, my brothers and Sharon and I learned to stay out of his way. Sometimes one of us would end up in the wrong place at the wrong time, and then we'd get hit. We used to sit around for hours thinking up excuses to tell our friends about where we got all our black eyes and bruises." He snorted. "As if any of our friends didn't know exactly what was going on. Most of them were living the same bad dream.

"You know, I used to pretend he wasn't really my father. I came up with this story about how I was some kind of mercreature that had gotten tangled in his nets one day when he was out in the fishing boat.''

Mia smiled. "Like Tasha pretending she's a Russian princess.''

Her smile was hypnotizing. Frisco could think of little but the way her lips had felt against his, and how much he wanted to feel that sweet sensation again. He resisted the urge to reach out and touch the side of her beautiful face. She looked away from him, her smile fading, suddenly shy, as if she knew what he was thinking.

"So there I was," Frisco continued with his story, "ten years old and living with this nightmare of a home life. It was that year—the year I was in fourth grade—that I started riding my bike for hours on end just to get out of the house."

She was listening to him, staring intently into her mug as if it held the answers to all of her questions. She'd kicked off her sneakers and they lay on their side on the floor in front of her. Her slender legs were tucked up beneath her on the couch, tantalizingly smooth and golden tan. She was wearing a gray hooded sweatshirt over her cutoffs. She'd had it zipped up at the hospital, but at some point since they'd returned home, she'd unzipped it. The shirt she wore underneath was white and loose, with a small ruffle at the top.

It was her nightgown, Frisco realized. She'd simply thrown her clothes on over her nightgown, tucking it into her shorts and covering it with her sweatshirt.

She glanced up at him, waiting for him to continue.

Frisco cleared the sudden lump of desire from his throat and went on. "One day I rode my bike a few miles down the coast, to one of the beaches where the SEALs do a lot of their training exercises. It was just amazing to watch these guys." He smiled, remembering how he'd thought the SEALs were crazy that first time he'd seen them on the beach. "They were always wet. Whatever they were doing, whatever the weather, the instructors always ran 'em into the surf first and got 'em soaked. Then they'd crawl across the beach on their bellies and get coated with sand—it'd get all over their faces, in their hair, everywhere. And *then* they'd run ten miles up and down the beach. They looked amazing—to a ten-year-old it was pretty funny. But even though I was just a kid, I could see past the slapstick. I knew that whatever they were going to get by doing all these endless, excruciating endurance tests, it had to be pretty damn good."

Mia had turned slightly to face him on the couch. Maybe it was because he knew she was wearing her nightgown under her clothes, or maybe it was the dark, dangerous hour of the night, but she looked like some kind of incredible fantasy sitting there like that. Taking her into his arms and making love to her would be a blissful, temporary escape from all of his pain and frustration.

He knew without a shadow of a doubt that one kiss would melt away all of her caution and reserve. Yes, she was a nice girl. Yes, she wanted more than sex. She wanted love. But even nice girls felt the pull of hot, sweet desire. He could show her—and convince her with one single kiss—that sometimes pure sex for the sake of pleasure and passion was enough.

But oddly enough, he wanted more from this woman than the hot satisfaction of a sexual release. Oddly enough, he wanted her to understand how he felt—his frustration, his anger, his darkest fear.

Try, she'd said. Try to make her understand.

He was trying.

"I started riding to the naval base all the time," he continued, forcing himself to focus on her wide green eyes rather than the soft smoothness of her thighs. "I started hanging out down there. I snuck into this local dive where a lot of the off-duty sailors went, just so I could listen to their stories. The SEALs didn't come in too often, but when they did, man, they got a hell of a lot of respect. A *hell* of a lot of respect—from both the enlisted men *and* the officers. They had this aura of greatness about them, and I was convinced, along with the rest of the Navy, that these guys were gods.

"I watched 'em every chance I could get, and I noticed that even though most of the SEALs didn't dress in uniform, they all had this pin they wore. They called it a Budweiser—it was an eagle with a submachine gun in one claw and a trident in the other. I found out they got that pin after they went through a grueling basic training session called BUD/S. Most guys didn't make it through BUD/S, and some classes even had a ninety-percent drop-out rate. The program was weeks and weeks of organized torture, and only the men who stayed in to the end got that pin and became SEALs.''

Mia was still watching him as if he were telling her the most fascinating story in all of the world, so he continued.

''So one day,'' Frisco told her, ''a few days before my twelfth birthday, I saw these SEALs-in-training bring their IBSs—their little inflatable boats—in for a landing on the rocks over by the Coronado Hotel. It was toward the end of the first phase of BUD/S. That week's called Hell Week, because it *is* truly hell. They were exhausted, I could see it in their faces and in the way they were sitting in those boats. I was sure they were all going to die. Have you seen the rocks over there?''

She shook her head, no.

''They're deadly. Jagged. And the surf is always rough—not a good combination. But I saw these guys put their heads down and do it. They could've died—men *have* died doing that training exercise.

''All around me, I could hear the tourists and the civilian onlookers making all this noise, wondering aloud why these men were risking their lives like that when they could be regular sailors, in the regular Navy, and not have to put themselves in that kind of danger.''

Frisco leaned closer to Mia, willing her to understand. ''And I stood there—I was just a kid—but I *knew*. I knew why. If these guys made it through, they were going to be SEALs. They were going to get that pin, and they were going to be able to walk into any military base in the world and get automatic respect. And even better than that, they would have self-respect. You know that old saying, 'Wherever you go, there you are'? Well, I knew that wherever they went, at least one man would respect them, and that man's respect was the most important of all.''

Mia gazed back at Frisco, unable to look away. She could picture him as that little boy, cheeks smooth, slight of frame and wire thin, but with these same intense blue eyes, impossibly wise beyond his tender years. She could picture him escaping from an awful childhood and an abusive father, searching for a place to belong, a place to feel safe, a place where he could learn to like himself, a place where he'd be respected—by others and himself.

He'd found his place with the SEALs.

"That was when I knew I was going to be a SEAL," he told her quietly but no less intensely. "And from that day on, I respected myself even though no one else did. I stuck it out at home another six years. I made it all the way through high school because I knew I needed that diploma. But the day I graduated, I enlisted in the Navy. And I made it. I did it. I got through BUD/S, and I landed my IBS on those rocks in Coronado.

"And I got that pin."

He looked away from her, staring sightlessly down at his injured knee, at the bruises and the swelling and the countless crisscrossing of scars. Mia's heart was in her throat as she watched him. He'd told her all this to make her understand, and she *did* understand. She knew what he was going to say next, and even as yet unspoken, his words made her ache.

"I always thought that by becoming a SEAL, I escaped from my life—you know, the way my life *should* have turned out. I should've been killed in a car accident like my brother Rob was. He was DUI, and he hit a pole. Or else I should've got my high school girlfriend pregnant like Danny did. I should have been married with a wife and child to support at age seventeen, working for the same fishing fleet that my father worked for, following in the old-bastard's footsteps. I always sort of thought by joining the Navy and becoming a SEAL, I cheated destiny.

"But now look at me. I'm back in San Felipe. And for a couple nights there, I was doing a damned good imitation of my old man. Drink 'til you drop, 'til you feel no pain."

Mia had tears in her eyes, and when Frisco glanced at her, she saw that his jaw was tight, and his eyes were damp, too. He turned his head away. It was a few moments before he spoke again, and when he finally did, his voice was steady but impossibly sad.

"Ever since I was injured," he said softly, "I feel like I've slipped back into that nightmare that used to be my life. I'm not a SEAL anymore. I lost that, it's gone. I don't know who I am, Mia—I'm some guy who's less than whole, who's just kind of floating around." He shook his head. "All I know for sure is that my self-respect is gone, too."

He turned to her, no longer caring if she saw that his eyes were filled with tears. "That's why I've got to get it all back. That's why I've got to be able to run and jump and dive and do all those things on that list." He wiped roughly at his eyes with the back of one hand, refusing to give in to the emotion that threatened to overpower him. "I want it back. I want to be whole again."

11

Mia couldn't help herself. She reached for Frisco.

How could she keep her distance while her heart was aching for this man?

But he caught her hand before she could touch the side of his face. "You don't want this," he said quietly, his eyes searching as he gazed at her. "Remember?"

"Maybe we both need each other a little bit more than I thought," she whispered.

He forced his mouth up into one of his heartbreakingly poignant half smiles. "Mia, you don't need me."

"Yes, I do," Mia said, and almost to her surprise, her words were true. She did need him. Desperately. She had tried. She had honestly tried not to care for this man, this *soldier.* She'd tried to remain distant, aloof, unfeeling, but somehow over the past few days, he had penetrated all of her defenses and gained possession of her heart.

His eyes looked so sad, so soft and gentle. All of his anger was gone, and Mia knew that once again she was seeing the man that he had been—the man all of his pain and bitterness had made him forget how to be.

He could be that man again. He was *still* that man. He simply needed to stop basing his entire future happiness on attaining the unattainable. She couldn't do that for him. He'd have to do it for himself. But she *could* be with him now, tonight, and help him remember that he *wasn't* alone.

"I can't give you what you want," he said huskily. "I know it matters to you."

Love. He was talking about love.

"That makes us even." Mia gently freed her hand from his, and touched the side of his face. He hadn't shaved in at least a day, and his cheeks and chin were rough, but she didn't care. She didn't care if he loved her, either. "Because I can't give you what *you* want."

She couldn't give him the power to become a SEAL again. But if she could have, she would.

She leaned forward and kissed him. It was a light kiss, just a gentle brushing of her lips against his.

Frisco didn't move. He didn't respond. She leaned forward to kiss him again, and he stopped her with one hand against her shoulder.

She was kneeling next to him on the couch, and he looked down at her legs, at the soft cotton of her nightgown revealed by her unzipped sweatshirt and finally into her eyes. "You're playing with fire," he said quietly. "There may be an awful lot of things that I can't do anymore, but making love to a beautiful woman isn't one of them."

"Maybe we should start a new list. Things you *can* still do. You could put 'making love' right on the top."

"Mia, you better go—"

She kissed him again, and again he pulled back.

"Dammit, you *told* me—"

She kissed him harder this time, slipping her arms up around his neck and parting his lips with her tongue. He froze, and she knew that he hadn't expected her to be so bold—not in a million years.

His hesitation lasted only the briefest of moments before he pulled her close, before he wrapped her in his arms and nearly crushed her against the hard muscles of his chest.

And then he was kissing her, too.

Wildly, fiercely, he was kissing her, his hot mouth gaining possession of hers, his tongue claiming hers with a breathtaking urgency.

It didn't seem possible. She had only kissed him once before, on the beach, yet his mouth tasted sweetly familiar and kissing him was like coming home.

Mia felt his hands on her back, sweeping up underneath her sweatshirt and down to the curve of her bottom, pulling her closer, seeking the smooth bareness of her legs. He shifted her weight toward him, pulling her over and on top of him, so that she was straddling his lap as still they kissed.

Her fingers were deep in his hair. It was incredibly, decadently soft. She would have liked to spend the entire rest of her life right there, kissing Alan Francisco and running her hands through his beautiful golden hair. It was all she needed, all she would ever need.

And then he shifted his hips and she felt the hardness of his arousal pressing up against her and she knew she was wrong. She both needed and wanted more.

He pulled at her sweatshirt, pushing it off her shoulders and down her arms. He tugged her nightgown free from the top of her shorts, and she heard herself moan as his work-roughened hands glided up and across the bare skin of her back. And then he pulled away from her, breathing hard.

"Mia." His lean, handsome face was taut with frustration. "I want to pick you up and take you to my bed." But he couldn't. He couldn't carry her. Not on crutches, not even with a cane.

This was not the time for him to be thinking about things he couldn't do. Mia climbed off of him, slipping out of his grasp. "Why don't we synchronize watches and plan to rendezvous there in, say…" She pretended to look at an imaginary watch on her wrist. "Oh two minutes?"

His face relaxed into a smile, but the tension didn't leave his eyes. "You don't need to say 'oh.' You could say 0430, but two minutes is just two minutes."

"I know that," Mia said. "I just wanted to make you smile. If that hadn't worked, I would have tried this.…" She slowly pulled her nightgown up and over her head, dropping it down into his lap.

But Frisco's smile disappeared. He looked up at her, his gaze devouring her bare breasts, heat and hunger in his eyes.

Mia was amazed. She was standing half-naked in front of this man that she had only known for a handful of days. He was a soldier, a fighter who had been trained to make war in more ways than she could probably imagine. He was the toughest, hardest man she'd ever met, yet in many ways he was also the most vulnerable. He'd trusted her enough to share some of his secrets with her, to let her see into his soul. In comparison, revealing her body to him seemed almost insignificant.

And she could stand here like this, she realized, without a blush and with such certainty, because she was absolutely convinced that loving this man was the right thing to do. She'd never made love to a man before without a sense of unease, without being troubled by doubts. But she'd never met a man like Alan Francisco—a man who seemed so different from her, yet who could look into her eyes, and with just a word or a touch, make her feel so totally connected to him, so instantly in tune.

Mia had never considered herself an exhibitionist before, but then again, no one had ever looked at her the way Frisco did. She felt her body tighten with anticipation under the scalding heat of his gaze. It was seductive, the way he looked at her—and nearly as pleasurable as a caress.

She reached up, slowly and deliberately, taking her time as she unfastened her ponytail, letting him watch her as she loosened her long hair around her shoulders, enjoying the sensation of his eyes on her body.

"You're not smiling," she whispered.

"Believe me, I'm smiling inside."

And then he did smile. It was half crooked and half sad. It was filled with doubt and disbelief, laced with wonder and anticipation. As she gazed into his eyes, Mia could see the first glimmer of hope. And she felt herself falling. She knew in that single instant that she was falling hopelessly and totally in love with this man.

Afraid he'd see her feelings in her eyes, she picked up her sweatshirt from the floor and turned, moving quickly down the hall to his bedroom. To his bed.

Frisco wasn't far behind, but she heard him stop at Natasha's room and go inside to check on the little girl.

"Is she all right?" she asked, as he came in a few moments later. He closed the door behind him. And locked it.

He stood there, a dark shape at the far end of the room. "She's much cooler now," he said.

Mia crossed to the window and adjusted the blinds slightly, allowing them both privacy and some light. The dim light from the landing streamed up in a striped pattern across the ceiling, giving the ordinary room an exotic glow. She turned back to find Frisco watching her.

"Do you have protection?" she asked.

"Yes. It's been a while," he admitted, "but…yes."

"It's been a while for me, too," she said softly.

"It's not too late to change your mind." He moved away from the door, allowing her clear access to make an escape. He looked away, as if he knew that his gaze had the power to imprison her.

"Why would I want to do that?"

He gave her another of his sad smiles. "A sudden burst of sanity?" he suggested.

"I want to make love to you," she said. "Is that really so insane?"

He looked up at her. "You could have your choice of anyone. Anyone you want." There was no self-pity in his voice or on his face. He was merely stating a fact that he believed was true.

"Good," she said. "Then I'll choose you."

Frisco heard her soft words, but it wasn't until she smiled and moved toward him that they fully sank in.

Mia wanted him. She wanted *him*.

The light from the outside walkway gleamed on her bare skin. Her body was even more beautiful than he'd imagined. Her breasts were full and round—not too big, but not too small, either. He ached to touch her with his hands, with his mouth, and he smiled, knowing he was going to do just that, and soon.

But she stopped just out of his reach.

Holding his gaze, she unfastened her shorts and let them glide down her legs.

He'd seen her in her bathing suit just that afternoon—he was well aware that her trim, athletic body was the closest thing to his idea of perfection he'd ever seen. She wasn't voluptuous by any definition of the word—in fact, some men might've found her too skinny. Her hips were slender, curving in to the softness of her waist. She was willowy and gracefully shaped, a wonderful combination of smooth muscles and soft, flowing lines.

Frisco sat down on the edge of the bed and she turned toward him. He reached for her and she went willingly into his arms, once again straddling his lap.

"I think this is where we were," she murmured and kissed him.

Frisco spun, caught in a vortex of pleasure so intense, he couldn't keep from groaning aloud. Her skin was so smooth, so soft beneath his hands, and her kisses were near spiritual experiences, each one deeper and longer than the last, infusing him with her joyful vitality and sweet, limitless passion.

She tugged at his T-shirt, and he broke free from their embrace to yank it up and over his head. And then she was kissing him again, and the sensation of her bare skin against his took his breath away.

He tumbled her back with him onto the bed, pulling her down on top of him, slipping his hand between them to touch the sweet fullness of her breasts. Her nipples were taut and erect with desire and he pulled her to his mouth, laving her with his tongue, suckling first gently then harder as she gasped her pleasure, as she arched her back.

"I like that," she breathed. "That feels so good...."

Her whispered words sent a searing flame of need through him and he pulled her even closer.

His movement pressed her intimately, perfectly against his arousal and she held him there tightly for a moment. He could feel her heat, even through her panties and his shorts. He wanted to touch her, to taste her, to fill her completely. He wanted her all. He wanted her now. He wanted her forever, for all time.

Her hair surrounded them like a sensuous, sheer, black curtain as he kissed her again, as she began to move on top of him, slowly sliding against the hard length of him. Oh, man, if she kept this up, he was going to lose it before he even got inside of her.

"Mia—" he groaned, his hands on her hips, stilling her movement.

She pulled back to look down at him, her eyes heavy-lidded with pleasure and desire, a heart-stoppingly sexy smile curving her lips. Flipping her long hair back over one shoulder, she reached for the button at the waistband of his shorts. She undid it quickly, deftly, then slid back, kneeling over his thighs to unfasten the zipper.

His arousal pressed up, released from his shorts, and she covered him with her delicate hands, gazing down into his eyes, touching him through his briefs.

She looked like some kind of extremely erotic fantasy kneeling above him, wearing those barely-there panties, the white silk contrasting perfectly with the gleaming golden color of her smooth skin. Her long, thick hair fell around her shoulders, several strands curving around her beautiful breasts.

Frisco reached for her, wanting to touch all of her, running his hands down her arms, caressing her breasts.

She pulled his shorts and his briefs down, watching his eyes and smiling at the pleasure on his face as her hands finally closed around him, closing her eyes in her own ecstasy as his hand tightened on her breast.

She leaned forward and met his lips in a hard, wild kiss, then pulled away, leaving a trail of kisses from his mouth, down his neck, to his chest, as with one hand she still held him possessively.

Her hair swept across him in the lightest of caresses and Frisco bit back a cry as her mouth moved even lower, as he nearly suffocated in a wave of exquisite, mind-numbing pleasure.

This was incredible. This was beyond incredible, but it wasn't what he wanted. He reached for her, roughly pulling her up and into his arms.

"Didn't you like that?" She was laughing—she knew damn well that he'd liked it. She knew damn well that she'd come much too close to pushing him over the edge.

He tried to speak, but his voice came out as only a growl. She laughed again, her voice musical, her amusement contagious. He covered her mouth in the fiercest of kisses, and he could feel laughter and sheer joy bubbling up from inside of her and seeping into him, flowing through his veins, filling him with happiness.

Happiness. Dear God, when was the last time he'd felt happy? It was odd, it was weird, it was *beyond* weird, because even remembering back to when he had been happy, before his injury, he had never associated that particular emotion with making love. He'd felt desire, he'd felt sexual satisfaction, he'd felt interested, amused, in control or even out of control. He'd felt confident, self-assured and powerful.

But he'd never felt so unconditionally, so inarguably *happy*. He had never felt anything remotely like this.

He'd also never made love to a woman who was, without a doubt, his perfect sexual match.

Mia was openly, unabashedly sexy and unembarrassed by her powerful sensuality. She was unafraid to take the lead in their lovemaking. She was confident and daringly fearless and bold.

If it hadn't been for that glimpse she'd given him in the hospital lobby of her sensual side, he never would have expected it. She was so sweet natured, so gentle and kind. She was *nice*. She was the kind of woman a man would marry, content to spend the rest of his life surrounded by her quiet warmth.

But Mia didn't carry her quietness with her into the bedroom. And she wasn't warm—she was incredibly, scaldingly, moltenly hot.

His hands swept down the smooth expanse of her stomach, down underneath the slip of silk that covered her. She was hot and sleek and ready for him, just as he'd known she would be. She arched up against his fingers, pushing him deeply inside of her, pulling his head toward her and guiding his mouth to her breast.

"I want to get on top of you," she gasped. "Please—"

It was an incredible turn-on—knowing this fiercely passionate woman wanted him so completely.

He released her, rolling onto his side to reach into the top drawer of his bedside table. He rifled through the clutter, and miraculously his hand closed on a small foil packet. He tore it open and covered himself as Mia pushed down her panties and kicked her legs free. And then she *was* on top of him.

She came down, and he thrust up, and in one smooth, perfect, white-hot movement, he was inside of her.

The look on her face was one he knew he'd remember and carry with him to his grave. Her eyes were closed, her lips slightly parted, her head thrown back in sheer, beautiful rapture.

He was making her feel this way.

She opened her eyes and gazed down at him, searching his face for God knew what. Whatever she was looking for, she seemed to have found it, because she smiled at him so sweetly. Frisco felt as if his heart were suddenly too large to fit inside of his chest.

She began to move on top of him, slowly at first. Her smile faded, but still she looked into his eyes, holding his gaze.

"Alan...?"

He wasn't sure he could speak, but he moistened his lips and gave it a try. "Yeah...?"

"This is really good."

"Oh, yeah." He had to laugh. It came bubbling up from somewhere inside of him, and he recognized his laughter as belonging to her.

She was moving faster now and he tried to slow her down. He wanted this to last forever, but at the rate they were going... But she didn't want to slow down, and he could refuse her nothing.

He pulled her down on top of him and kissed her frantically, fighting for his tenuous control. But he was clinging to the side of a cliff, and his fingerhold was slipping fast.

"Alan..." She gasped his name as she clutched him tightly, and he felt the first waves of her tumultuous release.

Frisco went over the edge. But instead of falling, he sailed upward, soaring impossibly high, higher than he'd ever gone before. Pleasure rocketed through him, burning him, scorching him, leaving him weak and stunned, shattered and depleted—yet still filled, completely and thoroughly, with happiness.

Mia's long, soft hair was in his face and he closed his eyes, just breathing in the sweet scent of her shampoo as he slowly floated back to earth.

After a moment, she sighed and smiled—he could feel her lips move against his neck. He wondered if she could feel his own smile.

Mia lifted her head, pulling her hair from his face. "Are you still alive?"

He felt his smile get broader as he met her eyes. Hazel was his new favorite color. "Definitely."

"I think we can safely add 'making love' to the list of things that you can still do," she said with a smile.

His knee. Man, he hadn't thought about his knee since he'd locked his door behind them. He *still* didn't want to think about it, and he fought to hold on to the peacefulness of this moment.

"I don't know," he said. "Maybe we should make sure that it wasn't some kind of fluke. Maybe we better try it again."

Mia's smile turned dangerous. "I'm ready when you are."

Frisco felt a surge of desire course through him, hot and sweet. "Give me a few minutes...."

He kissed her, a slow, deep kiss that promised her unlimited pleasure.

Mia sighed, pulling back to look at him again. "I'd love to stay, but..."

"But...?"

She smiled, running her fingers through his hair. "It's after six in the morning, Alan. I don't think it's smart for me to be here when Natasha wakes up. She's had enough turbulence recently in her life, without her having to worry about whether she's got to compete with me for your time and affection."

Frisco nodded. Mia was probably right. He was disappointed to see her leave so soon, but he had to consider the kid.

Mia slipped out of his arms and out of his bed. He turned onto his side to watch her gather her clothes from his floor.

"You called me Alan again," he said.

She looked up at him in surprise as she slipped on her shorts. "Did I? I'm sorry."

"You think of me as Alan, don't you?" he asked. "Not Frisco."

She zipped up her sweatshirt and then came and sat down next to him on the bed. "I like your name," she admitted. "I'm sorry if it keeps slipping out."

He propped himself up on one elbow. "It slipped out a lot while we were making love."

"God, I hope that didn't ruin it for you." She was half-serious.

Frisco laughed. "If you had called me Bob, that might've ruined it, but..." He touched the side of her face. "That was the first time in a long time that I've actually enjoyed being called Alan. And I *did* enjoy it."

She closed her eyes briefly, pressing her cheek against the palm of his hand. "Well, I certainly enjoyed calling you Alan, that's for sure."

"Who knows," he murmured, tracing her lips with his thumb. "If we keep this up, I might even get used to it."

Mia opened her eyes and gazed at him. "Do you…want to keep this up?" she asked. All teasing was gone from her voice, and for the first time all night, she sounded less than certain.

Frisco couldn't respond. It wasn't her question that shocked him—it was his own immediate and very certain answer. Yes. God, yes.

This was dangerous. This was extremely dangerous. He didn't want to feel anything but pleasure and satisfaction when he thought about this woman. He didn't want anything more than neighborly, casual, no-strings sex.

Yet there was no way he could let her walk out of here thinking that one night had been enough. Because it hadn't. Because the thought of her leaving simply to go home was hard enough to tolerate. He didn't want to think about how he would feel if she ever left for good. He *couldn't* think about that.

"Yes," he finally answered, "but I have to be honest, I'm not in any kind of place right now where I can—"

She silenced him with a kiss. "I want to, too," she told him. "That's all we both need to know right now. It doesn't have to be any more complicated than that."

But it *was* more complicated than that. Frisco knew just from looking at her. She cared for him. He could see it in her eyes. He felt a hot flash of elation that instantly turned to cold despair. He didn't want her to care for him. He didn't want her to be hurt, and if she cared too much, she would be.

"I just want to make sure you don't go turning this into some kind of fairy tale," he said quietly, unable to resist touching the soft silk of her hair, praying that his words weren't going to sting too badly. Still, a small sting now was better than a mortal wound in the long run. "I know what we've got going here looks an awful lot like *Beauty and the Beast*, but I need more than a pretty girl to turn me back into a prince—to make me whole again. I need a whole hell of a lot more to do that. And I've got to be honest with you, I…''

He couldn't say it. His throat closed on the words, but he had to make sure she understood.

''I'm scared that the doctors are right,'' he admitted. ''I'm scared that my knee is as good as it's going to get.''

Mia's beautiful eyes were filled with compassion and brimming with emotion. ''Maybe it would be a good thing if you could admit that—if you could accept your limitations.''

''A *good* thing…?'' He shook his head, exhaling his disbelief. ''If I give up trying, I'm condemning myself to a lifetime of this limbo. I'm not dead, but I'm not really alive, either.''

Mia looked away from him, and he knew what she was thinking. He'd certainly seemed full of life when they'd made love, just a short time ago. But this wasn't about sex. This wasn't about her. ''I need to know who I am again,'' he tried to explain.

Her head came up and she nearly burned him with the intensity of her gaze. ''You're Lieutenant Francisco, from San Felipe, California. You're a man who walks with a cane and a hell of a lot of pain because of that. You're a Navy SEAL— you'll always be a SEAL. You were when you were eleven years old. You will be when you die.''

She cupped his face with her hands and kissed him—a sweet, hot kiss that made him almost believe her.

''I haven't really known you that long,'' she continued, ''but I think I know you well enough to be certain that you're going to win. You're not going to settle for any kind of limbo. I know you're going to do whatever it takes to feel whole again. I know you'll make the right choices. You *are* going to live happily ever after. Just don't give up.'' She kissed him again and stood up. ''I'll see you later, okay?''

''Mia—''

But she was already closing his door quietly behind her.

Frisco lay back in his bed and gazed up at the ceiling. She had such faith in him. *Just don't give up.* She seemed convinced he would do whatever it took to get back into active duty.

He used to have that kind of faith, but it was worn mighty thin from time and countless failure, and now all of his doubts were showing through. And over the past several days, those doubts had grown pretty damn strong. It was becoming as clear as the daylight that was streaming in through his blinds that his recovery was not something that was in his control. He could bully himself, push himself to the edge, work himself until he dropped, but if his knee couldn't support his weight, if the joint was unable to move in certain ways, he would be doing little more than slamming his head against a stone wall.

But now he had Mia believing in him, believing he had what it would take to overcome his injury, to win, to be an active-duty SEAL again.

She cared more about him than she was letting on. Frisco knew without a doubt that she wouldn't have made love to him without feeling *some*thing for him. Was she falling in love with him? It was entirely likely—she was softhearted and kind. He wouldn't be the first down-on-his-luck stray she took into her heart.

Somehow he'd fooled her into thinking he was worth her time and emotion. Somehow he'd tricked her into believing his pipe dream. Somehow she'd bought into his talk of happily ever after.

He closed his eyes. He wanted that happily ever after. He wanted to stand up from this bed and walk into the bathroom without having to use his cane. He wanted to lace up his running shoes and clock himself five miles before breakfast. He wanted to head over to the naval base and join the team for some of their endless training. He wanted to be back in the game, to be ready for anything and everything, ready to be sent out at a moment's notice should the Alpha Squad be needed.

And he wanted to come home after a tough assignment to

the sweetness of Mia's arms, the heaven of her kisses and the warm light of love in her eyes.

God, he wanted that.

But would Mia want him if he failed? Would she want to spend her time always waiting for him to catch up? Would she want to be around a man trapped forever in the limbo between what he once was and what he hoped never again to be?

You're not going to settle for any kind of limbo, she'd told him. *I know you're going to do whatever it takes to feel whole again.*

You're going to win.

But what if he didn't win? What if his knee didn't allow him to rejoin the SEALs? And in his mind, rejoining the SEALs was the only way to win. Anything short of that, and he'd be a loser.

But Mia had faith in him.

He, however, no longer had her confidence. He knew how easy it was to lose when things were out of his control. And as much as he wanted it to be, his recovery was *not* in his control.

Frisco's knee began to throb, and he reached for his pain-killer.

He wished he had something that would work as quickly and effectively to ease the ache in his heart.

12

The man called Dwayne was walking across the condo parking lot.

Mia was in her kitchen, standing at the sink, and she just happened to look up and see him.

Not that he was easy to miss. His size called immediate attention to himself. He was wearing another well-tailored suit and a pair of dark sunglasses that didn't succeed in hiding the bandage across the bridge of his nose or the bruises on his face.

Mia went into her living room, where Natasha was sitting on the floor, working with painstaking care on a drawing. Crayons and paper were spread out in front of her on the wicker coffee table.

Trying to look casual, Mia locked and bolted her door, and then closed the living room curtains.

Dwayne's presence here was no coincidence. He was looking for Frisco. Or Natasha. But he wasn't going to find either of them.

Tasha didn't do more than glance up at Mia as she turned on the lamp to replace the sunlight that was now blocked by the curtains.

"Need more juice?" Mia asked the little girl. "You know, you'll get better faster if you have more juice."

Tasha obediently picked up her juice box and took a sip.

Frisco had knocked on Mia's door at a little after eleven. She almost hadn't recognized him at first.

He was wearing his dress uniform. It fit him like a glove—

white and starched and gleaming in the midmorning sun. The rows and rows and rows of colored bars on his chest also reflected the light. The effect was blinding. Even his shoes seemed to glow.

His hair was damp from a shower and neatly combed. His face was smooth shaven. He looked stern and unforgiving and dangerously professional. He looked like some kind of incredibly, breathtakingly handsome stranger.

And then he smiled. "You should see the look on your face."

"Oh, really? Am I drooling?"

Heat flared in his eyes, but then he turned and looked down, and Mia saw that Tasha was standing next to him.

"May we come in?" he asked.

Mia pushed open the screen. Tasha was already feeling much better. The little girl was quick to show Mia the second medal she'd had pinned to her T-shirt, awarded for following Frisco's rules all morning long. Of course, she'd been asleep nearly all morning long, but no one mentioned that.

She'd recovered from her high fever with the remarkable resilience of a small child. The antibiotic was working, and Tasha was back in action, alert and energetic.

Frisco touched Mia gently and lightly as he came inside— just a quick sweep of his fingers down her bare arm. It was enough to take her breath away, enough to remind her of the love they'd made just a few short hours ago. Enough to let her know he remembered, too.

He was wondering if she would mind watching Tasha for a few hours, while he went to the detox hospital and tried to see his sister. That was why he was all dressed up. He figured he had a better shot at getting past the "no visitors" rule if he looked like some kind of hero. One way or another, he was hell-bent on finding out exactly why Dwayne was after Sharon.

Mia volunteered to watch Natasha in Frisco's condo, but he'd told her he'd rather Tasha stay here at her place—he'd feel less as if he were bothering her. And despite Mia's re-assurances otherwise, her condo was where they'd ended up.

Now she had to wonder—had Frisco expected Dwayne to come looking for him again? Was that why he'd insisted she and Tash stay at her place instead of his?

Resisting the urge to peer out from behind her closed curtains to see if Dwayne was climbing up the stairs, Mia sat down next to Tasha. "What are you drawing?" she asked.

Her heart was drumming in her chest. Dwayne was going to ring Frisco's doorbell, and realize that no one was home. What then? Would he try the neighbors' doors in an attempt to find out where the man had gone? What if he rang her bell? What was she going to tell Tasha? How was she going to explain why she wasn't going to answer her door?

And, dear God—what if Frisco came home while Dwayne was still there?

Natasha carefully selected a red crayon from the brand-new box Frisco had bought her. "I'm making a medal," she told Mia, carefully staying within the lines she had drawn. "For Frisco. He needs a medal today, too. We were in the kitchen, and he dropped the milk and it spilled on the floor. He didn't say any bad words." She put the crayon back and took another. "He wanted to—I could tell—but he didn't."

"He's going to like that medal a lot," Mia said.

"And then," Natasha continued, "even though he was mad, he started to laugh." She chose another crayon. "I asked him if milk felt all funny and squishy between his toes, but he said he was laughing because there was something funny on the refrigerator. I looked, but I didn't see anything funny. Just a piece of paper with some writing on it. But I can't read, you know."

"I know." Mia had to smile, despite her racing heart. "He laughed, huh?" Before she'd left Frisco's condo early this morning, she'd started a new list and stuck it onto his refrigerator, next to his other list. Her new list included some of the things he *could* still do, even with his injured leg. She'd listed things like sing, hug Tasha, laugh, read, watch old movies, lie on the beach, do crossword puzzles, breathe and eat pizza. She'd begun and ended the list, of course, with "make love." And she'd peppered it thoroughly with spicy and sometimes extremely explicit suggestions—all of which she was quite sure he was capable of doing.

She was glad he'd laughed. She liked it when he laughed.

She liked it when he talked to her, too. He'd revealed quite a bit of himself last night. He had admitted he was afraid his knee wasn't going to get any better. Mia was almost certain he had been voicing his fears aloud for the very first time.

Frisco's friend Lucky had told her there was an instructor position waiting for Frisco at the base. Sure, it wasn't the future he'd expected or intended, but it *was* a future. It would take him out of this limbo that he feared. It would keep him close to the men he admired and respected. It would make him a SEAL again.

Mia went to the window. She moved the curtain a fraction of an inch then quickly dropped it back into place as she saw Dwayne pulling his large girth up the stairs.

She stood by her front door, listening intently, heart hammering. She could hear the faint sound of Frisco's doorbell through the thin wall that separated their two condos. It rang once, twice, three times, four.

Then there was silence.

Mia waited, wondering if the man had gone away, or if he was out in the courtyard—or standing in front of her own door.

And then she heard the sound of breaking glass. There was another sound, a crash, and then several more thumps—all coming from inside Frisco's condominium.

Dwayne had gone inside. He'd broken in, and from the sound of things, the son of a bitch was destroying Frisco's home.

Mia leapt for her telephone and dialed 911.

Police cars—three of them—were parked haphazardly in the condominium lot.

Frisco threw a ten-dollar bill at the taxi driver and pulled himself and his crutches as quickly as he could out of the cab.

His heart was in his throat as he raced into the courtyard. People were outside of their units, standing around, watching the police officers, several of whom were outside of both his and Mia's condos.

Both doors were open wide and one of the uniformed officers went into Mia's place.

Still on his crutches, Frisco took the stairs dangerously fast. If he lost his balance, he'd seriously hurt himself, but he wasn't going to lose his balance, dammit. He needed to get up those stairs.

"Mia," he called. "Tash?"

Thomas King stepped out of Mia's condo. "It's okay, Navy," he said. "No one was hurt."

But Frisco didn't slow down. "Where are they?"

"Inside."

He went in, squinting to adjust his eyes to the sudden dimness. Despite Thomas's reassurance, he had to see with his own eyes that they were okay. Mia was standing near the kitchen, talking to one of the policewomen. She looked all right. She was still wearing the shorts and sleeveless top she'd had on earlier. Her hair was still back in a single braid. She looked calm and composed.

"Where's Tasha?"

She looked up at him and a flurry of emotions crossed her face and he knew she wasn't quite as composed as she looked. "Alan. Thank God. Tasha's in my office, playing computer games. She's fine." She took a step toward him as if she wanted to reach for him, but stopped, glancing back at the police officer, as if she were embarrassed or uncertain as to his reception.

Frisco didn't give a damn who was watching. He wanted her in his arms, and he wanted her *now*. He dropped his crutches and pulled her close, closing his eyes and breathing in her sweet perfume. "When I saw those police cars…" He couldn't continue. He just held her.

"Excuse me," the policewoman murmured, slipping past them and disappearing out of the open condo door.

"Dwayne came looking for you," Mia told him, tightening her arms around his waist.

Dwayne. He held her tighter, too. "Dammit, I shouldn't have left you alone. Are you sure he didn't hurt you?"

"I saw him coming and we stayed inside," she said, pulling back to look up at him. "Alan, he totally trashed your living room and kitchen. The rest of the apartment's okay— I called the police and they came before he went into the bedrooms, but—"

"He didn't talk to you, didn't threaten you or Tash in any way?"

She shook her head. "He ran away when he heard the police sirens. He never even knew we were next door."

Frisco felt a rush of relief. "Good."

Her eyes were wide. "Good? But your living room is wrecked."

"To hell with my living room. I don't care about my living room."

He gazed down into her eyes, and at her beautiful lips parted softly in surprise, and he kissed her.

It was a strange kiss, having nothing to do with attraction and desire. He wasn't kissing her because he wanted her. He kissed her because he wanted to vanquish the last of his fears. He wanted to convince himself without a doubt that she truly was all right. It had nothing to do with sex and everything to do with the flood of emotions he'd felt while running up those stairs.

Her lips were warm and sweet and pliant under his own. She kissed him eagerly, both giving and taking comfort in return.

When they finally pulled apart, Mia had tears in her eyes. She wiped at them, forcing an apologetic smile. "I was scared out of my mind that Dwayne was going to somehow find you before you got home—"

"I can handle Dwayne."

She looked away, but not before he caught a glimpse of the skepticism in her eyes. He felt himself tense with frustration, but stopped himself from reacting. Why shouldn't she doubt his ability to protect himself? Just yesterday, she'd watched Dwayne beat the crap out of him.

He pulled her hand up, positioning it on the outside of his jacket, just underneath his left arm. There was surprise on her face as she felt the unmistakable bulge of his shoulder holster and sidearm.

"I can handle Dwayne," he said again.

"Excuse me, Lieutenant Francisco...?"

Frisco released Mia and turned to see one of the cops standing just inside the door. He was an older man, balding and gray with a leathery face and a permanent squint to his eyes from the bright California sun. He was obviously the officer in charge of the investigation.

"I'm wondering if we might be able to ask you some questions, sir?"

Mia bent down and picked up Frisco's crutches, her head spinning.

A gun. Her lover was carrying a *gun.* Of course, it made sense that he would have one. He was a professional soldier, for crying out loud. He probably had an entire collection of firearms. She simply hadn't thought about it before this. Or maybe she hadn't *wanted* to think about it. It was ludicrous, actually. She, who was so opposed to violence and weapons of any kind, had fallen in love with a man who not only wore a gun, but obviously knew how to use it.

"Thanks," he murmured to her, positioning his crutches under his arms. He started toward the policeman. "I'm not sure I can give you any answers," he said to the man. "I haven't even seen the damage yet."

Mia followed him out the door. Thomas was still standing outside. "Will you stay with Tasha for a minute?" she asked him.

He nodded and went inside.

She caught up with Frisco as he was stepping into his

condo. His face was expressionless as he gazed at what used to be his living room.

The glass-topped coffee table was shattered. The entertainment center that had held his TV and a cheap stereo system had been toppled forward, away from the wall. The heavy wood of the shelves was intact, but the television was smashed. All of his lamps were broken, and the ugly plaid couch had been slashed and shredded, and wads of white stuffing and springs were exposed.

His dining area and kitchen contained more of the same. His table and chairs had been knocked over and the kitchen floor was littered with broken glasses and plates swept down from the cabinets. The refrigerator was open and tipped forward, its contents smashed and broken on the floor, oozing together in an awful mess.

Frisco looked, but didn't say a word. The muscle in his jaw moved, though, as he clenched his teeth.

"Your...friend ID'd the man who broke in as someone named Dwayne...?" the policeman said.

His *friend.* As Mia watched, Frisco's eyes flickered in her direction at the officer's tactful hesitation. The man could have called her his neighbor, but it was obvious to everyone that she was more than that. Mia tried not to blush, remembering the bright-colored condom wrapper that surely still lay on Frisco's bedroom floor. These police officers had been crawling all over this place for the past twenty-five minutes. They surely hadn't missed seeing that wrapper—or the way Frisco had pulled her possessively into his arms when he'd arrived. These were seasoned cops. They were especially good at deductive reasoning.

"I don't know anyone named Dwayne," Frisco told the policeman. He unbuttoned his jacket, and carefully began maneuvering his way through the mess toward his bedroom. "Mia must've been mistaken."

"Alan, I saw—"

He glanced at her, shaking his head, just once, in warning. "Trust me," he murmured. Mia closed her mouth. What was he doing? He knew damn well who Dwayne was, and she *wasn't* mistaken.

"I appreciate your coming all the way down here, Officer," he said, "but I won't be pressing charges."

The policeman was respectful of Frisco's uniform and his rows of medals. Mia could hear it in the man's voice. But he was also obviously not happy with Frisco's decision. "Lieutenant, we have four different witnesses who saw this man either entering or leaving your home." He spread his hands, gesturing to the destruction around them. "This is no small amount of damage that was done here this afternoon."

"No one was hurt," Frisco said quietly.

Mia couldn't keep quiet. "No one was hurt?" she said in disbelief. "Yesterday someone was hurt...." She bit her lip to keep from saying more. Yesterday that man had sent Frisco to the hospital. His name had been Dwayne then, and it was still Dwayne today. And if Frisco had been home this afternoon...

But *trust me,* he'd whispered. And she did. She trusted him. So she had swallowed her words.

But her outburst had been enough, and for the first time since he'd stepped inside his condo, Frisco's face flashed with emotion. "This is not something that's going to go away by arresting this bastard on charges of breaking and entering and vandalism," he told her. "In fact, it'll only make things worse." He looked from Mia to the cop, as if aware he'd nearly said too much. With effort, he erased all signs of his anger from his face and when he spoke again, his voice was matter of fact. "Like I said, I don't want to press charges."

He started to turn away, but the policeman wouldn't let him go. "Lieutenant Francisco, it sounds like you have some kind of problem here. Maybe if you talked to one of the detectives in the squad...?"

Frisco remained expressionless. "Thank you, but no. Now, if you don't mind, I want to change my clothes and start cleaning up this mess."

"I don't know what's going on here," the cop warned him,

"but if you end up taking the law into your own hands, my friend, you're only going to have a bigger problem."

"Excuse me." Frisco disappeared into his bedroom, and after a moment, the policeman went out the door, shaking his head in exasperation.

Mia followed Frisco. "Alan, it *was* Dwayne."

He was waiting for her at his bedroom door. "I know it was. Hey, don't look at me that way." He pulled her inside and closed the door behind her, drawing her into his arms and kissing her hard on the mouth, as if trying to wipe the expression of confusion and apprehension off her face. "I'm sorry if I made you feel foolish in front of the police—claiming you were mistaken that way. But I didn't know what else to say."

"I don't understand why you won't press charges."

She looked searchingly up at him and he met her gaze steadily. "I know. Thanks for trusting me despite that." His face softened into his familiar half smile and he kissed her again, more gently this time.

Mia felt herself melt. His clean-shaven cheeks felt sensuously smooth against her face as she deepened their kiss, and she felt a hot surge of desire. His arms tightened around her, and she knew he felt it, too.

But he gently pushed her away, laughing softly. "Damn, you're dangerous. I've got a serious jones for you."

"A...jones?"

"Addiction," he explained. "Some guys get a traveling jones—they can't stay in one place for very long. I've had friends with a skydiving jones, can't go for more than a few days without making a jump." He crossed to his closet and leaned his crutches against the wall, turning back to smile at her again. "Looks like I've got myself a pretty severe Mia Summerton jones." His voice turned even softer and velvet smooth. "I can't go for more than an hour or two without wanting to make love to you."

The heat coursing through her got thicker, hotter. *I've got a serious jones for you*—the words weren't very romantic.

Yet, when Frisco said it, with his husky voice and his liquid-fire eyes, and that incredibly sexy half smile…it was. It was pure romance.

He turned away from her, somehow knowing that if he looked at her that way another moment longer, she'd end up in his arms, and they'd wind up in his bed again.

And there was no time for that now, as nice as it would have been. Thomas was back at her condo, watching Natasha. And Mia was still waiting for Frisco's explanation.

"Why won't you press charges?" she asked again.

She sat down on his bed, watching as he took off his jacket and hung it carefully in the closet.

"I saw Sharon," he told her, glancing back at her, his eyes grim and his smile gone. He was wearing a white shirt, and the dark nylon straps of his shoulder holster stood out conspicuously. He unfastened the holster and tossed it, gun included, next to her onto his bed.

Mia couldn't help but stare at that gun lying there like that, several feet away from her. He'd treated it so casually, as if it weren't a deadly weapon, capable of enabling him to take a human life with the slightest effort.

"It turns out that she *does* owe Dwayne some money. She says she 'borrowed' about five grand when she moved out of his place a few months ago." He hopped on one leg over to the bed and sat down next to her. Bending down, he pulled off his shoes and socks. His shirt was unbuttoned, revealing tantalizing glimpses of his tanned, muscular chest. But even that wasn't enough to pull Mia's attention away from the gun he'd thrown onto the bed.

"Please—I'd like it if you would move this," she interrupted him.

He glanced at her, and then down at his holstered gun. "Sorry." He picked it up and set it down, away from her, on the floor. "I should've known you wouldn't like firearms."

"I don't dislike them. I *hate* them."

"I'm a sharpshooter—*was* a sharpshooter, I'm a little rusty these days—and I know firearms so well, I'd be lying if I told

you I hated them. I'd also be lying if I told you I didn't feel
more secure when I'm carrying. What I do hate is when weapons get into the wrong hands.''

"In my opinion, *any* hands are the wrong hands. Guns
should be banned from the surface of the earth.''

"But they exist,'' Frisco pointed out. "It's too late to simply wish them away.''

"It's not too late to set restrictions about who can have
them,'' she said hotly.

"Legally,'' he added, heat slipping into his voice, too.
"Who can have them *legally*. The people who shouldn't have
them—the bad guys, the criminals and the terrorists—they're
going to figure out some way to get their hands on them no
matter *what* laws are made. And as long as *they* can get their
hands on firearms, I'm going to make damn sure that I have
one, too.''

His jaw was set, his eyes hard, glittering with an intense
blue fire. They were on opposite sides of the fence here, and
Mia knew with certainty that he was no more likely to be
swayed to her opinion than she was to his.

She shook her head in sudden disbelief. "I can't believe
I'm…'' She looked away from him, shocked at the words she
almost said aloud. *I can't believe I'm in love with a man who
carries a gun.*

He touched her, gently lifting her hand and intertwining
their fingers, correctly guessing at half of what she nearly said.
"We're pretty different from each other, huh?''

She nodded, afraid to look into his eyes, afraid he'd guess
the other half of her thoughts, too.

He smiled wryly. "Where do you stand on abortion? Or
the death penalty?''

Mia smiled despite herself. "Don't ask.'' No doubt their
points of view were one hundred and eighty degrees apart on
those issues, too.

"I like it this way,'' he said quietly. "I like it that you
don't agree with everything that I think.''

She *did* look up at him then. "We probably belong to opposite political parties."

"Is that so bad?"

"Our votes will cancel each other out."

"Democracy in action."

His eyes were softer now, liquid instead of steel. Mia felt herself start to drown in their blueness. Frisco wasn't the only one who had a jones, an addiction. She leaned forward and he met her in a kiss. Her hands went up underneath his open shirt, skimming against his bare skin, and the sensation made them both groan.

But when Mia would've given in, when she would have fallen back with him onto his bed, Frisco made himself pull away. He was breathing hard and the fire in his eyes was unmistakable. He wanted her as much as she wanted him. He may have been addicted, but he had a hell of a lot of willpower.

"We have to get out of here," he explained. "Dwayne's going to come back, and I don't want you and Tasha to be here when he does."

"I still don't understand why you won't press charges," Mia said. "Just because your sister owes this guy some money, that doesn't give him the right to destroy your condo."

Frisco stood up, shrugging out of his shirt. He wadded it into a ball and tossed it into the corner of his room, on top of his mountain of dirty laundry. "His name is Dwayne Bell," he told her. "And he's a professional scumbag—drugs, stolen goods, black-market weapons—you name it, he's involved. And he doesn't earn six figures a year by being nice about unpaid loans."

He glanced at her as he unfastened and stepped out of his pants. Mia knew she shouldn't be staring. It was hardly polite to stare at a man dressed only in utilitarian white briefs, but she couldn't look away.

"Sharon lived with him for about four months," he told her, hopping toward his duffel bags and searching through them. "During that time, she worked for him, too. According to Sharon, Dwayne has enough on her to cause real trouble. If he was arrested for something as petty as breaking and entering, he'd plea-bargain and give her up for dealing drugs, and *she'd* be the one who'd end up in jail."

Mia briefly closed her eyes. "Oh, no."

"Yeah."

"So what are we going to do?"

He found a pair of relatively clean shorts and came back to the bed. He sat down and pulled them on. "*We're* going to get you and Tasha out of here. Then *I'm* going to come back and deal with Dwayne."

Deal with Dwayne? "Alan—"

He was up again, slipping his shoulder holster over his arm and fastening it against his bare skin. "Do me a favor. Go into Tash's room and grab her bathing suit and a couple of changes of clothes." He bent down and picked up one of his empty duffel bags and tossed it to her.

Mia caught it, but she didn't move. "Alan…"

His back was to her as he searched his closet, pulling out a worn olive drab army fatigue shirt, its sleeves cut short, the ends fraying. He pulled it on. It was loose and he kept it mostly unbuttoned. It concealed his gun, but still allowed him access to it. He could get to it if he needed it when he "dealt with Dwayne." Unless, of course, Dwayne got to his own gun first. Fear tightened Mia's throat.

He turned to face her. "Come on, Mia. Please. And then go pack some of your own things."

She felt a flash of annoyance, hotter and sharper than the fear. "It's funny, I don't recall your *asking* me to come along with you. You haven't even told me where you're going."

"Lucky has a cabin in the hills about forty miles east of San Felipe. I'm going to call him, see if we can use his place for a few days."

Lucky. From Frisco's former SEAL unit. He was Frisco's friend—no, they were more than just friends, they were… what did they call it? Swim buddies.

"I'm asking for your help here," he continued, quietly. "I need you to come along to take care of Tash while I—"

"Deal with Dwayne," she finished for him with exasperation. "You know I'll help you, Alan. But I'm not sure I'm willing to go hide at some cabin." She shook her head. "Why don't we find someplace safe for Tasha to go? We could...I don't know, maybe drive her down to my mother's. Then I could come with you when you go to see Dwayne."

"No. No way. Absolutely not."

Her temper flared. "I don't want you to do this alone."

He laughed, but there was no humor in it. "What, do you really think *you're* gonna keep Dwayne from trying to kick my butt again? Are you going to lecture him on nonviolence? Or maybe you'll try to use positive reinforcement to teach him manners, huh?"

Mia felt her face flush. "No, I—"

"Dwayne Bell is one mean son of a bitch," Frisco told her. "He doesn't belong in your world—and you don't belong in his. And I intend to keep it that way."

She folded her arms across her chest, holding her elbows tightly so he wouldn't see that her hands were shaking with anger. "And which of those worlds do *you* belong in?"

He was quiet for a moment. "Neither," he finally said, unable to look her in the eye. "I'm stuck here in limbo, remember?"

Positive reinforcement. To use positive reinforcement to award positive behavior meant being as consistently blasé as possible when negative behavior occurred. Mia closed her eyes for a moment, willing herself not to fall prey to her anger and lash out at him. She wanted to shake some sense into him. She wanted to shout that this limbo he found himself in was only imagined. She wanted to hold him close until he healed, until he realized that he didn't need a miracle to be whole again—that he could be whole even if his knee gave out and he never walked another step again.

Wallowing in despair wouldn't do him a damn bit of good. And neither would her yelling at or shaking or even comforting him. Instead, she kept her voice carefully emotionless. "Well," she said, starting for the door with the duffel bag he'd tossed her. "I'll get Tasha's stuff." She turned back to him almost as an afterthought, as if what she was about to say to him didn't matter so much that she was almost shaking. "Oh, and when you call Lucky to ask about the cabin, it would be smart to tell him about all this, don't you think? *He* could go with you when you find Dwayne. He could watch your back, and *he* probably wouldn't resort to lectures on nonviolence as means of defense." She forced herself to smile, and was surprised to find she actually could. His insult had been right on target—and it wasn't entirely unamusing.

"Mia, I'm sorry I said that."

"Apology accepted—or at least it will be if you call Lucky."

"Yeah," Frisco said. "I'll do that. And I'll…" It took him a great deal of effort to say it, but he did. "I'll ask him for help."

He was going to ask for help. Thank God. Mia wanted to take one of the colorful medals from his dress uniform and pin it on to his T-shirt. Instead, she simply nodded.

"Then I'll stay with Tasha at Lucky's cabin," she said, and left the room.

13

Natasha pushed open the cabin's screen door, but then stopped, looking back at Frisco, who was elbow deep in dinner's soapy dishes. "Can I go outside?"

He nodded. "Yeah, but stay on the porch. It's getting dark." She was out the door in a flash, and he shouted after her, "Hey, Tash?"

She pressed her nose against the screen, peering in at him.

"Good job remembering to ask," he said.

She beamed at him and vanished.

He looked up to find Mia watching him. She was sitting on the couch, a book in her lap, a small smile playing about the corners of her mouth.

"Good job remembering to praise her," she told him.

"She's starting to catch on."

"Sure you don't want me to help over there?" she asked.

Frisco shook his head. "You cooked, I clean. It's only fair."

They'd arrived at Lucky's cabin just before dinnertime. It had been close to six years since Frisco had been up here, but the place looked almost exactly the same.

The cabin wasn't very big by any standards—just a living room with a fireplace and a separate kitchen area, two small bedrooms—one in the back, the other off the living room, and an extremely functional bathroom with only cold running water.

Lucky kept the place stocked with canned and dried goods—and enough beer and whiskey to sink a ship. Mia hadn't said a word about it, but Frisco knew she wondered about the temptation. She still didn't quite believe that alcohol wasn't a problem for him. But he'd been up here dozens of times with Lucky and some of the other guys from Alpha Squad, and he'd had cola while they made short work of a bottle of whiskey and a six pack of beer.

Still, he knew that she trusted him.

This afternoon, she'd followed his directions without so much as a questioning look as he'd asked her to leave the narrow back road and pull her car onto what was little more than a dirt path. They'd already been off the highway for what seemed like forever, and the dirt road wound another five miles without a sign of civilization before they reached an even smaller road that led to Lucky's cabin.

It was, definitely, in the middle of nowhere.

That made it perfect for SEAL training exercises. There was a lake not five hundred yards from the front porch, and countless acres of brush and wilderness surrounding the place.

It was a perfect hideout, too. There was no way on earth Dwayne Bell would find them here.

"How's your knee?"

Frisco glanced up to find that Mia had come to lean against the icebox, watching as he finished scouring the bottom of the pasta pot. He rinsed the suds from the pot by dunking it in a basin of clear, hot water, nodding his reply. "It's…improved," he told her. "It's been about eight hours since I've had to use the painkiller, and…" He glanced at her again. "I'm not about to start running laps, but I'm not in agony, either."

Mia nodded. "Good." She hesitated slightly, and he knew what was coming.

"When you spoke to Lucky…"

He carefully balanced the pot in the dish drain, on top of all the others. He knew what she wanted to know. "I'm meeting him tomorrow night," he said quietly. "Along with a couple other guys from Alpha Squad. The plan is for Thomas to come up in the afternoon and give me a lift back into San Felipe. You and Tash will hang out here.''

''And what happens when you actually find Dwayne?''

He released the water from the sink and dried his hands and arms on a dish towel, turning to look down into her eyes. ''I'm going to give him a thousand bucks and inform him that the other four thousand Sharon owes him covers the damages he caused by breaking into my condo. I intend to tell him that there's no amount of money in the world that would make retribution for the way he hit Natasha before she and Sharon moved out, and he's damned lucky that I'm not going to break him in half for doing that. I'm also going to convince him that if he so much as comes near Tash or Sharon or anyone else I care about, I will hunt him down and make him wish that he was dead.''

Mia's eyes were wide. ''And you really think that will work?''

Frisco couldn't resist reaching out and touching the side of her face. Her skin was so deliciously soft beneath his fingers. ''Yeah,'' he said. ''I think it'll work. By giving Dwayne some money—a substantial amount of money, despite the fact that it's only a fifth of what Sharon took—he doesn't walk away with nothing. He saves face.'' He paused. Unless this situation was more complicated than that. Unless there was something that Sharon hadn't told him, something she hadn't been quite honest about. But Mia probably didn't need to know that he was having doubts.

Unfortunately, she read his hesitation accurately. ''What?'' she asked, her gaze searching his face. ''You were going to say more, weren't you?''

He wanted to pull her close, to breathe in the sweet scent of her clean hair and luxuriate in the softness of her body pressed against his. He wanted that, but he couldn't risk touching her again. Even the sensation of her smooth cheek beneath his fingers had been enough to ignite the desire he felt whenever she was near—hell, whenever he so much as *thought* about her. If he pulled her into his arms, he would kiss her. And if he kissed her, he wouldn't want to stop.

"I got the sense Sharon wasn't one-hundred-percent honest with me," he finally admitted. Mia had been straightforward with him up to this point, sometimes painfully so. He respected her enough to return the favor. "I don't know—maybe I'm just being paranoid, but when I find Dwayne, I'm going to be ready for anything."

Mia's gaze dropped to his chest, to that hidden place near his left arm where his sidearm was snugly ensconced in his shoulder holster. Frisco knew exactly what she was thinking. He was going to go meet Dwayne with that weapon Mia disliked so intensely tucked under his arm. And it was that weapon that would help make him ready for anything.

She looked up at him. "Are you going to take that thing off when we make love tonight?"

When we make love tonight. Not if. When. Frisco felt the hot spiral of anticipation. Man, he'd hoped, but he hadn't wanted to assume. It was fine with him, though, if *she* wanted to assume that they were going to share a bed again tonight. It was more than fine.

"Yeah," he said, his voice husky. "I'll take it off."

"Good." She held his gaze and the air seemed to crackle around them.

He wanted to reach for her, to hold her, kiss her. He could feel his body's reaction to her nearness, to the soft curve of her lips, to the awareness in her eyes.

He wanted Mia now, but that wasn't an option—not with Tasha out sitting on the porch swing, rocking and singing a little song to herself. He tried to calculate the earliest he could get away with putting Tash to bed, tried to figure how long it would take her to fall asleep. Twilight was falling, and the cabin was already shadowy and dark. Even with no electricity, no bright lights and TV to distract the little girl, he had to guess it would be another hour at least before she'd agree to go to bed, another half hour after that before she was asleep.

He tried to glance surreptitiously at his watch, but Mia noticed and smiled. She didn't say a word, but he knew she was aware of everything he'd been thinking.

"Do you know where Lucky keeps the candles?" she asked, stepping away from him. "It's starting to get pretty dark."

He gestured with his head as he positioned his crutches under his arms. "In the cabinet next to the fireplace. And there's a kerosene lantern around here somewhere."

"Candles will be fine," Mia said, crossing to the cabinet. She threw him a very sexy smile over her shoulder. "I like candlelight, don't you?"

"Yeah," Frisco agreed, trying not to let his thoughts drift in the direction of candlelight and that big double bed in the other room. This next hour and a half was going to be the longest hour and a half of his entire life if he started thinking about Mia, with her long dark hair and her gorgeous, luminous eyes, tumbled onto that bed, candlelight gleaming on her satin smooth skin.

Mia found a box of matches on the fireplace mantel, well out of Tasha's reach, and lit one candle after another, placing them around the room. She looked otherworldly with the flickering candles sending shadows and light dancing across her high cheekbones, her full, graceful lips and her exotically tilted eyes. Her cutoff shorts were threadbare denim, and they hugged her backside sinfully snugly. Her hair was up in a braid. Frisco moved toward her, itching to unfasten it, to run his fingers through her silken hair, longing to see her smile, to hear her laughter, to bury himself in her sweetness and then hold her in his arms all night long. He hadn't had a chance to do that after they'd made love in the early hours of the morning, and now he found he wanted that more than he could believe.

She glanced at him again, but then couldn't look away, trapped for a moment by the need he knew was in his eyes.

"Maybe candlelight isn't such a good idea," she whispered. "Because if you keep looking at me like that I'm going to…"

"Oh, I hope so." Frisco moved closer, enough to take the candle from her hand and set it down on the fireplace mantel. "Whatever you're thinking about doing—I hope so."

Mia's heart was hammering. Lord, when he looked at her with such desire in his eyes, every nerve ending in her body went on red alert. He touched her lightly, brushing his thumb across her lips and she felt herself sway toward him, but he dropped his hand. She knew she shouldn't kiss him—not here, not now. Natasha was outside and she could come in at any moment.

She could read the same thoughts in Frisco's dark blue eyes. But instead of backing away as she'd expected, he lowered his head and kissed her anyway.

He tasted seductively sweet, like the fresh peaches they'd picked up at a local farm stand and sampled after dinner. It was a hard kiss, a passionate kiss, despite the fact that he kept both hands securely on the grips of his crutches, despite that the only place he touched her was her lips.

It was more than enough.

For now, anyway.

He pulled back and she found herself gazing into eyes the color of blue fire. And then she found herself reaching up, pulling his incredible lips down to hers again. She was wrong. Once was *not* enough.

"Are you gonna kiss again?"

Mia sprang away from Frisco as if she'd been burned.

She turned to see Natasha standing in the doorway, watching them. How long the child had been there, she couldn't begin to guess. She felt her cheeks flush.

Frisco smiled at Tasha. If he were the least bit perturbed, he was hiding it well. "Not right now."

"Later?"

His gaze flickered to Mia, and she could see genuine amusement lurking there. "I hope so."

Natasha considered this, head tilted to one side. "Thomas said if you broke Mia's heart, he was gonna kick you in the bottom." She sat down haughtily on the couch—the perfect

Russian princess. "He really said something else, but I don't say bad words."

The muscles in the side of Frisco's face twitched, but somehow he managed to hide his smile. "Well, Thomas and you don't have to worry. I have no intention of—"

"I made you a medal," Tash told him. "For not saying bad words, too. And for not drinking that smelly stuff," she added, almost as an afterthought, wrinkling her nose. She looked up at Mia. "Can I give it to him now?"

"Oh, Tasha, I'm afraid we left it back in my living room. I'm sorry…"

"It's beautiful," Tasha told Frisco, completely seriously. "You can have it when we go back. I'll give you the salute now, though, okay?"

"Sure…"

The little girl stood up and snapped off a military salute that would have impressed the meanest, toughest drill sergeant.

"Thanks, Tash." Frisco's voice was husky.

"Dwayne kissed Mommy and gave her a broke heart instead of getting married," she told them. "Are you going to get married?"

Frisco was no longer unperturbed. "Whoa, Tash, didn't we have this conversation already? And didn't we—"

"I would rather have a broke heart than Dwayne for a daddy," Tasha announced. "Why is it dark in here? Why don't we turn the lights on?"

"Remember that I told you there wasn't any electricity up here?"

"Does that mean that the lights are broke?"

Frisco hesitated. "It's kind of like that—"

"Is the TV broke, too?"

The little girl was looking up at Frisco, her eyes wide with horror. Frisco looked back at her, his mouth slightly open. "Oh, damn," he said, breaking her rule.

"Sweetie, there *is* no television up here," Mia said.

Natasha looked as if the end of the world were near, and Frisco's expression was nearly identical.

"I can't fall asleep without the TV on," Tasha whispered.

Frisco forced himself not to overreact as he went into Tash's bedroom for the third time in less than a half an hour. Yes, he'd seen Tasha in action on the night he'd accidentally turned off the TV set. She clearly depended on the damned thing to provide soothing background noise and light. She found it comforting, dependable and consistent. Wherever she'd been before this in her short life, there'd always been a television.

But she was a five-year-old. Sooner or later, exhaustion would win and she'd fall asleep. True, he'd hoped it would be sooner, but that was life. He'd have to wait a few more hours before Mia was in his arms. It wasn't *that* big a deal.

At least that's what he tried to convince himself.

As he sat on the edge of one of the narrow beds in the tiny back bedroom, Tasha looked up at him with wide, unhappy eyes. He kissed the top of her head. "Just *try* to sleep, okay?"

She didn't say a word. She just watched him as he propelled himself out of the room on his crutches.

Mia was sitting on one end of the couch that was positioned in front of the fireplace, legs curled up underneath her. Candlelight flickered, and she looked deliciously sexy. Carefully supporting his injured knee, he sat down, way at the other end of the couch.

"You're being very patient with her," she said softly.

He smiled ruefully. "You're being very patient with us both."

"I didn't come up here only for the great sex," she told him, trying to hide a smile. She failed and it slipped free.

"I had about two hours of sleep this morning, total," he said, his voice low. "I should be exhausted, but I'm not. I'm wide-awake because I know the kid's going to fall asleep, and I know that when she does, I'm going to take you into the other room, take off your clothes and make love to you, the way I've been dying to do again since you walked out of my bedroom this morning.''

He held her gaze. His own was steady and hot, and her smile quickly faded.

"Maybe we should talk about something else,'' she suggested breathlessly, and he forced himself to look away.

She was quiet for several long moments. Frisco could hear the second hand of her watch ticking its way around the dial. He could hear the cool night breeze as it swept through the trees. He heard the soft, almost inaudible creaking of the cabin as it lost the heat it had taken from the hot summer sun.

"I'm sorry I left the medal Tasha made for you at home,'' Mia finally said, obviously changing the subject. "We were in such a hurry, and I just didn't even think. She spent a long time on it. She told me all about what happened when you dropped the milk.''

Frisco couldn't help but think about that new list that Mia had attached to his refrigerator—the list of things he could still do, even with his injured knee. He'd seen it for the first time as he'd been mopping up the spilled milk. It had taken the edge off his anger, turning his frustration into laughter and hot, sweet anticipation. Some of the things she'd written down were mind-blowingly suggestive. And she was dead right. He *could* do all of those things. And he intended to, as soon as he got the chance....

He forced himself to focus on their conversation. Tasha. The medal she had made for him. But the little girl had said it was for more than his recently cleaned-up language. "I didn't think she'd notice that I haven't been drinking,'' he confessed. "I mean, I haven't been making that big a deal about it. I guess it's kind of...sobering, if you'll pardon the pun, that she *did* notice.''

Mia nodded, her eyes gentle. "She hasn't said anything to me about it.''

He lowered his voice even further, so that if Tasha were still awake, she wouldn't hear. "I ordered that couch.''

Mia looked confused, but then recognition flashed in her

eyes, and she clamped a hand over her mouth to keep from laughing out loud. "You mean the…?"

"Pink one," Frisco finished for her. He felt a smile spreading across his own face. "Yep. The other one was destroyed, and I figured what the hell? The kid wants it so badly. I'll just make sure she takes it with her when she goes."

When she goes. The thought was not a pleasant one. In fact, it was downright depressing. And that was strange. When Tash first arrived, he could think of nothing but surviving, about making the best of a bad situation until the time that she would go. It hadn't taken long for that to change. It was true that having the kid around made life more complicated— like right now for instance, when he desperately wanted her to fall asleep—but for the first time in years he was forced to think about something other than his injury. He was forced to stop waiting for a chance to live again, and instead actually do some living.

The truth was, he'd adored Tasha from the moment she'd been born.

"I helped deliver her. Did you know that?" he asked Mia.

"Natasha?" she said. "I didn't know."

"Lucky and I were on leave and he drove out to Arizona with me to see Sharon. She was about to have the baby, and we were about to be shipped out to the Middle East for God knows how long. She was living in this trailer park about forty miles east of Tucson. Twenty minutes after we arrived, she went into hard labor. The nearest hospital was back in Tucson, so we got her into my truck and drove like hell."

He smiled. "But Sharon never does anything the easy way. She must've had the shortest labor in history. We had to pull off the road because Tasha wasn't going to wait."

As Mia watched, Frisco was silent for a moment. She knew he was reliving that event, remembering.

"It was incredible," he said quietly. "When that baby came out, it was… It was one of the high points of my life."

He shook his head, the expression on his face one of wonder and awe, even after all this time. "I'd never seen a miracle before, but I saw one that day. And when Lucky put that tiny baby in my hands… She was all red and wrinkly, and so *alive*—this little new life, only a few seconds old.''

He glanced up at her, his smile tinged with embarrassment. ''Sounds pretty corny, huh?''

Mia shook her head, unable to answer him, unable to speak. It wasn't corny. It was incredibly, heart-wrenchingly sweet.

''I held Tasha all the way to the hospital,'' he continued. ''Sharon was out of it—which is pretty much her standard condition. So I wrapped that baby in my T-shirt and held her for what seemed like forever because she was crying, and Sharon was crying and the really stupid thing was that it was all I could do not to cry, too.'' He was quiet for a moment. ''But I finally got Tasha quieted down. I sang to her and talked to her, promised her that the hardest part of her life was over. She'd been born, and that's always rough, but if I had anything to say about it, it was going to be a breeze for her from here on in. I told her I'd take care of her, and I'd take care of her mom, too.

''And then we got to the hospital, and the nurses came out to take her away, and I didn't want to let her go.'' He forced a smile, and it made him look impossibly sad. ''But I did.''

He looked down at his injured knee. ''And three hours later, the CO called in all of SEAL Team Ten, and Alpha Squad shipped out on an emergency rescue mission.''

''That's when you were wounded,'' Mia said.

It wasn't a question, but he glanced at her and nodded. ''Yeah. That's when I was wounded.'' He was clenching his teeth and the muscle in the side of his jaw worked. ''I didn't keep any of those promises I made to that little baby. I mean, I sent Sharon money, but…'' He shook his head and forced another smile. ''So I'm buying the kid a pink couch, hoping that'll make up for all those years I wasn't around.'' His smile became more genuine. ''Lucky was going to go over with some of the guys and finish getting the place cleaned up. He'll be there to take delivery. I told him about the couch, but I'm not sure he believed me.'' He laughed. ''He'll believe me when he sees it, huh?''

Mia didn't know whether to laugh or cry. Every flicker of emotion on Frisco's face, every glint of pain or sorrow or joy in his eyes, every word that he spoke, every word that he shared with her filled her heart with a feeling of longing so deep, she could barely breathe.

She loved him.

He was everything she didn't need. His wounds were so deep and so catastrophic. She could handle his physical limitations. For her own self, she didn't give a damn whether or not he needed a cane or crutches or even a wheelchair to get around. In her mind, his emotional limitations were far more crippling. It was his emotional baggage—the bitterness and anger he carried with him—that had the bulk and the weight to engulf her and drag her down, too.

Still, despite that, she loved him.

Mia felt her eyes flood with tears, and she turned away, not wanting him to see. But he did, and he leaned forward, his eyes filled with concern.

''Mia…?''

She silently cursed her volatile emotions as she wiped her eyes. ''I'm sorry. I'm…being silly.''

He tried to make light of it. ''It *is* pretty silly to cry over a pink couch.''

''I'm not crying about the couch. I'm crying…'' Mia made the mistake of glancing up into his eyes, and now she was trapped, unable to look away, held as much by the gentleness of his concern as by the fire and the intensity that was also in his gaze. ''Because you've complicated my life beyond belief,'' she whispered.

He knew what she meant. He understood her unspoken message. Mia could see comprehension in his eyes, so she said the words aloud. ''I'm falling in love with you, Alan.''

Frisco's heart was in his throat. He'd suspected that Mia cared, but there was a big difference between a vague suspicion and hearing the words directly from her mouth. Falling. In love. With *him*.

Dear God, was she blind? How could she possibly be falling in love with this dried husk of a man he'd become? How could beautiful, lighthearted, joyful Mia possibly love someone who wasn't whole?

Her words should have elated him. Instead, he felt only despair. How could she *love* him?

He could hear Mia's watch ticking, its second hand traveling full circle again and again.

Finally she stood and crossed to the screen door, gazing out into the night as if she knew how much her softly spoken honesty had thrown him.

He had to say something. He knew from the tight set of her back that she wanted him to say something, *any*thing, but he couldn't think of a single response. "You're crazy" seemed inappropriate, as did "You're wrong."

"Frisco?"

He turned to see Natasha standing in the hallway. Her nightgown was several sizes too large, and it hung almost all the way down to the ground. She was holding her stuffed bear by one of its raggedy arms. Her hair was tangled around her face, and her eyes were filled with tears.

"I can't sleep," she told him. "It's too quiet. Too *nothing*. I don't like it. I can't hear *any*thing at all."

Frisco glanced at Mia, who had turned back, but wouldn't meet his eyes. Man, she'd just spilled her guts to him, and he hadn't responded. He'd said nothing, done nothing. At least he had to tell her that her declaration had totally blown him away.

"Tash, go on back into bed," he said. "I'll be there in a sec, but I need to talk to Mia first—"

Mia interrupted him. "No, it's okay. Alan, we can talk later." She forced a smile, but her eyes looked so sad. "It was...bad timing on my part."

She looked away, and there was silence in the room. Frisco

could hear his own heart beating, and Tasha's slight snuffle and that damned ticking watch....

The idea came to him in a flash.

Frisco pulled himself to his feet. "Come on." He led the way back into Tasha's bedroom. The little girl followed, but Mia didn't move. He stuck his head back out the door. "You, too," he told her.

He could see uncertainty in her eyes. "Maybe I should just wait out here...."

"Nope, we need you. Come on." He went back into the bedroom. "Back in bed, Tash."

Mia stood in the doorway, letting her eyes get used to the dark. She'd been in this bedroom, helping Tasha put on her nightgown. Even though it was dark, she could identify the different shapes that were the furniture. The bed Tasha had climbed into was against one wall. Another bed was directly opposite it. There was a small table and a chest of drawers, and several long windows that were open to the soft breezes of the summer night.

Frisco was sitting on the other bed, his back against the wall. "Come here," he said to Mia quietly.

She stepped hesitantly into the room, and he gently took her arm and pulled her down in front of him on the bed so that she was sitting between his legs, her back leaning against his chest. He looped his arms around her waist, holding her firmly in place.

She fought him for all of a half a second before giving in to the decadently glorious feeling of his arms around her. She let her head fall back against his shoulder and allowed herself the luxury of enjoying the sensation of his rough chin against her temple.

She knew she'd surprised him with her statement of love. Shoot, she'd surprised herself. But when he'd failed to react in any way at all, she'd assumed that unless she could somehow explain her feelings, he was intending to push her away.

But right now, he was doing anything but pushing her away. He was holding her close.

His lips brushed her cheek and she fought the sudden urge to cry again. Maybe the fact that she was falling in love with him didn't frighten him quite so much as she'd imagined. Maybe now that he'd had several minutes to get used to the idea, he actually *liked* it. Maybe...

"Tasha thinks it's absolutely silent in here," he said, his voice raspy and warm in the cool darkness.

"It *is*." The little girl sat up in the other bed.

"Gotta lie down," Frisco told her. "This will only work if you lie down."

She obeyed, but then popped right up again. "What are we doing?"

"*You* are lying down in your bed," he told her, waiting as she did so, amusement in his voice. "*We* are here to check on this odd silence you claim is in this room. And it's odd because it's far from silent out in the living room. And it's sure as he—*heck* not silent outside the cabin."

"It's *not?*" Tasha sat up again. This time she caught herself, and lay back down before Frisco could scold her.

"No way. Shh. Lie *very* still and listen."

Mia found herself holding her breath as Frisco and Tasha fell silent.

"Man," Frisco said after a moment. "You're wrong, Tash. This is one of the noisiest rooms I've ever been in."

The little girl sat up. "Noisy...?"

"Lie down," he commanded. "And listen again."

Again the silence.

"Listen to the wind in the trees," Frisco said quietly. Mia closed her eyes, relaxing even farther into his embrace, loving the sensation of his arms around her and his breath against her ear as his voice floated out across the darkness. "Listen to the way the leaves whisper together when a breeze comes through. And there's a branch—it's probably dead. It keeps bumping against the other branches, trying to shake itself free and drop to the ground. Do you hear it?"

"Yeah," breathed Tasha.

Mia did, too. But just a moment ago, she hadn't even been

aware of the noise at all. Another gust swept by, and she heard the sound of the leaves in the wind. Whispering, Frisco had said. His descriptions were poetic in their accuracy.

"And the crickets," Frisco said. "Hear them? And there must be some kind of locust out there, too, making their music, putting on a show. But they'll hush right up if a stranger comes around. The story the insects tell is the loudest when their music stops."

He was quiet again.

"Someone must be camping around the other side of the lake," he said quietly. "I can hear a dog barking—whining, probably tied up somewhere. And—shhh! Listen to that rumble. Must be train tracks not too far from here. Freight's coming through."

Sure enough, in the distance, Mia could hear the faint, lonely sound of a train whistle.

It was amazing. Although she made her living teaching U.S. history, she considered herself an artist, raised around artists, brought up surrounded by artists' sensitivities and delicate senses of detail. She'd never be able to paint like her mother, but she wasn't a half-bad photographer, able to catch people's quirks and personalities on film. On top of being an artist, she considered herself a liberal feminist, in tune with her world, always willing to volunteer at the local church homeless shelter, sensitive to the needs of others. She was a modern, sensitive, artistic, creative woman—who had never taken the time to truly stop and *listen* to the sounds of the night.

Unlike this big, stern-faced, gun-carrying, flesh-and-blood version of G.I. Joe, who ignored physical pain as if his heart and soul were made of stone—who had the patience to listen, and the sensitivity to hear music in the sound of the wind in the trees.

Mia had been amazed at herself for falling for a rough, tough professional soldier. But there was so much more to this man besides the roughness and toughness. So much more.

"The night is *never* silent," Frisco said. "It's alive, always

moving, always telling a story. You just have to learn to hear
its voice. You've got to learn how to listen. And once you
learn how to listen, it's always familiar, always like being
home. At the same time, it's never boring. The voice might
always be the same, but the story it tells is always changing.''

Another breeze shook the leaves, carrying with it the sound
of that distant dog barking. It was remarkable.

"And that's only *outside* the cabin," he told them. "Inside,
there's a whole pile of noises, too. Inside the cabin, *you* become part of the night's story."

"I can hear you breathe," Tasha said. Her voice sounded
sleepy and thick.

"That's right. And I can hear *you* breathing. And Mia, too.
She keeps holding her breath, thinking that'll help her be more
quiet, but she's wrong. Every time she exhales and then sucks
in another big breath, it's ten times as loud. If you don't want
to be heard, you need to breathe slowly and shallowly. You
need to become part of the night, breathing along with its
rhythms."

Mia could hear the distinct sound of his lips curving up
into a smile. She didn't need to see his face to know it was
one of his funny half smiles.

"Every now and then I can hear Mia's stomach rumble. I
don't know, Tash—maybe we didn't feed her enough at dinner," Frisco continued. "And I can also hear the second hand
on her watch. It's making a hell—heck—of a racket."

"Maybe it's *your* watch that you hear," Mia countered
softly, feeling much too noisy. Her breathing, her stomach,
her watch…next he was going to tell her that he could hear
her heart beating. Of course, due to her present position,
pressed firmly against him, her heart was pounding loudly
enough to be heard across the entire state.

"My watch has LED's," he breathed into her ear. "It's
silent."

She had to ask. "Where did you learn to listen like this?"

He was quiet for a moment. "I don't know. I did a lot of

night details, I guess. When it's just you and the night, you get to know the night pretty well.''

Mia lowered her voice. ''I've never known anyone like you.''

His arms tightened around her. ''The feeling is…very mutual.''

''Are you gonna kiss?'' Tasha's voice was *very* drowsy sounding.

Frisco laughed. ''Not in front of you, kid.''

''Thomas told me if you and Mia had a baby, it would be my cousin.''

''Thomas is certainly full of all kinds of information, isn't he?'' Frisco released his hold on Mia, giving her a gentle push up and off the bed. ''Go to sleep now, Tash. Remember, you've got the night keeping you company, all right?'' He picked his crutches up off the floor.

''All right. I love you, Frisco.''

''Love you, too, Tash.''

Mia turned away as Frisco bent over the little girl's bed and gave her a quick kiss.

''Sit with me for a minute?'' the little girl asked.

Mia heard Frisco sigh. ''All right. Just for a minute.''

Mia went into the living room, listening to wind in the trees, listening to the sound of her own breathing, the ticking of her watch. She stood at the screen door, looking out into the night, aware of the flames from the candles leaping and flickering behind her.

It may have been one minute or ten, but when she finally heard Frisco follow her out into the living room, she didn't turn around. She was aware of him watching her, aware that he didn't move any closer, but instead stopped, not even crossing to sit down on the couch.

She felt nervous at his silence, and she kicked herself for letting her feelings slip out the way they had. She hadn't been thinking. If she *had* been, she would've remembered that love wasn't on his agenda.

Still, the way he'd held her as they'd sat together in Tasha's room…

She took a deep breath and turned to face him. "I didn't mean to scare you. You know… Before."

"You didn't." He shook his head, as if he were aware he wasn't telling her the truth. "You *did*. I just… I don't…" It was his turn to take a deep breath. "Mia, I don't understand."

"What part are you having problems with?" she asked, taking refuge in her usual cheekiness. "The part where I said I love you, or… Well, no, that was the only part, wasn't it?"

He didn't laugh. He didn't even crack a smile. "A few days ago, you didn't even like me."

"No. A few days ago, I didn't like the person I thought you were," she told him. "I was wrong, though—you're incredible. I meant it when I said I've never met anyone like you. You're funny and smart and—"

"Dammit, stop," he said, pushing himself forward on his crutches, but then stopping in the middle of the room as if he were unsure of where to go, what to do. He ran one hand through his hair, leaving it messy—a visual testament to his frustration.

"Why? It's true. You're wonderful with Tasha. You're gentle and patient and kind, yet at the same time I don't doubt your ability to be anything *but* gentle in more aggressive situations. You're a soldier with an absolute code of honor. You're sensitive and sweet, yet you've got a willpower that's made of stone. You're—"

"Physically challenged," Frisco ground out through clenched teeth. "Don't leave *that* out."

14

"Yes, you're physically challenged, but you're also strong enough to deal with it." Mia took a step toward Frisco, and then another and another until she was close enough to touch him, until she *was* touching him.

When Mia touched him, it was so easy to forget about everything. When she touched him, the entire world went away. He pulled her toward him, needing the sanctuary of her kiss, but afraid she might take his silence for agreement. He stopped himself and forced himself to pull back.

"Mia, you don't understand. I—"

She kissed him. She kissed him, and he was lost. He was lost, but he was also suddenly, miraculously found.

She was fire in his arms, fire beneath his lips. She was an explosion of all that he wanted—only she wasn't out of reach. She was right here, well within his grasp.

Frisco heard himself groan, heard his crutches clatter to the floor, heard her answering sound of satisfaction as he kissed her harder now—deeper, longer, hotter kisses filled with all of his need and desire.

And then she pulled back. "Make love to me."

It wasn't an entreaty he needed to hear twice. "I'll check on Tash," he said hoarsely.

She slipped out of his arms. "I'll take some candles into our bedroom."

Candles. Candlelight. Yes. Frisco picked up his crutches and moved as silently as he could toward the room where

Tasha was sleeping. He could hear the child's slow and steady breathing before he even reached the doorway.

She was asleep.

For how long, he couldn't say. She might wake up in an hour or two. In fact, she'd *probably* wake up in an hour or two and be scared and confused. But for right now, she was asleep. For right now, he had the freedom to lock himself in that other bedroom with Mia and indulge in physical pleasures the likes of which he'd gotten a taste of early this morning.

For Mia, their joining would be more than mere physical satisfaction. Mia loved him. She actually believed that she loved him.

But sooner or later, just like Tasha, Mia would wake up, too. And then she'd see him without those rose-colored glasses that she always wore. She'd realize that he had been lying—lying both to her and even to himself.

His knee wasn't going to get any better. Steve Horowitz was right. Frisco had come as far as he could. He'd fought hard and long, but to keep fighting would only damage his joint further. It would be counterproductive. It would put him back into a wheelchair—maybe even for the rest of his life.

It was time to accept that which he'd denied for so many years.

He was permanently disabled. He wasn't going to be a SEAL ever again.

The truth crashed down around him, crushing him, squeezing him, and he nearly cried out.

He had to tell Mia. She said she loved him, but would she love him if she knew the truth?

He wasn't Lt. "Frisco" Francisco of SEAL Team Ten. He was Alan Francisco, disabled civilian. He didn't even know who Alan Francisco was. How could she possibly love him if he no longer knew who he was?

He had to tell her. Yet at the same time, he didn't want her to know. He couldn't bear the thought of her looking at him with pity in her beautiful hazel eyes. He couldn't bear to say

the words aloud. It was hard enough to admit he was temporarily disabled. But *permanently* disabled…

Mia's hair was down loose around her shoulders and she
was smiling as she came toward him. He closed his eyes as
she began unbuttoning his shirt, tugging him toward the bed
at the same time.

She took his crutches and laid them on the floor. Then she
gently pushed him down so that he sat on the bed, and swept
his shirt off his shoulders.

"Mia…" he rasped.

"Get rid of the gun, will you?" she murmured, pressing
feathery light kisses against his neck.

He unbuckled his shoulder holster and slipped it and his
sidearm into the top drawer of a rickety old bedside table. He
tried again, and again his voice sounded hoarse and strained.
"Mia. About my knee…"

She lifted her head, gazing directly into his eyes. "Does it
hurt?"

"No, it's all right. It's not—"

"Shh," she whispered, covering his mouth with hers.
"We've already talked enough tonight."

She kissed him again and he let himself drown in her sweetness. He'd tried to tell her, but she didn't want to talk. And
he really didn't want to say any of those awful truths aloud.

She was offering him a temporary escape, and he reached
for it eagerly. He grabbed it with both hands and held on tight
to the magic of right here and right now. In Mia's arms, reality
vanished, leaving only sheer perfection, only pure pleasure.

The outside world, with all of its problems and harsh truths
disappeared.

But only for an hour or two.

He rolled back with her onto the bed, covering her with his
body, kissing her, determined to take that hour or two and
use it to its fullest.

He pulled her shirt up and she helped get it over her head.
She was wearing a bra, and the black satin and lace against
her skin was enticingly sexy, but not nearly as sexy as the

candlelight would be, flickering across her bare breasts. He unfastened the front clasp, freeing her from its restraints.

He made a sound, deep in his throat as he touched her, and she pushed herself up onto her elbows. "Is your knee all right? Maybe I should be on top."

Her eyes were a swirl of yellow and brown, flecked with bits of green and concern.

"No," he murmured, lowering his mouth to where his hands had been just moments before, lightly encircling one hard bud of a nipple with the tip of his tongue.

He heard her sudden inhale of pleasure, felt her legs tighten around him and her hips rise to meet him. But just as quickly as she'd reacted, she released the pressure of her legs. "Alan, please, I don't want to accidentally hurt you.…"

He was balancing on his left leg. It was awkward, but with practice, he knew he would become more graceful. "You're not going to hurt me," he told her.

"But what if—"

"Mia, you're going to have to trust me on this, okay? Trust me enough to know that I'll tell you if I'm in pain. Right now, I'm not in pain." He pressed himself against her, fitting his arousal to her most intimately, to prove his point.

She moaned, arching up against him. "I *do* trust you."

Her words broke through the many layers of his desire—a pinprick of reality breaking through to this dreamworld. She trusted him. She *loved* him. His stomach tightened with remorse and despair, into a solid, cold block of deceit.

But her fingers were unfastening his shorts and her mouth covered his in a breathtaking kiss, warming him, melting him—at least a little bit, at least for a little while.

He awkwardly moved back, pulling her shorts and panties down her smooth, silky legs. She lay back against the pillows, her long dark hair fanning out across the white sheets, her eyes on fire as she gazed unsmilingly up at him. She was naked and so vulnerable in that position, yet she didn't try to cover herself. She didn't even move. She just waited. And watched as he pushed down his own shorts, as he released himself from his briefs.

She smiled then, gazing first at his arousal and then up into his eyes.

She watched, unmoving, as he covered himself, the heat in her eyes growing stronger, even more molten. She shifted her hips, opening herself even further to him, her invitation obvious.

Frisco inched himself forward, brushing the inside of her ankle with his mouth, trailing kisses up the smoothness of one calf while he caressed the soft inside of her other leg with his hand. He lifted his head when he reached her knees. She was up on her elbows again, her breasts rising and falling with each rapid breath. Her lips were parted and her hair tumbled down around her shoulders. As he met her eyes, she smiled a hot, sweet smile.

"Don't stop there," she told him.

Her smile was contagious and Frisco found himself grinning back at her before he lowered his head and continued his journey.

He heard her gasp, heard her soft cry of pleasure as he reached his destination. Her hands were in his hair, the softness of her thighs against his face as he tasted her sweet pleasure.

Maybe this would be enough.

The thought flashed through his mind as he took her higher, as he brought her closer to the brink of release.

Maybe he could find contentment or even happiness spending the rest of his life as Mia's lover. He could live forever in her bedroom, waiting for her to return from work, ready and willing to give her pleasure whenever she so desired.

It was, of course, a ridiculous idea.

How could she love a man who did nothing but hide?

Yet, hide was exactly what he'd been doing for the past few years. The truth had been there to see if he hadn't been so damn busy hiding from it.

Yeah, he was a real expert at evading the truth.

"Alan, please..." Mia tugged at his shoulders, pulling him up.

He knew what she wanted, and he gave it to her, filling her completely with one smooth thrust.

She bit down on her lip to keep from crying out, rising up to meet him.

His own pleasure was so intense, he had to stop, resting his forehead against hers while he struggled to maintain control.

"We fit together so well," she whispered into his ear, and when he lifted his head, he could see all of her love for him shining in her eyes.

And he knew at the moment that there was no way he could continue to deceive her. He had to tell her the truth. Not now. He couldn't tell her now. But soon. Very soon.

She began to move slowly underneath him and he matched her pace, watching her eyes, memorizing the pleasure on her face. He knew that once she knew the truth, she was as good as gone. How could he expect her to stay? He'd walk away from himself, if only he could.

"You're so serious tonight," she murmured, reaching up to touch the side of his face.

He tried to smile, but he couldn't, so he kissed her instead.

Her kiss was like magic, carrying him away to a place where there was only pleasure and light, where darkness and despair were set aside, if only temporarily.

They moved together faster now and even faster, bodies slick with heat and desire. There was no room between them for anything but the giving and taking of pleasure. Or love.

Frisco felt Mia's body tighten around him, felt her muffle her cries of passion with a deep, searing kiss. His body responded instantly to the sounds and sensations of her release, and he exploded with a fireball of pleasure that flared with a white-hot light behind his closed eyes.

The brilliant light brought clarity, and clarity brought another unwanted truth. He loved her.

He loved her.

Oh, Lord, he didn't love her. He *couldn't* love her.

His emotions were confused, and that, combined with the chemicals his body released at his climax, had given him this odd sensation that he had mistaken for love. It was nothing, and it would no doubt fade the same way his intense feelings of satisfaction and pleasure would eventually diminish.

Frisco slowly became aware of the soft hissing sounds of the candles' flames, of the ticking of Mia's watch from where it lay across the room on the dresser, of Mia's slow and steady breathing.

Damn, he was twice as big as she—he was crushing her. He rolled off of her, gathering her into his arms and cradling her close.

She sighed, opening drowsy eyes to smile up at him before she snuggled against his shoulder.

"Mia," he said, wondering how to tell her, how to begin. But she was already asleep.

It was not a big surprise that she was asleep—she'd been up all of the previous night, helping him take Tasha to the hospital. Like him, she'd probably only had around a two-hour nap in the morning. And then she'd had to endure the upset of Dwayne Bell's destructive visit to his apartment....

He gazed down at her, curled up against him, her hand pressed against his chest, covering his heart.

And that odd feeling that was surely just a strange chemical reaction made his heart feel tight and sore.

But that didn't mean that he loved her.

It didn't mean anything at all.

"Where's Tash?"

Frisco came out of the bathroom with his hair still wet from his shower, dressed only in a pair of shorts slung low on his lean hips, a towel around his neck. His question was phrased casually, but Mia couldn't miss the undercurrent of tension that seemed to flow from the man.

He looked tired, as if he hadn't slept well last night. He hadn't been in bed with her when she'd awoken this morning.

She had no idea how early he'd gotten up. Or why he'd gotten up at all.

She'd fallen asleep in his arms last night. She would have loved to have awakened that same way.

Mia set her book down on the end table, first marking her page with a leaf Natasha had brought inside to show her.

"Tasha's outside," she told him. "She asked, and I told her she could play right out front. I hope that's all right."

He nodded, sitting down across from her on the couch. He looked more than tired, Mia realized. He looked worn-out. Or burned-out and beaten down. He looked more like the grim angry man she'd first met. The glimpses of laughter and good humor and joy he'd let her see over the past several days were once again carefully hidden.

"I wanted a chance to talk to you while Tash was outside," he said, his voice uncommonly raspy. But then he didn't say anything else. He just cleared his throat and gazed silently into the cold fireplace.

"Well, Tasha's outside," Mia finally murmured. "And I'm listening."

He glanced up at her, briefly meeting her eyes and flashing one of his crooked smiles. "Yeah," he said. "I know. I'm just…you know, trying to find the right words." He shook his head and the flash of pain in his eyes nearly took her breath away. "Except there are no right words."

Mia couldn't believe what she was hearing. What had happened between last night and this morning? Last night they'd made love so perfectly, hadn't they? Or maybe it had only been perfect for her. He'd been quiet, almost subdued—she'd even commented on it. She leaned forward, wanting to reach for him, but suddenly, horribly afraid of his rejection.

He'd been honest with her, and told her he didn't love her. She in turn had told herself she didn't care, but that had been a lie. She *did* care. She wanted him to love her, and she'd foolishly hoped that the sex they shared would at least hold his attention until she could somehow, some way, make him love her, too.

She couldn't bear to know the answer, but still, she had to ask. "Are you trying to dump me?"

His blue eyes flashed as he looked up at her. "Hell, no! I'm… I'm trying to figure out how to tell you the truth." He held her gaze this time, and Mia was nearly overpowered by the sadness she saw there, mixed in among his quietly burning anger.

She wanted to reach for him, but his anger held her back. "Whatever it is, it can't be *that* bad, can it?"

"My knee's not going to improve," he said quietly, and she realized there were tears in his eyes. He gestured to his crutches. "This is as good as it's going to get. Hobbling around on crutches or with a cane."

Alan was finally facing the truth. Mia felt her own eyes flood with tears. Her heart was in her throat, filling her with relief. This wasn't about her, wasn't about *them*. It was about him.

She was so glad. He was facing the truth, and once he looked it in the eye, he could finally move forward.

At the same time, she grieved for him, knowing how hard it must've been for him to reach his conclusion.

He looked away from her, and his voice dropped even lower. "I'm not going to be a SEAL again. That's over. I have to accept the fact that I'm…permanently disabled."

Mia wasn't sure what to say. She could see the anger and bitterness beneath the pain in his eyes, and she realized that by telling her this, he was probably uttering these words aloud for the very first time. She decided to keep her mouth shut and simply let him talk.

"I know I told you that I was going to work past this," he said. "I know I made that list that's on my refrigerator, and if wanting something badly enough was all I needed to make it happen, damn, I'd be doing wind sprints right now. But my knee was destroyed and all the wishing and wanting in the world isn't going to make it better. This is it for me."

He looked up at her as if he wanted her to comment. Mia said the only thing she possibly could in the circumstances.

"I'm sorry."

But he shook his head. "No," he said tightly. "*I'm* sorry. I made you think that there would be something more. I let you believe that I had some kind of future—"

She couldn't let that one pass. "You *do* have a future. It's just not the one you thought you'd have back when you were eleven years old. You're strong, you're tough, you're creative—you can adapt. Lucky told me there's an instructor job waiting for you. If you wanted, you could choose to teach."

Frisco felt a burning wave of anger and frustration surge through him, devouring him. Teach. Man, how many times had he heard *that?* He could teach, and then watch his students graduate out of his classroom and do the things he would never do again. "Yeah, I'll pass on *that* barrel of laughs, thanks."

But Mia didn't let up. "Why? You'd be a *great* teacher. I've seen how patient you are with Natasha. And Thomas. You have an incredible rapport with him. And—"

His temper flared hotter, but the anger didn't succeed in covering up his hurt. There was nothing about this that didn't hurt. He felt as if he were dying. Whatever part of him that hadn't died back when his leg was nearly blown off, was dying now.

"Why the hell do *you* care what I do?" It wasn't exactly the question he was burning to ask her, but it would do for now.

She was shocked into silence, and gazed at him with her luminous eyes. "Because I love you—"

He swore, just one word, sharp and loud. "You don't even know me. How could you *love* me?"

"Alan, I *do* know—"

"*I* don't even know who I am anymore. How the hell could you?"

She nervously moistened her lips with the tip of her tongue, and Frisco felt his rage expanding. Dear God, he wanted her. He wanted her to stay. He wanted her to love him, because, dear Lord, he was in love with her, too.

The tight, uncomfortable feeling in his chest had never faded. He'd awakened repeatedly throughout the night to find it burning steadily, consuming him. It wasn't going to go away.

But she was. She was going to go away. Because, really, how could she love him? She was in love with a phantom, a shadow, an echo of the man he used to be. And sooner or later, even if he didn't tell her, she'd figure it out. Sooner or later she'd realize he was scamming her—that he'd been scamming her all along. And sooner or later, she would realize that she'd made a mistake, that he wasn't worth her time and laughter, and she would leave.

And then he'd be more alone than ever.

"Why should I bother to teach when I can sit home and watch TV and collect disability pay?" he asked roughly.

"Because I know that would *never* be enough for you." Her eyes were hot, her voice impassioned. How could she possibly have such faith in him?

Frisco wanted to cry. Instead he laughed, his voice harsh. "Yeah, and teaching's right up my alley, right? I certainly fit the old adage—'Those who can, do. Those who can't, teach.'"

She flinched as if he had struck her. "Is that *really* what you think about teachers? About *me*?"

"It wouldn't be an adage if there weren't some truth to it."

"Here's another adage for you—'Those who are taught, do. Those who teach, shape the future.'" Her eyes blazed. "I teach because I care about the future. And children *are* the future of this world."

"Well, maybe I *don't* care about the future," he shot back. "Maybe I don't give a damn about *anything* anymore."

She raised her chin. "I know that's not true. You care about Tasha. And I know, even though you won't admit it, that you care about me."

"You're as hopeless as I was when it comes to wishful thinking," he lied, wanting to push her over the edge, needing her to get mad enough to walk away, wanting her to stay forever, and knowing that she never would. How could she? He was nothing now, nobody, no one. "It's typical. You only see what you want to see. You moved to San Felipe from Malibu, thinking you're going to save the world by teaching underprivileged kids all about American history, when what those kids *really* need to learn is how to get through another day without some kid from the rival gang gunning them down when they walk to the store.

"You took one look at me and figured maybe I was worth saving, too. But just like the kids in your school, I don't need what you're teaching."

Her voice shook. "You're so wrong. You need it more than anyone I've ever met."

He shrugged. "So stick around, then. I guess the great sex is worth putting up with your preaching."

Mia looked dazed, and he knew he'd dealt their relationship the death blow. When she stood up, blinking back a fresh flood of tears, her face was a stony mask.

"You're right," she said, her voice trembling only slightly. "I don't know who you are. I thought I did, but..." She shook her head. "I thought you were a SEAL. I thought you didn't quit. But you have, haven't you? Life isn't working out exactly the way you planned it, so you're ready to give up and be bitter and angry and collect disability pay while you drink away the rest of your life, sitting on your couch in your lousy condominium, feeling sorry for yourself."

Frisco nodded, twisting his lips into a sad imitation of a smile. "That's right. That just about sums up my big plans for my exciting future."

She didn't even say goodbye. She just walked out the door.

15

"Yo, Navy, was that Mia I saw heading west, driving like she was behind the wheel of the Batmobile?"

Frisco looked up grimly from the peanut butter and jelly sandwich he was making for Natasha as Thomas King pushed open the screen door.

"Hey, Martian girl," the lanky teenager greeted Tash with one of his rare smiles.

"Thomas!" Tasha launched herself at the kid and immediately burst into tears. "Frisco yelled and yelled at Mia, and she went away!"

Thomas staggered back under the sudden unexpected weight of the little girl, but he managed to shift her into a position easier to hold on to. His dark eyes sought confirmation from Frisco over the top of Tasha's head. "Is that right?"

Frisco had to look away. "In a nutshell."

"I didn't want Mia to go," Tasha wailed. "And now she'll never come back!"

Thomas shook his head in disgust. "Oh, perfect. I come up here thinking *I'm* the one bearing bad news, and it turns out you guys have already done yourselves in without any outside help." He turned to the little girl still wailing in his arms. "You. Martian. Turn off the siren. Stop thinking only about yourself, and start thinking about Uncle Navy over here. If Ms. S. doesn't come back, *he'll* be the big loser, not you."

To Frisco's surprise, Tasha actually stopped crying.

"And you, Navy. Check yourself into a hospital, man. It's

time to get your head examined.'' Thomas lowered Tasha to the floor and picked up the plate that held her lunch. ''This yours?'' he asked her.

She nodded.

''Good,'' Thomas said, handing it to her. ''Go sit on that funny-looking swing on the porch while you eat this. I need to talk to Uncle Crazy here, all right?''

Tasha's lips were set at heavy pout, but she followed the teenager's order. As the screen door closed behind her, Thomas turned back to Frisco.

But instead of berating him about Mia's AWOL status, Thomas said, ''Your friend Lucky gave me a call. Apparently something came up. Said to tell you he's out of the picture until 2200 hours tomorrow night—whenever the hell *that* is. I mean, ten o'clock is ten o'clock—there's no need to get cute.''

Frisco nodded. ''It's just as well—I'm going to need to find someone to take care of Tash, now that…'' Mia's gone. He didn't finish the sentence. He didn't need to.

''I don't know what went down between you two,'' Thomas said, reaching into the bag of bread and pulling out two slices and laying them directly onto the counter. He pulled the peanut butter jar closer and began spreading the chunky spread onto the bread, ''but you oughta know that Ms. S. doesn't hang out with just anyone. I've known her for four years, and as far as I know, there's only been one other guy besides you that she's said good-night to after breakfast, if you know what I mean. She's been selective, Uncle Fool, and she's selected *you*.''

Frisco closed his eyes. ''I don't want to hear this.''

''Plugging your fingers in your ears so that you can't hear it doesn't change the truth, my man,'' Thomas told him, adding a thick layer of sweet, sticky strawberry jam to his sandwich. ''I don't know what she told you, but she wouldn't't've let you get so close if she didn't love you, with a capital *L*. I don't know what the hell you did to make her fall for you, but you'll be the biggest ass in the world if you don't take advantage of—''

Frisco's temper frayed. ''I'm not going to stand here and be lectured by some kid!''

Thomas took a bite of his sandwich and chewed it thoughtfully as he gazed at Frisco. ''Why are you always so angry, Navy?'' he finally asked. ''You know, I used to be just like you. I used to live and breathe anger. I thought it was the only way to stay alive. I was the meanest son of a bitch on the block. I didn't join a gang because I didn't *need* a gang— everyone was scared of me. I was tough enough to go solo. And I was on an express bus straight to hell. But you know what? I got lucky. I got the new teacher for history the year I was fifteen. I was six months away from dropping out, and Ms. S. did something no one ever did before. She looked me in the eye and somehow saw through all that anger, down to who I was underneath.''

Thomas gestured at Frisco with his sandwich. ''I remember, it was the day I pulled a knife on her. She told me to put the blade away and never bring it back to school again. She said I hid behind anger because *I* was the one who was scared— scared that everyone was right, that I was worthless and good for nothing.

''I mocked her, but she just smiled. She told me that she'd seen some of my test scores, and from what she saw, not only was I going to graduate from high school, but I was going to be valedictorian.'' He shook his head. ''She didn't give up on me, and when I turned sixteen, I kind of just kept putting off dropping out. I kept telling myself that I'd stay for another week, 'cause of the free lunches.'' He looked at Frisco. ''If I hadn't lucked out and had Ms. Summerton for a teacher, I would've ended up in jail. Or dead.''

''Why are you telling me this?''

''Because you don't seem to realize what was directly under your nose, Uncle Blindman.''

Frisco used his crutches to propel himself away from the

kitchen counter, his movements jerky. "I *do* know. You're wrong."

"Maybe. But one thing I'm right about is whatever it is you're scared of, whatever you're hiding under your anger, it's nothing compared to the fear you *should* be feeling about losing Ms. Mia Summerton. Be afraid of that, Navy, be *very* afraid."

Frisco sat on the couch, with his back to the cabinet that held enough whiskey to sink a ship.

It wouldn't take much. All he had to do was pull himself to his feet, set his crutches in place and then he'd be standing in front of that very same cabinet. The door would pop open with a pull of one hand...

Thomas and Natasha were down at the lake, not due to return until late afternoon, when they were all scheduled to leave for San Felipe. But right now there was no one around to protest. And by the time they returned, it would be too late. By then, Frisco wouldn't give a damn what anyone thought, what anyone said.

Not even little Tasha with her accusing blue eyes.

He closed his eyes. He would welcome the oblivion that a bottle of whiskey would bring. It would erase the picture he had in his mind of Mia's face right before she walked out the door.

He'd needed to tell her the truth. Instead he'd insulted her avocation and made it seem as if their relationship had been based purely on sex.

Why? Because he was so damned afraid that she would leave.

In fact, he *knew* Mia would leave. So he'd pushed her away before she could leave on her own initiative.

Very clever. He prophesied his own doom, and then went and made damn sure it happened. Self-sabotage, it was called in all the psychology textbooks.

Savagely Frisco pulled himself to his feet and set his crutches underneath his arms.

*   *   *

Mia pulled her car over the side of the road, swearing like a sailor.

She couldn't believe that she'd allowed herself to fall into such a classic trap. It had been *years* since she'd made this kind of mistake.

For the past few years, she'd been successful—she'd been able to work with and get through to the toughest, hardest cases in the high school. And she'd been able to do that by being thick-skinned.

She'd looked countless angry, hurt, and painfully frightened young men and women in the eyes. She'd let all of their harsh, insulting, sometimes shockingly rude words bounce off of her. She'd met their outbursts with calm and their verbal assaults with an untouchable neutrality. They couldn't hurt her if she didn't let them.

But somehow she'd let Alan Francisco hurt her.

Somehow she'd forgotten how to remain neutral in the face of this man's anger and pain.

And, God, he was in so much pain.

Mia closed her eyes against the sudden vision of him on the night they'd taken Tasha to the hospital. She'd seen him sitting on his bed, bent over from pain and grief, hands covering his face as he wept.

This morning Alan's darkest fears had been realized. He'd admitted—both to himself and to her—that he wasn't ever going to get his old life back. He wasn't going to be a SEAL again. At least not a SEAL on active duty. He'd come face-to-face with a harsh reality that had to have shattered the last of his dreams, crushed out the final flicker of his hope.

Mia knew Alan didn't love her. But if ever there was a time that he needed her, it was now.

And she'd let his angry words hurt her.

She'd run away.

She'd left him alone and on the edge—with only a five-year-old child and several dozen bottles of whiskey for comfort.

Mia turned her car around.

* * *

Frisco stared at the bottle and the glass he'd set out on the kitchen counter.

It was a rich, inviting amber color, with an instantly familiar aroma.

All he had to do was pick up the glass and he'd crawl into that bottle for the rest of the afternoon—maybe even for the rest of his life. He'd forget everything that he wasn't, everything that he couldn't be. And when he woke up, dizzy and sick, when he came eye to eye with what he'd become, well, he'd just have another drink. And another and another until once again he reached oblivion.

All he had to do was pick up that glass and he'd fulfill his family legacy. He'd be one of those good-for-nothing Francisco boys again. Not that they'd know any better, people had said, the way the father sits around drinking himself into an early grave....

That was his future now, too. Angry. Alcoholic.

Alone.

Mia's face flashed in his mind. He could see her beautiful hazel eyes, her funny smile. The hurt on her face as she walked out the door.

He gripped the edge of the counter, trying to push the image away, trying not to want what he knew he couldn't have.

And when he looked up, there was that glass and that bottle, still sitting on the counter in front of him.

Hey, why fight destiny? He was pegged to follow this path right from the start. Yeah, he'd temporarily escaped by joining the Navy, but now he was back where he'd started. Back where he belonged.

At least he'd had the integrity to know that Mia didn't deserve to spend her life in his personal hell. At least he had *that* much up on his old man.

Man, he loved her. Pain burned his stomach, his chest—rising up into his throat like bile.

He reached for the glass, wanting to wash away the taste, wanting not to care, not to need, not to feel.

I thought you were a SEAL. I thought you didn't quit.

Mia might as well have been standing in the room with him, her words echoed so loudly in his head.

"I'm not a SEAL anymore," he answered her ghostly presence.

You'll always be a SEAL. You were when you were eleven years old. You will be when you die.

The problem was, he'd already died. He'd died five years ago—he was just too stubborn and stupid to know it at the time. He'd lost his life when he'd lost his future. And now he'd lost Mia.

By choice, he reminded himself. He'd had a choice about that.

You do have a future. It's just not the one you thought you'd have back when you were a boy.

Some future. Broken. Angry. Less than whole.

I know you're going to do whatever it takes to feel whole again. I know you'll make the right choices.

Choices. What choices did he have now?

Drink the whiskey in this glass. Polish off the rest of the bottle. Kill himself slowly with alcohol the way his old man had. Spend the rest of his miserable life in limbo, drunk in his living room, with only the television for company.

He didn't want that.

You're strong, you're tough, you're creative—you can adapt.

Adapt. That's what being a SEAL had been all about. Sea, air or land, he'd learned to adapt to the environment, adapt to the country and the culture. Make changes to his method of operation. Break rules and conventions. Learn to make do.

But adapt to *this?* Adapt to forever walking with a cane? Adapt to knowing he would remain forever in the rear, away from the front lines and the action?

It would be so hard. It would be the hardest thing he'd ever done in his entire life. Whereas it would be so damn easy just to give up.

It would've been easy to give up during Hell Week, too, when he'd done the grueling training to become a SEAL.

He'd had the strength to keep going when all around him strong men were walking away. He'd endured the physical and psychological hardships.

Could he endure this, too?

I know you'll make the right choice.

And he *did* have a choice, didn't he? Despite what he'd thought, it came down to the very basic of choices.

To die.

Or to live.

Not just to be or not to be, but rather to do or not to do. To take charge or to lie back and quit.

But dammit, Mia was right. He *was* a SEAL, and SEALs *didn't* quit.

Alan Francisco looked down at the whiskey in his hand. He turned and threw it into the sink where the glass shattered and the whiskey trickled down the drain.

He chose life.

Mia's car bounced as she took the potholed dirt road much too fast.

She wasn't far now. Just another few miles until the turnoff that would lead directly to the cabin.

Determinedly, she wiped the last traces of her tears from her face. When she walked back in there, when she looked Alan in the eye, he was going to see only her calm offer of comfort and understanding. His angry words couldn't hurt her because she wouldn't let them. It would take more than that to drive her away.

She slowed as she rounded a curve, seeing a flash of sunlight on metal up ahead of her.

It was another car, heading directly toward her, going much too fast.

Mia hit the brakes and pulled as far to the right as she could, scraping the side of a tree as the other car went into a skid.

She watched it plunge down a sloping embankment, plowing through the underbrush and coming to a sudden jarring stop as it hit a tree.

Mia scrambled to unfasten her seat belt, fumbling in her haste to get out of her car and down to the wreck.

It was almost entirely hidden in the thick growth, but she could hear someone crying. She pushed away branches to get to the driver's side door, yanking it open.

Blood. There was blood on the man's forehead and face, but he was moving and...

Dwayne Bell. The man in the driver's seat was Dwayne Bell. He recognized her at the exact moment she recognized him.

"Well, now, it's the girlfriend. Isn't *this* convenient," he said in his thick Louisiana drawl. He reached up to wipe the blood from his eyes and face.

Natasha. The crying sound came from *Natasha*. What was *she* doing here...?

"Dammit, I think I must've hit my head on the windshield," Dwayne said.

Mia wanted to back away, to run, but Natasha was belted into the front seat. Mia couldn't simply just leave her there. But maybe Dwayne had hit his head hard enough to make him groggy.... Maybe he wouldn't notice if...

Mia quickly went around to the other side of the car. Tasha already had her seat belt unfastened and was up and in Mia's arms as soon as the door was opened.

"Are you okay?" she asked, smoothing back Tasha's hair from her face.

The little girl nodded, eyes wide. "Dwayne hit Thomas," she told Mia, tears still streaming down her face. "He fell down and was all bloody. Dwayne made him dead."

Thomas...? Dead? No...

"I screamed and screamed for Thomas to help me—" Tasha hiccuped "—but he wouldn't get up and Frisco couldn't hear me and Dwayne took me in his car."

Thomas was unconscious maybe, but not dead. Please God, not dead. Not Thomas King....

Moving quickly, Mia carried Natasha around the car and up the embankment, praying Dwayne was too dizzy to notice, hoping that if she didn't turn around to check, he wouldn't—

"Where you going in such a hurry, darlin'?" Dwayne drawled.

Mia froze. And turned around. And found herself staring down the muzzle of a very big, very deadly-looking gun.

Dwayne held a handkerchief to his forehead, but his gun hand was decidedly steady as he hefted his bulk out of the car.

"I think we'll take your car," he told her with a gap-toothed smile. "In fact, you can drive."

Frisco knew something was wrong. The woods were too quiet. There was no echo of laughter or voices from the lake. And he'd never known Tasha to be silent for long.

The footpath down to the water wasn't easy to navigate on crutches, but he moved as quickly as he could. And as he neared the clearing—out of force of habit—he drew his side-arm from his shoulder holster. He moved as silently as he could, ready to drop his right crutch should the need arise to use it.

He saw Thomas, crumpled on the beach, blood on his face.

There was no sign of Tasha—or anyone else. But there were fresh tire tracks at the boat drop. Whoever had been here had gone.

And taken Tasha with them.

Frisco holstered his weapon as he moved quickly toward Thomas.

The kid stirred as Frisco touched him, searching for a pulse. He was alive, thank God. His nose was bleeding and he had a nasty-looking gash on the back of his head. "Tasha," he gasped. "The fat man took Tash."

The fat man.

Dwayne Bell.

Took Tasha.

Frisco had been at the cabin, wrestling with his demons

while Dwayne had been down here kicking the living daylights out of Thomas and kidnapping Tash. Guilt flooded him, but he instantly pushed it aside. He'd have time to feel guilty later. Right now he had to move fast, to get Tasha back.

"How long ago?" Frisco tore a piece of fabric from his shirttail and used it to apply pressure to the back of Thomas's head as he helped the kid sit up.

"I don't know. He hit me hard and I went down." Thomas let out a stream of foul language that would've made a SEAL take notice. "I tried to fight it—I heard Tasha screaming for me, but I blacked out. Dammit. Dammit!" There were tears in his eyes. "Lieutenant, she's scared to death of this guy. We gotta find her and get her back."

Frisco nodded, watching as Thomas forced away his dizziness and crawled to the lake to splash water onto his face, washing away the blood. The kid probably had a broken nose, but he didn't so much as say ouch. "Can you walk, or should I get your car and bring it around?"

Thomas straightened up, wobbling only slightly. "I can walk." He felt his pockets and swore again. "The fat man took my car keys."

Frisco started up the path that led back to the cabin. "So we'll hot-wire it." He looked back. "Tell me if I'm going too fast for you." Now *that* was a switch, wasn't it?

"*You* know how to hot-wire a car?"

"It's something we're taught in the SEAL teams."

"Shoot," Thomas said. "I could be a SEAL."

Frisco looked back at him and nodded. "Yeah, you could."

16

"**I** need your help."

Frisco looked out the open car window, up at Lt. Joe Catalanotto, the Commanding Officer of SEAL Team Ten's Alpha Squad. Cat looked like he was ready to ship out on some high-level security training mission. He was dressed in fatigues and a black combat vest and wore his long dark hair back in a ponytail.

"Right now?" Cat asked, bending slightly to look inside the car, his sharp gaze taking in Thomas's battered appearance and bloody T-shirt.

"Yeah," Frisco said. "My sister's kid's been snatched. Sharon got herself in too deep with a drug dealer. He's the one that took the kid. I need help finding him and getting her back."

Joe Cat nodded. "How many guys you need?"

"How many you got?"

Frisco's former CO smiled. "How's all seven of Alpha Squad?"

Seven. Those seven were the six guys Frisco had served with—along with his own replacement. That was one man he *wasn't* looking forward to working with. But he nodded anyway. Right now he needed all the help he could get to find Natasha. "Good."

As Frisco watched, Cat slipped a microthin cellular phone from the pocket of his vest and dialed a coded number.

"Yeah, Catalanotto," he said. "Cancel Alpha Squad's flight out. Our training mission has been delayed—" he glanced up at the cloudless blue sky "—due to severe weather conditions. Unless otherwise directed, we'll be off base as of 1600 hours, executing local reconnaissance and surveillance training." He snapped the phone shut and turned back to Frisco. "Let's pay a visit to the equipment room, get the gear we need to find this guy."

"Whoa, Frisco, nice couch!"

With the exception of the glaringly pink couch, Frisco's apartment was starting to look like command central.

Lucky had finished cleaning the place up and had moved the sofa in yesterday. Now, under Joe Cat's command, Bobby and Wes—Bob, tall and built like a truck; Wes, short and razor thin, but inseparable since BUD/S training had made them swim buddies—had moved aside all unessential furniture and set the small dining room table in the center of the living room.

"You've gotta do the rest of the room in pink, too—it suits you, baby!" Six and a half feet tall, black and built like a linebacker, Chief Daryl Becker—nicknamed Harvard—possessed an ivy league education and a wicked sense of humor. He carried a heavy armload of surveillance gear, which he began to set up on the table.

Blue McCoy was the next to arrive. The blond-haired SEAL brought several large cases that made the muscles in his arms stand out in high relief. Assault weapons—God forbid they'd need to use them. Even the normally taciturn executive officer and second in command of Alpha Squad couldn't resist commenting on the pink couch.

"I'm dying to meet this new girlfriend of yours," Blue said in his soft Southern drawl. "Please tell me that sofa there belongs to her."

Mia.

Where the hell was she? She should have been back long before him.

But her apartment was still locked up tight. Frisco had gone out to check at least five times since he'd arrived. He'd even left a message on her answering machine, thinking she might phone in. He hadn't apologized—he'd need to do that in person. He'd simply told her that he was looking for her. Please call him.

"Okay," Harvard said, finishing hooking the computers and other equipment to Frisco's phone line. "We're all set. When this Dwayne calls, you keep him talking and we'll pinpoint his location in about forty seconds."

"*When* Dwayne calls. *If* Dwayne calls." Frisco couldn't keep his frustration from buzzing in his voice. "Dammit, I *hate* waiting."

"Gee, I forgot how much fun it was to work with the King of Impatience," Lucky said, coming in the door. Another man followed him. It was Ensign Harlan Jones, aka Cowboy—the hotheaded young SEAL who'd replaced Frisco in the Alpha Squad. He nodded a silent greeting to Frisco, no doubt subdued both by the seriousness of a kidnapped child and the strangeness of being in the home of the man whose place he'd taken for his own.

"Thanks for coming," Frisco said to him.

"Glad to be able to help," Cowboy replied.

Frisco's condo had never seemed so small. With eight large men and Thomas there, there was barely room to move. But it was good. It was like old times. Frisco had missed these guys, he realized. He just wished Natasha hadn't had to be kidnapped to bring them all together again.

And that had entirely been up to him. *He'd* been the one keeping his distance, pushing the squad away. Yeah, the fact that he wasn't one of them anymore stuck in his throat. Yeah, it made him jealous as hell. But this was better than nothing. It was better than quitting....

"You got anything to eat?" Wes asked, heading for the kitchen.

"Hey, Frisco, mind if I crash on your bed?" Bobby asked, also not waiting for an answer before he headed down the hall.

"Who hit *you* in the face with a baseball bat?" Lucky

asked Thomas, who'd remained silent and off to one side until now.

The kid was leaning back against the wall and he looked as if he should be sitting if not lying down. "Dwayne," he answered. "And it was the barrel of his gun, not a baseball bat."

"Maybe you should go home," Lucky suggested. "Take care of that—"

Thomas turned to give the other man a cool, appraising look. "Nope. I'm here until we get the little girl back."

"I think Alpha Squad…"

"I'm *not* leaving."

"…can probably handle—"

Frisco cut in. "The kid stays," he said quietly.

Blue stepped forward. "Your name's Thomas, right?" he said to the boy.

"Thomas King."

Blue held out his hand. "Pleased to meet you," he drawled. The two shook. "If you're going to be helping us, why don't I show you how some of this equipment works?"

Frisco sat down on the pink sofa next to Joe Cat as Blue and Harvard began giving Thomas a crash course in tracing phone calls. "I can't just sit here waiting," he said. "I've got to do something."

Wes came back out of the kitchen, having overheard Frisco's remark. "Why don't you make yourself a nice cup of hot tea," he teased in a lispingly sweet voice, "and curl up on your nice pink couch with your favorite copy of *Sense and Sensibility* to distract you?"

"Hey," Harvard boomed in his deep, subbass voice. "I heard that. I *like* Jane Austen."

"I do, too," Cowboy interjected.

"Whoa," Lucky said. "Who taught *you* to read?"

The room erupted in laughter, and Frisco restlessly stood up, pushing his way out the door and onto the landing. He knew that humor was the way the men of Alpha Squad deal with stress and a tense situation, but he didn't feel much like laughing.

He just wanted Natasha back.

Where was she right now? Was she scared? Had Dwayne hit her again? Dammit, if that bastard as much as *touched* that little girl…

Frisco heard the screen door open behind him and turned to see that Joe Cat had followed him.

"I want to go talk to my sister again," Frisco told the CO. "I think there's more to this than she's told me."

Cat didn't hesitate. "I'll drive you over. Just let me tell the guys where we're going." He stepped back into Frisco's condo, then came back out, nodding to Frisco. "Let's go."

As they headed down to the parking lot, Frisco glanced back one last time at Mia's lifeless condo. Where *was* she?

Mia carried Tasha across the well-manicured lawn to the front door of the big Spanish-style house.

This was ludicrous. It was broad daylight, they were in the middle of a seemingly affluent, upper-middle-class suburb. Down the street, several landscapers cleaned up a neighbor's yard. Should she scream for help, or try to run?

She did neither, well aware of that very large gun Dwayne Bell carried concealed in his pocket. If she had been alone, she might have risked it. But not with Natasha in her arms. Still, it gave her a chill to know that she could clearly identify the address where they'd been brought, and the man who'd brought them here.

"Shouldn't you have blindfolded us?" she asked as Dwayne opened the door.

"Can't drive if you're blindfolded. Besides, you're here as my guests. There's no need to make this more unpleasant than it has to be."

"You have a curious definition of the word *guest*, Mr. Bell," Mia said as Dwayne shut the door behind her. The inside of the house was dark with all the shades pulled down, and cool from an air conditioner set well below seventy degrees. She could hear canned laughter from a television somewhere in the big house. Tasha's arms tightened around her neck. "I've never held someone at gunpoint simply to invite them into my home. I think *hostage* is a more appropriate term."

"Actually, I prefer the word *collateral*," the overweight man told her.

A man appeared, walking toward them down the hall from a room that might've been a kitchen. His jacket was off and he wore a gun in a shoulder holster very similar to Frisco's. He spoke to Dwayne in a low voice, glancing curiously at Mia and Natasha.

"Have Ramon take care of it," Dwayne said, loudly enough for Mia to overhear. "And then I want to talk to you both."

There were at least two other men in the house—at least two of them carrying weapons. Mia looked around as Dwayne led them up the thickly carpeted stairs, trying to memorize the layout of the house, determined to gather any information that would be valuable for Frisco when he came.

Frisco would find them. Mia knew that as surely as she knew that the late-afternoon sun would soon slip beneath the horizon.

And then he would come.

"The stakes are higher than I thought," Frisco said tightly, coming out into the drug-and-alcohol rehab center's waiting room. Joe Catalanotto rose to his feet. "Sharon didn't steal five thousand from Bell—she stole *fifty* thousand. She fudged his bookkeeping—didn't think he'd notice."

He headed for the door, toward the parking lot and Joe Cat's jeep.

"Can she pay it back?" Cat asked.

Frisco snorted. "Are you kidding? It's long gone. She used most of it to pay off some gambling debts and blew the rest on drugs and booze." He stopped, turning to Cat. "Let me borrow your phone. Sharon gave me the address where she used to live with Bell," he told Cat as he dialed the number of the cellular phone link they'd set up back at his apartment.

The line was picked up on the first ring.

"Becker here." It was Harvard.

"It's just me, Chief," Frisco said. "Any calls?"

"Nothing yet. You know we would have relayed it directly to you if there were."

"I've got an address I want to check out. It's just outside of San Felipe, in Harper, the next town over to the east. Have Lucky and Blue meet me and Cat over there, all right?" He gave Harvard the street address.

"I've got that location on my computer," Harvard told him. "They're on their way, soon as I print them out a map. You need directions?"

Cat was listening in. "Tell H. to send a copy of that map to the fax in my jeep."

Frisco stared at Joe Cat. "You have a *fax* machine in your *jeep?*"

Cat smiled. "CO privileges."

Frisco ended the call and handed the phone back to Cat. But Cat shook his head. "You better hold on to it. If that ransom call comes in…"

Frisco met his friend's eyes. "If that ransom call comes in, we better be able to trace it," he said grimly.

"And pray that we're not already too late. Sharon told me Dwayne Bell has killed in revenge for far less than fifty thousand dollars."

"No one's home," Lucky reported as he and Blue McCoy silently materialized alongside Cat's jeep, down the street from the house Sharon had lived in with Dwayne Bell.

"I went through a basement window," Blue told Frisco and Joe Cat. "From what I could see from just a quick look around, Dwayne Bell doesn't live there anymore. There were kids' toys all over the place, and there was mail on the kitchen counter addressed to Fred and Charlene Ford. Looks like Bell moved out and these other folks moved in.''

Frisco nodded, trying not to clench his teeth. It would've been too easy if Bell had been there. He'd known that coming out here was a long shot to start with.

Cat was looking at him. ''What do you want to do?''

Frisco shook his head. Nothing. There was nothing they *could* do now but wait. ''I want the phone to ring.''

''He'll call and we *will* get Natasha back,'' Lucky said with far more confidence than Frisco felt.

Mia tried the window of the tiny bedroom where she and Tasha were being held. It was sealed shut. They wouldn't get out that way, short of breaking the glass. And even if they *could* break it without Dwayne and his goons hearing them, there was a *long* drop down to the ground.

Tasha sat on the bed, knees hugged tightly to her chest, her blue eyes wide as Mia made her way around the room.

The closet was minuscule—there was no way out there.

There were no secret doors, no hidden passages, no air ducts in the walls or crawl spaces underneath the throw rug. There was no hidden telephone with which she could make a furtive call for help, no gun in the dresser drawer that she could use to defend them.

The door was locked with a bolt on the outside.

They weren't going anywhere until Dwayne or his goons unlocked it.

There was nothing to do now but wait.

The phone rang.

They were halfway back to the condo, when the cell phone in Frisco's pocket chirped and vibrated against his leg. Joe Cat quickly pulled the jeep over to the side of the road as Frisco flipped the phone open.

''Frisco.''

It was Harvard. ''Call's coming in,'' he reported tersely.

"I'm linking it directly to you. Remember, if it's Bell, keep him talking."

"I remember."

There were several clicks, and then the soft hiss of an open line.

"Yeah," Frisco said.

"Mr. Francisco." It was Dwayne Bell's lugubrious voice. "You know who I am and why I'm calling, I assume."

"Let me talk to Tasha."

"Business before pleasure, sir," Bell said. "You have twenty-four hours to return to me the money that your charming sister stole. Fifty thousand, plus another ten in interest."

"It's going to take me longer than twenty-four hours to get together that kind of—"

"I'm already being very generous out of sentimentality for what Sharon and I once shared. It's nearly 6:00. If I don't have cash in hand by 6:00 p.m. tomorrow, I'll kill the girl. And if I don't have it by midnight, then I'll kill the child. And if you go to the police, I'll kill them both, and take your sister to prison with me."

"Whoa," Frisco said. "Wait a minute. What did you say? Both? The girl, *then* the child…?"

Bell laughed. "Oh, you don't know? Your girlfriend is a guest in my house as well as the brat."

Mia. Hell, Bell had Mia, too.

"Let me talk to her," Frisco rasped. "I want proof they're both still all right."

"I anticipated that." He must have turned away from the phone because his voice was suddenly distant. "Bring them in."

There was a pause and a click, and then Mia's voice came on the line. "Alan?"

The sound was boomy and Frisco knew Bell had switched to a speaker phone. "I'm here," he said. "Are you all right? Is Tash with you?"

Lucky appeared silently outside Joe Cat's car window. As

Frisco glanced at him, he pointed to his own cellular phone and signaled a thumbs-up.

Harvard had gotten the trace. They had a location.

"Yes," Mia was saying. "Listen, Alan. My parents have money. Go to them. Remember I told you they live near the country club in Harper?"

No, she'd told him her parents lived in Malibu.

"Just be careful of my dad—he's a little nuts, with all those guns he has in his collection, and his two bodyguards."

Harper. Guns. Two bodyguards. Damn, she had the presence of mind to tell him where they were and how many men there were guarding them.

"That's enough," Bell cut in.

"My parents have the money you want," Frisco heard Mia say sharply. "How is Alan going to get it if I don't tell him where to go?"

"I have the address," Frisco told her. "I'll take care of the money, you take care of Tasha. Tash—are you okay?"

"I wanna go home." Natasha's voice was wobbly.

"She doesn't have her medicine, so if her temperature goes up again, put her in the bathtub and cool her down. Do you understand?" Frisco said to Mia as quickly as he could. "Stay with her in the bathroom. And talk to her so she's not scared. You know how she gets when it's too quiet. I know she's too little to listen to the sounds of the night the way I can."

Man, he hoped she understood. If Mia and Tasha kept talking, the SEALs would be able to use high-tech, high-powered microphones to help pinpoint their location inside of the house. Frisco would need that information before he could figure out the best way to launch their attack against Bell and his men.

"Mia, I'll get that money soon. Right now, in fact, all right?"

"All right. Alan, be careful." Her voice shook slightly. "I love you."

"Mia, I—"

The line went dead. Frisco clicked off the telephone, cursing Dwayne Bell, cursing himself. But what, exactly, had he intended to say?

I love you, too.

God, the words had been right on the tip of his tongue. Forget about the fact that Cat and Lucky and Blue were listening in. Forget about the fact that a relationship with him was the last thing Mia needed.

But if after all he'd said and done she could still love him… No, she didn't *need* a relationship with him, but maybe, just maybe she wanted it.

God knows he did, despite the fact that he may well have burned his bridges with the awful things he'd said to her. Burned? Damn, he'd bombed the hell out of them.

Still, she'd told him that she *loved* him.

"We got it—273 Barker Street in Harper," Lucky leaned in the window to say. "Harvard's faxing a map and leaving Thomas at headquarters to relay any other calls. He and the rest of the squad will meet us over there."

Frisco nodded, hope flooding through him as he turned to Joe Cat. "Let's move."

Mia's stomach hurt as one of Dwayne Bell's cohorts followed her and Natasha back up the stairs.

Take care of Tasha, Frisco had told her. He'd given her as much carefully disguised information in his message as she'd tried to give him. *Stay with her in the bathroom. Put her in the bathtub.* If bullets started to fly, bullets like the ones that could be fired from Dwayne's enormous gun, bullets that could pass through walls and still have enough force to kill, then the bathtub, with its hard enamel, would be the safest place.

He'd told her to talk to Tasha. Why? *Talk to her so she's not scared.* Why would he want them to talk? It didn't make sense. But it didn't have to make sense. He'd asked—she'd do it.

Right now, Frisco had said. *I have the address.* Mia knew without a doubt that he was on his way. Somehow he'd found them. He'd be here soon.

She stopped in front of the open bathroom door, turning to look back at the man with the gun. "We need to use the bathroom."

He nodded. "Go ahead. Don't lock the door."

Mia drew Tasha inside the tiny room, closing the door behind her, taking a quick inventory.

Pedestal sink, grimy tub with a mildewed shower curtain, a less-than-pristine-looking toilet.

The window was tiny and sealed shut, the same as the window in the bedroom.

There was a narrow linen closet that held a few paper-wrapped rolls of toilet paper and several tired-looking washcloths and towels.

Mia took one of the washcloths from the closet and turned on the warm water in the sink, holding the small square of terry cloth underneath. "Okay, Tash," she said. "We're going to try to fool Dwayne and his friends into thinking that you're really sick, and that you might throw up, okay?"

The little girl nodded, her eyes wide.

"I need you to take a deep breath and hold it in for as long as you can—until your face turns *really* red, all right?"

Tasha nodded again, drawing in a big breath as Mia wrung out the washcloth.

"Now, this is going to be warm against your face, but we want you to feel kind of warm and sweaty so Dwayne will believe you've got a fever, okay?"

The little girl stood staunchly as Mia pressed the warm cloth against her forehead and cheeks. By the time Tasha exhaled, she was flushed and quite believably clammy.

"Can I get a drink?" she asked, turning on the cold water.

"Sure," Mia said. "But remember to look sick, okay?" She waited until Tash was done at the sink before she opened the bathroom door. "Excuse me. I think we better stay in here. Tasha's got a fever and—"

Behind her came the awful sound of retching, and Mia

turned to see Tasha leaning over the toilet, liquid gushing from her mouth.

"Oh, hell!" the man with the gun said in disgust, backing away and closing the bathroom door.

"Natasha," Mia started to say, alarmed.

But Tasha turned to look at Mia with a wicked light in her eyes. "I put lots of water in my mouth and spit it out," she whispered. "Do you think we fooled him?"

There was a sound from outside the door, and Mia opened it a crack. It was the man with the gun.

"I'm putting a bolt on the outside of this door," he said gruffly. "You're gonna have to stay in here. Dwayne don't want no mess. Can I get the kid some blankets or something?"

Mia nodded. "Blankets would be great."

She closed the door and turned back to Natasha, giving the little girl a big thumbs-up.

Now she had to keep talking. For some reason, Frisco wanted her to keep talking.

And she prayed that after this was all over, he'd still be alive to explain exactly why.

17

"**I**'ve got something," Harvard said, fine-tuning the dials of the ultrasensitive microphone that was aimed at the Barker Street house. "Sounds like a woman and a kid singing—I think it's 'The Alphabet Song.'"

He held out his padded earphones and Frisco slipped them on, staring out the darkened glass window in the side of Harvard's van at the house they were watching.

It was them. It had to be them. And then the song ended, and he heard Tash speak.

"Mia, why are we sitting in the bathtub?"

"Because your uncle thought we'd be safest here."

"'Cause Dwayne wants to make us dead, like he did to Thomas?"

"Honey, Frisco's not going to let that happen."

"Because he loves us?" the child asked.

Mia hesitated. "Yes," she finally said. "Because he loves…us."

Frisco knew she didn't believe what she was telling Tash. And why should Mia think he loved her after the terrible things he'd said? The thought of it made his chest ache. He handed the headphones back to Harvard. "It's them, Chief," he said. "Can you pinpoint their location?"

"Back of the house," Harvard told him, turning his dials. "I've got a TV up much too loud in the front of the house, along with sounds of someone eating."

Frisco nodded. That was a start. He'd have a better idea of Mia and Tash's exact location after Blue, Cowboy and Lucky checked in from their sneak and peek. In the early hours of the dusk, the three SEALs were checking over the yard and exterior of the house, looking for alarms or booby traps— anything that would tip Bell off as to their presence.

And Wes and Bobby were scanning with an infrared device that would help place the locations of Mia and Tash and their kidnappers. Bell and two others—that's what Mia had managed to tell him. All armed.

Three lowlifes against eight SEALs. There was no way the SEALs could lose.

Except for the fact that Frisco was determined that the SEALs would not open fire. Not with Mia and Tasha in the house, even despite the fact that they were protected by the bathtub. Because God help him if something went wrong and one of the two people he loved most in all of the world wound up in the cross fire.

No, they were going to have to do this by stealth—which currently was not one of his strengths. There was no way in hell he could climb up the side of the house silently.

"Hey! I found an extra headset and vest in the back of my jeep." Joe Catalanotto climbed into the van, tossing both in Frisco's direction.

"Man, do you know how long it's been since I've worn one of these?" Frisco asked, holding up the vest and lightweight headphones.

Cat nodded. "Yeah," he said. "I *do* know. Put 'em on. Blue and Lucky are starting to report in. You're gonna want to hear what they're saying."

Frisco slipped on the black combat vest. It was a newer version of the heavy-duty vest he'd damn near worn out during his five years as a SEAL. It was made from lighter fabric than his old vest and was more comfortable.

It felt good. He slipped on the headset and adjusted the lip microphone, plugging the wire into the radio unit in the vest. He adjusted the frequency and—

"...ly nothing in the yard." It was Blue McCoy, speaking in a low voice. "No extra alarms or movement sensors—

nothing. The alarm on the house is Mickey Mouse—Lucky already overrode it. There's also a trellis in the back—it's perfectly placed. Like an engraved invitation to the second floor.''

"I'm already up there.'' This was Cowboy's voice. "Windows seem tight. But there's a third floor—probably an attic. Windows there look good and loose. Easy access.''

"I got movement on the infrared,'' Bobby's deep voice reported. "Two are still stationary on the second floor, and three are downstairs, in the front of the structure, although one is moving now toward the back.''

"That's Cliff,'' Harvard reported. "He just told his homeboy Ramon that he's going into the kitchen to get more salsa for his corn chips. They're watching something on an adults-only channel. Not much dialogue but lots of cheesy music.''

Blue's voice again. "The house has seven rooms downstairs. A living room in the southeast corner. A dining room to the immediate west, and a kitchen and some kind of rec room stretches along the entire back of the house.''

Frisco grabbed paper and pen and sketched a rough floor plan as Blue continued to describe the layout, and the location of all doors and windows.

"Cat, you want me to insert through the attic?'' Cowboy asked.

"It's Frisco's show,'' Cat replied, turning to look at him.

Frisco looked up from his drawing and shook his head. "Not yet. Report back to the van,'' he said, speaking into his mike for the first time in five years. "Everyone but Bobby. I want you to stay on the infrared, Bob. I need to be dead sure that Mia and Tash aren't moved from that upstairs room.''

"You got it,'' Bobby replied.

It only took a few minutes for the rest of Alpha Squad to appear from the shadows and gloom of the early evening.

Frisco's plan was simple.

"I want Cat and Lucky to go in through the attic windows and work their way down to the second floor where Mia and Tash are held. The rest of us will make a silent entry through this back door." He pointed down to his drawing. "Except for Bobby, who's going to stay glued to the infrared and Harvard who's gonna keep listening in."

"Bor-ring," Bob's voice sounded over their headsets from somewhere out in the yard.

"Someone's got to do it," Joe Cat told him.

"Yeah, but why me? I mean, come on, a damn paraplegic in a wheelchair could handle *this* job...."

There was a sudden silence in the van. Nobody looked at Frisco or his crutches. Nobody so much as moved.

Bobby realized what he'd said and he swore softly. "Frisco, man—I didn't mean that the way it sounded.... I wasn't thinking."

"As usual," Wes added.

Frisco sat down, looking up at the uncomfortable expression on the faces of his friends.

"It makes sense for me to switch places with Bob," he said quietly. "Doesn't it?"

Joe Catalanotto was the first to look up and into his eyes. "This isn't going to be a difficult operation," he said. He glanced over at Blue. "We figured—"

And suddenly it was all clear to Frisco. "You figured you could let me play soldier one last time, huh?" he said, knowing that he spoke the truth. "You figured you could baby-sit me, and the fact that I can't run and can barely walk without crutches wouldn't put the squad in that much danger."

Cat respected him enough not to try to lie. But he couldn't bring himself to agree, either. So instead, he said nothing. But the answer was written plainly on his face.

"But still, my being there is going to put the squad in some danger," Frisco said.

"It's nothing we can't handle—"

"But if I'm not part of the team that goes in the back door, the chances of a snafu happening decreases."

"It's not that big a deal—"

Frisco pulled himself to his feet. "Bob, when we get ready to go, I'll switch with you."

Bob sounded as if he were in agony. "Frisco, I didn't mean to—"

"You'll have to wait until I get out there, because I want eyes on that infrared scanner at all times."

Lucky stepped forward. "Hey, buddy, we know how important it is for you to go in there and—"

"Working in a team means recognizing individual team members' strengths and weaknesses," Frisco told him evenly. "As much as I want to be the one to protect Mia and Natasha, I know I can't climb in the attic window. And the fact is, I have no business trying to sneak in that back door, either. I'll man the infrared." He took a deep breath. "Blue, you've got the point. You're in command once you're inside the house." He knew he could trust Blue McCoy to make the right decisions to apprehend Dwayne and his two men with the least amount of gunplay. "Okay, let's get into position."

One by one, the SEALs slipped out of the van, fading into the darkness of the night.

Frisco turned to Joe Cat. "Don't move Mia and Tash downstairs until you receive an all clear."

Cat nodded. "We'll wait for your signal."

Frisco clumsily swung himself out of the van and started toward the shrubs at the edge of the yard where Bobby and the infrared scanner were hidden. But Joe Cat stopped him.

"You know, it takes a real man to put others' welfare and safety before his own pride," Cat said.

"Yeah, right. I'm one hell of a hero," Frisco said. "Excuse me while I go hide in the bushes while the rest of you guys risk death to rescue my niece and my girlfriend."

"We both know that what you just did was impossibly hard and incredibly heroic," Cat countered. "If that were Ronnie in that house, I'm not sure I would've been able to assign myself out of the action."

"Yes, you would've," Frisco said quietly. "If you knew that putting yourself in the assault force would not only risk the lives of your men, but risk Ronnie's life..." He shook his head. "I had no choice. You would've had no choice, too."

Joe Cat nodded. "Maybe." He paused. "I'd like to think so."

"I'm counting on you to take care of Mia and Tash," Frisco said.

"These guys aren't going to hear us coming. If we do this right, the risk is minimal."

And doing it right meant that he wasn't in the way. Damn, as much as Frisco hated that, he knew it was true.

"Hey, you said it yourself. Working as a team means recognizing team members' strengths and weaknesses," Joe said as if he could read Frisco's mind. When Frisco would have nodded and turned away, Joe Cat stopped him again. "You can still be part of SEAL Team Ten, Lieutenant. God knows we need your strengths. I've got one hell of a shortage of dependable instructors and way too many raw recruits coming into the SEAL Teams to be able to teach 'em properly. You have a wealth of information to pass on to these kids. You could virtually have your pick of subjects to teach."

Frisco was silent. Teach. *Those who can, do. Those who can't, teach.* Except, what was it that Mia had said? *Those who are taught, do. Those who teach, shape the future.*

"And as for your weaknesses..." Joe Cat continued. "Do you remember the very end of Hell Week? You weren't in my boat team, but I know you probably heard the story. I was a half a day away from the end of the ordeal, and I got a stress fracture in my leg. Talk about pain. It was hell, but I wouldn't quit. I wasn't gonna quit after I'd come that far. But I was *damn* close to being taken out. One of the instructors— a real bastard nicknamed Captain Blood—was about to call for the medics and have me removed."

Frisco nodded. "I remember hearing that."

"But then Blue and the other guys who were left in my boat team told Captain Blood that I was okay, that I could make it. In fact, they said I'd run a mile down the beach to prove it. And the captain looked at me and told me if I could run that mile, he'd let me stay in 'til the end.

"There was no way in hell I could *walk,* let alone run, but

Blue and the other guys picked me up, and they ran that mile carrying me.''

Frisco *had* heard that story. With their incredible show of unity and loyalty, Cat and Blue and the rest of their boat team were rewarded by having the hard-nosed instructor announce them secure nearly six hours before the official end of Hell Week. It was unprecedented.

Joe Cat reached out and squeezed Frisco's shoulder. ''Right now you're letting us carry *you.* But don't think there's no way you can carry us in return, my friend. Because you can. By teaching those recruits who are going to back us up some-day, you'd be shouldering more than your share.''

Frisco was silent. What could he say?

''Think about it,'' Cat said quietly. ''At least think about it.''

Frisco nodded. ''I will—after you get Mia and Natasha safely out of that house.''

''I know you meant after *we* get them out of there. All of us—working as a team.''

Frisco smiled. ''Right. Slip of the tongue.''

From where he sat, Frisco could see the light coming from an upstairs window. This window was smaller than the oth-ers—it had to be the bathroom.

Mia and Natasha were on the other side of those panes of glass. So close, yet so damn far.

As he watched the infrared scanner, the reddish-orange spots that were the Alpha Squad moved closer to the house. Two who had to be Lucky and Cat moved up onto the house.

The other four—Blue, Bobby, Wes and Cowboy—were motionless now, waiting for Frisco's command.

Inside the house, according to his scanner, nothing had changed. Dwayne and his men were still in the living room. Mia and Tash were still upstairs.

Mia and Tash.

Both of them had given him unconditional love. Funny, he had no problem accepting it from the kid, but from Mia…

Frisco hadn't believed it was possible. It still seemed much too good to be true. She was filled with such joy and life while he was the poster model for despair. She had such strength of purpose while he was floundering and uncertain.

He hadn't told her he loved her. He could have. But instead he'd attacked her, attacked her avocation. He'd pushed her away. Yet still she loved him.

Was it possible that she'd somehow seen the desperate, frightened man that hid beneath the anger and pain of his verbal attack? Thomas had told him she'd done the same with him, making a critical difference in his life, altering his destiny, shaping his future.

Those who are taught, do. Those who teach, shape the future.

Frisco could picture Mia telling him that, her eyes blazing with passion and fire. She believed it so absolutely.

And right then, as Alpha Squad waited for his signal to move into Dwayne Bell's house, Frisco knew just as absolutely that he wanted a second chance.

His entire life was full of second chances, he realized. Another man might have died from the wounds he'd received. Another man would never have made it out of that wheelchair.

Another man would let Mia Summerton get away.

He thought of that list that she'd posted on his refrigerator—all the things he could still do. There *was* so much he could still do, although some of it was going to be extremely hard.

Like not being an active-duty SEAL. That was going to be damned hard. But it was going to be damned hard whether he spent the rest of his life drinking in his living room, or if he signed on as an instructor. His disappointment and crushed hopes would be a tough weight to carry, a rough road to walk.

But he was a SEAL. Tough and rough were standard operating procedure. He'd come this far. He could—and he would—make it the rest of the way.

"Okay," Frisco said into his lip microphone. "The three

targets haven't moved. Let's get this done. Quietly and quickly, Alpha Squad. Go.''

There was no response over his headset, but he saw the shapes on the infrared scanner begin to move.

Blue clicked once into his lip mike when the downstairs team were all inside.

"Moving slow in the attic," he heard Joe Cat breathe. "Beams are old—don't want 'em to creak."

"Take as long as you need," Frisco told him.

It seemed to take an eternity, but Frisco finally heard Cat report, "In place."

He and Lucky were outside the upstairs bathroom door. That was Blue's signal to move.

Frisco heard the flurry of movement and the sound of four automatic weapons being locked and loaded. That was when the noise started.

"Hands up," Blue shouted, his normally smooth voice hard and clipped. "Come on—let me see 'em. Hands on your heads!"

"Come on, get 'em up!" It was Cowboy. "Come on— *move!*"

"What the…" Frisco could faintly hear Dwayne's voice as he was picked up over all four microphones.

"Move it! Down on the floor, faces against the rug. Let's *go.*" That was Bobby, along with an accompanying crash as he helped someone down there.

"Who the hell are you?" Dwayne kept asking. "Who the hell are you guys?"

"We're your worst nightmare," Cowboy told him, and then laughed. "Hell, you don't know *how* many years I've been waiting to say that line!"

"We're Alan Francisco's friends," Frisco heard Blue tell Dwayne. "Okay, Frisco, Mr. Bell and his associates have all been relieved of their weapons."

"Take 'em out into the front yard and tie 'em up, Blue," Frisco ordered. He had already moved across the yard and was nearly inside the house. "H., use that fancy equipment of yours to dial 911. Let's get the police garbage removal squad to take away the trash. Cat, this is my official all clear. Let's get Mia and Tasha out of there.''

The bathroom door swung open, and Mia stared up into the face of an enormous dark-haired stranger carrying an equally enormous gun.

He must've seen the surge of panic in her eyes because he quickly aimed the gun down toward the floor. ''Lt. Commander Joe Catalanotto of the Alpha Squad.'' He identified himself in a rather unmistakable New York accent. ''It's all right now, ma'am, you're safe.''

''Dwayne's been detained—permanently.'' Another man poked his head in the door. It was Lucky O'Donlon. Both men were wearing army fatigues and some kind of black vest.

''Are you okay?'' the dark-haired man—Joe—asked.

Mia nodded, still holding Tasha close. In the distance, she could hear the sound of sirens. ''Where's Alan? Is he all right?''

Lucky smiled, coming forward to give them both a hand out of the bathtub. ''He's downstairs, waiting for the police to arrive. They're not going to be real happy to see us here, doing their job for them, so to speak.''

''I pretended to throw up so the bad man would lock us in the bathroom,'' Natasha told Lucky proudly.

''That's very cool,'' he told her, perfectly straight-faced. But when he looked up at Mia, there was a glint of amusement in his eyes. ''Barfing kid as weapon,'' he said to her under his breath. ''The thought makes the strongest man tremble with fear. Good thinking.''

''I want to see Alan,'' she said.

The man named Joe nodded. ''I know he wants to see you, too. Come on, let's go downstairs.''

''How many SEALs are here?'' she asked Joe as Lucky, Tasha in his arms, led the way down the stairs.

''All of Alpha Squad,'' he told her.

''How did you ever get him to agree to let you help?''

"He asked us."

Mia stared at Joe. Alan asked *them* for help? They didn't
volunteer and he grudgingly accept? God, she'd been so afraid
he'd come here on his own and get himself killed....

"It's hard for him, but he's learning," Joe said quietly.
"Give him time. He's gonna be okay."

"Frisco!" Tasha shouted.

Mia stopped halfway down the stairs, watching as the little
girl wriggled free from Lucky's arms and launched herself at
Alan Francisco.

He was dressed similarly to the other SEALs, complete
with black vest and some kind of headphone thing. His
crutches clattered to the living room floor as he caught Tasha
in his arms.

From across the room, over the top of Tasha's head, Alan
looked up at Mia. Their eyes met and he smiled one of his
sad, crooked, perfect smiles.

Then, God help her, she was rushing toward him, too—as
shamelessly as Natasha had.

And then she was in his arms. He held her as tightly as he
could with Tasha still clinging to him, too.

"I'm sorry," he whispered into her ear. "Mia, I'm so
sorry."

Mia wasn't sure if he was apologizing for his angry words
or Dwayne's abducting them. It didn't matter. What mattered
was they were safe and he was safe and he had actually *asked*
for help....

Flashing lights marked the arrival of police squad cars, and
Frisco loosened his hold on Mia and let Tasha slide down to
the floor.

"Can we talk later?" Frisco asked.

Mia nodded. "I was coming back, you know," she told
him. "To the cabin. To talk to you—talk, not fight. That was
when Dwayne nearly ran me off the road."

Her beautiful hazel eyes were shining with unshed tears.
She had been coming back to the cabin. She loved him
enough to swallow her pride.

And suddenly later wasn't good enough. Suddenly there were things he had to tell her, things that couldn't wait.

Frisco knew in that moment that even if right then and there, in a miraculous act of God, he suddenly regained full use of his injured leg, he would still be less than whole.

He knew with a certainty that took his breath away that it was only when he was with this incredible woman that he was truly complete.

Oh, he knew he could live without her—the same way he knew he could live without ever running again. It would be hard, but he could do it. It wasn't as if she'd saved him. She hadn't—he'd done that himself. With a little help. It had taken Natasha to nudge him back to the world of the living. And once there, Mia's warmth and joy had lit his path, helping him out of his darkness.

Frisco knew he'd probably never run again. But he also knew that he didn't have to live without Mia.

That was something he had at least a small amount of control over.

And he could start by telling her how he felt.

But there wasn't any time. The police had arrived, and the uniformed officers were less than pleased that the SEALs had taken matters into their own hands. Joe Cat had intercepted the officer in charge and was trying to calm him down, but back-up had to be called along with the police captain.

And instead of telling Mia that he loved her, Frisco turned to Lucky. "Do me a favor, man, and walk Mia and Tash out to Harvard's van. I want to get them out of here, but I've got to set one thing straight with the police before we leave."

"Absolutely."

Frisco picked up his crutches, positioning them under his arms as he looked back at Mia. "I'll try not to take too long."

She gave him a tremulous smile that added so much weight and meaning to her words. "That's okay. We'll wait."

Frisco smiled back at her, suddenly almost ridiculously happy. "Yeah," he said. "I know. But I don't want to keep you waiting any longer."

* * *

"I told the police captain that Sharon was willing to testify against Bell," Frisco told Harvard and Mia as they climbed out of the van and started toward the condo courtyard. "With her help, they can ID Bell as the perpetrator in a number of unsolved robberies and possibly even a murder."

"Sharon saw Dwayne *kill* someone?" Mia asked Frisco in a low voice.

He nodded, glancing at Harvard who was carrying a drowsy Tasha. But her five-year-old ears were as sharp as ever and she lifted her head. "I saw Dwayne kill someone, too," Tasha told them, her eyes filling with tears. "I saw him kill Thomas."

"Thomas isn't dead," Frisco said.

"Yes, he is," Tasha insisted. "Dwayne hit him and made him bloody, and he didn't get back up."

"Thomas is waiting for you, princess, up in the condo."

"Oh, thank God," Mia said. "Is he really all right?"

"A little shaky, maybe," Frisco said, "but, yeah. He's okay."

All signs of her drowsiness gone, Tasha squirmed free from Harvard's arms. Like a flash, she ran up the stairs. But the condo door was locked, and she pounded on it.

As Mia watched, it swung open, and sure enough, there was Thomas King, looking a little worse for wear. Tasha launched herself at him, and nearly knocked the teenager over.

"Hey, Martian girl," Thomas said casually and matter-of-factly, as if they'd run into each other on the street. But he held the child tightly. That and the sudden sheen of tears in his eyes gave him away.

"I thought you were dead," she told him, giving him a resounding kiss on the cheek. "And if you were dead, then you couldn't marry me."

"*Marry* you?" Thomas's voice slipped up an octave. "Whoa, wait a minute, I—"

"A Russian princess has to marry a king," Tasha told him seriously.

"You're kind of short," Thomas told her. "I'm not so sure I want a wife who's that *short*."

Tasha giggled. "I'll be taller, silly," she told him. "I'll be sixteen."

"Sixteen…" Thomas looked as if he were choking. "Look, Martian, if you're still interested when you're *twenty*-six, give me a call, but until then, we're friends, all right?"

Natasha just smiled.

"All right," Thomas said. "Now, come on inside and see what Navy bought for you."

They disappeared inside the house, and Mia could hear Tasha's excited squealing. She turned to Frisco, who was painstakingly pulling himself up the stairs. "Is it the couch?"

Frisco just shook his head. "Man, I forgot all about it."

"I didn't," Harvard said, laughter in his voice.

Curiosity overcame Mia, and she hurried to Frisco's door. And laughed out loud. "You got it," she said. "The couch. Dear Lord, it's so…"

"Pink?" Frisco volunteered, amusement and chagrin glinting in his eyes as he followed her inside.

Tasha was sitting in the middle of the couch, her ankles delicately crossed—the perfect Russian princess, despite the fact that her hair was tangled and her face dirty and tear streaked.

Harvard started packing up the array of equipment, and Thomas moved to help him.

"This stuff is so cool," Mia heard Thomas tell Harvard. "What do I have to do to become one of you guys?"

"Well, you start by joining the Navy," Harvard said. "And you work your butt off for about three years, and maybe, just maybe, then you'll be accepted into the BUD/S training."

"Hey," Frisco said to Natasha. "Don't I get a hug? Or any thanks?"

Tasha looked at him haughtily. "Russian princesses *don't* say thank you or give hugs."

"Wanna bet?" He sat down on the couch next to the little girl and pulled her into his arms.

She giggled and threw her arms around his neck. "Thank you, thank you, thank you, thank you, thank you—"

Frisco laughed. Mia loved the sound of his laughter. "Enough already," he said. "Go wash your face and get ready for bed."

Tash stood up, casting a look of longing back at the sofa.

"Don't worry," Frisco told her. "It'll be here in the morning."

"You bet it will," Harvard interjected. "And the morning after that, and the morning after *that…*"

"I don't know," Mia said. "It's starting to grow on me." She held out her hand to Tasha. "Come on. I'll help you."

Frisco watched them disappear into the bathroom. Tasha was dragging, clearly exhausted. It wouldn't be long before she was sound asleep. He turned back to Harvard. "Need help getting that stuff together?"

Harvard grinned, reading his mind. "All done. We're out of here. Gee, sorry we can't stay."

Frisco held out his hand, and Harvard clasped it. "Thanks, man."

"It was good seeing you again, Francisco. Don't be a stranger."

"I won't be," Frisco told his friend. "In fact, I'll probably be coming over to the base in a few days to talk to Cat."

Harvard smiled, his powerful biceps flexing as he easily lifted pounds and pounds of heavy equipment. "Good. See you then."

He followed Thomas outside and closed the door behind them.

The sudden silence and stillness was deafening. Frisco started toward Tasha's room, but stopped short at the sight of Mia quietly closing the little girl's door.

"She's already asleep," she told him. "She was exhausted."

Mia looked exhausted, too. Maybe this wasn't a good time to talk. Maybe she just wanted to go home.

"Do you want a cup of tea?" Frisco asked, suddenly horribly uncertain.

She took a step toward him. "All I want right now is for you to hold me," she said quietly.

Frisco carefully leaned his crutches against the wall and slowly drew her into his arms. She was trembling as she slipped her arms around his waist. He pulled her closer, held her tighter and she rested her head against his chest and sighed.

"Did you really ask the Alpha Squad for help?" she asked.

"Is that so hard to believe?"

Mia lifted her head. "Yes."

He laughed. And kissed her. She tasted so sweet, her lips were so soft. He'd been crazy to think he could ever give her up.

"Were you really coming back to the cabin?" he asked her.

She nodded.

"Why? You said damn near all that there was to say pretty concisely. Your vision of the way my future might've been was pretty accurate—although I'm willing to bet you didn't picture me drinking myself to death on a pink couch."

"The way your future might've been…?"

There was such hope in her eyes, Frisco had to smile. "That's not my future, Mia," he told her. "That was my past. It was my father who drank himself into oblivion every night in front of the TV set. But I'm not my old man. I'm a SEAL. You were right. I'm still a SEAL. And it's only my knee that got busted, not my spirit."

"Oh, Alan.…"

"Yeah, it hurts to know I'm not going to go on the active-duty list, but that's the hand fate dealt me. I'm done wallowing," he told her. "Now I'm going to get on with my *true* future. I'm going to talk to Joe Cat about that instructor position. And I've got Tash to think about, because Sharon's gonna have to do time on those DUI charges even if the man she hit lives.…"

Mia was crying. She was crying *and* she was laughing.

"Hey," Frisco said. "Are you all right?"

"I'm great," she told him. "And so are you. You made it, Alan. You're whole again." Her eyes filled with a fresh flood of tears. "I'm so happy for you."

He was whole? Frisco wasn't quite so sure. "I'm going to look for another place to live," he told her, searching her eyes. "I figure if I sell this place, I can maybe get something a little closer to the base, maybe something on the water—something on the ground floor. Something big enough for me and Tash and maybe…you, too…?"

"Me?" she whispered.

He nodded. "Yeah, I mean, if you want to…."

"You want me to live with you…?"

"Hell, no. I want you to *marry* me."

Mia was silent. Her eyes were wide and her lips slightly parted. She didn't say a word, she just stared at him.

Frisco shifted his weight nervously. "I know you're probably speechless with joy at the thought of spending the rest of your life with a man who owns a pink couch and—"

"Do you love me?"

Frisco could see from her eyes that she honestly didn't know. How could she not know? Well, he realized, because for starters, he'd never actually said the words….

"You know, up at the cabin, when I said all those horrible things…?"

Mia nodded.

"What I *really* meant to say was that I'd fallen absolutely in love with you, and that I was terrified—both of what I was feeling, and of the thought of you ruining the rest of your life by spending it with me."

She was indignant. "How could you have thought that?"

He smiled. "I still think it—I just figure I'll work really hard to keep you happy and smiling, and you won't even notice. You also won't notice that when we vote, we cancel each other out."

"Democracy in action," Mia said.

"And maybe, someday—if you want—we could add 'making babies' to that list you started on my refrigerator," he told her. "What do you say?"

"Yes," Mia told him, emotion making her voice tremble. "I say oh, yes."

Frisco kissed her.

And he was whole.

Man of Ice

DIANA PALMER

DIANA PALMER

has a gift for telling the most sensual tales with charm and humour. With over 40 million copies of her books in print, Diana Palmer is a bestselling romance author. Diana's hobbies include gardening, archaeology, anthropology, iguanas, astronomy and music. Diana met and married her husband within one week: 'It was just like something from one of my books.' Twenty-five years later they are still happily married and they have one son who is pursuing a career in law enforcement.

Prologue

Dawson Rutherford hesitated on the front steps of the Mercer home. As the butler held the carved wooden door open for him to enter, he was only absently aware of music and voices and the clink of ice in glasses. He couldn't remember ever feeling so unsure of himself. Would she welcome him? He smiled with cold mockery. When had Barrie Bell, his stepsister, ever welcomed his presence in recent years? She'd loved him once. But he'd killed her feelings for him, as he'd fought to kill all the violent emotions she inspired in him since her mother had married his father.

He pushed a big, lean hand through his short, wavy gold hair, only barely disrupting its neatness. His pale green eyes were thoughtful as he stood there, elegant and dramatically handsome, drawing the gaze of women. But he had eyes for none of them. They called him the "ice man." And it wasn't because he came from a cold country.

Through the open door he could see her on the steps, her

long, wavy black hair curling down her bare shoulders, sparkling in a silver dress. He was all she had left since both their parents had died, but she avoided him. He couldn't blame her, now that he knew at last about the other casualty of his turbulent relationship with Barrie; one that he'd only just found out about recently.

He hesitated to go in there, to see her again, to talk to her. They'd argued at their last meeting over the same issue he was going to bring up now. But this time he needed it as an excuse to get her back to Sheridan, Wyoming. He had to undo five years of pain and heartache, to make up to her for what she'd endured. In order to do that he was going to have to face some private demons of his own, as well as the fear he'd taught her to feel. He didn't look forward to it, but it was time to erase the past and start over. If they could...

One

There was a cardinal rule that people who gave parties never invited both Barrie Bell and her stepbrother, Dawson Rutherford, to the same social event. Since the two of them didn't have a lot of mutual friends, and they lived in different states, it wasn't often broken. But every rule had an exception, and tonight, Barrie discovered, was it.

She hadn't really wanted to go out, but Martha and John Mercer, old friends of the Rutherfords who'd taken a interest in Barrie since their move to Tucson, insisted that she needed a diversion. She wasn't teaching this summer, after all, and the part-time job that kept her bank account healthy had just ended abruptly. Barrie needed cheering up and Martha was giving a party that was guaranteed to accomplish it.

Actually it had. Barrie felt brighter than she had in some months. She was sequestered on the steps of the staircase in the hall with two admirers, one who was a bank executive

and the other who played guitar with a jazz band. She was
wearing a dress guaranteed to raise blood pressures, silver
and clinging from its diamanté straps at her lightly tanned
shoulders to her ankles, with a long, seductive slit up one
side of the skirt. The color of her high heels matched the
dress. She wore her long, wavy black hair loose, so that it
reached almost to her waist. In her creamy-complexioned,
oval face, bright green eyes shone with a happy glitter.

That is, they *had* been shining until she saw Dawson
Rutherford come in the front door. Her sophisticated chatter
had died abruptly and she withdrew into a shell, looking
vulnerable and hunted.

Her two companions didn't connect her stepbrother's entrance with Barrie's sudden change. Not, at least, until a few
minutes later when he spotted her in the hall and, excusing
himself to his hostess, came to find her with a drink in his
hand.

Dawson was more than a match for any man present,
physically. Some of them were spectacularly handsome, but
Dawson was more so. He had wavy blond hair, cut conventionally short, a deep tan, chiseled, perfect facial features
and deep-set pale green eyes at least two shades lighter than
Barrie's. He was tall and slender, but there were powerful
muscles in that lithe body, which was kept fit from hours
in the saddle. Dawson was a multimillionaire, yet being the
boss didn't keep him from helping out on the many ranches
he owned. It was nothing unusual to find him cutting out
calves for branding on the Wyoming ranches, or helping to
drive cattle across the spinifex plains of the several thou-
sand-square-mile station in Australia's Channel Country. He
spent his leisure hours, which were very few, working with
his thoroughbred horses on the headquarters ranch in Sheridan, Wyoming, when he wasn't buying and selling cattle
all over the country.

He was an elegant man, from his hand-tooled leather

boots to the expensive slacks and white silk turtleneck shirt
he wore with a designer jacket. Everything about him, from
his Rolex to the diamond horseshoe ring on his right hand,
screamed wealth. And with the elegant good looks, there
was a cold, calculating intelligence. Dawson spoke French
and Spanish fluently, and he had a degree in business.

Barrie's two companions seemed to shrink when he appeared beside them, a drink cradled in one big, lean hand.
He didn't drink often, and never to excess. He was the sort
of man who never liked to lose control in any way. She'd
seen him lose it just once. Perhaps that was why he hated
her so, because she was the only one who ever had.

"Well, well, what was Martha thinking, I wonder, that
rules were made to be broken?" Dawson asked her, his deep
voice like velvet even though it carried above the noise.

"Martha invited me. She didn't invite you," Barrie said
coldly. "I'm sure it was John. He's laughing," she added,
her gaze going to Martha's husband across the room.

Dawson followed her glance to his host and raised his
glass. The shorter man raised his in acknowledgment and,
catching Barrie's furious glare, turned quickly away.

"Aren't you going to introduce me?" Dawson continued,
unabashed, his eyes going now to the two men beside her.

"Oh, this is Ted and that's…what was your name?" she
somewhat abruptly asked the second man.

"Bill," he replied.

"This is my…stepbrother, Dawson Rutherford," she continued.

Bill grinned and extended his hand. It was ignored, although Dawson nodded curtly in acknowledgment. The
younger man cleared his throat and smiled sheepishly at
Barrie, brandishing his glass. "Uh, I need a refill," he said
quickly, because Dawson's eyes were narrowing and there
was a distinct glitter in them.

"Me, too," Ted added and, grinning apologetically at Barrie, took off.

Barrie glared after them. "Craven cowards," she muttered.

"Does it take two men at once to keep you happy these days?" Dawson asked contemptuously. His cold gaze ran down her dress to the low neckline that displayed her pretty breasts to their best advantage.

She felt naked. She wouldn't have dreamed of wearing clothing this revealing around Dawson normally. Only the fact that he'd come to the party unbeknownst to her gave him the opportunity to see her in this camouflage she adopted. But she wasn't going to spoil her sophisticated image by letting him know that his intent regard disturbed her. "There's safety in numbers," she replied with a cool smile. "How are you, Dawson?"

"How do I look?" he countered.

"Prosperous," she replied. She didn't say anything else. Dawson had come to her apartment only a few months ago, trying to get her back to Sheridan to play chaperone to Leslie Holton, a widow and former actress who had a piece of land Dawson wanted. She'd refused and an argument had resulted, which led to them not speaking at all. She'd thought Dawson would never seek her out again after it. But here he was. And she could imagine that the widow was still in hot pursuit of him—or so her best friend Antonia Hayes Long had told her recently.

He took a sip of his drink, but his eyes never left her face. "Corlie changes your bed every other day, hoping."

Corlie was the housekeeper at Dawson's Sheridan home. She and her husband Rodge had been in residence since long before Barrie's mother had married Dawson's father. They were two of her favorite people and she missed them. But not enough to go back, even for a visit. "I don't belong in Sheridan," she said firmly. "Tucson is home, now."

"You don't have a home any more than I do," he shot back, his voice cold. "Our parents are dead. All we have left is each other."

"Then I have nothing," she said harshly, letting her eyes speak for her.

"You'd like to think so, wouldn't you?" he demanded with a cold smile. And because the flat statement wounded him, he added deliberately, "Well, I hope you're not still eating your heart out for me, baby."

The accusation made her feel even more vulnerable. Her hands clenched in her lap. In the old days, Dawson had known too well how she felt about him. It was a weapon he'd used against her. She glared at him. "I wouldn't waste my heart on you. And don't call me baby!"

His eyes narrowed on her face and dropped to her mouth, lingering there. "I don't use endearments, Barrie," he reminded her. "Not in normal conversation. And we both remember the last time I used that one, don't we?"

She wanted to crawl under the stairs and die. Her eyes closed. Memories assailed her. Dawson's deep voice, husky with feeling and need and desire, whispering her name with each movement of his powerful body against hers, whispering, "Baby! Oh, God, baby, baby...!"

She made a hoarse sound and tried to get away, but he was too close. He sat down on the step below hers and settled back on his elbow, so that his arm imprisoned her between himself and the bannister.

"Don't run," he chided. "You're a big girl now. It's all right to have sex with a man, Barrie. You won't go to hell for it. Surely you know that by now, with your record."

She looked at him with fear and humiliation. "My record?" she whispered.

"How many men have you had? Can't you remember?"

Her eyes stared straight into his. She didn't flinch, although she felt like it. "I can remember, Dawson," she said with a forced smile. "I've had one. Only one." She actually shivered.

Her reaction took some of the antagonism out of him. He just stared at her, his pale eyes unusually watchful.

She clasped her arms tightly over her breasts and her entire body went rigid from his proximity.

He moved back, just a couple of inches. She relaxed, but only a little. Her posture was still unnatural. He wanted to think she was acting this way deliberately, in an attempt to resurrect the old guilt. But it wasn't an act. She looked at him with eyes that were vulnerable, but even if she cared as much as ever, she was afraid of him. And it showed.

The knowledge made him uncomfortable. More uncomfortable than he usually was. He'd taunted her with her feelings for him for years, until it was a habit he couldn't break. He'd even done it the night he lost his head and destroyed her innocence. He'd behaved viciously to push away the guilt and the shame he felt at his loss of control.

He hadn't meant to attack her tonight, of all times. Not after the argument he'd had with her months ago. He'd come to make peace. But the attempt had backfired. It was the way she was dressed, and the two eager young men sitting like worshipers at her feet, that had enraged him with jealousy. He hadn't meant a word he said, but she wouldn't know that. She was used to having him bait her. It didn't make him feel like a man to punish her for his own sins; it made him sick. Especially now, with what he'd only just found out about the past, and what had happened to her because of him...

He averted his eyes to her folded arms. She looked like a whipped child. She'd adopted that posture after he'd seduced her. The image was burned indelibly into his brain. It still hurt, too.

"I only want to talk," he said curtly. "You can relax."

"What could we possibly have to say to each other?"

she asked icily. "I wish I never had to see you again, Dawson!"

His eyes bit into hers. "Like hell you do."

She couldn't win an argument with him. It was better not to start one. "What do you want to talk about?"

His gaze went past her, to the living room, where people were laughing and drinking and talking. Happy, comfortable people. Not like the two on the staircase.

He shrugged and took another swallow from the glass before he faced her again. "What else? I want you to come home for a week or two."

Her heart raced. She averted her gaze. "No!"

He'd expected that reaction. He was ready to debate it. "You'll have plenty of chaperones," he informed her. "Rodge and Corlie." He paused deliberately. "And the widow Holton."

She looked up. "Still?" she muttered sarcastically. "Why don't you just marry her and be done with it?"

He deliberately ignored the sarcasm. "You know that she's got a tract of land in Bighorn that I have to own. The only way she'll discuss selling it to me is if I invite her to Sheridan for a few days."

"I hear that she's hanging around the ranch constantly," she remarked.

"She visits regularly, but not overnight," he said. "The only way I can clinch the land deal and get her to go away is to let her spend a few days at the ranch. I can't do that without you."

He didn't look pleased about it. Odd. She'd heard from her best friend, Antonia Long, that the widow was lovely and eligible. She couldn't understand why Dawson was avoiding her. It was common knowledge that she'd chased Powell Long, Antonia's husband, and that she was casting acquisitive eyes at Dawson as well. Barrie had no right to be jealous, but she was. She didn't look at him, because she didn't want him to know for sure just how vulnerable she still was.

"You must like her if you're willing to have her stay at the ranch," she said. "Why do you keep plaguing me to come and play chaperone?"

His pale green eyes met hers. "I don't want her in my bed. Is that blunt enough?"

She flushed. It wasn't the sort of remark he was in the habit of making to her. They never discussed intimate things at all.

"You still blush like a virgin," he said quietly.

Her eyes flashed. "And you're the one man in the world who has reason to know that I'm not!" she said in a harsh, bitter undertone.

His expression wasn't very readable. He averted his eyes to the carpet. After a minute he finished his drink. He reached through the bannister to put the glass on the hall table beyond it.

She pulled her skirt aside as he reached past her. For an instant, his deeply tanned face was on an unnerving level with hers. She could see the tiny mole at the corner of his mouth, the faint dimple in his firm chin. His upper lip was thinner than the lower one, and she remembered with sorrow how those hard lips felt on her mouth. She'd grieved for him for so long. She'd never been able to stop loving him, despite the pain he'd caused her, despite his suspicions, his antagonism. She wondered sometimes if it would ever stop.

He turned sideways on the step, leaning back against the bannister to cross his long legs in front of him. His boots were immaculate, as was the white silk shirt under his open dinner jacket. But, then, he made the most casual clothes look elegant. He was elegant.

"Why don't you get married?" he asked suddenly.

Her eyebrows went up. "Why should I?"

His quiet gaze went over her body, down her full, firm

breasts to her narrow hips and long legs. The side slit had
fallen open in the position she was sitting, and all too much
of her silk-clad leg was visible.

He watched her face very carefully as he spoke. "Because
you're twenty-six. In a few more years, it will be more
difficult for you to have a child."

A child… A child. The color drained out of her face, out
of her eyes. She swallowed a surge of nausea as she remembered the wrenching pain, the fear as she phoned for
an ambulance and was carried to the hospital. He didn't
know. He'd never know, because she wouldn't tell him.

"I don't want to marry anyone. Excuse me, I have to—"

She tried to get up, but his lean hand shot out and caught
her forearm, anchoring her to the steps. He was too close.
She could smell the exotic cologne he always wore, feel his
breath, whiskey-scented, on her face.

"Stop running from me!" he growled.

His eyes met hers. They were relentless, intent.

"Let me go!" she raged.

His fingers only tightened. He made her feel like a hys-
terical idiot with that long, hard stare, but she couldn't stop
struggling.

He ended the unequal struggle by tugging slightly and
she landed back on the steps with a faint thump. "Stop it,"
he said firmly.

Her eyes flashed at him, her cheeks flushed.

He let go of her arm all at once. "At least you look alive
again," he remarked curtly. "And back to normal pretending to hate me."

"I'm not pretending. I do hate you, Dawson," she said,
as if she was programmed to fight him, to deny any hint of
caring in her voice.

"Then it shouldn't affect you all that much to come home
with me."

"I won't run interference for you with the widow. If you want that land so badly…"

"I can't buy it if she won't sell it," he reminded her. "And she won't sell it unless I entertain her."

"It's a low thing to do, to get a few acres of land."

"Land with the only water on the Bighorn property," he reminded her. "I had free access when her husband was alive. Now I buy the land or Powell Long will buy it and fence it off from my cattle. He hates me."

"I know how he feels," she said pointedly.

"Do you know what she'll do if you're not there?" he continued. "She'll try to seduce me, sure as hell. She thinks no man can resist her. When I refuse her, she'll take her land straight to Powell Long and make him a deal he can't refuse. Your friendship with Antonia won't stop him from fencing off that river, Barrie. Without water, we'll lose the property and all the cattle on it. I'll have to sell at a loss. Part of that particular ranch is your inheritance. You stand to lose even more than I do."

"She wouldn't," she began.

"Don't kid yourself," he drawled. "She's attracted to me. Or don't you remember how that feels?" he added with deliberate sarcasm.

She flushed, but she glared at him. "I'm on vacation."

"So what?"

"I don't like Sheridan, I don't like you, and I don't want to spend my vacation with you!"

"Then don't."

She hit the bannister helplessly. "Why should I care if I lose my inheritance? I've got a good job!"

"Why, indeed?"

But she was weakening. Her part-time job had fallen through. She was looking at having to do some uncomfortable budgeting, despite the good salary she made. It only stretched so far. Besides, she could imagine what a woman like Mrs. Holton would do to get her claws into Dawson. The widow could compromise him, if she didn't do anything else. She could make up some lurid tale about him if he didn't give out…and there was plenty of gossip already, about Dawson's lack of interest in women. It didn't bear thinking about, what that sort of gossip would do to Dawson's pride. He'd suffered enough through the gossip about his poor father and Antonia Long, when there wasn't one shred of truth to it. And in his younger days, his success with women was painfully obvious to a worshiping Barrie.

"For a few days, you said," she began.

His eyebrows lifted. "You aren't changing your mind!" he exclaimed with mock surprise.

"I'll think about it," she continued firmly.

He shrugged. "We should be able to live under the same roof for that long without it coming to bloodshed."

"I don't know about that." She leaned against the bannister. "And if I decide to go—which I haven't yet—when she leaves, I leave, whether or not you've got your tract of land."

He smiled faintly. There was something oddly calculating in his eyes. "Afraid to stay with me, alone?"

She didn't have to answer him. Her eyes spoke for her.

"You don't know how flattering that reluctance is these days," he said, searching her eyes. "All the same, it's misplaced. I don't want you, Barrie," he added with a mocking smile.

"You did, once," she reminded him angrily.

He nodded. His hands went into his pockets and his broad shoulders shifted. "It was a long time ago," he said stiffly. "I have other interests now. So do you. All I want is for you to run interference for me until I can get my hands on that property. Which is to your benefit, as well," he added pointedly. "You inherited half the Bighorn property when George died. If we lose the water rights, the land is worthless. That means you inherit nothing. You'll have to depend on your job until you retire.''

She knew that. The dividend she received from her share of cattle on the Bighorn ranch helped pay the bills.

''Oh, *there* you are, Dawson, dear!'' a honied voice drawled behind him. ''I've been looking just everywhere for you!'' A slinky brunette, a good few years younger than Barrie, with a smile the size of a dinner plate latched onto Dawson's big arm and pressed her ample, pretty chest against it. ''I'd just love to dance with you!'' she gushed, her eyes flirting outrageously with his.

Dawson went rigid. If Barrie hadn't seen it for herself, she wouldn't have believed it. With a face that might have been carved from stone, he released himself from the woman's grasp and moved pointedly back from her.

''Excuse me. I'm talking to my stepsister,'' he said curtly.

The woman was shocked at being snubbed. She was beautiful and quite obviously used to trapping men with that coquettish manner, and the handsomest man here looked at her as if she smelled bad.

She laughed a little nervously. ''Of course. I'm sorry. I didn't mean to interrupt. Later, perhaps, then?''

She turned and went quickly back into the living room.

Barrie was standing where she'd been throughout the terse exchange, leaning against the bannister. Now she moved away from it and down the steps to stand just in front of Dawson. Her green eyes searched his quietly.

His jaw clenched. ''I told you. I'm not in the market for a woman—not you or anyone else.''

Her teeth settled into her lower lip, an old habit that he'd once chided her about.

He apparently hadn't forgotten. His forefinger tapped sharply at her upper lip. ''Stop that. You'll draw blood,'' he accused.

She released the stinging flesh. ''I didn't realize,'' she

murmured. She sighed as she searched his hard face. "You loved women, in the old days," she said with more bitterness than she knew. "They followed you around like bees on a honey trail."

His face was hard. "I lost my taste for them."

"But, why?"

"You don't have the right to invade my privacy," he said curtly.

She smiled sadly. "I never did. You were always so mysterious, so private. You never shared anything with me when I was younger. You were always impatient to get away from me."

"Except once," he replied shortly. "And see where that got us."

She took a step toward the living room. "Yes."

There was a silence, filled by merry voices and the clink of ice in glasses.

"If I ask you something, point-blank, will you answer me?" he asked abruptly.

She turned, her eyes wide, questioning. "That depends on what it is. If you won't answer personal questions, I don't see why I should."

His eyes narrowed. "Perhaps not."

She grimaced. "All right. What do you want to know?"

"I want to know," he said quietly, "how many men you've really had since me."

She almost gasped at the audacity of the question.

His eyes slid down her body and back up again, and they were still calculating, the way they'd been all evening. "You dress like a femme fatale. I can't remember the last time I saw you so uncovered. You flirt and tease, but it's all show, it's all on the surface." He scowled. "Barrie…"

She flushed. "Stop looking into my mind! I hated it when I was in my teens and I hate it now!"

He nodded slowly. "It was always like that. I even knew

what you were thinking. It was a rare kind of rapport. Some-where along the way, we lost it.''

''You smothered it,'' she said correcting.

He smiled coolly. ''I didn't like having you inside my head.''

''Which works both ways,'' she agreed.

He reached out and touched her cheek lightly, his fingers lingering against the silky soft skin. She didn't move away. That was a first.

''Come here, Barrie,'' he invited, and this time he didn't smile. His eyes held hers, hypnotized her, beckoned her.

She felt her legs moving when she hadn't meant to let them. She looked up at him with an expression that wasn't even recognizable.

''Now,'' he said softly, touching her mouth. ''Tell me the truth.''

She started to clamp down on her lower lip, and his thumb prevented her. It smoothed over her soft lower lip, exploring under the surface, inside where the flesh was moist and vulnerable . She jerked back from him.

''Tell me.'' His eyes were relentless. She couldn't escape. He was too close.

''I…couldn't, with anyone else,'' she whispered huskily. ''I was afraid.''

The years of bitterness, of blaming her for what he thought he'd made of her were based on a lie. All the guilt and shame when he heard about her followers, when he saw her with other men—he knew the truth now. He'd destroyed her as a woman. He'd crippled her sexually. And just be-cause, like his father, he'd lost control of himself. He hadn't known what she'd suffered until a week ago.

He couldn't tell her that he'd wrangled this invitation from John because he needed an excuse to see her. He hadn't realized in all the long years how badly he'd damaged her. Her camouflage had been so good. Now that he did know, it was unbelievably painful.

"Dear God," he said under his breath.

His hand fell away from her cheek. He looked older, suddenly, and there was no mockery in his face now.

"Surprised?" she taunted unsteadily. "Shocked? You've always wanted to think the worst of me. Even that afternoon at the beach, before it...before it happened, you thought I just wanted to show off my body."

He didn't blink. His eyes searched hers. "The only eyes you wanted on your body were mine," he said in a dead voice. "I knew it. I wouldn't admit it, that's all."

She laughed coldly. "You said plenty," she reminded him. "That I was a tramp, that I was so hot I couldn't—"

His thumb stopped the words and his eyes closed briefly. "You might not realize it, but you aren't the only one who paid dearly for what happened that night," he said after a minute.

"Don't tell me you were sorry, or that you felt guilty," she chided. "You don't have a heart, Dawson. I don't think you're even human!"

He laughed faintly. "I have doubts about that myself these days," he said evenly.

She was shaking with fury, the past impinging on the present as she struggled with wounding memories. "I loved you!" she said brokenly.

"Dear God, don't you think I know?!" he demanded, and his eyes, for that instant, were terrible to look into.

She went white, paper white. Beside her skirt, her hands clenched. She wanted to throw herself at him and hit him and kick him, to hurt him as he'd hurt her.

But slowly, as she remembered where they were, she forced herself to calm down. "This isn't the time or the place." She bit off the words. Her voice shook with emotion.

He stuck his hands into his pockets and looked down at her. "Come to Wyoming with me. It's time you got it all out of your system. You've been hurt enough for something that was never your fault to begin with."

The words were surprising. He was different, somehow, and she didn't understand why. Even the antagonism when he saw her had been halfhearted, as if he was only sniping at her out of habit. Now, he wasn't especially dangerous at all. But she didn't, couldn't, trust him. There had to be more to his determination to get her to Wyoming than as a chaperone.

"I'll think about it," she said shortly. "But I won't decide tonight. I'm not sure I want to go back to Sheridan, even to save my inheritance."

He started to argue, but the strain of the past few minutes had started to show in her face. He hated seeing the brightness gone from it. He shrugged. "All right. Think it over."

She drew in a steadying breath and walked past him into the living room. And for the rest of the evening, she was the life and soul of the party. Not that Dawson noticed. A couple of minutes after she left him in the hall, he went out the door and drove back to his hotel. Alone.

Two

It was a boring Saturday. Barrie had already done the laundry and gone to the grocery store. She had a date, but she'd canceled it. Somehow, one more outing with a man she didn't care about was more than she could bear. No one was ever going to measure up to Dawson, anyway, as much as she'd like to pretend it would happen. He owned her, as surely as he owned half a dozen ranches and a veritable fleet of cars, even if he didn't want her.

She'd given up hoping for miracles, and after last night, it was obvious that the dislike he'd had for her since her fifteenth birthday wasn't going to diminish. Even her one memory of him as a lover was nothing she wanted to remember. He'd hurt her, and afterwards, he'd accused her of being a wanton who'd teased him into seducing her. He could be kind to the people he liked, but he'd never liked Barrie or her mother. They'd been the outsiders, the interlopers, in the Rutherford family. Barrie's mother had married his father, and Dawson had hated them both from the moment he laid eyes on them.

Eleven years later, after the deaths of both their parents, nothing had changed except that Barrie had learned self-preservation. She'd avoided Dawson like the plague, until last night, when she'd betrayed everything to him in that burst of anger. She was embarrassed and ashamed this morning to have given herself away so completely. Her one hope was that he was already on his way back to Sheridan, and that she wouldn't have to see him again until the incident was forgotten, until these newest wounds he'd inflicted were healed.

She'd just finished mopping the kitchen floor in her bare feet and had put the mop out on the small balcony of her apartment to dry when the doorbell rang.

It was almost lunchtime and she was hungry, having spent her morning working. She hoped it wasn't the man she'd turned down for a date that evening, trying to convince her to change her mind.

Her wavy black hair lay in disheveled glory down her back. It was her one good feature, along with her green eyes. Her mouth was shaped like a bow and her nose was straight, but she wasn't conventionally pretty, although she had a magnificent figure. She was dressed in a T-shirt and a pair of worn jeans. Both garments had shrunk, emphasizing her perfect body. She didn't have makeup on, but her eyes were bright and her cheeks were rosy from all her exertions.

Without thinking, she opened the door and started to speak, when she realized who was standing there. It definitely wasn't Phil, the salesman with whom she'd turned down a date.

It was always the same when she came upon Dawson unawares. Her heart began to race, her breath stilled in her throat, her body burned as if she stood in a fire.

Eyes two shades lighter green than her own looked back

at her. Whatever he wore, he looked elegant. He was in designer jeans and a white shirt, with a patterned gray jacket worn loose over them. His feet were encased in hand-tooled gray leather boots and a creamy Stetson dangled from one hand.

He looked her up and down without smiling, without expression. Nothing he felt ever was allowed to show, while Barrie's face was as open as a child's book to him.

"What do you want?" she asked belligerently.

An eyebrow jerked over amused green eyes. "A kind word. But I've given up asking for the impossible. Can I come in? Or," he added, the smile fading, "isn't it convenient?"

She moved away from the door. "Check the bedroom if you like," she said sarcastically.

He searched her eyes. Once, he might have taken her up on it, just to irritate her. Not since last night, though. He hadn't the heart to hurt her any more than he already had. He tossed his hat onto the counter and leaned against it to watch her close the door.

"Have you decided whether or not you'll come back to Sheridan?" he asked bluntly. "It's only for a week. You're on summer vacation, and John told me that you'd been laid off at your part-time job." He looked at the counter and said with calculation, "Surely you can survive without your flock of admirers for that long."

She didn't contradict him or fly off the handle. That was what he wanted. She made points with Dawson by remaining calm.

"I don't want to play chaperone for you, Dawson," she said simply. "Get someone else."

"There isn't anyone else, and you know it. I want that land. What I don't want is to give Mrs. Holden any opportunities for blackmail. She's a lady who's used to getting what she wants."

"You're evenly matched, then, aren't you?" she replied.

"I don't have everything I want," he countered. His eyes narrowed. "Corlie and Rodge will be in the house, too. They miss you."

She didn't answer. She just looked at him, hating him and loving him while all the bad memories surfaced.

"Your eyes are very expressive," he said, searching them. There was so much pain behind the pretense, he thought sadly, and he'd caused it. "Such sad eyes, Barrie."

He sounded mysterious, broody. She sensed a change in him, some ripple of feeling that he concealed, covered up. His lean fingers toyed with the brim of his Stetson and he studied it while he spoke. "I bought you a horse."

She stared at him. "Why?"

"I thought you might respond to a bribe," he said carelessly. "He's a quarter horse. A gelding." He smiled with faint self-contempt. "Can you still ride?"

"Yes." She didn't want to admit that it touched her to have Dawson buy her a present. Even a plastic necklace would have given her pleasure if he'd given it to her.

His eyes lifted back to hers. "Well?"

"You have Rodge and Corlie to play chaperone. You don't need me."

His pale eyes held hers. "Yes, I do. More than you know."

She swallowed. "Look, Dawson, you know I don't want to come back, and you know why. Let's just leave it at that."

His eyes began to glitter. "It's been five years," he said coldly. "You can't live in the past forever!"

"The devil I can't!" she snapped. Her eyes hated him. "I won't forgive you," she whispered, almost choking on the words. "I won't ever, ever forgive you!"

His gaze fell, and his jaw clenched. "I suppose I should

have expected that. But hope springs eternal, don't they say?" He picked up his hat and turned back to her.

She hadn't gotten herself under control at all. Her slender hands were clenched at her sides and her eyes blazed.

He paused just in front of her. At close range, he was much taller than she was. And despite their past, his nearness disturbed her. She took a step backward.

"Do you think I don't have scars of my own?" he asked quietly.

"Men made of ice don't get scars," she managed to say hoarsely.

He didn't say another word. He turned and went toward the door. This wasn't like Dawson. He was giving up without a fight; he didn't even seem bent on insulting her. The very lack of retaliation was new and it disturbed her enough to call to him.

"What's wrong?" she asked abruptly, even as he reached for the doorknob.

The question, intimating concern, stopped him in his tracks. He turned as if he didn't really believe she'd asked that. "What?"

"I asked what was wrong," she repeated. "You aren't yourself."

His hand tightened on the doorknob. "How the hell would you know whether I am or not?" he returned.

"You're holding something back."

He stood there breathing roughly, glaring at her. He shifted, restless, as highly strung as she remembered him. He was a little thinner these days, fine-drawn. His eyes narrowed on her face.

"Are you going to tell me?" she asked him.

"No," he said after a minute. "It wouldn't change anything. I don't blame you for wanting to stay away."

He was hiding something. She knew instinctively that he didn't want to tell her. He seemed vulnerable. It shocked her into moving toward him. The action was so unexpected, so foreign, that it stilled his hand on the doorknob. Barrie hadn't come toward him in five years.

She stopped an arm's length away and looked up at him. "Come on, tell me," she said gently. "You're just like your father, everything has to be dragged out of you. Tell me, Dawson."

He took a deep breath, hesitated, and then just told her.

She didn't understand at first.

"You're what?" she asked.

"I'm impotent!"

She just looked at him. So the gossips weren't talking about a cold nature when they called him the "ice man." They were talking about a loss of virility. She hadn't really believed the rumors she'd heard about him.

"But...how...why?" she asked huskily.

"Who knows?" he asked irritably. "What difference does it make?" He took off his hat and ran a lean hand through his hair. "Mrs. Holton is a determined woman, and she thinks she's God's gift to manhood." His face clenched and he averted it, as if it tormented him to tell her all of it. "I need that damn tract of land, but I have to let her come to Sheridan to talk to me about selling it. She wants me, and she'll find out, if she pushes hard enough, that I'm...incapable. Right now it's just gossip. But she'd make me the news item of the century. Who knows? Maybe that's her real reason for wanting to come in the first place, to check out the gossip."

Barrie was horrified. She moved back to the sofa and sat down, hard. Her face was drawn and pale, like his. It shocked her that he'd tell her such a thing, when she was his worst enemy. It was like offering an armed, angry man a bullet for his gun.

He saw her expression and grew angry. "Say something."

"What could I possibly say?" she whispered.

"So you do have some idea of how devastating it is," he murmured from a rigid face.

She folded her hands in her lap. "Then I'm to run interference for you? Will the threat of a sister stop her?"

"That isn't how you'd come back to Sheridan."

She lifted both eyebrows. "How, then?"

He fished a small velvet box out of his pocket and tossed it to her.

She frowned as she opened it. There were two rings inside, a perfect emerald in a Tiffany setting and a matching wedding band set with diamonds and emeralds.

She actually gasped, and dropped the box as if it were red-hot.

He didn't react, although a shadow seemed to pass over his eyes. "Well, that's a novel way of expressing your feelings," he said sardonically.

"You can't be serious!"

"Why can't I?"

"We're related," she blurted out, flushing.

"Like hell we are. There isn't one mutual relative between us."

"People would talk."

"People sure as hell would," he agreed, "but not about my...condition."

She understood now, as she hadn't before, exactly what he wanted her to do. He wanted her to come back to Sheridan and pretend to be engaged to him, to stop all the gossip. Most especially, he wanted her there to run interference while Mrs. Holton was visiting, so that she wouldn't find out the truth about him in a physical way while he tried to coax her into selling him that vital piece of land. He could kill two birds with one stone.

To think of Dawson as impotent was staggering. She couldn't imagine what had caused it. Perhaps he'd fallen in love. There had been some talk of him mooning over a woman a few years ago, but no name was ever mentioned.

"How long ago did it happen?" she asked without thinking.

He turned and his green eyes were scorching. "That's none of your business."

Her eyebrows arched. "Well, excuse me! Exactly who's doing whom the favor here?"

"It doesn't give you the right to ask me intimate questions. And it isn't as if you won't benefit from getting her to sell me the land."

She flushed and averted her face.

He rammed his hands into his pockets with an angry murmur. "Barrie, it hurts to talk about it," he snapped.

She should have realized that. A man's ego was a surprisingly fragile thing, and if what she'd read and heard was correct, a large part of that ego had to do with his prowess in bed.

"But you could...you did...with me," she blurted out.

He made a rough sound, almost a laugh. "Oh, yes." He sounded bitter. "I did, didn't I? I wish I could forget."

That was surprising. He'd enjoyed what he did to her, or she certainly thought he had. In fact, he'd sounded as if the pleasure was... She shut out the forbidden thoughts firmly.

He bent and retrieved the jewelry box from the floor, balancing it on his palm.

"It's a very pretty set," she remarked tautly. "Did you just buy it?"

"I've had it for...a while." He stared at the box and then shoved it back into his pocket before he looked at her. He didn't ask. He just looked.

She didn't want to go back to Sheridan. She'd learned last night and this morning that she was still vulnerable with him. But the thought of Dawson being made a laughingstock disturbed her. He had tremendous pride and she didn't want that hurt. What if Mrs. Holton did find out about him and went back to Bighorn and spread it around? Dawson might have recourse at law, but what good would that do once the rumors started flying?

She remembered so well the agony her stepfather and Antonia Hayes had suffered over malicious gossip. Dawson must be remembering as well. There was really no way to answer suspicious looks and whispers. He seemed to have had a bad enough time from just the gossip. How would it be for him if everyone knew for certain that he wasn't capable of having sex?

"Barrie?" he prompted curtly.

She sighed. "Only for a week, you said?" she asked, lifting her eyes to surprise a curious stillness in the expression on his lean, handsome face. "And nobody would know about the 'engagement' except Mrs. Holton?"

He studied his boots. "It might have to be in the local papers, to make it sound real." He didn't look at her. "I doubt it would reach as far as Tucson. Even if it did, we could always break the engagement. Later."

This was all very strange and unexpected. She hadn't really had time to think it through. She should hate him. She'd tried to, over the years. But it all came down to basics, and love didn't die or wear out, no matter how viciously a heart was treated. She'd probably go to her grave with Dawson's name on her lips, despite the lost baby he didn't even know about, and the secret grief she'd endured.

"I need my mind examined," she said absently.

"You'll do it?"

She shrugged. "I'll do it."

He didn't say anything for a minute. Then the box came out of his pocket. "You'll have to wear this."

He knelt just in front of her, where she sat on the sofa, and took out the engagement ring.

"But it might not fit…"

She stopped in midstatement as he slid the emerald gently onto her ring finger. It was a perfect fit, as if it had been measured exactly for it.

He didn't say a word. He had her hand in his and, as she watched, he lifted it to his mouth and kissed the ring so tenderly that she stiffened.

He laughed coldly before he lifted his eyes to hers, and if there had been any expression in them, it was gone now. "We might as well do the thing properly, hadn't we?" he asked mockingly, and got gracefully to his feet.

She didn't reply. She still felt his warm mouth on her fingers, as if it were a brand. She looked down at the ring, thinking how perfect the emerald was. Such a flawless stone was easily worth the price of a diamond of equal size.

"Is it synthetic?" she asked absently.

"No. It's not."

She traced around it. "I love emeralds."

"Do you?" he asked carefully.

She lifted her eyes back to his. "I'll take good care of it. The woman you originally bought it for, didn't she want it?" she asked.

His face closed up. "She didn't want me," he replied. "And it's a good thing, considering the circumstances, isn't it?"

He sounded angry. Bitter. Barrie couldn't imagine any sane woman not wanting him. She did, emotionally if not physically. But her responses had been damaged, and he hadn't been particularly kind to her in the aftermath of their one intimacy.

Her eyes on the emerald she asked, "Could you, with her?"

There was a cold pause. "Yes. But she's no longer part of my life, or ever likely to be again."

She recognized the brief flare of anger in his deep voice.

"Sorry," she said lightly. "I won't ask any more questions."

He turned away, his hands back in his pockets again. "I thought I might fly you up to Wyoming today, if you don't have anything pressing. A date, perhaps."

She stared at his back. It was strangely straight, almost rigid. "I had the offer of a date," she admitted, "but I refused it. That's who I thought you were. He said he wouldn't take 'no' for an answer...."

Just as she said that, an insistent buzz came from the doorbell. It was repeated three times in quick succession.

Dawson went toward it.

"Dawson, don't you dare!" she called after him.

It didn't even slow him down. He jerked open the door, to reveal a fairly good-looking young blond man with blue eyes and a pert grin.

"Hi!" he said pleasantly. "Barrie home?"

"She's on her way out of state."

The young man, Phil by name, noticed the glare he was getting and the smile began to waver. "Uh, is she a relative of yours?"

"My fiancée," Dawson said, and his lips curled up in a threatening way.

"Fi...what?" Phil's breath exploded.

Barrie eased around Dawson. "Hi, Phil!" she said gaily. "Sorry, but it only just happened. See?" She held out her ring finger. Dawson hadn't budged. He was still standing there, glaring at Phil.

Phil backed up a step. "Uh, well, congratulations, I'm sure. I'll, uh, see you around, then?"

"No," Dawson replied for her.

Barrie moved in front of him. "Sure, Phil. Have a nice weekend. I'm sorry, okay?"

"Okay. Congratulations again," he added, trying to make the best of an embarrassing situation. He shot one last glance at Dawson and returned down the hall the way he'd come, very quickly.

Dawson muttered something under his breath.

Barrie turned and glowered up at him. "That was unkind," she said irritably. "He was a nice man. You scared him half to death!"

"You belong to me for the duration of our 'engagement,'" he said tautly, searching her eyes. "I won't take kindly to other men hanging around until I settle something about that tract of land."

She drew in a sharp breath. "I promised to pretend to be engaged to you, Dawson," she said uneasily. "That's all. I don't belong to you."

His eyes narrowed even more, and there was an expression in them that she remembered from years past.

He looked as if he wanted to say more, but he hesitated. After a minute, he turned away.

"Are you coming with me now?" he asked shortly.

"I have to close up the apartment and pack…"

"Half an hour's work. Well?"

She hesitated. It was like being snared in a net. She wasn't sure that it was a good idea. If she'd had a day to think about it, she was certain that she wouldn't do it.

"Maybe if we wait until Monday," she ventured.

"No. If you have time to think, you won't come. I'm not letting you off the hook. You promised," he added.

She let out an angry breath. "I must be crazy."

"Maybe I am, too," he replied. His hands balled into fists in his pockets. "It was all I could think of on the spur of the moment. I didn't plan to invite her. She invited herself, bag and baggage, in front of half a dozen people and in such a way that I couldn't extricate myself without creating a lot more gossip."

"There must be other women who would agree to pose as your fiancée," she said.

He shook his head. "Not a one. Or didn't the gossip filter down this far south, Barrie?" he added with bitter sarcasm. "Haven't you heard? It would take a blowtorch, isn't that what they say? Only they don't know the truth of it. They think I'm suffering from a broken heart, doomed to desire the one woman I can't have."

"Are they right?" she asked, glancing at the ring on her finger.

"Sure," he drawled sarcastically. "I'm dying for love of a woman I lost and I can't make it with any other woman. Doesn't it show?"

If it did, it was invisible. She laughed self-consciously. She'd known there were women in Dawson's life for years, but she and Dawson had been enemies for a long time. She was the last person who'd know about a woman he'd given his heart to. Probably it had happened in the years since they'd returned from that holiday in France. God knew, she'd stayed out of his life ever since.

"Did she die?" she asked gently.

His chin lifted. "Maybe she did," he replied. "What difference does it make?"

"None, I guess." She studied his lean face, seeing new lines in it. His blond hair had a trace of silver, just barely visible, at his ears. "Dawson, you're going gray," she said softly.

"I'm thirty-five," he reminded her.

"Thirty-six in September," she added without thinking.

His eyes flashed. He was remembering, as she was, the birthdays when he'd gone out on the town with a succession of beautiful women each year. Once Barrie had tried to give him a present. It was nothing much, just a small silver mouse that she'd saved to buy for him. He'd looked at the present with disdain, and then he'd tossed it to the woman he was taking out that night, to let her enthuse over it. Barrie had never seen it again. She thought he'd probably given it

to his date, because it was obvious that it meant nothing to
him. His reaction had hurt her more than anything in her
life ever did.

"The little cruelties are the worst, aren't they?" he asked,
as if he could see the memory, and the pain, in her mind.
"They add up over the years."

She turned away. "Everyone goes through them," she
said indifferently.

"You had more than most," he said bitterly. "I gave you
hell every day of your young life."

"How are we going to Sheridan?" she asked, trying to
divert him.

He let out a long breath. "I brought the Learjet down
with me."

"It's overcast."

"I'm instrument rated. You know that. Are you afraid to
fly with me?"

She turned. "No."

His eyes, for an instant, were haunted. "At least there's
something about me that doesn't frighten you," he said
heavily. "Go and pack, then. I'll be back for you in two
hours."

He went out the door this time, leaving her to ponder on
that last statement. But she couldn't make any sense of it,
although she spent her packing time trying to.

Three

It was stormy and rain peppered the windscreen of the small jet as Dawson piloted it into his private airstrip at Sheridan. He never flinched nor seemed the least bit agitated at the violent storm they'd flown through just before he set the plane down. He was as controlled in the cockpit as he was behind the wheel of a car and everywhere else. When he'd been fighting the storm, Barrie had seen him smile.

"No butterflies in your stomach?" he taunted when he'd taken off his seat belt.

She shook her head. "You never put a foot wrong when the chips are down," she remarked, without realizing that it might sound like praise.

His pale green eyes searched her face. She looked tired and worried. He wanted to touch her cheek, to bring the color back into her face, the light back into her eyes. But it might frighten her if he reached toward her now. He might have waited too late to build bridges. It was a sobering

thought. So much had changed in his life in just the past
two weeks, and all because of a chance meeting with an old
buddy at a reunion and a leisurely discussion about Tucson,
where the friend, a practicing physician, had worked five
years earlier in a hospital emergency room.

Barrie noticed his scrutiny and frowned. "Is something
wrong?"

"Just about everything, if you want to know," he remarked absently, searching her eyes. "Life teaches hard lessons, little one."

He hadn't called her that, ever. She'd never heard him
use such endearments to anyone in normal conversation.
There was a new tenderness in the way he treated her, a
poignant difference in his whole manner.

She didn't understand it, and she didn't trust it.

A movement caught his eye. "Here comes Rodge," he
murmured, nodding toward the ranch road, where a station
wagon was hurtling toward the airstrip. "Ten to one he's
got Corlie with him."

She smiled. "It's been a long time since I've seen them."

"Not since my father's funeral," he agreed curtly. He
left the cockpit and lowered the steps. He went down them
first and waited to see if she needed help. But she'd worn
sneakers and jeans, not high heels. She went down as if she
were a mountain goat. She'd barely gotten onto the tarmac
when the station wagon stopped and both doors opened.
Corlie, small and wiry and gray-haired, held her arms out.
Barrie ran into them, hungry for the older woman's warm
affection.

Beside her, Rodge shook Dawson's hand and then waited
his turn to give Barrie a hug. He was at least ten years older
than Corlie, and still dark-headed with a few silver streaks.
He was dark-eyed and lean. When he wasn't managing the
ranch in Dawson's absence, he kept busy as Dawson's sec-

retary, making appointments and handling minor business problems.

The two of them had been with the Rutherfords for so long that they were more like family than paid help. Barrie clung to Corlie. She hadn't realized how much she'd missed the woman.

"Child, you've lost weight," Corlie accused. "Too many missed meals and too much fast food."

"You can feed me while I'm here," she said.

"How long are you staying?" Corlie wanted to know.

Before Barrie could answer her and spill the beans, Dawson caught her left hand and held it under Corlie's nose. "This is the main reason she came back," he said. "We're engaged."

"Oh, my goodness," Corlie exclaimed before a shocked Barrie could utter a single word. The older woman's eyes filled with tears. "It's what Mr. Rutherford always prayed would happen, and me and Rodge, too," she added, hugging Barrie all over again. "I can't tell you how happy I am. Now maybe he'll stop brooding so much and smile once in a while," she added with a grimace at Dawson.

Barrie didn't know what to say. She got lost in the enthusiasm of Rodge's congratulations and Dawson's intimidating presence. He must have had a reason for telling them about the false engagement, perhaps to set the stage for Mrs. Holton's arrival. She could ask him later.

Meanwhile, it was exciting to look around and enjoy being back in Sheridan. The ranch wasn't in town, of course, it was several miles outside the city limits. But it had been Dawson's home when she came here, and she loved it because he did. So many memories had hurt her here. She wondered why it was so dear to her in spite of them.

She found herself installed in the back seat of the station wagon with Corlie while Dawson got in under the wheel and talked business with Rodge all the way up to the house.

The Rutherford home was Victorian. This house had been built at the turn of the century, and it replaced a much earlier structure that Dawson's great-grandfather had built. There had been Rutherfords in Sheridan for three generations.

Barrie often wished that she knew as much about her own background as she knew about Dawson's. Her father had died when she was ten, too young to be very curious about heritage. Then when her mother married George Rutherford, who had been widowed since Dawson was very young, she was so much in love with him that she had no time for her daughter. Dawson had been in the same boat. She'd learned a bit at a time that he and his father had a respectful but very strained relationship. George had expected a lot from his son, and affection was something he never gave to Dawson; at least, not visibly. It was as if there was a barrier between them. Her mother had caused the final rift, just by marrying George. Barrie had been caught in the middle and she became Dawson's scapegoat for the new chaos of his life. George's remarriage had shut Dawson out of his father's life for good.

Barrie had tried to talk to Dawson about his mother once, but he'd verbally slapped her down, hard. After that, she'd made sure personal questions were kept out of their conversation. Even today, he didn't like them. He was private, secretive, mysterious.

Rodge took her bags up to her old room on the second floor, and she looked around the hall, past the sliding doors that led to the living room on one side and the study on the other, down to the winding, carpeted staircase. Suspended above the hall was a huge crystal chandelier, its light reflected from a neat black-and-white-tile floor. The interior of the house was elegant and faintly unexpected on a ranch.

"I'd forgotten how big it is," Barrie mused.

"We used to do a lot of entertaining," Corlie reminded her. She glared at Dawson. "Not anymore."

"I'll remember you said that," he replied. "Perhaps we'll throw a party for Mrs. Holton when she gets here."

"That would make a nice change," Corlie said. She winked at Barrie. "But I expect she's going to be something of a nuisance to a newly engaged couple. I'll help run interference."

She smiled and went off to make coffee.

"Oh, dear," Barrie murmured, seeing more complications down the road.

Dawson shoved his hands into his pockets and searched her face. "Don't worry," he said. "It will all work out."

"Will it?" She grimaced. "What if Mrs. Holton sees right through us?"

He moved a little closer, near enough that she could feel the warmth of his body. "Neither of us is used to touching or being touched," he remarked when she stiffened. "That may be awkward."

She remembered how he'd pushed away the woman at the party in Tucson. Barrie was afraid to come that close, but they were supposed to be engaged and it would look unnatural if they never touched each other.

"What are we going to do?" she asked miserably.

He sighed heavily. "I don't know," he said honestly. Slowly his hand went out, and he touched her long, wavy dark hair. His fingers were just a little awkward. "Maybe we'll improve with some practice."

She bit her lower lip. "I...hate being touched," she whispered in a rough whisper.

He winced.

She lowered her eyes to his chest. "Didn't you notice, at the party? I had two men at my feet, but did you see how much distance there was between us? It's always like that. I don't even dance anymore...!"

His hand withdrew from her hair and fell to his side.

"God forgive me," he said miserably. "I don't think I can ever forgive myself."

Her eyes came up, shocked. He'd never admitted guilt, or fault before. Something must have happened to change him. But what?

"We'll have to spend some time together before she gets here," he said slowly. "And get to know each other a little better. We might try holding hands. Just to get used to the feel of each other."

Tentative. Like children on a first date. She wondered why she was being so whimsical, and smiled.

He smiled back. For the first time in recent memory, it was without malice or mockery.

"Antonia said that Mrs. Holton was very attractive," she remarked.

"She is," he agreed. "But she's cold, Barrie. Not physically, but emotionally. She likes to possess men. I don't think she's capable of deep feelings, unless it's for money. She's very aggressive, single-minded. She'd have made a good corporate executive, except that she's lazy."

"Did her husband leave her well-fixed?" she asked curiously.

"No. That's why she's trying to find a man to keep her."

She bristled. "She ought to go back to school and keep herself," she said shortly.

He laughed softly. "That's what you did," he agreed. "You wouldn't even take an allowance from George. Or from me."

She flushed, averting her eyes. "The Rutherfords put me through college. That was more than enough."

"Barrie, I never thought your mother married my father for his money," he said, reading the painful thought in her mind. "She loved him, just as he loved her."

"That wasn't what you said."

His eyes closed. "And you can't forget, can you? I can't

blame you. I was so full of hatred and resentment that I lashed out constantly. You were the most easily reachable…and the most vulnerable.'' His eyes opened again, cold with self-contempt. ''You paid for every sin I accused your mother of committing.''

''And how you enjoyed making me pay,'' she replied huskily.

He looked away, as if the pain in her eyes hurt him. ''Yes, I did,'' he confessed bluntly. ''For a while. Then we went to the Riviera on holiday with George.''

She couldn't think about that. She didn't dare let herself think about it. She moved away from him. ''I should unpack.''

''Don't go,'' he protested. ''Corlie's making coffee. She'll probably have cake to go with it.''

She hesitated. Her big green eyes lifted to his, wary and uncertain.

His face hardened. ''I won't hurt you,'' he said roughly. ''I give you my word.''

He was old-fashioned that way. If he made a promise, he kept it. But why should he stop sniping at her now, and so suddenly? Her eyes mirrored all her uncertainties, all her doubts.

''What's changed?'' she asked miserably.

''*I've* changed,'' he replied firmly.

''You suddenly woke up one morning and decided that you'd give up an eleven-year vendetta?''

He searched over her face with an enigmatic expression on his darkly tanned face. ''No. I discovered how much I'd lost,'' he said, his voice taut with some buried feeling. ''Have you ever thought that sometimes our whole lives pivot on one decision? On a lost letter or a telephone call that doesn't get made?''

''No, I don't suppose I have, really,'' she replied.

"We live and learn. And the lessons get more expensive with age."

"You're very reflective, lately," she said, curious. A strand of hair fell over her eyes, and she pushed it back from her face. "I don't think in all the time we've known each other that we've really talked, until the past day or so."

"Yes. I know." He sounded bitter. He turned away from her to lead the way into the spacious living room. It had changed since she'd lived on the Rutherford ranch. This was the very room where Dawson had so carelessly tossed the little silver mouse she'd given him to his date. But it wasn't the same at all. The furniture was different, Victorian and sturdy in its look, but wonderful to sink into.

"This room doesn't look like you at all," she remarked as she perched herself in a delicate-looking wing chair that was surprisingly comfortable.

"It isn't supposed to," he replied. He sat down on the velvet-covered sofa. "I hired a decorator to do it."

"What did you tell her, that you wanted to adopt someone's grandmother and install her here?" she asked.

He lifted an eyebrow. "In case you didn't notice, the house is late Victorian. And I thought you liked Victorian furniture," he added.

She shifted, running her hand along the arm of the chair. "I love it," she confessed in a subdued tone. Questions poised on the tip of her tongue, and she almost asked them, but Corlie came in with a tray of cake and coffee, beaming.

"Just what the doctor ordered," she said smugly, putting the tray on the big coffee table.

"Great huge coffee tables aren't Victorian," Barrie muttered.

"Sure they are. Victorians drank coffee," Corlie argued.

"They drank tea," she replied, "and out of dainty little china cups and saucers."

"They also ate cucumber sandwiches," Corlie returned. "Want a few?"

Barrie made a face. "I'll be quiet about the coffee table if you won't offer me those again."

"It's a deal. Call if you need anything else." Corlie went out, closing the sliding doors behind her.

She helped herself to coffee and cake and so did he. As always he took his coffee black while Barrie put cream and sugar in hers.

"Antonia said that you'd been offered a job heading the math department at your high school next fall," he remarked. "Are you going to take it?"

She looked up over the rim of her coffee cup. "I don't know," she replied. "I love teaching. But that job is mostly administrative. It would take away the time I had with my students, and plenty of them require extra tutoring."

He searched her down-bent face. "You…like children, don't you?"

"Oh, yes." She toyed with her coffee cup, trying not to think about the child they'd made, the one she'd lost so many years ago.

He sat, waiting, hoping that she might finally decide to tell him her secrets. But the moment passed. She went right on eating cake and drinking coffee, and she didn't make another remark. He was hesitant about bringing it up himself. They had a long way to go before she might feel comfortable talking about something so intimate and painful with him.

He changed the subject and conversation reverted to impersonal topics. He went into his study to make some phone calls and she went upstairs to unpack.

She wondered at the change in him, but she was still too raw from the past to let her guard down.

Supper was a cheerful affair, with Rodge and Corlie sitting at the table with Barrie and a taciturn Dawson. They talked. He listened. He seemed preoccupied, and he excused himself to work in the study. He didn't come back, even when Barrie said good-night to Corlie and Rodge and went up to her old room to go to bed.

She lay awake for a long time. Being in the house again brought back memories, so many memories, of Dawson and his antagonism. Then, inevitably, her mind went to the Riviera....

It had been a beautiful summer day. Sea gulls had dived and pitched above the white beach where Barrie sat on a big beach blanket and worried about her conservative appearance. Many people were nude. Most of the women were topless. Nobody seemed to pay the least attention, either.

Barrie wanted to sunbathe without white lines, but she was inhibited at twenty-one, and a little intimidated by Dawson in his white trunks. He was exquisite, and she couldn't keep her eyes off him. A thick thatch of curly gold hair, darker than that on his head, covered his broad chest and narrowed down his flat stomach into his trunks. Long, elegantly powerful legs had the same tan as the rest of his body. She imagined that he normally sunbathed without any trunks at all, although she didn't know for sure.

The path of her thoughts embarrassed her and she averted her eyes. But her hands toyed with the ties of her bikini top as she thought daringly how it would be to let it fall, to know that Dawson's gaze was on her bare breasts. She shivered with just the thought of it, and wished she were sophisticated and chic like his usual companions, that she had the nerve just once to do something outrageous and shocking.

She'd glanced at him in what might have seemed a coquettish way as her fingers toyed with the straps and she'd smiled nervously.

Dawson hadn't realized how inhibited she was. He'd formed the idea that Barrie was a born flirt, that she collected men. He'd always seen her shy attempts at affection as deliberate coquetry, because it was the sort of game the sophisticated women he knew played.

So when Barrie had darted that curious glance at him, he'd thought she wanted him to coax her into taking off the top. And because she had a lovely young body, and he wanted very much to look at it, he'd played along.

"Go ahead," he'd murmured in a deep, tender voice. "Untie it, Barrie. I want to look at you."

She remembered looking into his eyes and seeing the lazy sensuality in them, the calculating narrowness of them.

"Why the hesitation?" he'd taunted. "You're drawing attention because you're being so damned conservative. None of the other women have any hang-ups about their bodies."

He nodded toward two young women about Barrie's age, dancing along the beach with only bikini bottoms covering their womanliness.

She bit her lip, hesitating, turned just sideways from him, toward the beach.

He'd been beside her, facing her on his knees, his lean hands resting on his muscular thighs. "Barrie?" he'd coaxed softly. And when she looked at him his voice softened and deepened. "Take it off."

He hypnotized her with forbidden longings, with long-buried needs. Her hands fumbled with the single tie at the back of her neck and she loosened it. Her fingers reached around to the other single fastening under her shoulder blades. She looked into his pale green eyes, trembling with new sensations, flushing at the enormity of what she was doing. And she let the top fall away.

She remembered even now the feel of his eyes, the soft intake of his breath as he'd looked at her. She had high, firm, full breasts, pale pink, with darker pink crowns that went rigid under the impact of his level gaze.

She trembled helplessly as he looked his fill. There was a dark flush along his high cheekbones, and he made no pretence of not staring.

Unexpectedly his eyes lifted to hold hers. Whatever he'd seen there must have told him what he wanted to know, because he'd made a sound deep in his throat and stood up. He seemed to vibrate with some violent emotion. Suddenly he'd bent and slipped his arms under her knees and her back and lifted her off the sand. His eyes stared into hers as he slowly, exquisitely, brought her upper body to his so that her breasts flattened gently in the thick hair that covered his broad chest. His skin was as cool from the breeze as hers was hot from the feelings he aroused in her virginal body. She'd stiffened at the shock of the contact.

"No one is looking," he said roughly. "No one gives a damn. Put your arms around me and come closer."

It was shocking, the need she felt. She obeyed him, forgetting her shyness as she ached to feel his body against hers. She remembered burying her hot face in his throat, drinking in the scent of him, feeling his heavy, harsh pulse against her bare breasts as his arms tightened and he walked toward the water with her.

"Wh…why?" She choked.

"Because I'm so damned aroused that I can't hide it," he said half angrily. "The only escape is right into the ocean. Or don't you feel it, too, Barrie? A burning deep in your belly, an emptiness that wants filling, an ache that hurts?"

Her arms contracted and she moaned softly.

"Yes, you feel it," he breathed as he began to wade into the water. His face slid against hers and his mouth suddenly opened as it sought and found her parted lips. She didn't remember the shock of the water. There was nothing in life except that first, burning sweetness of Dawson's hard mouth on her lips, nothing more than the feel of him in her arms, against her bare breasts.

Vaguely she was aware that they were in the warm water, that his arms had released her so that he could pull her into an even more intimate embrace. His long legs tangled with hers, and for the first time, she felt the force of his desire for her. They kissed and kissed, there in the water, oblivious to the whole world, to the line of hotels above the shore, the other swimmers, the noise on the beach.

He moved her, just enough to let his lean hand find and swallow one swollen breast. His tongue eased into her open mouth. His free hand lifted and pulled her, fit her exactly to the hard thrust of him. And she almost lost consciousness at the stabbing ache of pleasure he kindled in her trembling body, there in the water, there in the blue ocean....

She fell asleep with the memories deep in her mind. Unfortunately, those sweet memories merged with some that were much darker. Dawson had finally gained temporary control of himself, and left her alone in the sea to recover from their feverish embraces. But all through the evening meal with George, he'd watched Barrie with eyes that made her feel hunted. The idiotic way she'd smiled at him and encouraged his watchfulness could still make her cringe. She'd thought he was falling in love with her, and she was doing her best to show him that she already felt that way about him. She'd had no idea how he was interpreting her shy flirting.

But it had all become clear after she'd gone to bed that night. The sliding door on her balcony had opened and Dawson had come through it. He'd been wearing a robe and nothing else. Barrie remembered the sweep of his hand as he tore the sheet away from her body, clad only in thin briefs because of the heat and the failing air-conditioning. Her body had reacted at once to his eyes, and even the shock and faint fear hadn't robbed her of the desire that was all too visible to a man of Dawson's experience.

"Want me, Barrie?" he'd whispered as he threw off his robe and joined her on the bed. "Let's see how well you follow up on those teasing little glances you've been giving me all night."

She hadn't had the presence of mind to explain that she hadn't been teasing him. She wanted to tell him that she loved him, that he was her life. But his hands on her body were shocking, like the things he whispered to her in the moonlight, like the feel of his mouth surging over her taut breasts while he made love to her as if he were some demon of the night.

If she'd been the experienced woman he thought her, it would have been a night to remember. But she'd been a virgin, and he'd been completely out of control. She remembered the faint tremor in the hands that had gathered her hips up to the fierce thrust of his body, his cry of pleasure that drowned out her cry of pain. He whispered to her all through it, his body as insistent as his mouth, his hands, until finally he arched up as though he were on some invisible rack, his powerful body cording with ripple after ripple of ecstasy until he convulsed with hoarse, fierce cries and his hands hurt her.

She felt no such pleasure. Her body felt torn and violated. She was almost sick with the pain that had never seemed to stop. When he pulled away from her finally, exhausted and sweaty, she winced and cried out, because that hurt, too.

She wept, curled into a ball, while he got to his feet and put his robe back on. He'd looked down at her sobbing form with eyes she couldn't see, and she didn't like remembering the things he'd said to her then. His voice had been as brutal as his invasion of her, and she'd been far too innocent to realize that he was shocked and upset by her innocence, hitting out to disguise his own stark guilt. It could have been

so different if he'd loved her. But in the darkness of her
dream, he was a bird of prey, tearing at her flesh, hurting
her, hurting her…

She didn't realize that she'd screamed. She heard the door
open and close, felt light against her eyelids, and then felt
hands shaking her.

"Barrie. Barrie!"

She came awake with a start, and the face above her was
Dawson's. He was wearing a robe, as he had been that night.
His hair was damp from a shower, and her mind reverted
to the night she'd spent in his arms in France.

"Don't…hurt me…anymore!" she whispered, sobbing.

He didn't reply. He couldn't. The terror in those eyes
made him sick right through to his soul. "Dear God," he
breathed.

Four

Barrie saw his face contort and as she came back to awareness, she noticed the room around her, the light fixture overhead. "It's…not France," She choked. Her eyes closed. "Oh, thank God, thank God!"

Dawson got up from the bed and moved to the window. He moved the curtain aside and looked out into the darkness. He wasn't looking at anything. He was seeing the past, the horror in Barrie's eyes, the pain that he'd caused.

Barrie sat up. She noticed his lean hand clenching the curtains. It had gone white. He looked beaten, exhausted.

She swallowed hard. Her hands went to her pale cheeks and smoothed over them and then pushed back the tangled dark hair that fell over her breasts. She was wearing a long cotton gown that completely covered her except for her arms and a little of her slender neck. She never slept just in her briefs these days, not even in summer.

"I didn't realize that you still had nightmares about it,"

he said after a minute. His voice was dull and without expression.

"Not very often," she said. She couldn't tell him that most of them ended with her losing the baby, crying out for Dawson. That hadn't happened tonight, thank God. She couldn't bear for him to know it all.

He turned away from the window and moved back to the side of the bed, but not close. His hands closed in the pockets of his robe.

"It wouldn't be that way a second time," he said stiffly. Her eyes widened in fear, as if he'd suggested seducing her all over again. The realization infuriated him, but he controlled the surge of anger. "Not...with me." He bit off the words, averting his face. "I didn't mean that."

She drew her knees up and wrapped her arms around them. The sound of the fabric sliding against her skin was abnormally loud. She glanced up at him and the memories began to recede. If she was hurting, so was he. He couldn't fake the sort of pain she saw in his drawn face.

"Haven't you even been curious since then, for God's sake?" he asked. "You're a woman. You must have friends, people you could ask. Surely someone told you that first times are notoriously bad."

She smoothed one hand over the other. Her body slumped with a long sigh. "I can't talk to anyone about it," she said finally. "I only have one best friend. And how could I possibly ask Antonia, when she's known us both for years? She wouldn't need two guesses to figure out why I was asking."

He nodded. "You were a virgin. You needed time to be properly aroused, especially with me, and I lost control much too soon," he added. His eyes searched her face grimly. "That was a first for me. Until you came along, there had never been a woman who could throw me off-balance in bed."

Her face lowered. It was an accomplishment of sorts, she supposed.

"I damaged both of us that night," he said gently. "Until I had you, I genuinely thought you were experienced, Barrie, that you were only teasing on the beach when you had to be coaxed into removing your top."

That brought her eyes up to his, shocked. "But I would never have done such a thing!" she protested.

"I had to find that out the hard way," he replied. "Maybe I used it as an excuse, too. I wanted you and I convinced myself that you'd surely had men at your age, that it had all been playacting on your part, all that coy shyness. But it didn't take me long to realize why you'd given in without a struggle. You loved me," he said huskily.

Her eyes closed. She couldn't bear to hear him say it again. He'd taunted her with her feelings after that disastrous night.

She felt the bed depress as he sat down slowly beside her. His hand tipped her head back toward his, making her look at him. "Guilt will drive a man to violence, Barrie," he said, his voice deep and soft in the silence of her room. "Especially when he's done something unforgivable and knows he'll never find forgiveness for it. I taunted you because I couldn't live with what I'd done to you. It doesn't make much sense, now. But at the time, blaming you was the only thing that kept me from putting a gun to my head."

She hadn't said a word. Her big eyes were locked into his as she struggled to understand him.

"I couldn't stop." He took an unsteady breath. "God, Barrie, I tried. I tried. But I couldn't...stop." He leaned forward, his head down bent, defeated. "For months after it happened, I could hear your voice in my nightmares. I knew I was hurting you, but I couldn't draw back."

She didn't understand desire of that sort, pleasure too blind to feel pity. She'd never felt it, although the way he'd kissed her in the ocean had made her hungry for something. "I wanted you, too."

He lifted his head and looked down at her. "You don't understand, do you?" he asked gently. "You've never felt desire that overwhelming. Your only knowledge of real intimacy is forever embedded in pain."

"I didn't know you had nightmares," she said slowly.

"I still have them," he said on a cold laugh. "Just like you."

Her gaze went over his face like searching hands. "Why did you come to my room that night?" she asked softly.

He moved, one long arm going across her body to support him as he leaned closer, so that his face filled her entire line of vision. "Because I wanted you so much that I would have died to have you," he said through his teeth.

The subdued violence in the flat statement surprised her. Perhaps she'd known on some unspoken level how desperately hungry he'd been for her, but he'd never actually said the words before.

"I wanted you so much that I was almost sick with it. I came to you because I couldn't stop myself. And it does no good whatsoever five years after the fact to tell you that I'm sorry."

"*Are* you sorry?" she asked sadly.

He nodded, without blinking an eye. "Sorry. Bitter. Hurt. All the things you were. But there was more to it than just physical pain on your part." He didn't move. He didn't seem to breathe. He took a slow, deliberate breath. "You never told me that I gave you a baby that night. Or that, several weeks later, you lost it. Did you think I wouldn't find out, someday?" he concluded heavily, the pain lying dark and dull in his eyes as he saw the shock register on her face.

Her heart skipped and ran away. "I...how did you find out?" she faltered. "I never even told Antonia!"

"Do you remember the intern who attended to you in the emergency room?"

"Yes. Richard Dean," she recalled. "He'd been a student in your graduating class. But you never saw him, he even said that you didn't mix socially. Besides, he was a doctor, he took an oath never to talk about his patients…!"

"We met at a class reunion a few weeks ago," he confided. "He thought I knew. You're my stepsister, after all, he reminded me. He assumed that you'd told me."

She gnawed her lower lip, staring up at him worriedly.

His lean hand came to touch her mouth, disturbing the grip of her teeth. "Don't," he said softly.

"I forget sometimes," she murmured.

His thumb traced over her mouth gently. He searched her eyes. "He said…that you were utterly devastated," he whispered. "That you cried until he had to sedate you." His face drew up with bitterness. "He said you wanted the baby desperately, Barrie."

She dragged her eyes down to his chest. "It was a long time ago." Her voice sounded stiff.

He let out a heavy breath. "Yes, and you've done your grieving. But I've only just started. I didn't know until Richard told me. It's been a little rough, losing a child I didn't even know I'd helped create."

His face was averted, but she could see the pain on it. It was the first time they'd really shared grief, except when his father had died. But that had only been a few words, because she couldn't stand to be near him so soon after the Riviera.

"Would you have told me?" he asked, staring at the wall.

"I'm not sure. It seemed senseless, after so long a time. You didn't know about the baby. I wasn't sure you'd want to know."

He caught her slender hand in his and linked his fingers with it. "I got drunk and stayed drunk for three days after

I got back from my class reunion," he said after a minute. Then he added, expressionlessly, "Richard said that you asked a nurse to call me from the emergency room."

She stared at the big hand holding hers so closely. "Yes, in a moment of madness."

"I didn't know she was a nurse. She mentioned your name and before she could say why she was calling, I hung up on her."

His fingers had tightened painfully. "Yes," she said.

He drew her hand to his lips and kissed it hungrily.

His head was bent over her hand, but she saw the faint wetness at the corner of his eye and she gasped, horrified.

As if his pride wouldn't take that sort of blow, letting her see the wetness in his eyes, he let go of her fingers and got up, going back to stand at the darkened window. He didn't speak for a full minute, his hand gripping the curtain tightly. "Richard said it was a boy."

She rested her forehead against her knees. "Please," she whispered gruffly. "I can't talk about it."

He moved from the window, back to the bed. He tore the covers away and scooped her up into his arms, sitting down to hold her tight, tight, across his legs, with his face against her soft throat.

"I've got you," he whispered roughly. "You're safe. Nothing will ever hurt you again. Cry for him. God knows I have!"

The tender gruffness in his deep voice broke the dam behind which her tears had hidden. She gave way to them, for the first time since the miscarriage. She wept for the son she'd lost. She wept for her pain, and for his. She wept for all the lost, lonely years.

A long time later, she felt him dabbing at her eyes with a corner of the sheet. She took it from him and finished the job. And still he held her, gently, without passion. Her cheek felt the regular, hard beat of his heart under the soft fabric of the robe. She opened her hot, stinging eyes and stared across at the dark window, all the fire and pain wept out of her in salty tears.

"It's late," he said finally. "Mrs. Holton arrives first thing in the morning. You need to get some sleep."

She stretched, boneless from exhaustion, and looked up into his quiet, watchful eyes. Involuntarily his own gaze went down to the soft thrust of her breasts under the cotton gown. He remembered the beauty of her body, years after his last glimpse of it.

She watched him staring at her, but she didn't move or flinch.

"Don't you want to run?" he taunted.

She shook her head. Her eyes looked straight up into his. She slid her fingers over the lean, strong hand that was lying across her waist. She tugged at it until it lifted. She smoothed it up her side, over her rib cage, and then gently settled it directly over one soft breast.

His intake of breath was audible, and his body seemed to jump.

"No," he said curtly, jerking his hand down to her waist. "Don't be stupid."

She felt less confident than she had before, but there was a faint film of sweat over his upper lip. He was more shaken than he looked.

"Don't make me ashamed. It's hard for me, to even think of this, much less…do it," she said. "I only wanted to know if I could let you touch me," she finished with a rueful smile.

The cold hauteur left him. "I can't take the risk, even if you're willing to." He started to move her aside, but she clung.

"What risk?" she asked.

"Don't you know? You don't need to find out the hard

way that I can still want you." He laughed coldly. "I'm not sure I want to know, either."

While she was working that one out, he lifted her and placed her gently onto the pillows. He got up and moved back from the bed. "Go to sleep."

"What if you could…want me?" she persisted, levering up on her elbows.

He looked unutterably weary. "Barrie, we both know that you'd scream the minute I touched you with intent," he said. "You couldn't help it. And even if I could feel anything with you, it might be just the way it was before. I might lose my head again, hurt you again."

"I'm not a virgin anymore," she said without thinking.

His face was quiet, expressionless as he looked down at her. "It's a moot point. My body is dead, as far as sex is concerned. For both our sakes, let well enough alone. It's too soon for experimenting."

Before she could speak, he'd gone out the door, closing it behind him with a firm snap. Barrie lay back, turning what he'd said over in her mind.

He knew, finally, about the baby they'd lost. She didn't know if she was sorry or glad, but it had been cathartic to have it all out in the open. He grieved for their child, at least, as she did. But he had nothing to give her, and she still loved him. It was a problem that had no easy resolution, and in the morning a new complication was due to present itself. She wondered how she was going to react to the widow Holton. It would be an interesting introduction, at the very least.

Leslie Holton blew in the next morning like a redheaded tornado, driving a brand-new shiny black Jaguar. Peering through the lacy curtains in the living room when she drove up, Barrie couldn't help thinking that the car suited her. Mrs. Holton was sleek and dangerous-looking, a powerhouse no less than the car she drove. She was wearing a black-and-white suit. Its starkness made her pale skin even paler and presented a backdrop for her fiery hair. Wickedly Barrie wondered how much of it came out of a bottle, because the widow was obviously over twenty-one. Way over.

She went out into the hall and met up with Dawson who had just come out of his study. There were dark circles under his eyes. He appeared worn, as if he hadn't slept. He looked across at Barrie, and she realized that he hadn't slept at all.

She moved toward him. Last night had calmed some old terrors, the way they'd talked had changed things in some subtle way. She stopped in front of him and looked up.

"You haven't had any sleep," she said gently.

His face hardened. "Don't push your luck."

Her eyebrows lifted. "Am I?"

"Looking at me like that is chancy."

She smiled. "What will you do?" she chided.

Something equally reckless flared in his pale eyes. "Want to see?"

He moved forward with an economy of motion to scoop her up against his chest. He held her there, searching her eyes at point-blank range.

Her arms tightened around his strong neck and she looked back at him curiously. He'd wanted the baby, too. That knowledge had changed the way she envisioned him. Even though there was some residual fear of him in her, the memory of the grief she'd seen in his face last night tempered it.

"Doesn't anybody hear the doorbell ringing?" Corlie muttered as she came out of the kitchen and suddenly spotted Dawson holding Barrie off the floor in his arms. "Well, excuse me." She chuckled, sparing them a wicked glance as she went toward the front door.

Barrie started to speak but Dawson shook his head. "Don't disillusion her," he whispered. "Let her hope."

Something in the way he said it made her look at him curiously. His pale eyes fell to her mouth and he hesitated.

"If you wanted to kiss me, you could," she said boldly. "I mean, I wouldn't scream or anything."

"Cheeky brat," he muttered, but he was still looking at her mouth.

"I can always tell when you've been on a trip to the station in Australia," she whispered.

"Can you?" His head bent closer, his mouth threatening her soft lips. His arms contracted a little. Somewhere in the distance, a stringent voice was demanding that Corlie have someone get luggage out of the Jaguar.

"Yes," she whispered at his lips. "You always come back using Aussie slang."

He chuckled softly.

Barrie felt the vibration of his laughter all the way to her toes. It was the old magic, without the fear. She loved him. His arms were warm and strong and safe, and her hands clasped together behind his neck. She lifted herself closer to that hard, beautiful mouth and parted her lips.

"No self-preservation left, Barrie?" he whispered huskily. His own lips parted and moved down slowly. "Baby," he breathed into her mouth. "Baby, baby…!"

The pressure became slow and soft and insistent. It began to deepen and she caught her breath, anticipating the hunger that she could already taste…

"Dawson!"

Their faces jerked apart. Dawson stared at the newcomer just for a moment with eyes that didn't quite focus. "Leslie," he said then. "Welcome to White Ridge." He lowered Barrie gently to her feet and, keeping a possessive arm around her, held his hand out to Leslie.

Mrs. Holton made an indignant sound. "Hello, Dawson,"

she said impatiently. "My goodness, isn't that your stepsister?"

"She was," Dawson replied coolly. "Yesterday, she became my fiancée. We're engaged."

Mrs. Holton was clearly surprised. "But isn't that against the law?"

"Barrie and I aren't blood-related in any way," he said. "My father married her mother."

"Oh." Leslie stared at Barrie, who grinned at her. "I'm glad to meet you, Miss Rutherford."

"Bell," Barrie corrected her, extending a hand. She was quivering inside, all raw nerves and excitement. "Barrie Bell."

"I didn't expect this," Mrs. Holton said. She eyed Dawson carefully. "Of course, it's very sudden, isn't it?" She smiled with feline calculation. "In fact, I seem to remember hearing that the two of you didn't even speak. When did that change?"

"Yesterday," Dawson said, unperturbed. He looked down at Barrie. "It was sudden, all right. Like a bolt of lightning." His eyes fell to her soft mouth as he said it, and she caught her breath at the surge of feeling the stare provoked.

Leslie Holton wasn't blind, but she was determined. "You do, uh, still want to discuss my tract of land near Bighorn?" she asked with a calculating smile.

"Of course," Dawson replied, and he smiled back. "That was the purpose of your visit, wasn't it?"

She shrugged a thin shoulder. "Well, yes, among other things. I do hope you're going to show me around the ranch while I'm here. I'm very interested in livestock."

"Barrie and I will be delighted, won't we, baby?" he added with a glance at Barrie that made her toes curl.

She pressed close to his side, shocked at her surge of

hunger to be near him. It was equally shocking to hear his faint breath and feel his arm tighten around her shoulders.

"Certainly," she said. She smiled at Mrs. Holton, but she sounded, and felt, breathless.

"Corlie will show you to your room, and Rodge will bring your bags right up," Dawson said. "I'll be right back." He let go of Barrie with a smile and went to call Rodge on the intercom.

"You teach, don't you?" Mrs. Holton asked Barrie. "You must be on summer vacation."

"Yes, I am. What do you do?" Barrie shot right back.

"Do? My dear, I'm rich," Leslie said with hauteur. "I don't have to work for a living." Her eyes narrowed with calculation. "And neither will you after you marry Dawson. Is that why you're marrying him?"

"Of course," she murmured wickedly. She glanced at Dawson, who was just coming out of the study again. "Dawson, you do know that I'm only marrying you for your money, don't you?" she asked, raising her voice.

He chuckled. "Sure."

Leslie was confused. She looked from one of them to the other. "What a very odd couple you are."

"You have no idea," Barrie murmured dryly.

"Amen," he added.

"Well, I'll just slip upstairs and rest for a few minutes, if you don't mind," Leslie said. "It's been a long, tiring drive." She paused in front of Dawson and smiled up at him seductively. "I might even soak in the hot tub for a little while. If you'd like to wash my back, you're welcome," she added teasingly.

Dawson didn't reply. He just smiled.

Leslie glowered at him, glanced at Barrie irritably and followed an impatient Corlie up the staircase.

Barrie moved closer to him. "Do we have hot water, or is it still subject to fits of temperament in the spring?"

"We have bucketsful of hot water," he replied. "And a whirlpool bath in every bathroom." He looked down at her. "One of them holds two people."

She had mental images of being naked in it with Dawson, and her face paled. She withdrew from him without making a single move.

He tilted her chin up to his eyes. "I'm sorry. That could have been less crude."

She sighed. "It's early days yet," she said apologetically.

"Very early days." He pushed back her long, soft hair. "You let me kiss you," he added quietly. "Was it all an act, for her benefit?" He jerked his head toward the staircase.

"I don't act that well."

"Neither do I." His gaze fell to her mouth. "If we make haste slowly, we may discover that things fall into place."

"Things?"

He touched the very tip of her nose with his forefinger. "We might get rid of our scars."

She was worried, and looked it. "I don't know if I can—" she began uncertainly.

"That makes two of us," he said interrupting her.

She grimaced. "Sorry."

His chest rose and fell heavily. "One day at a time."

"Okay."

They took Leslie Holton riding that afternoon. She was surprisingly good on a horse, lithe and totally without fear. She seemed right at home on the ranch. If only she hadn't been making eyes at Dawson, Barrie could have enjoyed her company.

But Leslie Holton wanted Dawson, and she was working on ways to get him. The sudden engagement was very strange and she knew for a fact that Dawson had a reputation for avoiding women altogether. She thought Barrie was helping him put on an act, and if it took her every minute of her time here, she was going to unmask them. If Dawson really was cold, Leslie was going to find out why before she left.

Five

Unaware of Leslie Holton's plotting, Barrie was trying to concentrate on what Dawson was telling them about the history of the area they were riding through. But her eyes kept straying to the tall, proud way he rode, as if he were part of the horse. He looked good on horseback.

He looked good any way at all.

He caught her staring and smiled gently. Her heart skipped beats. He'd never been this way with her in all the time they'd known each other, and she couldn't believe he was faking it. There was a new tenderness in his eyes. He didn't talk to her in the old, mocking way. If she was different, so was he.

And through it all, there was an attraction that had its roots in the past. But Barrie was still afraid of intimacy with him. It was one thing to kiss him and hold hands with him. It was quite another to think of him in bed with her, demanding, insistent, totally out of control, hurting her…!

He glanced at her and saw that flash of fear, understood it without a word being spoken.

As Leslie rode ahead, he fell back beside Barrie. "Don't brood on it," he said seriously. "There's no rush. Give it time."

She sighed as she glanced toward him. "Reading my mind?"

"It isn't that difficult," he told her.

She toyed with the reins. "Time won't help," she said miserably. "I'm still afraid."

"My God, what is there to be afraid of?" he asked shortly. "Didn't you hear what I told you? I meant it. I can't, Barrie. I can't!"

She searched his eyes slowly. "You can't with other women," she corrected.

"I can't with you, either," he muttered. "Hell, don't you think I'd know after last night?"

She glanced warily ahead where Leslie was riding. "Last night you were holding back," she said.

"Yes, I was," he admitted. "You'd just had a nightmare and you were terrified. I didn't want to make it worse. But even this morning," he said heavily, averting his eyes to the horizon. His broad shoulders rose and fell. He couldn't bring himself to admit that even the hungry kiss he'd started to share with Barrie hadn't been able to arouse him.

Barrie noticed his reticence and kept her silence. She glanced around at the budding trees. Spring was her favorite season, although it certainly came later to Wyoming than it did to Arizona, even if May was basically the same in both places. Closer than the budding trees, however, was the irritated way Leslie Holton was glaring back at them.

"We aren't fooling her, you know," she said suddenly, and lifted her eyes to search his. "She thinks we're pretending."

"Aren't we?" he asked with a bitter laugh.

She supposed they were. Only it hadn't felt like pretense that morning on her part.

"That was a bald-faced lie," he murmured after a minute, and the saddle leather creaked as he reined in his horse and turned to look at her. His eyes were level and penetrating. "Suppose we try."

She felt her eyes widen. "Try...?"

"What you suggested last night. Or have you already forgotten where you put my hand?" he asked outrageously.

"Dawson!"

"You should look shocked. That was how I felt."

"That's right," she agreed, "pretend it was the first time a woman ever offered you any such thing!"

He managed a wistful smile. It had been a very long time since he'd been able to laugh about his body's lack of interest in women. "I can't," he admitted.

"That doesn't surprise me."

He drew up one long leg and wrapped it around the pommel, straining his powerful muscles against the thick fabric of his designer jeans. He leaned against it to study her, pigtailed and wearing similar clothing, jeans and a loose shirt. "You don't wear revealing clothes around me."

She shrugged. "No. Because I don't have to fight you off."

He cocked an eyebrow inquiringly.

She grimaced. "Well, men come on to me all the time, and I don't want any sort of physical relationship. So I flaunt my figure and flirt and talk about how much my family wants to see me get married and have a big family. You'd be amazed at how fast they find excuses to stop seeing me."

He chuckled. "Suppose someday a man calls your bluff?"

"That hasn't ever happened."

"Hasn't it?"

She realized what he meant, and her cheeks burned.

"I don't suppose I even bothered to tell you that I'd never seen a body more perfect," he continued quietly. "Barrie, undressed, you could pose for the Venus de Milo. I'm not sure that you wouldn't make her jealous."

She wasn't sure if it was a compliment or a dig, because their relationship had shifted in the past two days.

"I mean it," he explained, so that there wasn't any doubt. "And if I were still the man I was five years ago, you'd need a dead bolt on your door."

She searched his eyes. "I suppose at one time or another someone's ventured the opinion that your problem is mental and not physical?"

"Sure. I know that already. The thing is," he added with a faint smile, "how to cure it. And you seem to have a similar hang-up."

She shrugged. "From the same source."

"Yes, I know."

She traced around her pommel. "The obvious solution…"

He swung his leg back down and straightened as Leslie, missing them, came back to find them. "I'm not capable," he said shortly.

"I wasn't offering," she muttered. She glared toward Mrs. Holton. "Of course, she would, in a New York minute!"

He cocked an eyebrow. "Maybe I should let her try," he said cynically. "She probably knows tricks even I haven't learned."

"Dawson!"

He glanced at her, and he didn't smile. "Jealous?"

She moved restlessly in the saddle. "I…don't know. Maybe." She searched his face. "I wish I could offer you the same medicine she could. But you'd have to get me stinking drunk," she said on a pained laugh. She averted her eyes. "I'd never forgive you if you did."

"Did what? Get you stinking drunk?"

"No!" she said at once. "Do it...with her," she explained.

His caught breath carried, but before he could reply, Leslie reined in beside them. "Aren't you two coming along?" she drawled. "It's lonely trying to explore a ranch this size on my own."

"Sorry," Dawson said, easing his horse into step beside hers. "We were discussing plans."

"I have a few of my own," Leslie murmured sweetly. "Want to hear them?"

Barrie fell back a little, glaring at them. But Dawson wasn't having that. He stopped and motioned to her to catch up, with eyes that dared her to hesitate. Reluctantly she rode up beside him and kept pace, to Leslie's irritation, all the way home.

She'd thought Dawson would forget what she'd said before Leslie interrupted them. But he didn't. While Leslie was changing clothes before supper, Dawson caught Barrie by the hand and led her into his study that overlooked the cottonwood-lined river below.

He closed the door behind them and, as an afterthought, locked it.

She stood by the desk at the window, watching him warily. "I gather that you wanted to talk to me?" she asked defensively.

"Among other things." He perched himself on the edge of the desk facing her, and searched her wary face. He folded his arms across his broad chest. "You kissed me back this morning," he said. "You weren't doing it in case Leslie was watching, either. You've buried everything you used to feel for me, but it's still there. I want to try to dig it back up again."

She studied her hands in her lap. It was tempting, because, despite everything that had happened, she loved Dawson. But the memories were too fresh even now, the pain too real. She couldn't block out the years of sarcastic remarks, cutting words, that had wounded her so badly.

She didn't know what he was offering, other than an attempt at a physical relationship. He'd said nothing about loving her. She knew he felt guilty about the baby she'd lost, and the knowledge of her miscarriage was very new to him. When he had time to cope with the grief, he might find that all he really felt for her was pity. She wanted much more than that.

She traced a chipped place on one neat fingernail.

"Well?" he asked impatiently.

She lifted her eyes. "I agreed to pretend to be engaged to you," she said quietly. "I don't want to live in Sheridan for the rest of my life, or give up the promotion I've been offered at my school in Tucson." He started to speak, but she held up her hand. "I know all too well how wealthy you are, Dawson, I know that I could have anything I wanted. But I'm used to making my own way in the world. I don't want to become your dependent."

"There are schools in Sheridan," he said shortly.

"Yes. There are good schools in Sheridan, and I'm sure I could get a position teaching in one. But they'd know my connection to you. I could never be sure if I got the job on my merit or yours."

He glared at her. This wasn't at all what he'd expected, especially after the way she'd softened toward him since last night.

"Don't you feel anything for me?" he asked.

She dropped her eyes to the emerald ring on her engagement finger. "I care for you, of course. I always will. But marriage is more than I can give you."

He got off the desk and turned away to the window. "You blame me for the baby, is that it?"

She glanced at his straight back. "I don't blame anyone. It wasn't preventable."

His head lifted a little higher. At his nape, his blond hair had grown slightly over his collar and it had a faint wave in it. Her eyes searched over his strong neck lovingly. She wanted nothing in life more than to live with him and love him. But what he was offering was a hollow relationship. Perhaps once he was over his guilt about the baby, he'd be able to function with a woman again. It was only a temporary problem, she was certain, caused by his unexpected discovery that she'd become pregnant and lost their child. But marriage wasn't the answer to the problem.

"We can have therapy," he said after a minute, grudgingly. "Perhaps they can find a cure for my impotence and your fear."

"I don't think your problem needs any therapy," she said. "It's just knowing about the baby that's caused it..."

He whirled, his eyes flashing. "I didn't know about the baby five years ago!" he said curtly.

She stared at him blankly for a minute, until she understood what he'd just said. Her face began to go pale. "Five years!" she stammered.

He glowered at her. "Didn't you realize what I was telling you?"

"I had no idea," she began. Her breath expelled sharply. "Five years!"

He looked embarrassed. He turned back to the window. He didn't speak.

She couldn't find any words to offer him. It hadn't occurred to her that a man could go for five years without sex. She eased out of her chair and went to the window to look up at him.

"I had no idea," she said again.

His hands were clasped behind him. His eyes were staring blankly at the flat horizon. "I haven't wanted anyone," he

said. ''When I found out about the baby, I was devastated.
And yes, I felt guilty as well. One reason I asked you back
here was to share the grief I felt, because I was pretty sure
that you felt it, too, and had never really expressed it.'' He
glanced down at her wistfully. ''Maybe I hoped I could feel
something with you, too. I wanted to be a whole man again,
Barrie. But even that failed.'' His eyes went back to the
window. ''Stay until Leslie leaves. Help me keep what little
pride I have left. Then I'll let you go.''

She wasn't sure what to say to him. That he was devastated was obvious. So was she. Five years without a woman.
She could hardly imagine the beating his ego had taken. It
was impossible to offer comfort. She had her own feelings
of inadequacy and broken pride.

''Everything would have been so different if we hadn't
gone to France that summer,'' she said absently.

''Would it?'' He turned to look at her. ''Sooner or later,
it would have happened, wherever we were. I know how
my father felt,'' he added enigmatically.

''I'll stay until the widow leaves. But what about your
land? She doesn't seem excited about selling.''

''She will be, when I make her an offer. I happen to know
that Powell Long is temporarily strapped for ready cash because of an expansion project on his ranch. He won't be
able to match what I offer, and she's in a shaky financial
situation. She can't afford to wait a long time for a buyer
who'll offer more.''

She was curious now. ''Then if you know she'll sell, why
am I here?''

''For the reason I told you in the beginning,'' he replied.
His eyes were old and tired. ''I can't let her find out that
everything they've said about me is true. I do have a little
pride left.''

She grimaced. ''It won't do any good if I tell you that...''

He touched his forefinger to her mouth. "No. It won't do any good."

She searched his eyes quietly. She felt inadequate. She felt sick all over. Somewhere in the back of her mind, she knew that the only hope he had of regaining a normal appetite was with her. The problem had begun in France. Only she would have the power to end it. But she didn't have the courage to try.

"Don't beat a dead horse," he said heavily, and managed a smile. "I've learned to live with it. I'll get along. So will you. Go back to Tucson and take that job. You'll do them proud."

"What will you do?" she asked. "There must be a way, someway…!"

"If there was, I'd have found it in five years' time," he said. He turned away from her and started toward the door. "We'd better make an appearance."

"Wait."

He paused with his hand on the lock.

She ran her hands through her hair, drew a finger over her mouth, opened the top button of her blouse and drew part of the shirttail out.

He understood what she was doing. He pulled out his handkerchief and gave it to her. She drew it lightly over the corner of her mouth and handed it back.

Then he unlocked the door, to find Leslie sitting on the bottom step of the staircase. She eyed them suspiciously and when she saw Barrie's attempts at reparation, she made an impatient sound.

"Sorry," Dawson murmured. "We forgot the time."

"Obviously," Leslie said shortly, glaring at Barrie. "I did come here to talk about land."

"So you did. I'm at your disposal," Dawson said. "Would you like to talk over a cup of coffee?"

"No, I'd like to drive into town with you and see some of the sights," she said. She glanced at Barrie. "I suppose she'll have to come, too."

"Not if you'd rather have my undivided attention," Dawson said surprisingly. "You don't mind, do you, honey?" he added.

Barrie was unsettled, but she forced a smile to her tight lips. "Of course not. Go right ahead. I'll help Corlie bake a cake."

"Can you cook?" Leslie asked indifferently. "I never bothered to learn how. I eat out most of the time."

"I hate restaurant food and fast food," Barrie remarked, "so I took a culinary course last summer. I can even do French pastries."

Dawson was watching her. "You never mentioned that."

She shrugged. "You never asked," she said coolly.

"How odd," Leslie interjected. "I thought engaged people knew all about each other. And she *is* your stepsister," she added.

"We've spent some time apart," he explained. "We're still in the learning stages, despite the engagement. We won't be long," he told Barrie.

"Take your time."

He hesitated, and Barrie knew why. She didn't want to give Leslie any excuse to taunt him. She went forward, sliding her arms around his waist and trying not to notice how he stiffened.

"Remember that you're engaged," she said in a stage whisper, and went on tiptoe to put her lips to his.

They were as cold as ice, like the eyes that never closed, even though he gave the appearance of returning her caress.

"We'll expect something special on the table when we get back," he said, and gently put her away from him.

Barrie felt empty somehow. She knew he wasn't capable of giving her a full response, but she'd hoped for more warmth than he'd shown her. He looked at her as if he hated her. Perhaps he still did.

Her sad eyes made him uncomfortable. He took Leslie's arm with a smile and led her out the door toward the garage behind the house.

"Trouble in your engagement already?" Leslie mused as they drove out of town in Dawson's new silver Mercedes. "I notice that you're suddenly very cool toward your fiancée. Of course, there is a rather large age difference between you, isn't there?"

Dawson only shrugged. "Every engagement has a few rough spots that need smoothing over," he said carelessly.

"This one was sudden."

"Not on my part," he replied as he slowed to make a turn.

"I begin to understand. Unrequited love?"

He laughed bitterly. "It seemed that way for a few years."

Leslie stared at him curiously, and then all at once she began laughing.

His eyebrows lifted in a silent query.

"I'm sorry." She choked through her laughter. "It's just that there were these rumors going around about you," she confessed. "I don't know why I even believed them."

"Rumors?" he asked, deadpan.

"Oh, they're too silly to repeat. And now they make sense. I suppose you simply gave up dating women you didn't care about."

He hadn't expected that Leslie might be so easy to placate about those rumors. He glanced at her, scowling.

She only smiled, and this time without overt flirting. "It's kind of sweet, really," she mused. "Barrie didn't suspect?"

He averted his eyes. "No."

"She still doesn't suspect, does she?" she asked curiously. "You're engaged, but she acts as if it's difficult for her even to kiss you. And don't think I was fooled by that very obvious lipstick smear on your handkerchief," she added with a grin. "There wasn't a trace of it on your face, or a red mark where you might have wiped it off. She's very nervous with you, and it shows."

He knew that, but he didn't like hearing it. "It's early days yet."

She nodded slowly. "You might consider that she has less experience with men than she pretends," she added helpfully. "She hasn't got that faint edge of sophistication most women of her age have acquired. I don't think she's very worldly at all."

He pulled the car into a parking spot in front of the old county courthouse. "You see a lot for someone who pretends to have a hard edge of her own," he said flatly, pinning her with his pale green eyes.

She leaned back in her comfortable seat. "I was in love with my husband," she said unexpectedly. "Everybody thought I married him for his money, because he was so much older than I was. It wasn't true. I married him because he was the first person in my life who was ever kind to me." Her voice became bitter with memories. "My father had no use for me, because he never believed I was his child. My mother hated me because I had to be taken care of, and she wanted to party. In the end, they both left me to my own devices. I fell in with bad company and got in trouble with the law." Her thin shoulders lifted and fell. "I was sentenced to a year in prison for helping my latest boyfriend steal some cigarettes. Jack Holton was in court at the time representing a client on some misdemeanor and he started talking to me during the recess." She smiled, remembering. "I was a hard case, but he was interested and very persistent. I was married before I knew it." She stared at her skirt, distracted by memories. "When he died, I went

a little mad. I don't think I came to my senses until today."
She looked up. "Barrie has something in her past, something that's hurt her. Go easy, won't you?"

He was surprised by her perception. But it was beyond
him to admit to a relative stranger how Barrie had been hurt,
and by whom. "I'll keep it in mind," he replied.

She smiled at him with genuine fondness. "I do like you,
you know," she said. "You're a lot like Jack. But now that
I know how things stand, you're off the endangered list.
Now how much do you want to offer me for that tract of
land?"

He chuckled. He hadn't expected it to be this easy, but
he wasn't looking a gift horse in the mouth.

When he came back with Leslie, his arm around her
shoulder and all smiles, Barrie was immediately on the defensive. She had all sorts of ideas about why they were both
smiling and so relaxed with each other. She was furiously
jealous and hurt, and she didn't know how to cope with her
own reactions.

She was silent at the dinner table, withdrawn and intro-
spective, speaking only when addressed. It was the first
glimmer of hope that she'd given a pensive Dawson. If she
could still feel jealous about him, there was hope that he
hadn't killed all her feelings for him.

So he laid it on with Leslie.

"I think we ought to have a celebration party," he announced. "Friday night. We'll phone out invitations and
have a dance. Corlie will love making the arrangements."

"Can she do it, on such short notice?" Leslie asked.

"Of course! Barrie will help, too, won't you?" he added
with a smile in his fiancée's direction.

"Certainly," Barrie replied in a lackluster voice.

"I have some wonderful CDs, just perfect for dancing
to," Leslie added. "Including some old forties torch

songs,'' she added flirtatiously. "Do you dance, Barrie?"
she asked.

"I haven't in quite some time,'' the other woman replied
politely. "But I suppose it's like riding a bicycle, isn't it?''

"It will come back to you,'' Dawson assured her. His
eyes narrowed as he stared at her. "If you've forgotten the
steps, I'm sure I can teach you.''

She glanced up, flushing a little as she met his calculating
stare. "I'm learning all the time,'' she said shortly.

He lifted an eyebrow and grinned at Leslie. "We'll have
a good time,'' he promised her. "And now, suppose we go
over that contract I had my attorney draw up, just to make
sure it's in order? Barrie, you won't mind, will you?'' he
added.

Barrie lifted her chin proudly. "Certainly not,'' she replied. "After all, it's just business, isn't it?''

"What else would it be?'' he drawled.

What else indeed! Barrie thought furiously as she
watched him close the study door behind himself and the
widow Holton.

She went up to her room and locked the door. She'd never
been so furious in all her life. He'd wanted her to come here
and pretend to be engaged to him to keep the widow at bay,
and now he was behaving as if it were the widow he was
engaged to! Well, he needn't expect her to stay and be a
doormat! He could have his party Friday, and she'd be on
her way out of town first thing Saturday morning. If he liked
the widow, he could have her.

She lay down on the bed and tears filled her eyes. Who
was she kidding? She still loved him. It was just like old
times. Dawson knew how she felt and he was putting the
knife into her heart again. What an idiot she'd been to believe anything he told her. He was probably laughing his
head off at how easily he'd tricked her into coming here, so
that he could taunt her some more. Apparently she was still

being made to pay for his father's second marriage. And
she'd hoped that he was learning to care for her. Ha! She
might as well cut her losses. She'd tell him tomorrow, she
decided. First thing.

Six

Barrie told Dawson that she'd be leaving after the party. Her statement was met with an icy silence and a glare that would have felled a lesser woman.

"We're engaged," he said flatly.

"Are we?" She took off the emerald ring and laid it on his desk. "Try it on the widow's finger. Maybe it will fit her."

"You don't understand," he said through his teeth. "She's only selling me the tract. There's nothing to be jealous of."

Her eyebrows lifted. "Jealous?" she drawled sarcastically. "Why, Dawson, why should I be jealous? After all, I've got half a football team of men just panting to take me out back in Tucson."

He hadn't had a comeback. The remark threw him completely off-balance. By the time he regained it, cursing his own lack of foresight, she'd gone out the door. And until the night of the party, she kept him completely at bay with plastic smiles and polite conversation.

It had been a long Friday evening, and all Barrie wanted was to go back to her room and get away from Dawson. All night she'd watched women, mostly Leslie Holton, fawn over him while he smiled that cynical smile and ate up the attention. He wasn't backing away from Leslie tonight. Odd, that sudden change.

Barrie had been studiously avoiding both of them all night, so much so that Corlie, helping serve canapés and drinks, was scowling ominously at her. But Barrie couldn't help her coldness toward Dawson. She felt as if he'd sold her out all over again.

The surprise came when Leslie Holton announced that she was going to leave and went to her car instead of her room. Barrie watched from the doorway as Leslie reached up and kissed Dawson deliberately. And he didn't pull away, either. It was the last straw. She went back inside with bottled fury. Damn him!

He came back inside just as Barrie was saying goodbye to the last of their few guests. She tried to ease out, but while he said good-night to the departing guest, Dawson's arm came across the doorway and blocked her exit. He seemed to know that she'd withdraw instinctively from his touch, because he smiled without humor when she stepped back.

The visitor left. Dawson closed the door with a snap and turned to her, his narrow green eyes cold and calculating.

"Why?" she asked and tried not to sound afraid.

His eyes ran the length of her, from her loosened wavy dark hair to her trim figure and long, elegant legs in the short black dress.

"Maybe I'm tired of playing games," he said enigmatically.

"With me or Leslie Holton?" she demanded.

"You don't know why I played up to Leslie?" he drawled. "You can't guess?"

Her face colored delicately. "I don't want to know why. I want to go to bed, Dawson," she said, measuring the distance to the door.

He let out a long, weary sigh and moved closer, noticing with resignation her rigid posture and the fear that came into her eyes.

"You run. I run. What the hell difference has it made?" he asked. His hands shot out and caught her shoulders. He pulled her to him, ignoring her struggles, and held her against the lean warmth of his powerful body. "If I ruined your young life, you damn sure ruined mine," he said under his breath, staring at her mouth. "I thought we were getting closer and now we're worlds apart, all over again. Come here."

Two neat whiskies had loosened all his inhibitions. He dragged her to him without caring that he couldn't feel anything physically. He could kiss her, at least…

And he did, with aching need, his mind yielded to the feel and touch and taste of her. He groaned as he drew her even closer, feeling her go rigid against him as his mouth parted her soft lips. But her resistance didn't stop him. He gave in to his hunger without any thought except to show her that he couldn't be aroused by even the most ardent kiss.

But what he expected to happen, didn't. He drew her hips to his and the sudden touch of her long legs against his made him shudder and all at once, his body exploded with hunger, need, anguished desire. His intake of breath was audible, shocking as he felt a full, raging arousal for the first time in almost five years.

He dragged his mouth from hers and looked down at her with horror and dawning realization. The curse he spat out shocked even Barrie, who'd heard them all at one time or another from very modern grammar school students. His face looked frightening and his hands tightened until they hurt.

She reacted purely with instinct, fighting the pain he was unknowingly inflicting. She struggled away from him, breathing roughly, rubbing the arms he'd held in that steely grip.

He wasn't even aware of having hurt her. He just stood there, glaring at her, shivering with the force of his desire for her. He wanted her with pure obsession and she couldn't bear him to touch her. It was ironic. Tragic. He'd only just discovered that he was still capable with one woman at least, and she had to be the one woman on earth who couldn't bear him to touch her.

He stared at her with narrow, bitter eyes. "God, that was all it needed!" he said in anguish, his face tormented as he met her eyes. "That was damn all!"

He was looking at her as if he hated her, with wild eyes, while she stood gaping at him. He'd said he couldn't feel anything! She didn't realize that she'd said it aloud.

He ran a rough hand through his wavy blond hair and drew it over his brow as he turned away. "I thought I was dead from the waist down, that I was immune to any woman. I never realized why, even if I suspected it…I might as well be dead!" he said huskily. "My God, I might as well be!"

He threw open the door and went out it as if he'd forgotten Barrie's presence altogether, reaching his car in long, angry strides. He jerked the door open, started it, and took off.

Barrie watched him as if she were a sleepwalker until it suddenly dawned on her that he was acting totally unlike himself. She'd seen him down two neat whiskies, but would that have been enough to make him lose control so completely?

"Dawson," she said to herself, because he was already out of sight.

She stood helplessly in the doorway, trying to decide what to do. He was in no condition to be driving. How could she go to bed now? On the other hand, how could she stay down here? He might be even more violent when he returned. She remembered, oh, too well, what Dawson was like when he was out of control. Corlie and Rodge had gone to bed. She couldn't bear the thought of being alone with him... But the way he'd driven off had been frightening too. What if he hurt himself?

With a concern that grew by the minute, she rushed to get her wrap and purse and the keys to Dawson's MG that hung by the back door. She'd drive down the road, she thought, just to make sure he hadn't run into a ditch or something. That would make her feel better. And if she didn't see him, she could assume that he was all right and go back to her room. Not that it was going to make her stop worrying. She'd never seen him so shaken, so wild. Dawson never lost control. Well, only that once. But even that hadn't been such a total loss of reason. The alcohol would have made it worse, too.

Her mind made up, she started off in the general direction Dawson had taken. The headlights of the sports car picked up nothing on the side of the road for at least two miles down the deserted highway, and she breathed a sigh of relief. He was probably on his way back to the house even...

Her heart jumped when she saw the flashing lights over the next rise. She knew, somewhere deep inside her, that Dawson was where they were. She stepped on the accelerator and began to pray as a cold sickness grew in the pit of her stomach.

It could have been worse, but not much. The car had overturned. She caught sight of skid marks on the black pavement, and the sheriff's deputy patrol car on the side of the road. Even as she pulled off the road and stopped, she could hear an ambulance in the distance.

She threw the MG out of gear and left it idling and ran frantically to the median where Dawson's Jaguar lay crushed with its wheels in the air.

"Dawson!" she screamed. Her heart was beating so fast that she shook with it. "Oh, God!"

The sheriff's deputy stopped her headlong flight.

"Let me go." She wept piteously, fighting him. "Please, please…!"

"You can't help him like this," he said firmly. "You recognize the car?"

"It's Dawson," she whispered. "Dawson Rutherford. My stepbrother…is he…dead?"

It seemed forever before he answered. "Not yet," he said. "Calm down."

She looked up at him in the glare of the flashing lights. "Please!" she whispered, reduced to begging as she tugged against his firm hold. "Oh, God, please, please…!"

The officer was basically a kind man, and that look would have touched a career criminal. With a rough sigh, he let go of her.

Heart pounding savagely, eyes wide with fear, she ran headlong to the car, where Dawson lay in a curious position in the wreckage. Blood was coming from somewhere. When she touched his jacket, she felt it on her hands. She knew not to try to move him. His face was turned away. She touched his hair with trembling hands. It was icy cold, like the skin on his face. Her hands cradled what she could reach of him, as if by touching and holding, she could keep him alive.

"You mustn't…die," she whispered brokenly. "Dawson, please! Oh, God, please, Dawson, you mustn't die!"

There was no movement at all, no answer. He seemed to be pinned. She couldn't tell where in the darkness. Behind her, the ambulance siren came closer. She heard it stop, heard voices. Another vehicle pulled up, too.

Gentle, but firm hands moved her away, back into the care of the deputy. This time she stood silently, unmoving, watching, waiting. She'd thought so many times that she hated Dawson, especially since he'd played up to Leslie, but she'd only been lying to herself. She might have legions of dates, men who wanted her, but there was only one man that she loved. Despite the pain and anguish of the past, her heart was lying in that tangled wreckage. And she knew then, for certain, that if Dawson died, part of her would die with him. She only wished that she'd had time to tell him so.

They had to cut him out of the Jaguar. When they put him on the stretcher, he didn't move. His face was almost white. They covered him with a blanket and carried him to the waiting ambulance. Barrie stared at him, at the ambulance, with dull, dead eyes. Was he gone? He didn't move. Perhaps he was already dead and they didn't want to cover him up in front of her. But her heart was still beating. She was still breathing. Surely if he was dead, she would be, too.

"Come on," the deputy said gently. "I'll drive you to the hospital."

"The...car," she faltered numbly.

"I'll take care of it." With the ease of years of practice, he attended to the car, loaded her into the patrol car and followed the ambulance back to the private hospital in Sheridan.

Barrie drank five cups of coffee before anyone came to tell him how he was. She didn't think at all. She sat staring out the window into the darkness, praying.

"Miss Rutherford?"

She looked up. "Bell," she corrected dully. "Dawson is my stepbrother." Her eyes pleaded for miracles.

And the doctor had one. He smiled wearily, his green mask dangling from his neck, lying on his stained surgical uniform. Blood, she noticed idly. Dawson's blood.

"He'll make it," he told her abruptly. "He was unconscious when they brought him in, probably due to the concussion he's sustained. But, miraculously, there was no internal damage. He didn't even break any bones, isn't that...Miss Bell!"

She came to lying on a bed in the emergency room. She saw the lights overhead and the whiteness of the ceiling. Dawson was going to live. The doctor had said so. Or had she dreamed it?

She turned her head, and a nurse smiled at her.

"Feeling better?" she asked. "You've had quite a night, I gather. Mr. Rutherford is in a private room, and he's doing fine. He came around a little while ago and asked about you."

Her heart jumped. "He was conscious?"

"Oh, very," she replied dryly. "We assured him that you were in the waiting room and he didn't say another word. He's going to be all right."

"Thank God," she breathed, closing her eyes again. "Oh, thank God."

"You must be very close," the nurse remarked.

Barrie could have laughed. "We don't have family," she said evasively. "Only each other."

"I see. Well, what a lucky thing that he was wearing his seat belt. He's very handsome," she added, and Barrie looked again, noticing the nurse's pretty blond hair and brown eyes.

"Yes, he is, isn't he?" Barrie replied.

The nurse finished working on her chart. "He's on my ward. Lucky me." She grinned.

Yes. Lucky you, Barrie thought, but she didn't say anything. She got up, with the nurse's help, and went to the rest room to freshen up. She tried not to think on the way. She'd had enough for one night.

After she'd bathed her face and retouched her makeup and combed her hair, she went along to Dawson's room. She peered around the door cautiously, but he was in a private room and alone. He was conscious, as the nurse had said.

His head turned as he heard her step and she grimaced at the cuts on one side of his handsome face. There was a bruise on his cheek and at his temple. He seemed a little disoriented, and it wasn't surprising, considering the condition the Jaguar had been in. She shuddered, remembering how he'd looked then.

His eyes narrowed. He breathed slowly, watching her approach. "Sorry," he managed to say in a hoarse tone.

She winced and tears overflowed her eyes. "You idiot!" she raged, sobbing. "You crazy idiot, you could have been killed!"

"Barrie," he said softly, holding out a hand.

She ran to him. The walls were well and truly down, as if they'd never existed. She all but fell into the chair beside the bed and lay across him, careless of the IV they were giving him, shivering as she felt his hands on her shoulders, holding her while she wept.

"Here, now," he chided weakly. "I'm all right. Lucky I hit my head and not some more vital part."

She didn't answer. Her body shook with sobs. She clung. She felt his hand in her hair, smoothing it, soothing her.

"Damn," he breathed roughly. "I'm so weak, Barrie."

"Weak is better than dead," she muttered as she finally lifted her head. Her red, swollen eyes met his. "You're going to have a dandy bruise," she told him, sniffing, dabbing with her fingers at her wet cheeks and eyes.

"No doubt." He moved and winced. "God, what a headache. I don't know if it's the whiskey or the wreck." He frowned. "Why was I driving?" he added, struggling to regain complete control of his faculties after the concussion.

Her heart jumped. "I don't know, exactly," she said evasively. "You…got angry and stormed out to the car."

He whistled softly through pursed lips and smiled half-humorously. "Nice epitaph—dead for unknown reasons."

"Don't," she said, dabbing at her eyes with a tissue from the box by his bed. "It isn't funny."

"Were we arguing again?" he asked.

She shook her head. "Not really."

He frowned. "Then what…?"

The door opened again, and the pretty blond nurse danced in with a clipboard. "Time for vital signs again," she informed them. "This will only take a minute." She glanced at Barrie. "If you'd like to get a cup of coffee…?"

She didn't have the heart for an argument. "I'll be back soon," she said.

Dawson looked as if he wanted to say something, but the nurse popped her electronic thermometer in his mouth and he grimaced.

* * *

Later, Barrie went back to the house and phoned Antonia to tell her what was going on. She'd called Corlie and Rodge the night before, and they were waiting for her when she arrived. She took time to fill them in on Dawson's condition before she phoned her best friend in Bighorn.

"Do you want me to come over and sit with you?" Antonia asked.

"No," Barrie said. "I just needed someone to talk to. He'll be in for another day or so. I didn't want you to worry in case you tried to get in touch with me and wondered where I was. Especially after I'd told you I'd be back in Tucson today."

"Can we do anything?"

Barrie laughed. "No, but thanks. I'll keep you in mind. He's getting plenty of attention right now from a very pretty young nurse. I don't think he'll even miss me when I go."

There was a pause. "You aren't going to leave before they release him?"

"No," Barrie said reluctantly.

"You don't know why he was driving so recklessly?"

"Yes, I think I do," she said miserably. "It was partly my fault. But he'd had too much to drink, too. And he's the one who's always lecturing people about not driving under the influence."

"We can blackmail him for years on this," Antonia replied with a smile in her voice. "Thank God he'll be alive so that we can."

"I'll tell him you said so. If I can get his attention."

She hung up and went into the study, because she felt closer to Dawson there. She hadn't told him the truth about last night. She had a suspicion about why he'd gone out. He'd said it himself. He was only capable with one woman...the one woman he'd scarred too much to ever want sex again. And he couldn't bear the thought of it. How horribly ironic.

It did make sense, somehow. She went to the window to look out. The sky was gray and low with dark clouds. It was going to snow. She needed to get out before the roads became impassable, but she couldn't leave Dawson. What was she going to do? The first thing was to go back to the hospital.

But Corlie refused to let her. "You need food and rest. You've been up all night. Rodge and I will sit with him until you have a little rest."

"You don't have to do that," she began.

"Barrie, you know better than that. He's like our own child, mine and Rodge's. You eat something and we'll stay until you get back to be with him tonight."

"Okay."

Corlie seemed to take it for granted that Barrie was going to stay the night with him. Of course. Everyone still thought they were engaged. She grimaced. Dawson wasn't going to like that one bit. When he was back to himself he was going to hate her all over again. She was his one and only big mistake. He'd been furious at her when he'd stormed out. He seemed to actually hate her because he was aroused by her.

But he was subtly different. When she arrived back at the hospital, he watched her come in with eyes that were alert and searching.

"Feel better?" he asked quietly.

"That's my line," she murmured, smiling at Corlie and Rodge.

Corlie got up and hugged her warmly. "Honey, you're freezing," she chided. "Don't you have something heavier than that windbreaker to wear?"

"It doesn't exactly freeze in Tucson," Barrie reminded her.

"Go to Harper's and buy a coat," Dawson said. "I've got an account there."

"I don't need a coat," she said on a nervous laugh. "And I won't be here long enough to use it. Anyway, it's just a little nip in the air. It's spring."

He didn't reply. His eyes were watchful, curious. "Corlie, you know what size to buy?"

"Yes," Corlie said, grinning.

"Get her one."

"I'll do it first thing tomorrow."

"But...!" Barrie began.

"Hush, child. He's right, you'll freeze in that thing you're wearing. We'll be back early in the morning." She hugged Barrie again.

"Might as well not argue," Rodge said with a grin. "I haven't won an argument with her in thirty-five years. What chance would you have?"

"Not much," Barrie sighed.

They said their goodbyes to Dawson and went out the door, waving.

Barrie edged toward the chair beside the bed, feeling vulnerable now that they were alone. He was much too alert to suit her.

He watched her sit down, his eyes following her. He caught her gaze and held it relentlessly until she flushed and looked away.

"I've remembered," he said.

She bit her lower lip. "Have you?"

"And apparently you've realized why I lost my temper."

The flush got worse. She looked at the floor.

He laughed bitterly. "That's right, Barrie, try to pretend it didn't happen. Run some more." His hand shot out and caught her arm. "Stop that," he said curtly. "Your lip's bleeding."

She hadn't even felt the pain. She pulled out a tissue and held it to her lip. It came away red. "It's a habit," she faltered.

He let go of her arm and sank back against the pillows. He looked older. There were new lines in his face, around his eyes. He looked as if he'd never smiled once in his life.

She clutched the tissue in her hand. "Dawson?"

His gaze came back to hers, questioning.

"Why is it that you weren't…cold…with me?" she asked hesitantly. "I mean, all those other women, like Mrs. Holton… and she's a knockout."

He searched her eyes. "I don't know why, Barrie," he replied. "Maybe it's because I hurt you so badly. Maybe it's what hell really is. I want you and you're physically afraid of me. Ironic, isn't it? Do you have any idea, any idea at all, how it makes a man feel to know that he's impotent?"

She shook her head. "Not really."

"All these long years," he said, brushing the unruly hair back from his broad forehead. His eyes closed. "It makes me sick when women touch me, fawn over me. I don't feel anything, Barrie. It seemed to be like that with you. That's why I pulled you against me that way, I wanted to show you what you'd done to me." He laughed with bitter irony. "And I got the lesson, didn't I? It was the most violent, raging arousal I've ever had in my life—with the one woman who shudders at my touch." His eyes closed.

She clenched her teeth as she studied him. She'd loved him all her life, it sometimes seemed. And then in one short night, he'd destroyed her love, her future, her femininity. If his life was hopeless, so was hers.

He glanced at her. "It's been that bad for you, too, hasn't

it?'' he asked suddenly, with narrowed eyes that seemed to see right through her. "All those damn men parading through your life in a constant, steady stream, in threes and fours. And you've never let one of them touch you, not even in the most innocent way."

She shivered. It was too much. It was too much, having him know that about her. He might as well have stripped her soul naked.

She started to jump up, but he caught her wrist with surprising strength for a man in his condition and jerked her firmly right back down into the chair again.

"No," he said, glaring at her. "No, you don't. You aren't running this time. I said, you've never let anyone touch you, in any way, even to kiss you, since me. Go ahead. Tell me I'm lying."

She swallowed. Her face gave him the answer.

His lips parted. He exhaled softly. "Damn me, Barrie," he said huskily. "Damn me for that."

He let go of her wrist and lay back on the bed. "For the first time in my life, I don't know what to do," he confessed dully.

He sounded defeated. Dawson, of all people. She hated that uncertainty in his deep voice. She hated what they'd done to each other. He was her whole world.

She reached out, very slowly. Her cold fingers just barely touched his bare arm, just at the elbow.

As if he couldn't believe what his senses were telling him, he turned his head and looked at her pale hand on his arm. His eyes lifted to hers, curious, intent.

She bit her lip again. "I don't want you to die," she said unsteadily.

He looked at her fingers, curled hesitantly around his arm. "Barrie…"

Before he could get the words out, the door opened and

the pretty nurse was back again, smiling, cheerful, full of optimism and already possessive about her handsome patient.

"Supper," she announced, putting a tray on the table. "Soup and tea, and I'm going to feed you myself!"

"Like hell you are," Dawson said curtly.

The nurse started. His eyes weren't welcoming at all. They had a very cobralike quality, flashing warnings at her. She laughed with a sudden loss of confidence and pushed the high, wheeled tray over to the bed. "Well, of course, if you feel like feeding yourself, you can." She cleared her throat. "I'll be back to pick it up in a few minutes. Try to eat it all, now."

She smiled again, but with less enthusiasm, and went out the door much more quickly than she'd come in.

Dawson took a pained breath. His head turned toward Barrie. "Help me," he said quietly.

It was intimate, helping him eat. She watched every mouthful disappear past those thin, firm lips, and without wanting to, she remembered the feel of them on her mouth in passion. She'd been innocent and very frightened. He hadn't realized that. His kisses had been adult, passionate, giving no quarter. She knew that he'd never even suspected that she was a total innocent until…

Her flush was revealing. Dawson swallowed the last of the soup and caught her gaze.

"I have my own nightmares," he said unexpectedly. "If I could take it back, I would. Believe that, at least."

She moved restlessly as she put the soup bowl back on the table and helped him sip some of the hot tea. He made a terrible face.

"It's good for you," she said stubbornly.

"It may be good as a hand warmer in a cup on a cold day," he muttered. "If it's good for anything else, I wouldn't know." He lay back down. "If they want to shovel caffeine in me, why can't I have coffee?"

"Ask someone who knows."

He chuckled without humor. His eyes searched hers. "Going to stay with me tonight?"

"It seems to be expected."

His face hardened. "Don't let me put you out. I'm perfectly capable…"

She winced.

He closed his eyes. Beside his thigh, his fist clenched until the knuckles went white.

She pulled her chair closer. Her fingers spread tremulously over his big fist and lingered there. "Dawson, don't," she whispered. "Of course I'll stay. I want to."

He didn't say a word. And still, his hand clenched.

Her fingers pressed down, became caressing.

She knew when his head turned, when his eyes opened. She knew that he was watching her. With a long, helpless sigh, she lifted his hand and put it to her lips. And he shuddered.

She dropped it abruptly, horrified at her own action, and started to get up, red-faced.

But he had her hand now, turned in his, firmly held. He drew it until he could press the palm to his hard mouth. His eyes closed and he made a sound deep in his throat. When he looked at her again, what she saw in his face made her go hot all over.

"Come here," he said huskily.

Her knees became weak. She felt the imprint of his mouth on her palm as if it were a brand. She never knew whether or not she would have obeyed that heated command, though, because the door opened and the doctor, making rounds, came in smiling. Dawson let go of her hand and the moment was lost.

But not forgotten. Not at all, not through the long night when he slept, because of the pills they gave him, and she lay in the chair and watched him sleep. They seemed to have reached some sort of turning point. Her life lay in that hospital bed now. She had no desire whatsoever to leave him. And it seemed to be the same for him.

When he woke the next morning, a new young nurse came in with soap and a towel and a basin of water. Her eyes were bright and flirting, but when she offered to bathe him, he gave her a look that made her excuse herself and leave.

"You're intimidating the nurses," Barrie remarked with a faint smile. She was tired and half-asleep, but the look he'd given the nurse amused her.

"I don't want them touching me."

"You're not up to bathing yourself," she protested.

His eyes searched hers without amusement, without taunting. "Then you do it," he said quietly. "Because yours are the only hands I want on my body."

She stared at him helplessly. He wasn't chiding her now. His eyes were warm and quiet and soft on her face.

She got up, a little hesitant. "I've never bathed anyone except myself," she said.

He untied the hospital gown at the neck and, holding her eyes, sloughed it off, leaving the sheet over his lean hips.

She colored a little. She'd never seen him undressed, despite their intimacy.

"It's all right," he said, soothing her. "I'll leave the cover where it is. I can do the rest myself, when you finish."

She didn't stop to ask why he couldn't do it all. Her hands went to the cloth. She wet it, and put soap on it. Then, with gentle motions, she drew it over his face and throat and back, rinsing it and him before she put more soap on the cloth again and hesitated at his arms and chest.

"I'm not in a place, or in a position, to cause you any worry," he said gently.

She managed a smile. She drew the cloth down his arms, to his lean, strong hands, and back up to his collarbone. She rinsed it again before she began to smooth it, slowly over the thick hair on his chest. Even through the cloth, she could feel the warm muscles, the thickness of the hair. She remembered just for an instant the feel and smell and taste of his chest under her lips, when she'd been all but fainting with desire for him.

He felt her hesitate. His hand pressed down on hers. "It's only flesh and bone," he said quietly. "Nothing to be afraid of."

She nodded. Her hand smoothed down to his navel, his flat stomach. He groaned suddenly and caught her fingers, staying them.

His breath came erratically. He laughed abruptly. "I think…you'd better stop there."

Her hand stilled. Involuntarily her eyes slipped past it, and she stared.

"One of the pitfalls of bathing a man," he said, swallowing hard. "Although I won't pretend not to enjoy it. For years, that hasn't happened at all."

Her eyes were curious as they met his.

"You don't understand," he mused.

She smiled faintly. "Not really."

"That doesn't happen with other women," he explained slowly. "Not at all."

"And if it doesn't, you can't—" She stopped.

He nodded. "Exactly."

Evading his intent gaze, she lifted the cloth and rinsed it

and then soaped it again. She handed it to him. "Here. You'd better…"

His hand touched hers. He searched her eyes. "Please," he whispered.

She bit her lip. "I can't!"

"Why?" He didn't even blink. "Is it repulsive, to touch me like that, to look at me?"

Her face was a flaming red. "I've never…looked!"

"Don't you want to?" he asked gently. "Honestly?"

She didn't speak. She didn't move, either. His hand went to the sheet and he pulled it away slowly, folding it back on his powerful thighs.

"We made love once," he said quietly. "You were part of me. I'm not embarrassed to let you look. And I'll tell you for a fact, I'd never let another woman see me helpless like this." He took a long, slow breath and felt the tension drain out of him. He was weak and disoriented, and his body relaxed completely. It worried him a little that he couldn't maintain the tension, but when he was well again, perhaps he could find out if he really was capable completely. Unaware of his misgivings, Barrie bit down hard on her lip, and let her eyes slide down. She looked and then couldn't look away. He was…beautifully made. He was like one of the nude statues she'd seen in art books. But he was real.

She tried to use the cloth, but it was just too much too soon. With a smile and a grimace she finally gave in to her shyness and turned away while he finished the chore.

"Don't feel bad," he said gently when he was covered again, and the bath things were put aside. "It's a big step for both of us, I guess. These things take time."

She nodded.

He tugged her down into the chair beside the bed. "Do you realize that we made love and never saw each other undressed?"

"You shouldn't talk about it," she faltered.

"You were innocent and I was a fool," he said. "I rushed at you like a bull in heat, and I never even realized how innocent you were until I hurt you. And I couldn't accept that you were, Barrie," he confessed heavily. "Because if I admitted that, I had to accept what I'd done to you, how I'd scarred you. Maybe my body was more honest than I was. It didn't want another woman after you. It still doesn't. The reaction you get, I can't give to anyone else."

She met his eyes. "I don't...want anyone else, either," she said softly.

"Do you want me?" he asked bluntly. "Are you able to want me?"

She smiled sadly. "I don't know, Dawson."

He took her hand and held it tight. "Maybe that's something that we're both going to have to find out, when I leave here," he said, and it sounded as if he dreaded the outcome as much as she did.

Seven

They let Dawson go home three days after he was admitted. The doctor insisted that he be cautious about returning to work, and that if he had any recurring symptoms from the head injury, he was to get in touch. Barrie wasn't happy about them discharging him, but she did have every sympathy with the nursing staff. Dawson in a recovered state was better off without time on his hands. He made everyone uncomfortable.

He'd progressed from the bed to the desk in his study and he'd taken Barrie in there with him to discuss the tract of land Leslie Holton had agreed to sell him.

She stared at the contract on the desk, which had arrived by special courier that morning. "She wasn't that eager to sell at first. How did you change her mind?" she asked with barely contained irritation.

He leaned back in his chair, his forehead still purplish from its impact with the steering wheel, marred by the thin line of stitches that puckered the tanned flesh.

"How do you think I convinced her?" he taunted.

She didn't say a word. But her face spoke silently.

He smiled cynically. "And that's a false conclusion if I ever saw one," he mused. "I can't do that with anyone except you, Barrie."

She flushed a little. "You don't know that."

"Don't I?" His pale eyes slid down her body which was in a loose knit shirt and jeans, and lingered on the thrust of her high breasts. "Then let's say that I'm not interested in finding out if I can want anyone else."

"You'd been drinking," she reminded him.

"So I had." He stood up. "And you think it was the whiskey?"

She shrugged. "It might have been."

He moved away from the desk, glanced at her thoughtfully for a moment, and then on an impulse, went to close and lock the office door. "Let's see," he murmured deeply, and moved toward her.

She jumped behind a wing chair and gripped it for dear life. Her eyes were wide, wild. "No!"

He paused, searching her white face. "Calm down. I'm not going to force you."

She didn't let go of the chair. Her eyes were steady on him, like a hunted animal's.

He put his hands into his pockets and watched her quietly. "This isn't going to get us anywhere," he remarked.

She cleared her throat. "Good."

"Barrie, it's been five years," he said irritably. After the closeness they'd shared while he was in the hospital, now they seemed to be back on the old footing again. "I've been half a man for so long that it's a revelation to have discovered that I'm still capable of functioning with a woman. I only want to know that it wasn't a fluke, a minute out of time. I want to…make sure."

Her big eyes searched his. "I'm afraid of you like that."

"You weren't just after you had the nightmare," he reminded her. "You weren't the next morning. In fact, you weren't in the hospital when I let you bathe me."

Her hands released the back of the chair. Her short nails had left fine marks in the soft leather. She stared at them. "You weren't…aroused when you pulled back the sheet," she faltered.

"That's what bothers me most, that it didn't last until you tried to bathe me," he said heavily. "Maybe it was just a flash in the pan, the whole thing," he said with black humor. "But either way, I want to know. I *have* to know."

There was something in the way he looked that made Barrie feel guilty. Her own fear seemed a poor thing in comparison with the doubt in his hard face. It was devastating for a man to lose his virility. Could she really blame him for wanting to test it, to know for sure if he'd regained what he'd lost?

Slowly, hesitantly, she stepped away from the chair and let her hands fall to her sides. After all, she'd seen him totally nude, she'd felt his body against hers when it was aroused, and she hadn't succumbed to hysteria. Besides, she loved him. He was here with her, alive and vital. Her mind wouldn't let go of the picture it held—Dawson in the overturned car, his face covered with blood. She looked at him with her heart in her eyes.

His eyes traced her face in its frame of long, wavy dark hair to her soft, parted lips. His hands were still in his pockets, and he didn't move, despite the fact that her expression made him feel violent. She looked as if she cared.

"Are you just going to stand there?" she asked after a minute.

He searched her eyes. "Yes."

She didn't understand for a moment, and then he smiled faintly, and she realized what he wanted. "Oh," she said. "You want me to…kiss you."

He nodded. He still didn't move.

His lack of action made her less insecure. She moved toward him, went close, so that she could feel the heat from his tall, powerful body, so that she could smell the clean scents of soap and cologne that always clung to him. He'd shaved. There was no rasp of beard where she reached up and hesitantly touched his cheek. Involuntarily her fingers slid down to his long, firm lower lip and traced it.

His breath drew in sharply. She felt him tense, but his hands stayed in his pockets.

Curious, she let her fingers become still on his face. There was something in his eyes, something dark and intense. She searched them for a long moment, but she couldn't read the expression.

At least, she didn't understand until she took an involuntary step closer and felt his body against hers.

"No fluke," he said through his teeth. His voice sounded odd. "Now I don't want to frighten you," he continued shortly, "so if you're getting cold feet, this is your last chance to move away."

She wasn't sure if she meant to hesitate, but she did. His hands came out of his pockets and slid to cradle her by the hips. He pulled her, very gently, against him, and then moved her slowly against the raw thrust of his body, shivering.

It wasn't so frightening that way. She was fascinated by what she saw.

"Yes," he said through his teeth. "You recognize vulnerability, don't you?" he asked impatiently, hating the helpless desire he felt even while he thanked God for the ability to feel it. "My legs are shaking. Can you feel them?" He drew her a little closer, to make sure that she could. "I'm swelling. You can feel that, too, can't you?"

It was embarrassing to hear him telling her such intimate things, especially in that angry tone. She flushed, but when she tried to drop her eyes, he caught her chin and made her look at him.

"Stop cringing. I'm not a monster," he said roughly. "I lost control with you at the worst possible time, and I hurt you. I won't hurt you again."

She swallowed. The feel of his body in such close contact made her nervous, but it also excited her to feel him wanting her. She grew dizzy with confused sensations. She shifted uneasy yet exhilarated at the same time.

He drew in a sharp breath and groaned, and then he laughed. "God, that feels good!" He bit off the words. He actually shivered. His eyes met hers and he moved her against him in the same exotic little motion she'd made without thinking. His teeth ground together and the laughter came again. "I'd forgotten what it felt like to be a man."

His pleasure affected her in the oddest way. She buried her face in his chest, half afraid, half excited. She shivered, too, as his arms enfolded her.

"So you feel it, too, do you?" he asked at her ear. His hands tightened on her hips and he repeated the rough, deft motion and heard her cry out. "Do you like being help-less?" he asked, and his head bent. "Do you like wanting me and feeling powerless to draw away?"

She could hear the resentment, mingled with heated de-sire, in his deep voice. She opened her mouth to respond and his lips moved over it, opening to fit the shape of it before they settled with a rough, hungry, demanding pres-sure that made her stiffen with unexpected pleasure.

Pictures of tidal waves flew through his mind as he groaned and forced her body into even more intimacy with his. He wanted her. God, he wanted her. It was a fever that burned so high and bright that he couldn't hide his need. It grew and swelled, the pressure hard against her soft stom-ach. He could feel her embarrassment as she tried to move her hips away from his, but he wouldn't permit it. He couldn't. He needed her softness against the flare of his masculinity.

He needed her.

His arm forced her closer as his mouth deepened the slow kiss into stark intimacy. She felt the slow, soft penetration of his tongue, the hard caress of his lips, the aching deep groan that shuddered out of his chest.

Her arms were under his and around him. She could feel the heat from the hard muscles under her hands. She could feel his belt digging into her midriff. His powerful legs were trembling as he moved her against him and he groaned again, in anguish.

While he kissed her, his hands went deftly under the knit top to the front catch of her lacy bra, quickly loosening the catch before she could protest. His hands slowly took the weight of her bare breasts, caressing their hard tips, while the kiss went on and on. He felt her body tremble again and heard her soft cry go into his mouth. He couldn't stop. It was just like France, just like that night in her room. Some part of him stood away and saw his own helpless headlong rush into seduction, but he was too far gone to fight it now. He hadn't been a man for years. Now he was in the grip of the most desperate arousal he'd ever felt and he had to satisfy it. He wanted her, needed her, had to have her.

He was practiced, an expert in this most basic of arts. She was, for all her fears, still a novice who'd never known pleasure. He was going to give her that. He was going to make her want the satisfaction his body demanded.

Slowly he began to to slide the fabric of her blouse from her body while his mouth bit at hers in the kind of kisses that were a blatant prelude to intimacy. They threw her off-balance so that she made no protest when he removed the top and bra and dropped them onto the carpet. His hands caressed her soft, bare breasts and he drew away a breath so that he could watch them under the tender mastery of his hands.

"They're beautiful," he whispered tenderly, aware at some level of her dazed, wide-eyed stare. His hands caught her waist and he lifted her to his mouth. He traced the hard tips with soft wonder, savoring their taste with lips that cherished her. "You taste of rose petals and perfume," he breathed, nipping her tenderly.

She made a sound that brought his head up. He looked into her eyes, seeing the excitement, the shock of wonder in them. No, she couldn't stop him now. He recognized that blank, set expression on her face. She was in the throes of passion. There was no way she could draw back now, even if she'd wanted to.

Confident, he let her slide down his body and he moved back a step. She didn't try to cover her breasts. After a minute he caught the hem of his own knit shirt and pulled it over his head, tossing it onto the floor with her things.

His chest was sexy, she thought through a haze of pleasure, staring at it, bronzed and muscular with a thick curling mat of hair just a few shades darker than the hair on his head. Without volition, she moved forward and leaned into him, closing her eyes with a shaky sigh as she felt his bare chest against her breasts.

His big hands flattened just under her shoulder blades and drew her closer in erotic little motions that made her shiver.

She felt the heavy, hard beat of his heart under her ear. She traced the nipple beside her mouth and felt him tauten. Then he groaned and his mouth slid down and found hers. He lifted her clear off the floor and stood holding her, kissing her, in the middle of the sunlit room. For an instant he looked up and glared around the room. There was only the sofa or the desk or the carpet. He groaned.

He had no more time for decisions. Shaking with the

terrible need to have her, he couldn't risk having her come back to her senses before…

He laid her down on the carpet in front of the picture window that overlooked the lawn half a story below. Her body, there in the light, had the shimmer of a pearl. He knelt beside her and slowly, tenderly, stripped the clothing from her body, leaving it bare and trembling, all the while tracing her softness with his lips, with his hands, in skilled caresses that made it impossible for her to draw back.

He removed his own clothes then, still a little uncertain that his body was going to cooperate with him despite its tense need. So many years, so much pain, so much hunger. He looked at her and felt his whole body clench as he stood above her, shivering a little in the fullness of his arousal.

She looked at him with faint fear in a single moment of sanity. It hadn't been this intimate before. In the darkness, she'd had hardly a glimpse of him. Now, standing over her that way, she saw the magnitude of his arousal and flushed.

"I'll be careful," he said quietly.

He eased down beside her, restraining his own desire. He smoothed the hair back from her flushed face and bent to kiss her with aching tenderness, stemming the rush of words that rose to her lips. She wanted to tell him that she was unprotected, to ask him if he was going to take precautions. But his mouth settled hard on her breast and she arched, shivering with hot pleasure, and her last grasp on reason fell away.

The slow, easy movements of his hands and mouth relaxed her. She lay watching him touch her, hearing the deep tenderness of his voice as he whispered to her. The words became indistinguishable as he touched her more intimately. Her body lifted, shivered, opened to him. Her eyes, wide with awe, sought his as the pleasure built to some unexpected plateau and trembled there on the edge of ecstasy as he moved over her at last and his body began, very slowly, to join itself to hers.

She stiffened at first, because it was suddenly difficult, and her eyes flew open, panicked.

He paused, breathing heavily, and bent to kiss her wild eyes closed. He couldn't lose control, he told himself. Not this time. He had to fight his own desperate hunger for her sake. "I won't hurt you," he whispered roughly. His hand caressed over her flat stomach, lightly tracing, soothing. "I won't hurt you, baby. Try to relax for me."

Her eyes opened again, hesitant and uncertain. "You're…so…so…!" she blustered, swallowing. "What if I can't…?"

He groaned, because he was losing control, losing it all over again when he'd sworn he wouldn't, that he could contain the raging desire she kindled. But he couldn't. The feel of her body cost him his restraint.

He moved helplessly against her. "You did before," he said. "God, Barrie, don't tense like that!" he whispered urgently. "Oh, baby, I can't stop…!" His hand suddenly slid between them and he began to touch her expertly, feeling her body respond immediately, uncoiling, lifting helplessly. "Yes!" he groaned. "Yes, yes…!" He shuddered and suddenly his tongue was in her mouth probing, like his body, teasing, penetrating…!

She sobbed. He was doing something to her, something that made a rush of pleasure shoot through her like fiery shafts, that made her body crave what he was doing, what she was feeling…

There was a fullness that grew unexpectedly, that teased and provoked and excited. She was empty and now, now, she felt the impact of the fullness, shooting through her like fireworks, making her body throb in a new rhythm, making her blood flow faster. She could hear herself breathing, she could hear him breathing, she could feel his hips moving, his skin sliding sensuously against hers, above her, as his body moved closer and closer. She couldn't breathe for the hectic beat of her heart. She opened her eyes, her nails biting into his muscular upper arms as she tried to look down, to understand what was happening to her.

"No, don't look," he snapped when she tried to see. He kissed her eyelids, so that they had to close, and his mouth found hers again. His hand was still between them, and she was feeling things so intense that they made her mind spin.

"What are you…doing?" she gasped against his devouring mouth, shivering as the pleasure suddenly gripped her and made her body convulse.

"My God…what do you think I'm doing?" he cried out, shuddering as his hips pushed down in a pressure that sent the sun shattering behind her eyelids in a burst of pleasure so primitive that she sobbed like a child.

She couldn't tell how he was touching her now, she didn't care. She was moving with him, helplessly. Her taut body felt hot and tight and swollen. She felt it opening to the fullness that was alien and familiar all at once. This, she thought blindly, must be how a man prepared a woman for his body, this…!

His mouth never left her own. She was buffeted in a hard, quick rhythm that increased the fullness and the pressure, and it wasn't enough to fill the emptiness she had inside. Her legs felt the rough brush of his as she heard the anguish that came gruffly from the lips possessing hers. She could hear someone pleading, a sobbing high voice that sounded oddly like her own. She went rigid as the feeling stretched her as tight as a cord and suddenly snapped in the most unbelievable rush of hot pleasure she'd ever known in her entire life.

She felt intimate muscles stretching, stretching, felt her body in rhythmic contractions that threatened to tear her apart. And even as they took her to a level of ecstasy she'd

never dreamed existed, the plateau she'd reached fell away
to reveal one even higher, more intense...

She cried out, shivering, sobbing, drowning in pleasure.
She must have opened her eyes, because his face was above
hers, taut and rigid, his eyes so black they might have been
coals. His teeth were clenched and he was trying to say
something, but he suddenly cried out and his face flooded
with color. She watched him in rapt wonder, saw his eyes
go black all at once, saw the helpless loss of control, the
set rigor of climax that made his face clench. The pressure
inside her exploded and she felt his body go rigid, convuls-
ing under her fascinated eyes as his voice cried out hoarsely
in an endless moan of pleasure. His chest strained up, away
from her, his arms shivering with the convulsive pleasure.
He shuddered again and again,and all the while she watched
him, watched him...

He felt her eyes, hated them, hated her, even while the
world was exploding under him. He thought he was going
to faint with the onrush of ecstasy, reaching a level he'd
never dared achieve before it left him helpless. Always, he'd
been in control. He'd watched women in this anguished ric-
tus, but he'd never allowed a woman to see it happen to
him. Until now. He was helpless and Barrie could see. She
could see...what he really felt. Oh, God, no...! He wanted
to close his eyes, but he couldn't. She could see everything...*everything*.

The room seemed to vanish in the violence of his rapture.
It was a long time before he could open his eyes and see
the carpet where his cheek lay against her body. He was
shaking. Under him, he felt her labored breathing, felt her
cool skin touching his, felt her hands touching his hair,
heard her voice whispering shaken endearments, whispering, whispering. Damn her. Damn her!

As she held him, her breasts were wet, like the rest of
her body. He was heavy, lying on her. She felt his shoulders

and they were cool and damp. She moved her hands and felt his thick gold hair, wet with sweat. When she moved, she felt the pressure of him deep inside her body. She gasped.

When he could breathe completely again, he lifted his head and searched her eyes with barely contained fury at his loss of command, raising himself on both elbows so that she came into focus. He looked odd. He poised above her with a dark scowl.

His jaw tightened. "I saw you watching me," he said. "Did you enjoy it? Did it please you to watch me lose control to the extent that I couldn't even turn my face away?"

The angry words shocked her after the intimacy they'd just shared. She didn't understand the anger that flared in his face. He looked at her with contempt, almost hatred, his lips making a thin line. He took a rough breath and began to lift away, but she hated to lose the intimacy, the oneness he'd shared with her. Her body gripped him in protest at his upward movement, but then she suddenly cried out and her fingernails bit into him.

"Dawson, don't!" she whispered frantically, clutching at him.

He stopped moving at once, afraid that he'd hurt her. He scowled. "What's wrong?" he asked curtly.

Her face was rigid. She could feel the contractions inside her body. "It...hurts when you move," she said, embarrassed. She licked her dry lips. He muttered something that made her color and started to withdraw again, but this time he did it gently, with a slow, steady pressure. It was still uncomfortable, but not painful.

She looked down and blushed as red as a rose as he lifted himself completely away from her.

He rolled away from her and got to his feet, his muscles trembling from the violence of his fulfillment and the fear her cry had aroused. Memories of the night in France came back and he couldn't look at her.

He'd hurt her again. He jerked his clothes back on, hating his helplessness. He was just like his father, he thought furiously, a victim of his own uncontrollable desire. He wondered if Barrie had any idea how it frightened him to be at the mercy of a woman or why.

Barrie didn't understand his coldness, but slowly her pride came to the rescue. She couldn't bear to think of the risk she'd just taken, of the things he'd said to her. She'd welcomed him without a thought for the future, walking like a lamb into the slaughter, just as she had five years ago. Would she never learn? she wondered bitterly.

She drew herself up, wincing at the unfamiliar soreness, embarrassed and hurt as she reached for her things and began to dress, more clumsily than he had. She didn't understand what had made him so angry. He'd wanted her. Had it only been to prove his manhood after all? He'd given her pleasure that she never expected, and at first he'd been tender, almost loving. Now he wouldn't even look at her.

He was breathing a little unsteadily still. She didn't seem to be damaged, at least, thank God. But as his fear for her subsided, his anger at himself only increased. His body ached with the pleasure he'd had from her, but his pride was lacerated. He'd lost himself in her. He'd been helpless, so in thrall to desire that he'd have taken her in the hall, in the car...

He turned away, unable to bear even the sight of her. He was like his father. He was a slave to his desire. And she'd seen him that way, vulnerable, helpless!

She bit her lower lip until she drew blood. "Dawson?"

He couldn't look at her. He stared out the window with his hands tight in his pockets.

She felt cold. Her arms clenched around her body. It was impossible not to understand his attitude, even if she didn't want to. "I see," she said quietly. "You only wanted to know if you…could. And now that you do, I'm an embarrassment, is that it?"

"Yes," he said, lying through his teeth to save his pride.

She hadn't expected him to agree. She stared at him with eyes that had gone dark with shock. The clock had turned back to France, to that night in her hotel room. The only difference was that he hadn't hurt her this time. But she felt just as cheap, just as used, as she had then.

There was really nothing else to say. She looked at him and knew that the love she'd felt for him since her teens hadn't diminished one bit. The only difference was that now she knew what physical love truly was. She'd gloried in it, drowned in the wonder of his desire for her, given all that he asked and more. But it still wasn't enough for him. Now she knew that it never would be. He hated his hunger for her, that was obvious even to a novice, despite the fact that he'd indulged it to the absolute satiation of his senses. He wanted her, but it was against his will, just as it had been five years ago. Maybe he hated her, too, for being the object of his desire. How ironic that he was impotent with everyone else. How tragic.

She knew that it would do no good to conduct a postmortem. He was uncommunicative, and all her efforts weren't going to dent his reserve. She turned and went to the door, unlocking it with cold hands. Even when she went through it, he never looked her way or said a single word. Nor did she expect him to. He'd frozen over.

She took a bath and changed her clothes. Her shame was so sweeping that she couldn't bear to look at herself in the mirror. There was another fact that she might have to face. He hadn't even tried to protect her, and she'd been so hopelessly naive as to welcome the risk of a child. If she'd had any sense at all, she'd have let him writhe with his insecurities about being a man. If she'd had any sense at all, she'd have run like the wind. Which was, of course, what she was about to do.

It only took her a few minutes to pack. She put everything into her suitcase and garment bag and carried the lot down the staircase by herself. Rodge and Corlie were busy with their respective chores, so they didn't see or hear her go out the front door. Neither did Dawson, who was still cursing himself for his lack of restraint and pride.

He didn't realize she'd gone until he heard the car engine start up. He got to the front door in time to see her turning from the driveway onto the main highway that led to Sheridan.

For a few seconds, he watched in anguish, his first thought to go after her and bring her right back. But what would that accomplish? What could he say? That he'd made a mistake? That giving in to his passion for her had been folly and he hoped they wouldn't both live to regret it?

He closed the front door and rested his forehead against it. He'd wanted to know that he was still a whole man, and now he knew that he was. But only with Barrie. He didn't want any other woman. The desire he felt for Barrie was sweeping and devouring, it made him helpless, it made him vulnerable. If she knew how desperately he wanted her, she could use him, wound him, destroy him.

He couldn't give anyone the sort of power over him that Barrie's mother had held over George Rutherford. He'd actually seen her tease George into a frenzy, into begging for her body. Barrie didn't know. She'd never known that her mother had used George's desire for her to make him do anything she liked. But Dawson knew. A woman with that kind of power over a man would abuse it. She couldn't help herself. And Barrie had years of Dawson's own cruelty to avenge. How could he blame her if she wanted to make him pay for the way he'd treated her?

He didn't dare let Barrie stay. She'd seen him totally at
the mercy of his desire, but she didn't, thank God, know
how complete her victory was. He could let her leave thinking he'd turned his back on her, and that was for the best.
It would save his pride.

From his childhood, he'd known that women liked to find
a weakness and exploit it. Hadn't his own mother called
him a weakling when he'd begged to be held and loved as
a toddler? She'd made him pay for being born. And then
George had married Barrie's mother, and he'd seen the destructive pattern of lust used as a bargaining tool, he'd seen
again the contempt women had for a man's weaknesses.
He'd seen how his father had been victimized by his own
desire and love. Well, that wasn't going to happen to him.
He wasn't going to be vulnerable!

Barrie thought he'd only wanted to prove his manhood;
she'd think he'd used her. Let her. She wouldn't get the
chance to gloat over his weakness, as her mother had
gloated over his father's. She wouldn't ever know that his
possession of her today had been the most wondrous thing
that had ever happened to him in his life, that her body had
given him a kind of ecstasy that he'd never dreamed he was
capable of experiencing. All the barriers had come down,
all the reserve, all the holding back.

He'd…given himself to her.

His hands clenched violently. Yes, he could admit that,
but only to himself. He'd gone the whole way, dropped all
the pretense, in those few seconds of glorious oblivion in
her arms. He hated that she'd seen his emotions naked in
his eyes while he was helpless, but that couldn't be helped
now. It was the first time in his life that he'd ever been able
to give himself to pure physical pleasure, and it was probably only due to the enforced abstinence of sex. Yes. Surely
that was the only reason he'd had such pleasure from her.

Of course, she'd had pleasure from him, too. It touched

something in him to realize how completely he'd satisfied her in spite of her earlier fear. He felt pride that he'd been able to hold back at least that far, that he'd healed the scars he'd given her during their first intimacy.

But wouldn't it be worse for her, now that she knew what kind of pleasure lay past the pain? And wouldn't she be hurt and wounded even more now by his rejection, after she'd given in to him so completely? His only thought had been for his pride, but now he had to consider the new scars she was going to have. Why hadn't he let her go while there was still time? He groaned aloud.

"Dawson?" Corlie called from the kitchen doorway. "Don't you and Barrie want any lunch?"

"Barrie's gone," he said stiffly, straightening, with his back to her.

"Gone? Without saying goodbye?"

"It was…an emergency." He invented an excuse. "A call from a friend in Tucson who needed her to help with some summer school project. She said she'd phone you later."

She hadn't said that at all, but he knew she would phone. She loved Corlie and Rodge. She wouldn't want to hurt their feelings, even if she was furious with Dawson.

"Oh," Corlie said vaguely. "I must not have heard the phone ring." She was curious about his rigid stance and the scowl between his eyes when he glanced at her, but Dawson in a temper wasn't someone she wanted to antagonize. "All right, then. Do you want some salad and sandwiches?"

He shook his head. "Just black coffee. I'll come and get it."

"You've quarreled, haven't you?" she asked gently.

He sighed heavily as he walked toward the kitchen. "Don't ask questions, Corlie."

She didn't, but it took every last ounce of her willpower. Something had gone terribly wrong. She wondered what.

Barrie, meanwhile, was well on her way back to Arizona. She stopped at the first café she came to, certain that she wouldn't have to worry about Dawson following her. The very set of his head had told her that he wouldn't.

She ordered coffee and soup and then sat barely touching it while she relived her stupidity. Would she never learn that Dawson might want her body, but never her heart? This was the second time she'd given in to him. She'd gotten pregnant the very first. Would she, from something so insanely pleasurable? It seemed almost fated that such an experience would produce a child, even if he didn't love her...

Her hand touched her flat stomach and she let herself dream for a space of precious seconds, her eyes closed. Dawson's child, in her body. It would be wonderful to be pregnant again. Somehow she'd carry the child to term. Even if she had to stay in bed forever, she wouldn't lose it...!

She opened her eyes and came back to her senses. No. She removed her hand. She was being fanciful. It wouldn't happen, and even if it did, how would she cope? Dawson didn't want her. She repeated that, refusing to recall his anguish at her loss of their first child, his hunger for a baby. She couldn't let herself dream about Dawson's reaction if he knew she was pregnant. Besides, she thought, lightning rarely struck twice.

She'd simply go back to Tucson and forget Dawson. She'd done it once before. She could do it again!

Eight

But it wasn't that easy to forget him. Barrie had started losing her breakfast the day she got back to Tucson, just as she had after that disastrous night in France. She, who never had nausea a day in her life! She'd been home for two weeks now, and it hadn't stopped. It was the absolute end, she thought as she bathed her face at the sink, the absolute end that she could get pregnant so easily with him.

Now that lightning did appear to strike twice, what in the world was she going to do?

She hadn't let any of her lukewarm suitors know she was back in town, so there were no phone calls. She didn't have to worry about a part-time job because, apparently, Dawson had settled the deal with Leslie Holton over her tract of land. He'd have those water rights and he could keep his cattle on the Bighorn land that Barrie owned with him.

Her eyes went to the emerald engagement ring he'd given her such a short time ago. She hadn't meant to take it with her, she'd meant to leave it, but she'd been upset at the time, and she'd forgotten about it. She would have to send it back. Her fingers touched the beautiful ring and she sighed as she thought about what might have been. How wonderful if Dawson had bought her a set of rings years ago, knowing that she loved emeralds, if he'd bought them with love and asked her to marry him and told her that he loved her. Oh, what lovely dreams. But it was reality she had to face now.

She curled up in an armchair, still a little nauseous, and began to make decisions. She could go on teaching, presumably, although it was going to be tricky, under the circumstances. She would be an unwed mother and that wouldn't sit well considering the profession she followed. What if she lost her job? The money she got from her share of George Rutherford's estate, while it helped make her life comfortable, was hardly enough to completely support her. She couldn't risk losing her job. She'd have to move somewhere else, invent a fictitious husband who'd deserted her, died…!

Her stomach churned and she swallowed a rush of nausea. How shocking to be able to tell that she was pregnant so soon after conception, she thought. But it had happened just that way after she'd returned from France. In fact, in some mysterious way, she'd known even while Dawson was taking her. Her eyes closed. Taking her. Taking her. She could feel the harsh thrust of his muscular body, feel all over again the insane pleasure that had spread into her very blood.

She made a sound deep in her throat and opened starkly wounded eyes as the knock on the door coincided with her groan.

She blinked away the memories and got up, swaying a little as she made her way to the door. She didn't want company. She didn't want to talk at all. She leaned her forehead against the cold wood and looked through the peephole. Her heart froze in her chest.

"Go away!" she cried hoarsely, wounded to the heart that Dawson should be standing there.

He looked toward the door, his face pale and set. "I can't."

That was all he said, and not very loudly, but she heard him. Surely he wouldn't know, *couldn't* know. She smiled at that naive imagining. Of course, he knew, she thought fatally as she sighed and unlocked the door. There was some mysterious mental alchemy that had always allowed them to share their thoughts.

She didn't look up as he entered the apartment, bareheaded, reserved. She closed it and turned away, to sit back down in the armchair.

He stood over her, his hands in the pockets of his gray suit and looked at her pale, pinched face. Her lack of makeup and the dark circles under her eyes told their own story.

"I know," he said uncomfortably. "God only knows how, but I do."

She looked up, her wounded eyes searching his pale, glittery ones. She shrugged and stared at her clenched hands instead. She was barefoot, wearing a loose dress instead of jeans, because of the nausea. He probably knew that, too.

He let out a long, rough sigh and sat down on the sofa opposite her, leaning toward her with his hands clasped over his knees.

"We have to make some quick decisions," he said after a minute.

"I'll manage," she said tightly.

He turned the diamond horseshoe ring on his right hand. "You're an educator. Not the most liberal of professions. You won't get that promotion. You may not even be able to keep your job, despite the enlightenment of modern life." He looked up, his pale green eyes lancing into her own. "I want this baby,'' he said gruffly. ''I want it very much. And so do you. That has to be our first concern.''

She couldn't believe this was happening, that he was so certain, that she was pregnant. ''You can't tell until six weeks. It's only been two,'' she began, faintly embarrassed.

''We knew while we were making him,'' he said through his teeth. ''Both of us. I didn't take precautions, and I knew without asking that you weren't using anything, either. It wasn't an accident.''

She'd known that, at some level. She didn't try to deny it.

''We have to get married,'' he said.

She laughed bitterly. ''Thanks. As proposals go, that's a honey.''

His face was tight and uncommunicative. ''Think what you like. I've made the arrangements and applied for the license. We'll both need blood tests. It can be done in Sheridan.''

She looked up at him, her eyes furious. ''I don't want to marry you,'' she said flatly.

''I don't want to marry you, either,'' he snapped right back, his face mocking and angry. ''But I want that baby you're carrying enough to make any sort of sacrifice, even having to live with a woman like you!''

She jumped to her feet, her eyes flashing, her body shivering with rage, with hatred, with outrage. ''If you think I'm going to…!'' she shouted at him, when all at once, her face went white and she felt the nausea boiling up into her throat, into her mouth. ''Oh, God!'' She choked, running toward the bathroom.

She barely made it. There had been a grim satisfaction in seeing the guilt on Dawson's lean, tanned face when he realized what he'd caused. Good, she thought through waves of nausea, she hoped he suffered for it.

She heard footsteps, and then water running. A wet cloth

was held against her forehead until the nausea finally passed. She was vaguely aware of him coping with his normal cold efficiency, handling everything, helping her to bathe her face and wash the taste out of her mouth. He lifted her then and carried her into the bedroom, laying her gently on the covers. He propped two pillows behind her and went away long enough to fetch a cold glass of water and help her take a sip. The cool drink settled her stomach, but she glared at him just the same.

He was sitting on the side of the bed. His lean hand went to her damp, tangled hair. He smoothed it gently away from her face and studied her features with faint guilt. He'd tried so hard to stay away, to let go. But the past two weeks had been pure torment. He'd spent them going from ranch to ranch, checking stock and books, and it hadn't helped divert him. He'd missed Barrie as never before. And in some mysterious way, he'd known there was going to be a child. That had brought him here. That, and the feelings he didn't want to have for her.

"I'm sorry," he said tersely. "I didn't mean to upset you."

"Yes, you did," she replied. "You don't want to be here at all. And I'm not marrying any man who has the opinion of me that you do!" she added hotly.

He stared at his hands for a long moment. He didn't speak. The skin of his face was pulled taut by clenched muscles.

She put her hands over her eyes with a shaky sigh. "I feel horrible."

"Were you sick like this…after France?" he asked.

"Yes. It started the very next morning, just like this time. That's how I knew," she said wearily. She didn't open her eyes.

He turned and looked at her, wincing at the fatigue he could see in every line of her face, in the very posture of her body. Without conscious volition, his lean hand went to her belly and pressed lightly there, through the fabric, as if he could feel the child lying there in the soft comfort of her body.

She moved her hands, shocked by the touch of his hand, and saw his high cheekbones ruddy with color as he looked at her stomach.

He felt her gaze and met it them with his own. There was no expression at all in his face, but his eyes glittered with feeling.

"Why?" she said heavily, her voice thick with tears. "Oh, why, why…?"

His arms slid under her. He lifted her across his powerful thighs and enveloped her against him, one hand pressing her cheek to his chest in a rough gesture of comfort. She cried, and he held her, rocked her. Outside were the sounds of car horns and pulsing engines and brakes and muffled voices. Inside, closer, there was the sound of her choked sobs and her ragged breathing.

"Don't," he said huskily at her ear. "You'll make yourself sicker."

Her hand clenched against his broad chest. She couldn't remember when she'd been so miserable. He'd made her pregnant and now he was going to marry her, so that their child would have the security of parents. But some part of him hated her, resented her. What sort of life would they have?

As she thought it, the words slipped out, muffled by tears.

His chest rose and fell heavily, his breath audible as it stirred her hair. "We haven't many options," he answered her quietly. His hand smoothed her disheveled hair. "Unless you want to stop this pregnancy before it begins," he added, his voice as cold as winter.

She laughed bitterly. "I can't step on an ant and you think I could…"

His thumb stopped the words. "I know you can't, any more than I can," he said shortly. "I didn't mean it."

"Then why say it?" she demanded.

He tilted her face back and looked into it pensively. "You and I are two of a kind," he said absently. "I strike out and you strike back. You've never been really afraid of me, except in one way." His eyes narrowed as she flushed. "And now you aren't afraid of me that way anymore, either, are you?" he taunted softly. "Now you know what lies beyond the pain."

She pushed at his chest, but he wouldn't let go.

Something glittered in his pale eyes, something fierce and full of contempt and anger. His hand tangled in her thick hair and clenched, pulling so that her face arched up to his.

"That hurts," she protested.

His grip loosened, but only a little. His heart was beating heavily, roughly. She could feel it against her breasts. She could feel something else as well: the involuntary burgeoning of his body and the instant response of her own to it.

He laughed bitterly as he heard her soft gasp. "I was so hot that I couldn't hold back. I couldn't protect you. I couldn't even breathe at the last." His voice grew icy with self-contempt and his hand contracted again, angrily. "I want to make you that helpless in my arms. I want to make you beg me, plead with me, to satisfy you. I want you so maddened with desire that you can't go on living if I don't take you!"

He was saying something to her. Something more than just words. She looked into his face and saw bitterness and self-contempt. And fear.

Fear!

He didn't realize what he was giving away. His anger had taken control of him. "You think you can break me, don't you?" he demanded, dropping his eyes to her mouth. "You think you can lead me around by the nose, make me do anything because I want you!''

She hadn't said a word. She was still overcome by the enormity of what she was learning about him. She didn't even protest the steely hand in her hair. She lay quietly in his embrace and just listened, fascinated.

"Well, I'm not your toy," he said harshly. "I won't come running when you call or follow you around like a whipped dog begging for favors!"

Odd, she thought, that he didn't really frighten her like this, when he looked ferocious with that scowl between his flashing eyes.

"Can't you talk?" he demanded.

"What would you like me to say?" she asked softly, searching his eyes.

The calm tone eased some of the tension from his body. His hand unclenched and he winced, as if he'd only just realized his loss of control. His jaw tautened and his breathing became deliberate at once.

"You were angry because I watched," she prompted, remembering how unduly enraged he'd been about that.

The color flared along his high cheekbones.

She saw the self-consciousness in his anger. Her hand reached up hesitantly and touched his cheek. He actually flinched.

Her whole body relaxed, forcing him to shift his weight so that he could take hers. She hung in his arms, her eyes quietly clinging to his, and her fingers went from his hard cheek down to the corner of his mouth and then lightly brushed the long lower lip.

"Why didn't you want me to look?" she asked softly.

He didn't speak. His breathing grew rough.

"For heaven's sake, isn't that what sex is all about?" she faltered. "I mean, isn't the whole point of it to let go of inhibitions and restraints with another person?"

"Not for me," he said flatly. "Not ever. I don't lose myself with women."

"No," she agreed, studying him. She could almost see the answer. "No, the whole point of the thing is to make a woman lose all her inhibitions, to humble her so that she…"

"Stop it!"

He put her aside and got to his feet, his breathing unsteady. He rammed his hands into his pockets and paced to the window, viciously pulling the curtains aside.

She sat up on the bed, propped on her hands, staring at him as all of it jelled in her mind and brought a startling, shattering conclusion.

"That's why you were so vicious to me in France," she said. "You lost control."

He drew in a breath. His fingers went white on the curtain.

"That hasn't ever happened to you, not before, not with any woman," she continued in a hushed tone, knowing it was the truth without a word from him. "And that's why you hate me."

His eyes closed. It was almost a relief to have it said, to have her know it. His broad shoulders slumped as if relieved of some monumental burden.

Barrie had to lie back against the pillows. She felt faint. He wasn't admitting anything, but she knew all the same. She knew so much about him, so many things that she understood on a less conscious level. So why hadn't she realized that it wasn't Barrie he was punishing with his cutting words? It was himself, for losing command of his senses, for wanting her so desperately that he couldn't hold back.

"But, why?" she continued. "Is it so terrible to want someone like that?"

The muscles in his jaw moved convulsively. "I came across them in the hall one day," he said in a rough whisper. "She was teasing him, the way she always teased him,

aunting him with her body and then drawing back. She did
hat to make him give in, to make him do what she wanted.''

"She?'' she queried, puzzled.

He didn't seem to hear her. "That day, she wanted him
o trade cars. She had her heart set on a sports car, and he
vasn't ready to give up the luxury sedan he always drove.
So she teased him and then told him she wouldn't give in
o him if he didn't let her have her way.'' He let out a cold
breath. "He begged her.'' His eyes closed. "He was crying
ike a little boy, begging, begging…! And in the end, he
couldn't contain it, and he pushed her against the wall
and…''

He leaned his forehead against the cold glass, shivering
vith the memory. "She laughed at him. He was all but
aping her, right there in full view of the whole damn house-
old, and she was laughing that he couldn't even make it
o the bedroom.'' He turned, his eyes blazing in a white
ace. "I got out before they saw me, and then I was sick. I
actually threw up. You can't imagine how I hated her.''

She was getting a horrible premonition. She'd seen her
mother tease George Rutherford, but only with words. And
once or twice, she'd heard her mother make some remark
about him. But Barrie and her mother had never been close,
and she'd spent as little time at home as she could manage,
irst at boarding school in Virginia and then at college. She
made a point of staying out of her mother's way and out of
Dawson's. So she'd known very little about her mother's
econd marriage at all. Until now.

"It was…my mother,'' she said in a ghostly tone.

"Your mother,'' he said with contempt. "And my father.
She treated him like some pitiful dog. And he let her!''

Her breathing was oddly loud in the sudden stillness of
he room. She looked at Dawson and went white. Everything
e felt, remembered, hated in all the world was in his eyes.

She understood. Finally it made some terrible sort of

sense. She dropped her eyes to her lap. Poor Dawson, to
have to witness something like that, to see the father he
adored humiliated time and time again. No wonder he drew
back from what he felt with Barrie. He didn't want to be
helpless, because he didn't trust her not to treat him with
the same contempt her mother had had for George Ruther
ford. He couldn't know that she loved him too much to want
to hurt him that way. And of course, he didn't trust her
because he didn't love her. His was nothing more than a
helpless physical passion without rhyme or reason, a hated
weakness that he couldn't help. He looked at love as a
woman's weapon.

"I'm so sorry," she said quietly. "I didn't know."

"How could you not know what she was like? She was
your mother!"

"She never wanted me," she confessed stiffly, and it was
the first time she'd ever talked about her mother to him, or
to anyone else. Her face felt frozen. "She told me once that
if abortion had been legal at the time, she'd never have had
me in the first place."

He was shocked. His heavy brows drew into a frown as
he looked at her, sitting as stiff as a poker in the bed. "Good
God."

She shrugged. "My father loved me," she recalled with
determined pride.

"He died when you were very young, right?"

"Yes," she said.

He didn't even blink. "You were sixteen when she mar
ried my father." His eyes narrowed. "How many men did
she go through before she found him, Barrie?" he asked
with sudden insight.

She bit her lip almost through, wincing at the pain.

"Stop biting your lips," he muttered impatiently.

She smoothed her finger over it resignedly. "She had

lovers, if that's what you're asking.'' She glanced at him. ''That's why you thought I'd had them,'' she realized.

He nodded. He moved to the bed and sat down in the chair beside it, fatigue in his face, in his eyes. ''She was a bitch.''

''Yes,'' she said, not offended. She searched his face, looking for weaknesses, but he was mending the wall already. ''I know you loved your father.''

''I tried to,'' he said shortly. ''She came along just when he and I were beginning to understand each other. After that, he had no time for me. Not until he was dying.'' He looked away. He didn't want to talk about that.

She didn't push. He'd already given away more than he'd meant to, she knew.

After a minute he took a quick breath and his pale eyes searched her thin face. ''You've lost weight,'' he remarked abruptly.

She managed a weak smile. ''I started losing meals the day I left the ranch,'' she confessed, and flushed as she remembered the circumstances.

''I couldn't eat for the rest of the day,'' he recalled. He stared at the floor. ''I shouldn't have let you go like that, without a word.''

''What could you have said?'' she asked. ''I felt used...''

''No!'' He was really angry now. ''Don't you ever say anything like that to me again. Used! My God!''

''All right, cheap, then!'' she countered, sweeping back an annoying strand of hair. ''Isn't that how you wanted me to feel?''

''No!''

She glared at him, her lower lip trembling with emotion.

He made a curt gesture with one big hand and his lips flattened. ''Damn.'' He leaned forward, his head bowed, his hands supporting it as he braced his elbows on his splayed thighs.

She picked at the bedspread nervously. "You only wanted to see if you were capable with a woman," she muttered. "You said so."

His hands covered his face and pushed back into his hair. "I had an orgasm," he said roughly.

She recognized the resentment in the words even though she didn't quite understand their content. "What?"

He looked up, glared up, at her. "Don't you know what it is?"

She flushed. "I read books."

"So do I," he replied, "and until France and then that afternoon, that's the only way I knew what it meant."

"You're in your mid-thirties," she said pointedly.

"I'm repressed as hell!" he snapped back. "I never liked losing control, in any way at all with a woman, so I never permitted myself to feel anything…anything like that," he added uncomfortably. His head bent. "I got by on little tastes of pleasure, now and again."

What she was hearing shocked her. He was admitting, in a roundabout way, that he'd never been completely satisfied by a woman until he'd made love to Barrie.

"Oh."

The husky little reply made his head lift. She didn't look like a cat with the cream. She didn't even look smug. She looked…

"You're embarrassed," he said unexpectedly.

She averted her eyes. "That's nothing new, with you," she muttered, and blushed even harder.

Her inhibition made him less irritable, and much less threatened. He watched her with open curiosity.

"Don't stare at me," she grumbled. "I'm not some sort of Victorian exhibit."

"Aren't you?" He leaned forward, with his arms crossed over his splayed thighs. His wavy gold hair fell roguishly onto his wide forehead, tangled from his restless fingers in it. He hadn't remembered how soft her skin was, how radiant it was at close range. It had the sheen of a pink pearl. He'd bought her a string of them once, and balked at giving them to her. They were still in the safe back in Sheridan.

"Did you have one, too?" he asked suddenly.

Nine

She didn't know how to answer that. She was intimidated and embarrassed.

He became more relaxed when he saw her expression. She still hadn't smiled, or acted as if his fall from grace in her arms had made her want to gloat.

He leaned back and crossed his legs. "Well, well," he murmured, his eyes narrowing. "What a blush. Are you embarrassed?" he added, emphasizing the word with a mocking smile.

"Yes." She bit her lip. He got up and sat down beside her, his thumb forcing her teeth away from it. His hand spread onto her cheek, gentle and caressing while he studied her pale, pinched face.

"So am I," he confessed unexpectedly. "But maybe the reason we're embarrassed is because we've never talked about being intimate with each other."

"You've already said quite enough," she muttered stiffly.

He let out an odd, amused sound. "Miniskirts," he mused, "silk hose, four boyfriends at a time, low-cut blouses. And it never occurred to me that it was all an act. You little prude."

Her eyes flashed. "Look who's calling who a prude!!" she raged at him.

His eyebrows went up. "Who, me?"

"Yes, you!" She took a shaky breath. "You gave me hell, shamed me, humiliated me, and all because I opened my eyes at the wrong time! I couldn't really see you anyway," she blurted out, "because what I was feeling was so sweet that—" She stopped in midsentence as she realized what she was admitting.

But if she was embarrassed, he wasn't. His face changed as if by magic, his body became less taut.

He drew in a quiet breath. "Thank you," he said huskily.

She didn't recognize the expression on his handsome, darkly tanned face. "What for?"

His eyes dropped to his hands. "Making the memory bearable."

"I don't understand."

He picked at his thumbnail. "I thought you watched because you wanted to enjoy seeing me helpless."

Tears stung her eyes. She'd always thought of Dawson as invincible, stoic. This man was a stranger, someone who'd known pain and grief and humiliation. She wondered if what he'd let her know about him today was only the tip of the iceberg, if there were other painful memories that went back even farther in his life. Surely it had taken more than her mother's taunts to George Rutherford to make Dawson so bitter about women and his own sexuality.

Hesitantly, she reached out and touched his hand, lightly, her cold fingers unsteady as she waited to see if she was allowed to touch him.

Apparently she was. His hand opened, his fingers curled

warmly around hers and then linked slowly with them. He turned his head, searching her eyes.

"Couldn't step on an ant, hmm?" he asked absently, and his eyes softened. "I don't suppose you could. I remember you screaming when you saw a garter snake trapped under the wheelbarrow you were using in the flower beds, and then moving it so the poor thing could escape."

She liked the way it felt to hold hands with him. "I don't like snakes."

"I know."

Her fingers slowly moved against his and she lifted her eyes quickly to make sure that he didn't mind.

His lips twitched with amusement. "You're not very sure of yourself with me after all these years."

She smiled briefly. "I'm never sure how you're going to react," she confessed.

He held her eyes. "Tell me what you felt when we made love in my study."

She flushed. She tried to look away, but he wouldn't let her avoid him.

"We've gone too far together for secrets," he said. "We're going to be married. I hurt you when I pulled back. How?"

She shook her head and dropped her eyes.

"Talk to me!"

She grimaced. "I can't!"

There was a long pause. When she got the courage to look up, he was watching her with an expression she couldn't analyze.

She felt his hand still holding hers. She looked at it, admiring the long, deeply tanned fingers wrapped in her own. Her hand looked very small in that powerful grasp.

"Reassure me, then," he said quietly. "I hurt you. But it wasn't all pain, was it?"

"Oh, no," she said. "There was so much pleasure that

thought I might die of it. I opened my eyes and I saw you, but I felt just barely conscious. Then, you started to draw away and it had been so sweet that I wanted to stay that close to you, so I resisted…'' She swallowed. ''That's when it started to hurt.''

His breath was audible. ''You should have told me what you really wanted.''

''I couldn't. You looked as if you hated me.''

He made a sound deep in his throat. His fingers contracted around hers. ''I hated myself,'' he said roughly. ''I've hated myself since we were in France, when I went to your room and all but raped you.''

''It wasn't that,'' she replied. ''I wanted you, too. It was just that I didn't know how.''

''You were a virgin.'' He brought her hand to his lips and touched it softly with them. ''But I wanted you so desperately that I found excuses to have you.''

He was afraid that he'd injured her because he'd lost control. In fact, he was afraid that he might do it again. She felt warm inside, as if he'd shared something very secret with her. And he had. Certainly his loss of control was part of the problem along with bad memories of his stepmother and how she'd humiliated his father.

She touched his wavy hair gently. ''After I lost…after the baby,'' she said. ''The doctor told me that I should have had a complete gynecological examination before I was intimate with anyone. I was very…intact.''

''I noticed,'' he muttered. He looked down at her, enjoying the feel of her fingers against his hair. ''You said that it hurt when I pulled back, Barrie.''

She flushed. ''Dawson, I can't talk about this!''

He bent and brushed his mouth softly over her forehead. ''Yes, you can,'' he whispered. ''Because I have to know.'' His cheek rested against hers as he spoke, so that she didn't have to look at him. "In the study, just at the last, when I lost control and pushed down, did it hurt you at all, inside?"

She colored at the memory of how exquisitely he'd lost control. "No."

"Thank God! I hated your mother because of what she did to my father," he said, and his lean hand brushed back her hair."But that was never your fault. I'm sorry I made you pay for something you didn't do, Barrie," he added bitterly.

"Why didn't you ever talk to me about my mother and George?"

"At first because you were so naive about sex. Then, later, I'd built too many walls between us. It was hard to get past them." He drew her hand to his chest and held it there. "I've lived inside myself for most of my adult life. I keep secrets. I share with no one. I've wanted it that way, or I thought I did." His eyes searched hers. "We'll both have to stop running now," he said abruptly. "You can't run from a baby."

She gaped at him. "Well, I like that!"

"Yes, you do, don't you?" he asked with a gentle smile. "I like it, too. What were you going to do, go away and invent a fictional husband?"

She colored. "Stop reading my mind."

"I wish I could have read it years ago," he returned. "It would have saved us a lot of grief. I still don't know why it never occurred to me that you could become pregnant after that night on the Riviera."

"Maybe I wasn't the only one trying to run," she remarked.

His face closed up. Yes, he had tried to run, tried not to think about a baby at all. Was she rubbing it in? Gloating? Surely she didn't know about his mother, did she? He started to move away, but her hands clung to him, because she knew immediately why he'd withdrawn from her.

"There's a very big difference between teasing and sarcasm," she reminded him bluntly. "Sarcasm is always meant to hurt. Teasing isn't. I'm not going to live with you if you take offense at everything I say to you."

His eyebrows went up. "Aren't you assuming a lot?"

"Not at all. You thought I was making fun of you. I'm not my mother, and you're not your father," she continued firmly. She felt belligerent. "I can't even kill a snake, and you think I could enjoy humiliating you!"

Put that way, he couldn't, either. Barrie didn't have the killer instinct. She was as gentle as her mother had been cruel. He hadn't given that much thought. Now he had to.

He sat back down again, his eyes solemn as they searched over her face. "I don't know you at all," he said after a minute. "We've avoided each other for years. As you reminded me once, we've never really talked until the past few weeks."

"I know that."

He laughed shortly. "I suppose I'm carrying as many emotional scars as you are."

"And you don't look as if you have a single one," she replied. Her eyes fixed on him. "Did you give her the silver mouse?"

He knew at once what she was referring to. He shook his head. "I keep it in the drawer by my bed."

That was surprising, and it pleased her. She smiled shyly. "I'm glad."

He didn't return the smile. "I've done a lot of things I regret. Making you look foolish over giving me a birthday present is right at the top of the list. It shamed me, that you cared enough to get something for me, after the way I'd treated you."

"Coals of fire?"

"Something like that. Maybe it embarrassed me, too. I never gave you presents, birthday or Christmas."

"I never expected them."

He touched her disheveled hair absently. "They're in my closet."

She frowned. "What's in your closet?"

"All the presents I bought you and never gave to you."

Her heart skipped. "What sort of presents?"

His shoulder lifted and fell. "The emerald necklace you wanted when you were nineteen. The little painting of the ranch the visiting artist did in oils one summer. The Book of Kells reproduction you couldn't afford the year when the traveling European exhibition came through Sheridan. And a few other things."

She couldn't believe he'd done that for her. "But you never gave them to me!"

"How could I, after the things I'd said and done?" he asked. "Buying them eased the ache a little. Nothing healed it." He picked up her hand and his thumb smoothed over the emerald ring she was wearing on her engagement finger. "I bought you this set when you left France."

That was a statement that left her totally breathless. "Why?"

"Shame. Guilt. I was going to offer you marriage."

"You never did," she whispered in anguish.

"Of course I didn't," he said through his teeth. "When I came by your apartment a week after you'd left France, a man answered the door and told me you were in the shower. He was wearing jeans—nothing else, just jeans, and he was sweating."

She wouldn't have understood that reference once. Now, remembering the dampness of her own body after Dawson's fierce lovemaking, she understood it too well.

"That was Harvey," she said miserably." He was my landlord's son at the apartment house where I lived back then. He and his brother were building cabinets in the kitchen. They took a break and while they were doing that, had a quick shower. I'd been helping them…'' She paused. ''Harvey never said I'd had a visitor!''

He winced.

"You thought he was my lover," she guessed.

He nodded. "It seemed fairly obvious at the time. I went away eaten up with jealousy, believing that I'd set you off on a path to moral destruction. I was so disheartened that I flew all the way back to France."

She could have cried. If Harvey hadn't been there, if she hadn't been in the shower, if, if, if. Her face told its own story.

"You see what I meant, the morning I came to take you to Sheridan with me?" he asked quietly. "All it takes is a missed message, a lost letter, a phone call that doesn't get answered. And lives are destroyed."

He was still holding her hand, looking at the ring on her finger.

"You knew that I loved emeralds," she said softly.

"Of course I knew." He wasn't admitting how he knew, or why he'd gone to so much trouble to find a wedding set exactly like that one.

Suddenly she remembered. "I saw a ring like this in a magazine, one of those glossy ones," she recalled. "I left it open on the sofa, to show Corlie, because I loved it so much. That was about the time I left for college."

"You had on a pink tank top and cutoffs," he recalled. "You were barefoot, your hair was halfway down your back. I stood in the doorway and watched you sprawled on the carpet with that magazine, and I had to get out of the house."

She searched his eyes. "Why?"

He gave a short laugh. "Can't you guess? Because the same thing happened that always happened when I get close to you. I got aroused."

"But you acted as if you couldn't bear the sight of me!" she blurted.

"Of course I did! I'd have given you the perfect weapon to use against me if I'd let you know how I felt!" he replied without thinking.

He really believed that. She could see it in his pale eyes as they searched her face. He'd spent all those long years protecting himself, avoiding intimacy or even affection because he thought of it as a weakness that any woman would exploit. It was no wonder that they called him the "ice man." In so many ways, he was. She wondered if anything would thaw him out. Perhaps the baby would be a start. *The baby!* With wonder, her hands went absently to her flat stomach.

The involuntary action brought Dawson out of his unpleasant memories. He followed the motion of her hands and the bitterness left his face.

He reached out and placed one of his big hands over both of hers. "I'll take care of you this time," he said quietly, "even if it means hiring a hospital staff and keeping you in bed for the full nine months."

Her hands slid over his and rested there. "I won't lose this one," she said with certainty.

He made an odd sound and there was a glimmer of real affection in his eyes. "I still can't quite believe it," he said with poignant hesitation.

"Neither can I. Well, so much for that promotion," she murmured dryly. "I'm not living in Tucson alone."

He cocked an eyebrow. "You can teach in Sheridan."

"When he starts school," she agreed.

He searched her eyes. "He?"

"I hate dolls," she murmured shyly. "But I love football and baseball and soccer and wrestling."

He chuckled with genuine amusement. "Chauvinist."

"I am not. I wouldn't mind a daughter, really. I think

Antonia's stepdaughter, Maggie, is precious. I'm sure they're as crazy about her as they are about their new son, Nelson.'' She shrugged. ''Besides, Maggie hates dolls, too. But she loves to read and she knows almost as much about cattle as her dad.''

''I like Antonia,'' he replied.

''You can get used to Powell. Can't you?'' she coaxed.

He pursed his lips. ''I don't know. Will you make it worth my while?'' he murmured with a slow, steady appraisal of her relaxed body.

She couldn't believe she was hearing that. It was the first time in memory that he'd actually teased her. He even looked rakish, with his disheveled wavy gold hair on his forehead and his pale green eyes affectionate. He was so handsome that he took her breath away, but she'd have loved him if he'd been the ugliest man on earth.

''I've shocked you,'' he mused.

''Continually, ever since you walked in the door,'' she agreed. She smiled up at him. ''But to answer the question, yes, when I feel better, I'll do my best to make it worth your while.''

''No more fear?'' he asked, and was solemn.

''I don't think so,'' she replied. ''If it's going to be like last time from now on. And if you won't get furious afterward again.''

He took her hand in his and held it tightly. ''I'll make sure it's like the last time. As for getting upset...'' He grimaced. ''It's difficult for me.''

''Because you don't trust me yet,'' she said perceptively.

''I know. You'll just have to learn how, I suppose. But I don't think making fun of people is any way to carry on a relationship, if it helps. And I don't think less of you for enjoying what we do together.'' She blushed. ''In bed, I mean.''

"We didn't do it in bed. We did it on the carpet." His face hardened. "Like animals..."

She sat up and put her hand over his lips. "Not like animals," she said. "Like two people so hungry for each other that they couldn't wait. There's nothing to be ashamed of in that."

He took a deliberate breath, but his eyes were still full of storms and bitterness.

She traced his long, sensuous mouth with her forefinger. "I'm sorry that my mother made you hate what you feel when we're together, Dawson," she said quietly. "But I'm not like her, you know. I couldn't hurt you. I couldn't even tell you about the baby we lost, because I knew it would devastate you."

He reached for her roughly and enveloped her bruisingly close against him. There was a fine tremor in his arms as he buried his face in the thick hair at her throat.

She smoothed his hair with gentle hands, nestling closer. "But we won't lose this one, my darling," she whispered. "I promise you, we won't."

There was a stillness in him all at once. He didn't lift his head, but his breathing was suddenly audible. "What did you call me?" he whispered gruffly.

She hesitated.

"What?" he persisted.

"I said...my darling," she faltered self-consciously.

He drew back enough to let him see her flushed face. "No!" he said quickly. "Don't be embarrassed! I like it."

"You do?"

He began to smile. "Yes."

She sighed with pure delight as she looked at him.

He studied her flushed face in its frame of disheveled dark, wavy hair. His hands gathered it up and tested its silkiness with pleasure that was visible. "Feeling better?"

She nodded. "I'm a little queasy, but it's natural."

"My doctor can probably give you something for it."

She shook her head. "No. I won't even take an aspirin tablet while I'm carrying him. I won't put him at the slightest risk."

He dropped his eyelids so that she couldn't see the expression in his eyes. "Do you want the baby because of that maternal instinct, or do you want him because he's my child?"

"Are you going to pretend that you don't know?" she mused. "You used to taunt me about how I felt—"

"Yes, I knew." He interrupted curtly and met her eyes. "It hurt, damn it. I was cruel to you and even that didn't make any difference. You can't imagine what torment it was to know that all I had to do was touch you and I could have you, any time I wanted to. But I had too much honor to do it." His eyes narrowed with pain. "All the same, I hope I haven't killed that feeling in you. I don't know much about love, Barrie. But I want you to love me, if you can."

Tears burned in her eyes as she felt his lips touch her forehead, her eyebrows, her wet eyelids. The tears fell and she couldn't seem to stop them. "I've loved you since the first time I saw you," she whispered unsteadily. "So much, Dawson. So much, so much…!"

He kissed her. His mouth was hungry at first, insistent, almost cruel in its devouring need. But he felt her weakness and his arms loosened their tight grip. His mouth became caressing, tender.

When he lifted his head, he looked dazed. This was his woman. She loved him. She had his child under her heart. She was going to be his wife. He felt as stunned as he looked.

"We can…if you want to," she murmured sheepishly. "I mean, I'm not that sick."

He smoothed back her damp hair. "I wouldn't be much of a man if sex was all I had in mind right now," he replied quietly. "You're carrying my child. I could burst with pride."

It was an odd way to put it, but it touched her. She smiled shyly. "One time and I'm pregnant," she said pensively. "If we don't want twenty kids, I suppose one of us is going to have to do something after the baby comes."

"I'll do something," he said. "I don't want you taking anything that might put you at risk."

"I don't have to take something. I can use something."

"We'll see."

She touched his face, his shoulder, his chest. "I could get drunk on this."

"On what?"

"On being able to touch you whenever I want to," she said absently, unaware of the effect the words had on the man holding her. "I used to dream about it."

"Even after France?" he asked with sudden bitterness.

"Even after France," she confessed. She looked up. "Oh, Dawson, love is the most stubborn emotion on earth."

"It must be," he said.

She leaned forward and kissed his eyelids closed. "When do you want to leave for Sheridan?"

"Now."

"Now? But...!"

"I want to get married," he said firmly. "I want to do it quickly, before you change your mind."

"But, I wouldn't!"

He wasn't sure of that. He'd made so many stupid mistakes already that he couldn't risk another one. "And we won't sleep together again until the ring is on your finger," he added.

"Why, you blackmailer," she said.

He cocked an eyebrow. "I beg your pardon?"

"Withholding your body to make me marry you. Well, I never!"

"Yes, you did," he murmured.

She liked the way his eyes twinkled when he was amused. She smiled. He might not love her, but he liked her, and he wanted her.

"Yes, I did," she agreed. "Okay, if you're in such a hurry to give up your freedom, who am I to stand in your way? I'll pack right now!"

Ten

Corlie wasn't at all surprised to see Dawson walk in with a radiant Barrie. She hugged them both and went away with a smug expression to make them a pot of coffee.

"Coffee," Barrie began. "I really should have milk…"

Dawson put his finger over her lips and looked sheepish. "Don't. I'll go and tell her we both want milk."

"She'll be even more suspicious of that," she whispered.

He shrugged. "Maybe I'm overreacting. Maybe you are, too," he continued. "We don't even know for sure yet."

She leaned into his body with her eyes closed, feeling secure and at peace for the first time in years. "Yes, we do," she said.

He rocked her in his arms. "Yes, we do," he agreed after a minute. He closed his own eyes and refused to give in to the fear. It would be wonderful to have a child with her. Surely nothing would go wrong, as it had with his mother. And she wasn't going to make him jump through hoops.

His eyes opened and he stared past her. He felt troubled and turbulent. Trust came hard to a man with his history. He didn't know how he was going to cope with what lay ahead.

They were married quietly in the local Methodist church with Corlie and Rodge for witnesses. Antonia Long and her husband sent flowers and congratulations, but the baby had a cold and they wouldn't leave him, even for such a momentous occasion as to see Barrie and the "ice man" get married.

Dawson kissed her with a tenderness she'd never expected from him and Barrie felt on top of the world. Since their return to Sheridan, he hadn't touched her except to hold her hand or brush a light kiss across her mouth.

But tonight was their wedding night. She marveled at her excited anticipation, remembering the pleasure his body had taught hers to feel. It wasn't fear she was feeling now when she thought of lying in Dawson's arms in the darkness. And surely, after the honesty he'd shown her about his past, they could cope with his emotional scars. If he wanted to make love with the lights out, to conceal his vulnerability, she wouldn't even mind that. She only wanted to lie in his arms and love him.

But if she expected the wedding band to make an immediate difference in their relationship, she was in for a shock. Because that afternoon Dawson, who'd been restless and prowling ever since the reception, suddenly packed a bag and announced that he just had to see a man in California about a seed bull.

"On our wedding day?" Barrie exclaimed, aghast.

He looked more uncomfortable than ever. "It's urgent. I wouldn't go otherwise. He's threatening to sell it to someone else."

"You could just buy it," she suggested.

"Not without seeing it first." He closed his bag. "It won't take long. A few days."

"Days?"

He grimaced at her expression. He tried to speak and made a curt gesture with one hand instead. "I won't be away long. Corlie's got the number where I can be reached if you need me."

"I need you already. Don't go."

He paused to tilt her face up to his worried eyes. "I have to." He ground out the words.

She had a feeling that the confinement of marriage was already making him nervous. He'd faced so many things in the past few weeks, including a sudden marriage and a pregnancy. He was trapped and straining at the ropes. And if she didn't let him go now, she might lose him for good. She was wise enough to know that he needed a little time, a little room. Even if it was on their wedding day. She couldn't corner him. She had to let go.

"Okay." She smiled instead of arguing. "If you have to go, you have to go."

He seemed surprised at her lack of protest. His impatience to leave lessened. "You don't mind?"

"Yes, I mind," she said honestly. "But I understand, perhaps better than you realize."

He glared at her. "It's only a business trip. It has nothing to do with our marriage or the baby."

"Of course not."

He didn't like the expression in her eyes. "You think you know everything about me, don't you?"

Her eyebrows raised. "I haven't even scratched the surface, yet."

"I'm glad you realize it."

She reached up and kissed him beside his mouth, very gently, feeling his tall body tense at the unexpected caress "Do you mind if I kiss you goodbye?" she asked.

He stared at her. "No."

She grinned. "Have a safe trip. Are you taking the Learjet or a commercial flight?"

"Commercial," he said surprisingly. "I don't feel like worrying with maps and vectors today."

"Good. As long as you don't feel compelled to tell the pilot how to fly," she added tongue in cheek, remembering an incident in the past when Dawson had actually gone into the cockpit to instruct the pilot to change his altimeter.

He averted his eyes. "He was a novice commuter pilot and he was so nervous that he had his altimeter set wrong. Good thing I noticed. He'd have crashed."

"I suppose he would have, at that. And he never flew again, either."

"He realized he wasn't cut out for the stress of the job, and he had the guts to admit it." He looked down at her with calmer eyes, searching over her face. "You look better than you did in Tucson," he said. "But don't overdo, okay?"

"Okay."

"And try to eat more."

"I will."

"Don't drive anywhere unless Rodge and Corlie know where you're going."

"Okay."

"And if something goes wrong, call me. Don't try to handle it yourself."

"Anything else?"

He began to look uncomfortable. "Stay away from the horses. You shouldn't go riding until we know for certain."

"You're a case," she murmured with twinkling eyes. "Imagine that, you worrying about me."

He didn't react with humor, as she'd expected. In fact, he looked more solemn than ever. He took a long strand of her hair and tested its soft texture, looking at it instead of her while he spoke. "I've always worried about you."

She sighed, admiring his rare good looks in the tan suit he wore. "I can't believe that you actually belong to me, now," she reminded him, noting his shocked expression.

It should have pleased him to hear the note of possession in her voice. It didn't. Combined with his fears of being vulnerable in her arms, it made him angry. He dropped her hair and moved away. "I'll phone you tonight. Stay out of trouble."

She colored at the snub, because that's what it was. She wasn't through walking on eggshells with him, she realized at once. She'd only just begun.

"Dawson?"

He paused, looking back with obvious reluctance.

She hesitated, frowning. She was going to have trouble approaching him at all from now on. She had to do it right the first time.

"Marriage doesn't just happen," she said, choosing her words carefully. "It takes some cooperation, some compromise. I'll go halfway, but no further."

He looked puzzled. "What do you mean?"

"You're my husband," she said, tingling as she said the word.

"And now you think you own me, because I married you?" he asked in a dangerously soft tone.

Her face felt tight. She just stared at him for a minute before she spoke. "Just remember that I didn't ask you to marry me," she said quietly. "It was *you* who came after *me*. Not the reverse."

His eyebrows rose at the haughty tone. "I came after you to save you from an unwed pregnancy," he informed her with a mocking smile. "Or did you think I had other motives? Do I look like a man who's dying for love of you?" he added with biting sarcasm.

"Of course not," she said in a subdued tone. "I know that you don't love me. I've always known."

He didn't understand the need he felt to cut her, especially now. He'd drained all the joy out of her green eyes, all the pleasure out of her radiant face. She looked tired. If she really was pregnant, as they suspected, upsetting her was the very last thing he should be doing. But she had him now, and he burned for her. He wanted her with a headlong, reckless passion that could place him forever in her power. And that wasn't the only fear he was nursing. He had cold feet and they were getting colder by the minute. He had to get away now, to be alone so that he could get a grip on himself. Dear God, why did she have to look that way? Her very silence made him feel guilty.

Her chin lifted and she managed a smile. "Have a good trip."

His eyes narrowed. "You won't run away while I'm gone?" he asked abruptly, and watched her face color. "Damn it...!"

"Don't you swear at me!" she snapped back. Her lower lip was trembling, her hands clenched at her sides, her eyes glittered with tears of anger and hurt. "And I'm not the one who's running, you are! You can't bear the thought of a wife, can you, especially me!"

Her loud voice brought Corlie into the hall. The housekeeper stopped dead, aghast at the scene before her eyes. There was Dawson with a suitcase, looking as unapproachable as she'd ever seen him, and Barrie crying, shivering.

"You've only just got married," she said hesitantly, looking from one of them to the other.

"Why don't you tell her the truth, Dawson? We didn't get married for love. We got married because we had to!" Barrie sobbed. "I'm pregnant, and it's his fault!"

Dawson's face went white as the words stabbed him like a knife right out of the past. He was oblivious to Corlie's shocked expression as he glared at Barrie. "Don't make it sound like that. You couldn't possibly know for sure yet!" he snapped at her.

"Yes, I could," she said in a ghostly tone. "I used one of those home pregnancy kits, and it says I am!" she growled.

Thinking it was one thing. Hearing it, knowing it, being sure—that was something entirely different. He stood with the suitcase in his hand and he didn't move. She was really pregnant. His eyes went to her stomach, where one of her hands was flattened protectively, and then back up to her hurt, wet face. But he wasn't seeing Barrie. He was seeing his mother, blaming him for her marriage, blaming him, and then at the last, in the casket, with the little casket beside her…

"Well, you're married," Corlie said, trying to find a glimmer of optimism. "And you both love children…"

Barrie wiped her wet eyes. "Yes, we love children." She glared at Dawson. "What are you waiting for? There's a bull standing in a pasture in California just dying for you to rush out there and buy him, isn't there? Why don't you go?"

Corlie glanced at him. "You're going to California to buy a bull on your wedding day?" she asked, as if she couldn't have heard right.

"Yes, I'm going to buy a bull," he said belligerently. He slammed his hat on his head, ignoring his guilt at the way Barrie looked. "I'll be home in a few days."

He stalked to the front door and jerked it open. He knew both women were watching him, and he didn't care. He wasn't going to go rushing to Barrie's bed like a crazed animal begging for favors, and she needn't expect it. She had to learn right from the beginning that he had the upper hand, and that he wasn't going to be some sort of sexual toy for her. She already blamed him for getting her pregnant,

for ruining her life. She was going to be like his mother,
she was going to torment him. He had to escape while he
could.

That he was behaving irrationally didn't even occur to
him. Not then, at least.

But by the time he was ensconced in his California hotel
suite, the world seemed to snap quite suddenly back into
focus.

He looked around him with vague shock. He'd walked
out on his wife of two hours, left her alone and pregnant,
to go and buy a bull. He couldn't believe what he'd done,
what he'd said to her. He must have been out of his mind.

Perhaps he really was, he thought. He'd tortured himself
with thoughts of making love to Barrie, but once again he'd
have to submit to the madness she created in his body. He'd
be helpless, vulnerable, weak. She'd watch him…she'd see
not only his surrender to her body, but what he really felt.
In the heat of ecstasy he wouldn't be able to hide it from
her.

He took a long breath. He'd never faced his own vulnerability with her. In fact, he'd gone to extreme lengths to
make sure he didn't have to face it. It had been impossible
for him to lower the barriers between them, for fear that
she'd want revenge even now for the way he'd treated her.
If he let her see the extent of his desire, she'd use it against
him. Hadn't his own mother taunted him with his childish
weaknesses, ridiculed him, made him look small in front of
his father and his friends? Hadn't she pointed out that he
was a sissy because he'd cried when his German shepherd
had been hit by a car? Hadn't she spent his childhood making fun of him, making him pay, unbeknownst to his father,
for a marriage she'd never wanted in the first place? Dawson
had been a mistake, she often told him, and she'd had to
marry a man she didn't really love because of it…

Funny that he hadn't let himself remember those words

until today. Barrie was pregnant and she'd cried that she'd had to marry Dawson because of it. If she hadn't said that, he'd never have gone out the door. Ironic that her own mother had said the same thing about her, he thought, recalling what she'd told him in Tucson. Maybe women didn't really want babies at all except as a means of torturing men and making them feel guilty. He wondered if that thought was quite coherent.

He sprawled on the luxurious sofa in the sitting room, remembering other things, remembering Barrie's soft skin under his, her sweet cries of passion as he drove her into the carpet beneath the heated thrust of his body. He groaned aloud as the memory of the ecstasy she'd given him poured into his mind and made him shiver. Could he live without ever again knowing that pleasure, regardless of the price?

His eyes closed as he lay back. He could always turn out the lights, he thought with dry humor. Then she couldn't look at him. It wouldn't matter if she heard him. He'd hear her, too. She was none too quiet when they made love. His eyes blazed with feeling as he recalled her own shocked pleasure that morning on the carpet. She'd known only pain from him before. He'd taught her that she could expect far more than that.

She'd said she loved him. Good God, how could she love him, when he kept pushing her away? Why couldn't he accept her love, why couldn't he accept his own addiction to her? She was pregnant, and he'd left her in Sheridan on their wedding day out of nothing more than cold fear because he…because he…

He opened his eyes and took a slow, painful breath. Because he loved her. There. He couldn't admit it to her, but he couldn't hide it from himself. He loved her. He'd loved her since she was sixteen, since she'd given him a silver mouse on his birthday. He'd loved her in France, hated himself for taking advantage of what she felt for him in an attempt to deny that love. But it had grown and grown until it consumed him. He couldn't get rid of it. He couldn't stop. He couldn't give in to it. What was he going to do?

Well, he thought as he managed to get to his feet, there was one thing he could do. He could have a drink, and then he was going to call Barrie and set her straight on a few things!

Barrie was surprised when she heard Dawson's thick voice on the telephone. She hadn't really expected him to call after the furious way he'd left. She'd spent the rest of the day alternately crying and cursing, while Corlie did her best to comfort and reassure her. She'd gone to bed early, sick and disappointed because her new husband couldn't even stand to be in the same house with her. And after the tenderness she'd felt in him in Tucson, too. It had been utter devastation.

Now, here he was on the phone trying to talk to her, and unless she missed her guess, he was blind, stinking drunk!

"Did you hear me?" he demanded. "I said, from now on, we're only going to make love in the dark!"

"I don't mind," she said, confused.

"I didn't ask if you minded," he muttered. "And you can't look at me while we do it."

"It would never occur to me," she said placatingly.

"And don't say you own me. You don't own me. No woman is going to own me."

"Dawson, I never said that."

"You said I belonged to you. I'm not a dog. Did you hear me?"

"Yes, I heard you." She smiled to herself at his efforts to enunciate properly. The anguish and disappointment of the afternoon had vanished as he poured out his deepest fears without even realizing it. It was a fascinating glimpse at the real man, without the mask.

"I don't belong to you," he continued. He felt hot. He pushed back his hair. He was sweating. Maybe he should turn on the air conditioner. If he could only find it. He bumped into the table and almost upset the lamp. In the tangle, he dropped the phone.

"Dawson?" Barrie called, concerned when she heard the crash.

There were muttered, half-incoherent curses and a scrambling sound as he retrieved the receiver. "I walked into the table. And don't laugh!"

"Oh, I wouldn't dream of it," she assured him.

"I can't find the air conditioner. It must be in this room somewhere. How the hell can they hide something that big?"

She almost lost it then. She had to stifle a burst of laughter. "Look under the window," she instructed.

"What window? Oh, that one. Okay."

There was another pause and some odd sounds, followed by a curse and a thud. "I think I turned on the heat," he said. "It's hot in here."

"You might call housekeeping and ask them to check," she said hesitantly.

"Check what?"

"The air conditioner."

"I already checked it," he muttered. "It's under the window."

She wasn't going to argue. "Did you see the bull?" she asked.

"What bull?" There was a pause. "Listen, there's no bull in here, are you crazy? This is a hotel!"

By now, Barrie was rolling on the floor.

"Are you laughing?" he asked furiously.

"No," She choked. "I have a cough. I'm coughing." She coughed.

There was another pause. "I was going to tell you something," he said, trying to focus. "Oh, I remember. Listen here, Barrie, I can live without sex. I don't even need it."

"Yes, Dawson," she agreed gently.

"But if you want to sleep with me, you can," he continued generously.

"Yes, I would like that, very much," she said.

He cleared his throat. "You would?"

"I love sleeping with you," she said softly.

He cleared his throat again. "Oh," he said after a minute.

The opportunity was too good to miss. He was talking to her as if he'd had truth serum. "Dawson," she began carefully, "why did you go to California?"

"So I wouldn't make love to you," he said drowsily. "I didn't want you to see...how much I wanted to. How much I cared."

Her heart began to swell, to lift, to soar. "I love you," she whispered.

He sucked in a sharp breath. "I know. I love you, too," he said drowsily. "Love you...so much. So much, Barrie, so much, so much...!" He swallowed. He couldn't quite talk.

Which was just as well, because Barrie was as speechless as he was. She gripped the receiver like a life jacket, staring into space with her heart in her mouth. "But I don't want you to know it," he continued quite clearly. "Because women like having weapons. You can't know how I feel, Barrie," he continued. "You'd torment me with it, just like your mother tormented George because he wanted her so much."

She felt the pain right down to her toes. She'd never known these things about Dawson.

"Listen, I have to go to bed now," he said. He frowned, trying to remember something. "I can't remember why I called you."

"That's all right, darling," she said softly. "It doesn't matter."

"Darling," he repeated slowly. He took a heavy breath. "You don't know how it hurts when you call me 'darling.' I'm buried inside myself. I can't dig my way out. I miss you," he whispered, his voice husky and deep. "You don't know how much. Good night...sweetheart."

The line went dead. Barrie stayed on it, waiting. After a minute the switchboard came on the line. She heard the operator's voice with a sense of fate. She smiled.

"May I help you?" the operator repeated.

"Yes, you may. Can you tell me how to get to your hotel?"

Corlie muttered all the way to the airport in Sheridan, but she was smiling just the same. She put Barrie on the commuter flight to Salt Lake City, Utah, where she caught the California flight. It was tiring and she was already fatigued, but it seemed somehow the right thing to do, to get to her reluctant husband before he sobered up completely.

She arrived at the hotel very early the next morning and showed the hotel clerk her marriage license. It didn't take much persuasion after that to coax him into letting her have a key to Dawson's room.

Feeling like a conspirator, she let herself in and looked around the suite with a little apprehension. But timidity hadn't brought her this far; courage had.

She opened the door to what must be the bedroom, and there he was, sprawled nude on the covers, as if he'd passed out before he could get under them. Not that he needed to. Bread could have been baked on the floor, judging by the temperature.

Barrie went to the air conditioner and found the switch turned off. She clicked it on high and cool air began to blow in. She stood there for a minute, because she was feeling a little nauseous from the heat. As the cool air filtered up to her face, she began to breathe more easily.

There was a sound and when she turned, Dawson was propped on one elbow, watching her through bloodshot eyes.

Eleven

"**G**ood morning," she said, shy now that she was actually facing him after their extraordinary conversation of the previous night.

"Good morning." His eyes searched over her body in jeans and a tank top with a lined jacket over it. Her long hair was a little disheveled, and she looked flushed. He still wasn't certain that she wasn't a mirage. He scowled. "What are you doing here?"

"Turning on the air-conditioning," she said.

He cocked an eyebrow. "Pull the other one."

She lifted her chin and colored a little as her eyes registered his blatant masculinity. He wasn't only nude, he was already aroused, and apparently not the least shy anymore about letting her see. "I'm getting educated."

He smiled mockingly. "We're married. If you don't want to look at me, nobody's making you."

She glared at him. The wall was back up. She'd come all

this way on hope, exhilaration that he'd finally admitted his feelings for her, only to find that she'd overstepped her limit again. He wasn't going to admit anything. He was going to go right on keeping her at a distance, refusing to let her see into his heart. The baby wouldn't make any difference. They'd live together like strangers with the child as their only common ground. She could see down the long, lonely years of loving without any visible return of her feelings for him, without hope.

"I came to tell you that I'm going back to Tucson," she said coldly. "That's what you want, isn't it?" she added when he looked shocked. "That's what this trip is all about. You married me because you felt you had to, but now you're sorry and you don't want me around. I make you lose control, and you can't stand that." She straightened. "Well, no more worries on that score. I've got my bags packed and I'll be out of your house by tomorrow!"

He threw his legs off the bed and got up. Nude, he was more than intimidating. He moved toward her and abruptly lifted her up in his arms, turning to carry her back to bed.

"Put me down!" she snapped at him. "What do you think you're doing?"

"I'll give you three guesses." He tossed her onto the bed and followed her down, catching her flailing hands. He pressed her wrists into the mattress and poised there above her, his eyes pale and steady and totally unreadable.

"I hate you!" she said furiously. Her eyes stung with unshed tears as he blurred in her vision. "I hate you, Dawson!" she sobbed.

"Of course you do." His voice sounded almost tender, she thought through the turmoil of emotions. But surely it wasn't. His hands slid up to melt into hers, tangling with her fingers as he bent and drew his lips softly, tenderly, over her mouth. His chest eased down, his long legs slid against hers in a silence that magnified her ragged breathing and the sound of his body moving against hers.

He drew her arms around his neck. His hands slid under her, disposing of catches and buttons and zippers. In a melting daze, she felt him undressing her, and all the while, his mouth was making her body sing. He nuzzled her breasts, tasting their hard tips, suckling them, while he removed the layers of fabric until she was as nude as he was. The thick hair on his chest tickled her skin at first, and then made her body tauten with desire.

He never spoke. He kissed her from head to toe, in ways he never had before, his hands touched her with a mastery that would have made her insanely jealous of the women he'd learned it with if she'd been able to think at all. His mouth teased and tempted and finally devoured hers. And all the while, he caressed her as if her pleasure was the most important thing in the world to him. He kindled fires and all but extinguished them over and over again until she was on the edge of madness, sobbing aloud for relief from the tension his expert caresses built in her.

But it was a long, long time later before he finally eased down between her legs and very gently probed the dark, sweet mystery of her body, covering her mouth with his just as he pushed softly and felt her open to absorb him.

She stiffened just a little, but there was no resistance at all to his passage, and he shifted just enough to make her gasp and cling to him before he probed even deeper. All the while, he was tender as he'd never been in the past, slow and quiet and utterly loving. *Loving.* She didn't open her eyes once. She didn't try to look at him. She lay drowning in the pleasure each slow, soft movement of his hips created, sobbing rhythmically under the exquisite throb of pleasure that grew deeper and deeper, like a drum beating in her body, beating, beating...

With maddening precision he built the pleasure to a cres-

cendo that left her whimpering like a wounded thing, clinging fiercely, whispering things to him in her need that would
shock her minutes later. But for now, there was no future,
no shame. She pleaded helplessly, her whole body rising,
shivering in a painful arch, a silent plea for fulfillment. And
recognizing the end of her endurance, he moved sharply,
suddenly, into complete possession in a slow, deep, endless
rhythm that sent her spinning right up into the sun. Her nails
bit into his back helplessly as she shuddered, sobbing under
his mouth, crying out in anguished delight, tears raining
down her cheeks as she endured the most incredible ecstasy
she'd ever felt, so deep and throbbing that it was almost
pain.

Only then, only when he felt her body convulse in the
final spasms of completion did he drive fiercely for his own
fulfillment. It was as before, spasms of aching pleasure that
built and built and suddenly blazed in his taut body in an
explosion of heat and light, making him mindless, shapeless,
formless. He was part of her, as she was part of him. There
was nothing in the world, only the two of them. Only...
this...!

He saw the ceiling without seeing it. He was lying on his
back, still trembling from the violence of his satisfaction.
He could hear Barrie breathing raggedly. He could feel the
dampness of her body where it lay so close and so far from
his.

"They say that muscular contractions that violent could
break bones without the narcotic of ecstasy to make them
bearable," he remarked drowsily when he had his breath
back.

She didn't say anything. She was lying on her stomach,
half-dead with pleasure and so miserable that she wanted to
hide. Sex. Only sex. He hadn't said a word, all the while,

and now he was treating her to a scientific explanation of
sexual tension.

He rolled over onto his side and looked at her. She
averted her face, but he pulled her against him and tilted
her chin up.

"Well, do you still want to leave me after *that?*" he
asked. "Or would you like to try and convince me that all
those outrageous, shocking things you whispered to me were
the result of a bad breakfast…Barrie!"

She'd torn out of his arms in a mad dash for the bathroom, and only barely made it in time. She knelt there, her
heart breaking in her chest, her eyes red with tears, while
she lost her breakfast and everything in between. *The monster!* The monster, taunting her about a response she
couldn't help! And where had he learned such skills anyway, the licentious, womanizing…!

While she was thinking it, she was saying it.

Dawson wrapped a towel around his waist and with a
resigned sigh, he wet a facecloth and knelt beside her. When
the nausea finally passed, he bathed her face and carried her
back to bed, tucking her gently under the sheet.

"I want my clothes." She wept. "I can't leave like this!"

"No problem there. Because you aren't leaving." He
picked up her clothes, opened the window and threw them
out.

She lay in a daze, watching him perform the most irra-
tional act of their long acquaintance. She actually gasped
out loud.

He calmly closed the window. Below there was a loud
squeal of brakes. He cocked an eyebrow at her. "That lacy
bra probably landed on some poor soul's windshield and
shocked him into panic," he mused. "You shouldn't wear
things like that in your condition, anyway. It's scandalous."

She held the sheet tucked against her while she struggled
with the possibility that Dawson's mind had snapped.

He laughed softly as he stood over her, the towel just barely covering his lean hips. Her expression amused him. "What's the matter?" he asked.

Her hand clenched on the cool cotton fabric. "I didn't bring a change of clothes," she said stiffly. "And now even my underwear—my underwear, for God's sake!—is out there being handled by total strangers! How am I supposed to leave the room, much less the hotel?"

"You aren't," he replied. His eyes slid over her soft, faintly tanned shoulders and he smiled. "God, you're pretty," he said. "You take my breath away without your clothes."

She didn't say anything. She wasn't sure it would help the situation.

He sat down beside her with a rueful smile. "I guess I can't expect you to understand everything at once, can I?" He smoothed back her hair and his eyes were tender on her pale face. "While you're struggling with your situation, I'll have them send up something to settle your stomach. How about some strawberry ice cream and melon?"

Her favorite things. She hadn't realized that he knew. She nodded slowly.

"And some hot tea."

"The caffeine…"

"Cold milk," he amended, smiling.

She nodded again.

He picked up the phone, punched room service and gave the order. Then he went to his suitcase and pulled out one of his nice, clean shirts and laid it on the bed within reach. "I don't wear pajamas," he said. "But that will make you decent when room service comes."

"How about you?" she asked uncomfortably.

He gave her a rueful look. "No guts?" he chided. "Don't want to be seen with a naked man, even if you're married to him?"

She flushed.

"And you were calling me a prude." He got up, tossed the towel onto a chair and pulled on his slacks.

"Better?" he asked when he'd fastened the belt in place around them.

Better. She stared at him with pure pleasure, her eyes drifting over his broad, hair-covered chest down to his narrow waist and lean hips and long, powerful legs. He even had nice feet. She loved looking at him. But that was going to get her in trouble again so she averted her eyes to the bed.

He knew why. He sat back down with a long, heavy sigh and smoothed his big, warm hand over her bare shoulder. It was cool and damp to the touch. Her face was too pale, and a little pinched.

"Go ahead," he invited. "Look at me. It doesn't matter anymore. I suppose I told you all there was to tell last night. I don't remember too much of what I said, but I'm sure I was eloquent," he added bitterly.

She lifted her eyes warily to meet his. She didn't say anything, but her face was sad and resigned and without life.

He grimaced. "Barrie…"

She burrowed her face into the pillow and gripped it. "Leave me alone," she whispered miserably. "You've had what you wanted, and now you hate me all over again. It's always the same, it's always…!"

He had her up in his arms, close, bruisingly close. His face nuzzled against her soft throat through a cushion of thick wavy dark hair. "I love you," he said hoarsely. "I love you more than my own life! Damn it, isn't that enough?"

It was what he'd said last night, but he was sober now. She wanted so badly to believe it! But she didn't trust him.

"You don't want to love me," she whimpered, clinging closer.

He sighed heavily, as if he was letting go of some intolerable burden. "Yes, I do," he said after a minute, and he sounded as if he were defeated. "I want you and our baby. I want to hold you in the darkness and make love to you in the light. I want to kiss away the tears and share the good times. But I'm afraid."

"Not you," she whispered, smoothing the hair at his nape. "You're strong. You don't feel fear."

"Only with you," he confessed. "Only *for* you. I never had a weakness until you came along." His arms contracted. "Barrie," he said hesitantly, "if I lose you, I can't live."

Her heart jumped. "But, you aren't going to lose me!" she said. "I'm not going to walk out on you. I didn't really mean it. I thought you wanted me to go."

"No!" he said huskily, lifting his head. He looked worried. Really worried. He traced her soft cheek. "That's not what I meant. I meant that I could lose you when you have the baby."

"Oh, for heaven's sake...!" she exclaimed, stunned.

"Women do still die in childbirth," he muttered uncomfortably . "My mother...did."

She was learning things about him that she would never have dared ask, that she hadn't known at all. She searched his eyes slowly. "Your mother died in childbirth?"

He nodded. "She was pregnant. She didn't want to be, and she tried to have an abortion, but my father found out and made so many threats about cutting off the money she liked to spend that she gave in. She went into labor and something went wrong. They were out of the country, on a trip she'd insisted on taking even that late in her pregnancy. The only medical care available was at a small clinic. It was primitive, there was only an intern there at the time." He sighed heavily. "And she died. He loved her, just as he'd loved your mother. It took him years to get over it. He felt responsible. So would I, if something happened to you.''

Her fingers twined around his. It was humbling to realize that he loved her that much. He didn't want to get rid of her at all. He'd gone to the other extreme. He was terrified that he might lose her.

''I'm strong and healthy and I want this baby. I want to live,'' she said softly. ''I couldn't leave you, Dawson,'' she added firmly. ''Not even to die.''

He looked down into her wet eyes and his face was strained, taut. He looked so stoic and immovable that it shocked her when he traced her mouth with a finger that wasn't quite steady.

''You'll learn to trust me one day,'' she said softly. ''You'll learn that I'll never deliberately hurt you, or belittle you, or try to make you feel less of a man because you care about me. And our child will never be mocked or spoken to with sarcasm.''

His hand stilled on her face. ''And you won't leave me,'' he added with a bitter laugh.

She smiled. ''No,'' she said gently. ''I have no life without you.'' She took his hand and slid it under the cover to lie on the soft, bare swell of her stomach. ''I'm pregnant,'' she said. ''We have a future to think about.''

''A future.'' His hand flattened where she'd placed it. ''I guess I'm going to have to stop living on bad memories. It's hard.''

''The first step is to look ahead,'' she told him.

He shrugged. He began to smile. ''I suppose so. How far ahead?''

''To the nearest department store,'' she said with sudden humor. ''I can't spend the day without underwear!''

He pursed his lips and for the first time since she'd arrived, he looked relaxed. ''Why not?'' he asked. ''Are you sore already?''

She stared up at him uncertainly.

"Are you?" he persisted, and his hand moved insinuat-ingly. "Because I want to make love again."

"It's broad daylight," she said pointedly.

His broad shoulders rose and fell. "It was broad daylight a few minutes ago," he reminded her. His face was solemn. "You kept your eyes closed. Don't do it again. I won't make any more snide remarks about it. I'm sorry I made you ashamed of wanting to watch something so beautiful."

She wasn't sure how to take this apparent change in him. She searched his pale eyes, but there were no more secrets there. He wasn't hiding anything from her.

"I know," he murmured ruefully. "You don't quite trust me, either, do you? But we'll work it out."

"Can we?"

The knock at the door interrupted what he might have replied. Barrie quickly slipped on his shirt and buttoned it while he let the waiter in, signed the bill and handed the man a tip on his way out.

"Take that off," he murmured when he'd locked the door again, nodding toward the shirt.

"I won't," she replied.

"Yes, you will. But we'll let your stomach get settled first," he conceded. He picked up the small dish of home-made strawberry ice cream and sat down on the bed, lifting half a spoonful of it to her lips.

She was surprised, and looked it.

"You fed me when I had the wreck," he reminded her. "Turnabout is fair play."

"I'm not injured," she replied.

"Yes, you are," he said quietly. "Right here." He put the spoon into the hand holding the small crystal goblet and with his free hand he touched her soft breast through the shirt. He felt its immediate response, but he didn't follow up. He lifted the spoon again to her mouth. "Come on," he coaxed. "It's good for you."

She had a sudden picture of Dawson with a toddler, smiling just like that, coaxing food into a stubborn small mouth and she managed a watery smile as she took the ice cream.

"What are you thinking about?" he wondered.

"A little mouth that doesn't want medicine or spinach," she said quietly.

He understood her. His eyes darkened, but not with irritation. He took a long breath and held another spoonful of ice cream to her mouth. Eventually he smiled. "I guess I might as well learn to change diapers and give bottles, too," he mused softly.

"No bottles," she said firmly. "I want to nurse the baby."

His hand stilled halfway to her mouth. He searched her eyes, shocked at the way the statement aroused him.

She could tell from the tautness of his body and the darkness of his eyes, from the faint flush across his cheekbones what he was feeling. She felt her own breath catch in her throat. She could see him in her mind, watching as she nursed the baby...

"You're trembling," he said unsteadily.

She moved restlessly and a self-conscious laugh passed her lips. "I was thinking about you watching me with the baby," she said shyly.

"So was I."

She let her eyes fall to his hard mouth, tracing the firm, sensuous lips. She caught her breath as a wave of hunger swept over her body.

"Good God." He whispered it reverently. He set the goblet aside carefully, because his hands weren't steady. And when he turned back to her, she had the shirt open. She pulled the edges aside, red-faced and taut, and watched him as he looked at her hard-tipped breasts.

Shakily her hands went to his face and she tugged as she lay back on the bed, dragging his mouth to her breast. He suckled her hungrily, fiercely, pressing her back into the mattress with a pressure that was nothing short of headlong passion.

"I'm too hungry. I'll hurt you," he warned off, as he gave in to it.

"No, you won't." She drew him closer, arching under the heat of his mouth. "Oh, Dawson, Dawson, it's the sweetest sensation!"

"You taste of rose petals," he growled. "God, baby, I don't think I can hold it back this time!"

"It's all right," she repeated breathlessly. Her hands helped him get the fabric out of the way. She moved, fixed her body to his, helped him, guided him into sudden, stark intimacy. It should have been uncomfortable, but it wasn't.

He felt the ease of his possession and lifted his head to look into her eyes as he levered above her, softly kissing her. "I'll let you…watch," he whispered, shivering as he felt the tension building in his loins. "I don't mind. I love you. I love you, Barrie. I love you…!"

She watched his face tauten, the flush that spread to his cheekbones as his eyes began to dilate and the movements quickened into fierce, stark passion. He lifted his chest away from hers, his teeth clenched.

"Look…" he managed before he lost control completely.

Barrie went with him every step of the way. She lifted to the harsh, violent demand of his body for the satisfaction hers could give it. She opened herself to him, clung to him, as he cried out in great shuddering waves of ecstasy. Then she, too, cried out as her body exploded into pulsing shards of exquisite color, burning so high from the pleasure that the whole world spun around her.

His voice came from far away and it sounded concerned. "What's wrong?" he asked gently.

"I'm fine." Her eyes opened, wide and green and dazed with satiation. She traced the whorls of damp hair on his body. "I said the most shocking things," she said uncomfortably.

"Wicked, sexy things," he agreed. He smiled. "I loved it."

"Oh."

He bent and brushed his mouth over hers. "There shouldn't be limits on what we can say to each other in bed, what we can do to each other," he explained gently. "I won't ever tease you about it."

"That goes for me, too." She searched his face. "I watched you," she whispered.

He flushed. "I know. I wanted you to."

She smiled self-consciously. "But I couldn't really see much," she added shyly. "Stars were exploding in my head."

"That was mutual. And I couldn't really watch you for the same reason." He chuckled. "I suppose I'm losing my inhibitions, bit by bit."

"Maybe I am, too." She pushed back his damp hair gently. "I like being intimate with you. I like feeling you as close as you can get to me."

He drew her close and rolled onto his back with a long sigh. "Intimacy is new to me," he revealed.

She hit him. "Ha! Where did you learn all those things you did to me this morning? No!" She put her hand over his mouth. "No, don't you tell me, I don't want to know!"

He lifted her onto his chest and searched her angry eyes. "Yes, you do. And I'm going to tell you. I learned them with a succession of carefully chosen, emotionally alienated one-night stands. I learned them without any real participation except for a superficial one. No, don't look away. You're going to hear this." He turned her flushed face back to his. "I have had sex. But until I touched your body, I had never made love. That day on the floor of my study was the first time in my life that I gave myself completely and deliberately to a woman.''

She felt hot all over. ''You didn't like it.''

''I loved it,'' he said harshly. ''I didn't like having you watch it happen to me. I didn't trust you enough.'' His eyes calmed. ''I'm sorry about that, too. We made a baby in the heat of that exquisite loving. I'm sorry I didn't make it a happier memory for you...for both of us.''

''I'm not sorry about the baby. Or about watching you,'' she whispered wickedly. ''It was the most exciting, embarrassing thing that ever happened to me.''

''I can imagine,'' he replied quietly. ''Because I kept my head long enough to watch you this morning, all through it.'' His eyes began to glitter. ''And now I understand why you had to see my face.''

She eased down over his chest and kissed him softly, nibbling his upper lip. ''Because you wanted to see the love in my eyes,'' she whispered.

''Yes. And that's what you saw in mine, above and beyond the desire that was making me helpless, wasn't it?'' he asked.

She nodded after a minute. ''I didn't recognize it at the time. But, yes it was. It was the love that you didn't want me to see,'' she realized.

''Yes.'' He traced her nose with his forefinger, enjoying the lazy intimacy of their sprawled bodies. ''I could have saved myself the trouble. You honestly didn't know how I felt until I told you in a drunken rage last night, did you?''

''No, I didn't,'' she confessed with a chuckle. ''And it knocked me so hard that I got on the first plane out here to see if you meant it.'' She glared at him. ''I thought you didn't want me here.''

''I was surprised that you came, and delighted at being spared the trouble of flying right out to Sheridan to show you how completely I'd given in to my own feelings toward you.''

Her body lay open to his eyes, and he looked at her with wonder and obvious pleasure. ''I couldn't even do this before, did you realize it?'' he asked quietly. ''It made me feel uncomfortable to see you nude, to look at you openly.''

''Then we're making progress.''

''Apparently.'' He traced around her taut nipple and frowned as he saw the blue veins that had become prominent. The nipple was darker, bigger. His hand slid down to her belly and he felt the thickening of her waist. A smile pulled up the corners of his mouth. ''My, how you're changing.''

She smiled complacently. ''I'll be as big as a pumpkin by Christmas.''

His hand caressed her. ''So you will.'' He bent and drew his mouth gently over her stomach. ''We didn't hurt him, did we?''

''Babies are very tough,'' she said. She knew he was remembering the one they'd lost. ''This one wants to be born,'' she added. ''I feel it.''

He lifted his head and searched her eyes. He didn't say anything for a long time. His eyes said all too much.

''You won't lose me,'' she said deliberately. ''I promise you won't.''

He took a long breath and let it out. ''Okay.''

She sat up, pressing close to him. ''I'm sleepy.''

''So am I. I think a nap might be a good idea. Do you feel better?''

''Oh, yes. I didn't ever feel bad,'' she murmured with a chuckle. ''On the contrary, I felt entirely too good.''

He drew her closer. ''So did I. I wonder if two people ever achieved such a high at the same time?''

''Should we call the people at the record book and ask…ouch!''

He'd pinched her behind. He chuckled at her outraged expression. "I'll repent. Come here. We'll sleep for a while."

"A while?" she teased as he ensconced them together under the sheet.

His hand cradled her belly. "Life can be sweet after all."

"Hmmm," she murmured drowsily. Her eyes closed. She went to sleep with the sound of Dawson's heart beating softly at her ear.

Twelve

The phone was ringing off the hook. Barrie opened her
eyes, disoriented. The phone was on the bedside table, on
the other side of a broad, very hairy chest. She stared at that
chest for a moment trying to get her bearings. Then she
remembered where she was.

She smiled as she poked him in the ribs and felt him
jump, coming awake immediately.

"Phone," she said, shaking him gently.

He reached over and picked it up. "Rutherford," he said
shortly. He was quiet for a moment, then he rolled over
onto his back and ran a hand through his hair. "What?" he
said then. He made a rough sound in his throat. "Hell, no!
Good God, man, what sort of person do you think I am?"
There was the sound of hurried, apologetic conversation.
"You'd damn well better apologize, if you expect me to
stay here again or book my people in for another conference.
You didn't? Well, that's no excuse. Yes, I should think you

are! Very well.'' He slammed the receiver down and then started laughing.

"What was that all about?'' she asked curiously.

He rolled onto his side to prop on his elbow and looked down at her. "It seems that the prestige of the hotel was briefly lowered when one of the guests threw a woman's dress and very skimpy underwear out of a window. Naturally I had no idea why they should suspect me of... Stop that!'' He flicked her cheek with a long forefinger when she started laughing. "You have no idea who did it, either. Remember that. I spend a lot of time here when I travel, and I do want to come back again.''

"I still can't believe you threw my clothes out the window!''

He grinned. "It seemed the best way to keep you from leaving.'' He lifted the sheet and looked at her with eyes as appreciative as any artist's. He shook his head. "God almighty,'' he breathed. "I've never seen anything so beautiful.''

She grinned back. "Lecher.''

He drew her against him and held her close with a long, lazy sigh as his legs tangled softly with hers. "Sore?''

"Very.''

"So am I,'' he confessed, chuckling at her expression. "Men aren't made of iron, you know.''

"No kidding!''

His arms tightened. "I suppose we'll have beautiful memories for the next few days, at least.''

"Several.'' She touched the faint cleft in his chin gently. "Dawson, I can't go back to Sheridan naked.''

"You can't?''

She hit him.

"All right. I'll go shopping.'' He grinned wickedly. "How about a maternity dress?''

"I don't even show yet,'' she scoffed.

"Why waste time wearing normal clothes until you do?" he wanted to know. "A man has his pride, Barrie. I'm rather anxious to show off what I've accomplished in such a short time."

Her eyebrows lifted. "*I'm* an accomplishment?!"

"By God, you are," he said huskily. "The most wonderful accomplishment of my life, you and this baby. I must have a guardian angel sitting on my shoulder."

She slid her arms around his neck and reached over to kiss him lazily. "Then so must I, I guess, because you're certainly my most wonderful accomplishment."

He searched her loving eyes with pride and a lingering sense of wonder. "I'm sorry it took me so long to deal with the past," he said. "I wish I'd told you when you were sixteen that I was going to love you obsessively when you were old enough."

Her eyes twinkled. "Did you know so long ago?"

"Part of me must have," he replied, and he was serious as he searched her green eyes. "I was violent about you from the very beginning."

"And I never even suspected why," she agreed. She smoothed her hand over his thick gold hair, tracing the wave that fell onto his broad forehead. "What would have become of us if you hadn't dragged me back to Sheridan to act as chaperone for you and Leslie Holton?"

"I'd have found another excuse to get you home."

"Excuse?"

"I've been managing flirtatious women for a lot longer than five years, honey," he said with a deliberate grin.

"You said you were desperate to get that land!"

"I was desperate to get *you* home," he replied lazily. "There's another tract of land on the north end of the property that's just become available, and I bought it before Powell Long even had time to get a bid in. I didn't need

Leslie's tract anymore. Of course, she didn't know that. Neither did you.''

''I'm in awe of you,'' she said, aghast.

He lifted a rakish eyebrow. ''That's just right. A woman should always be in awe of her husband.''

''And a man in awe of his wife,'' she returned pertly.

He grinned. ''I'm in awe of you, all right.''

''Good. I'll do my best to keep you that way.''

He stretched drowsily and drew her close. ''We can sleep a bit longer. Then we should go home.''

''I didn't leave labels in any of my clothes,'' she pointed out. ''The ones you threw out the window, I mean. There's no way they could identify you as the mystery lingerie tosser.''

''That's not why I want to go home. It's been just about six weeks, hasn't it? And despite the home pregnancy test, I want proof. I want something I can take up on the roof and wave at people.''

She nuzzled her cheek against his chest. ''You'll get it,'' she promised.

And he did. The doctor confirmed not only that Barrie was pregnant, but that she was disgustingly healthy and should be over her morning sickness in no time.

As she and Dawson settled down in Sheridan, she thought back over the long, lonely years they'd been apart and how wonderful it was to have their future settled so comfortably.

Dawson was still sensitive to teasing just at first, but as he and Barrie grew together he became less defensive, more caring, more tender. Over the months of her pregnancy, Dawson was as attentive and supportive as any prospective mother could wish her husband to be. He seemed to have finally dealt with all his fears, even the one of childbirth.

But the most incredible revelation Barrie was ever to see

was the look on Dawson's handsome face when he held
their twin sons in his arms. As he looked into her worn,
delighted face, the expression in his pale green eyes would
last her the rest of her life. He looked as if he had the world
in that small hospital room. And, as he later told Barrie, he
did!

*   *   *   *   *

Watch out for exciting new covers on your favourite books!

Every month we bring you romantic
fiction that you love!
Now it will be even easier to find your favourite
book with our fabulous new covers!

We've listened to you – our loyal readers, and as of
August publications you'll find that...

We've improved:

☑ *Variety between the books*
☑ *Ease of selection*
☑ *Flashes or symbols to highlight mini-series
and themes*

We've kept:

☑ *The familiar cover colours*
☑ *The series names you know*
☑ *The style and quality of the stories you love*

*Be sure to look out for next months titles so
that you can preview our exciting new look.*

SILHOUETTE

Secret agents
bound by
love, loyalty
and the law

COLORADO
Confidential

Amanda
Stevens

**Jasmine
Cresswell**

Debra
Lee Brown

On sale 16th July 2004

*Available at most branches of WHSmith,
Tesco, Martins, Borders, Eason, Sainsbury's
and all good paperback bookshops.*

0804/009/SH76

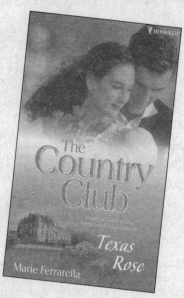

Ready
for love

The Country Club

A race
against
time...and
danger

The Country Club